# BARBARIAN'S TOUCH

*Berkley Titles by Ruby Dixon*

*Ice Planet Barbarians*

ICE PLANET BARBARIANS

BARBARIAN ALIEN

BARBARIAN LOVER

BARBARIAN MINE

BARBARIAN'S PRIZE

BARBARIAN'S MATE

BARBARIAN'S TOUCH

# BARBARIAN'S TOUCH

RUBY DIXON

BERKLEY ROMANCE
New York

BERKLEY ROMANCE
Published by Berkley
An imprint of Penguin Random House LLC
penguinrandomhouse.com

Library of Congress Cataloging-in-Publication Data

Names: Dixon, Ruby, 1976– author.
Title: Barbarian's touch / Ruby Dixon.
Description: First Berkley Romance edition. | New York: Berkley Romance, 2024. |
Series: Ice Planet barbarians
Identifiers: LCCN 2023020253 | ISBN 9780593639474 (trade paperback)
Subjects: LCGFT: Romance fiction. | Monster fiction. | Science fiction. |
Erotic fiction. | Novels.
Classification: LCC PS3604.I965 B378 2024 | DDC 813/.6—dc23/eng/20230605
LC record available at https://lccn.loc.gov/2023020253

*Barbarian's Touch* was originally self-published, in different form, in 2016.

First Berkley Romance Edition: January 2024

Printed in the United States of America
1st Printing

Book design by Kristin del Rosario

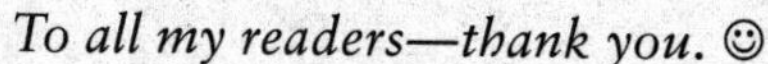

*To all my readers—thank you.* ☺

# BARBARIAN'S TOUCH

# What Has Gone Before

Aliens are real, and they're aware of Earth. Fifteen human women have been abducted by aliens referred to as "Little Green Men." Some are kept in stasis tubes, and some are kept in a pen inside a spaceship, all waiting for sale on an extraterrestrial black market. While the captive humans staged a breakout, the aliens had ship trouble and dumped their living cargo on the nearest inhabitable planet. It is a wintry, desolate place, dubbed Not-Hoth by the survivors.

On Not-Hoth, the human women discover that they are not the only species to be abandoned. The sa-khui, a tribe of massive, horned blue aliens, live in the icy caves. They hunt and forage and live as barbarians, descendants of a long-ago people who have learned to adapt to the harsh world. The most crucial of adaptations? That of the *khui*, a symbiotic life-form that lives inside the host and ensures its well-being. Every creature of Not-Hoth has a khui, and those without will die within a week, sickened by the air itself. Rescued by the sa-khui, the surviving human women take on a khui symbiont, forever leaving behind any hopes of returning to Earth.

The khui has an unusual side effect on its host: if a compatible pairing is found, the khui will begin to vibrate a song in each host's chest. This is called resonance and is greatly prized by the sa-khui. Only with resonance are the sa-khui able to propagate their species. The sa-khui, whose numbers are dwindling due to a lack of females in their tribe, are overjoyed when several males begin to resonate to human females, thus ensuring the bonding of both peoples and the life of the newly integrated tribe. A male sa-khui is fiercely devoted to his mate.

The humans have now been on the ice planet for over a year and a half, and most have adapted to tribal life. New babies are being born of human and sa-khui pairings, and the tribe stirs with life once more. The last of the human castaways resonate, and the remaining men despair of ever having a mate. Josie, who ran from her resonance to Haeden, stumbles across the wreckage of the spaceship that Kira destroyed and discovers the unthinkable: two more human women are trapped in stasis there. Josie and Haeden return to tell the rest of the tribe, and a rescue party is sent out to retrieve the new women.

This is where our story picks up.

# CHAPTER ONE
## Rokan

I am the only one not in a foul mood as we approach the strange cave that carried new humans to our world. Raahosh and Haeden walk in front, both surly and unpleasant because of the long journey. They wish to be home with their mates, curled up beside the fire and sharing furs. My brother Aehako walks behind them, his arm around his mate, Kira. They miss their kit and do not want to be here, either, but Kira feels obligated.

Near me, Hassen, Taushen, and Bek bicker over the human females we are traveling to retrieve. Bek and Hassen are both convinced that the females will take one look at them and resonate, like Vektal did to Shorshie. Their snappish retorts have made Taushen unhappy; if they will both get a mate, will there be one left for him? He does not like the odds.

Me? I walk silently, listening to their conversations with amusement. The day is cold but pleasant, and we are healthy, so I have no complaint. My brother is here if I am lonely and need company—but I do not. My younger brother Sessah is home with my father and mother. I have no mate waiting for me. I am content.

But my mood is light because my body is humming with anticipation.

Something big is coming. I do not think it is resonance, but my strange "knowing" feeling is prickling over my skin. I feel it when a large storm is rolling in, or when someone in the tribe is in danger. My brother's mate, Kira, calls it *een-too-itchen*. Humans have many words, and I do not grasp most of them. To me, it is just knowing. Like I can look at Bek and know that he will not find a mate here. Not here, not now. The time is not right. I know that in my heart as much as I know something life-changing is down in that strange human cave.

What, I do not know. But I am eager to see it.

I do not share this, though. Bek is still struggling to find his pride after Claire left his furs for Ereven. It has been a long journey here, and will be a long journey home. It will be that much longer if he is filled with anger the entire time. I study the others as they bicker to see if I get a similar feeling from them, but there is nothing. I shrug. It does not always work.

"What about you, Rokan?" Taushen asks, rousing me from my reverie. "What color mane would you want on your mate? Red like Har-loh or brown like Tee-fah-nee? Or yellow like Leezh?"

I shrug. "If there is a mate for me, I do not care what color she is." Humans have many strange features, but when I see Aehako looking at Kira's flat, smooth face with adoration, I know it does not matter. She can have three noses, and if I resonate to her, I will cherish all three of them.

Hassen makes a hissing sound of irritation. "Why do you bother to ask him, Taushen? He refuses to play this game. He does not care if he mates. That means the females are for us that care."

"That is not how it works and you know that," I add, amused at Hassen's possessiveness. "Just ask Haeden."

Haeden simply snorts, but his response has no real ire behind it. He misses his mate too much.

I increase the pace of my steps, pulling away from the others. If they wish to argue and ruin the day, they will do so without me. I pull out my bow and nock an arrow, scanning the skies. Raahosh and Leezh have been giving me lessons and now I am as good with this weapon as with my spear, if not better. It will give me more leverage against a sky-claw if one should appear. There are many in the area, which is concerning, especially to Aehako. We are big enough to be ignored, but my brother's mate is just small enough to be carried off. He keeps a rope tied at his waist, linking them together in case of attack, and Kira walks in the center of our party. So far the sky-claws have avoided our band, but it never hurts to be vigilant.

I have good reason to be cautious. Half-eaten dvisti litter the landscape, blood spattering the white hills. The sky-claws found a herd here recently and shredded their kills. They are messy eaters, and I frown as we pass another carcass with the belly torn out and not much else eaten. The creature's body is frozen, the blood forming icicles on the rib cage, but all I can think is how much meat has been wasted. My tribe would make use of all of the animal, right down to the bones and hooves. On the next crest is a metlak carcass, freshly dead. The stench of its filthy fur makes Taushen complain.

A peaceful journey, this is not. But it is a necessary one.

At least two humans have been found in the remains of one of the strange caves that Kira and her people swear fly through the stars. They sleep, unaware that they are on our world, and Kira is determined to rescue them. As the tribe still has several unmated males—myself included in those numbers—the thought of more mate-able females is an exciting one. Sometimes I cannot grasp how much our tribe has changed in a handful of seasons. Before, there were four females and three kits. Now there are sixteen females and the caves swarm with newly born kits.

I have not resonated, but this is not surprising to me. I know each human female, and though they were attractive enough in their human way, they did not set off my knowing feeling. Now they are all mated, so it does not matter. Maybe I shall never mate.

"There," says Raahosh, pausing ahead. He gestures in the distance. "The ship is below, in the valley. I see the red flame, just like you said, Haeden."

Haeden nods, staring off in the same direction. I move to their sides and gaze down, getting my first look at the flying cave. I remember the one that Shorshie and the other humans arrived in, with its strange square shape and odd black-stone walls. This one is of a similar shape, though the cave mouth looks more like a backpack that has been torn open to spill its contents.

Near the entrance, a strange red "flame" blinks and then goes black. A scarce breath later, it blinks into brilliant light again. Strange. Around it, the snow has melted and a semicircle of sky-claw carcasses surround it.

"Is that fire?" I ask, watching it blink out and return again. "How does it remain burning after so long?"

"It is a light like the ones in the ancestors' cave," Haeden explains. "It—"

A sky-claw screams overhead, the shadow of wings falling over us. I aim my bow even as Aehako shouts and dives to cover his mate. I squint, aim my arrow, and then instinctively move it ahead of the target and let it fly. A moment later, it connects in the exact spot my knowing tells me it will be, and it sinks deep into the creature's gut. Blood splatters onto the snow like rain, but the creature doesn't circle back to us. Rather, it flaps harder, continuing into the valley, heading right for the flame, which blinks back into existence once more.

As I ready another arrow, Raahosh makes a sound of disbelief. My gaze rips back to the cave, and as I watch, the sky-claw dives. Its maw opens, and a moment later, there's a terrible cracking noise that rips through the valley as it slams into the light and then crumples, wings spread, to the ground, piling on top of the others.

"It just broke its neck," Haeden says in a low voice, and rubs his own throat, staring down into the valley.

I lower my arrow slowly. "Is that what is killing the sky-claws? They do not like the flame?"

Raahosh snorts. "We need one of those fires in front of our cave."

Haeden gives him a surly look. "What, and draw every sky-claw on this side of the mountains to us?"

The two exchange irritated glances and then Raahosh stomps farther along the trail, heading for the valley. I follow close behind. This place is strange. I have hunted here before, but never has it felt as eerie and unwelcoming as now. Even the mountains seem uneasy with the new landscape.

"Let us get the females and leave this place," Haeden says, gripping his spear and moving forward. "The sooner they are retrieved, the sooner we are homeward bound."

I glance back at my brother. Aehako has helped his snow-covered mate back to her feet. She nods as Taushen approaches and offers a hand. "I'm good. Let's just go. Haeden's right—the sooner we're done here, the sooner we're home."

They are right. The sooner we leave this place, the better. I do not need my "knowing" to tell me that. Even without the threat of sky-claws and the strange alien cave, this is deep into metlak territory, and they do not like sa-khui.

We make our way down through the valley, sidestepping the sky-claw corpses, and enter the cave. It's a large, dark room, as big as the enormous central cave of the tribal home. The floor is covered with a fine sheen of snow, which melts as we step on it, but there are no tracks and no dead animals. Traces of the days Haeden and his mate, Jo-see, spent here remain, and we start a fire in the abandoned pit, because Kira is shivering.

The bickering does not stop now that we have arrived, though. Taushen and Bek make fire, squabbling the entire time. Hassen guards the entrance, casting looks back at Kira as she sits by the fire to warm herself. Raahosh and Haeden work on sweeping out the cave and I work on carving up the frozen quill-beast carcass I have carried slung at my belt for the morning, thanks to a lucky arrow near dawn. It will make a warm meal for Kira, who cannot handle the cold as well as we sa-khui.

*Kira* and *the new humans,* I remind myself. I glance over at Hassen, who has his arms crossed over his chest, scowling. Impatience vibrates through his body and it does not take my "knowing" to see that he's soon to explode. I slice chunks of tender meat off the hide and drop them into the hanging pouch for stewing. Tension fills the cave, broken only by the chatter of Kira's square little human teeth. Nearby, Bek stokes the fire higher while Aehako shakes out furs, freeing them of ice.

I drop the last bit of meat into the stew pouch and open my drinking skin, adding water and a bit of my mother's favorite spices. I stir it with a long thigh bone and then drop it into the broth to add flavor.

"Well?" Hassen explodes. I look up as he stalks away from the entrance, spear forgotten. He is vibrating with frustration. "We are here! Free the females! Where are they?"

Aehako jumps to his feet, a snarl on my brother's normally laughing face. "Let my mate thaw her fingers before you demand—"

"It's okay," Kira says in her soft voice, interrupting before the argument gets ugly. She blows on her fingers to warm them and then gets to her feet, a faint smile on her face. "Everyone's excited. I get that."

Aehako growls. "Sit by the fire—"

She shakes her head. "I can do it." Ignoring her mate's protests, she pats his arm and then wanders to the back of the strange cave, her gaze fixed on the wall. "It's just finding the *releez hatsh*."

"The what?" Hassen charges forward, and Aehako steps between him and Kira, glaring. I get to my feet; if we choose sides, of course I will choose my brother. Raahosh moves to Aehako's side as well, glaring at Hassen's impatience. Haeden moves to the entrance, picking up the guard post that Hassen has abandoned.

I look over just as Kira touches the strange, bubbled wall of the cave. A moment later, a hissing noise cuts through the air, and steam fills the air. Haeden hesitates, and Aehako turns to his mate, rushing to her side.

Something pale and human-sized falls out of the wall and into Kira's arms. It is a female, all snow-colored limbs and a mane of dark, wet hair, which clings to her soft skin like vines. Her thin clothing is damp and sticks to her body, outlining high breasts and a curving waist.

A groan escapes me before I realize it. I did not realize that the female would be so perfect. I touch my chest. My khui is silent but I cannot deny that the sight of the new human female has hit me like a thunderbolt.

Haeden glares at me, grabbing a discarded fur wrap from the flooring and moving forward to cover the female up. He takes her from Kira's and Aehako's grasp and settles her gently on the ground.

Her eyes flutter open—pale white with a glassy green center. Her strange eyes blink, and I take a step back. I do not wish to scare her.

# CHAPTER TWO
## Lila

My first waking thought? How cold everything is. So damn cold. Like frost in my veins. It's like I've been dumped in a freezer with nothing but a wet nightie on. No panties, no shoes, no nothing. Just my nightshirt, which clings to my prickling, shivering skin.

Then I wonder why I'm nearly naked, wet, and freezing my butt off. What's happening? Why am I here instead of back home in the apartment I share with my sister, Maddie?

Dizzy, I vaguely realize someone's helping me sit up. My eyes are having trouble focusing, and my mouth feels like I chewed on a dirty sock. I blink repeatedly, even as something soft and fuzzy is wrapped around me, and the worst of the bone-chilling cold dampens a bit. It's quiet, unnervingly so. Is everyone waiting for me to say something? Like why I'm here? Wherever here is?

Something blue moves in and out of my blurry vision. Things are slowly coming into view; it's dark wherever I'm at, and there's a faint scent of smoke in the air. Was there a fire? I rub my forehead, and everything aches. It's like I've got a fever of some kind.

Maybe that's why I'm so cold. I try to remember what I did before I went to bed, but vague memories of television and working on the computer waft through my mind, completely unmemorable. The blue thing moves again, and my gaze crystallizes and focuses in.

The blue thing is . . . a face.

A devil's face—enormous, horned, the brows creased with bony ridges. His face is hard and scowling, his nose and cheekbones prominent. The devil is holding me, his face inches from mine.

Jerking away, I scream. At least, I try to. I push out of his arms, and my mouth is open but I can't hear anything.

That's when I realize I can't hear *anything*. At all. And a new fear cascades through me.

The devil releases me and I shoot backward. My feet get tangled in the furry thing—a cape? a pelt?—and then my back slams into something metal. I can't go back any more. I just scream and stare. There are other figures in this shadowy place, and a fire dances in the distance. My horrified gaze flicks from the devil sitting near me to another, and another. God, how many are there?

Am I in hell?

Did I die and now I'm in hell?

My fingers go to my ears and I run my fingers along the shell, looking for the familiar tubing that should be there. Ten years ago, I got cochlear implants. Ten years ago, I went from completely deaf to being able to hear—one of the greatest joys in my life. But as I touch my ears, I feel nothing—no tubes, no wires. I reach farther back, to the circle on my scalp where the implant goes into my skull—and there's nothing but smooth scar tissue and a bald patch the size of a penny.

I whimper—I think. I can't hear it.

And that sends me into further panic.

Where's Maddie? Where's my sister? I squeeze my eyes shut, my world going black and silent as I touch my implant-less ears and try to grasp what's happening. My mind is whirling and frantic, and I'm on the verge of hyperventilating. I need Maddie.

I need her.

Ever since I was little, Maddie's been there for me. She's been the arm that guided me when we went to school, because I couldn't hear traffic. She's been my interpreter when we met people that didn't understand ASL—American Sign Language. After I got my implants, she's taken more of a back seat, but we're still best friends, sisters, and closer to each other than anyone else in the world. I lean on her in everything.

I'm lost without her.

Hot tears splash down my cheeks and I sob into the darkness. It's so quiet. I feel trapped, and I can't stop shivering. I'm trembling because of cold, and of fear. I don't know what's going on and I don't know what to do. No one's touching me, for which I'm thankful. I huddle in the fur blanket and weep.

I want this all to go away. I want my hearing back.

Hands touch my arm, and I open my eyes and jerk away, a little scream erupting from my throat again.

A familiar face is there, round with the same green eyes I have, and a wealth of messy blonde hair. It's Maddie, her full lips pressed into a hard line. She touches my cheek and says something, but in the shadows, it's hard for me to make it out. *Lila? You okay?* I think she says.

I'm not. I'm so not okay. I do the ASL gesture for *can't* and then tap my ear quickly.

Maddie's eyes widen and her hand goes to my ear, looking

for my implant. She realizes it's gone and then signs to me: *We will figure this out.*

I feel a surge of relief and nod. Maddie's got me, no matter what else happens. I huddle in the blankets, feeling small and like that isolated twelve-year-old I once was, not the twenty-two-year-old grown woman I am. I watch as Maddie surges to her feet and confronts the nearest person. I can't hear any of it, but I'm guessing Maddie's yelling. Her body is stiff with anger and she shakes a fist as she speaks.

I'm not strong, not like Maddie. My first instinct isn't to fight. It's to hide. *I'd give anything to be able to hide right now,* I think as I watch my sister.

Since her back is to me and she's standing in front of the person she's yelling at, I can't read lips to try and follow along. I glance at my surroundings, trying to make sense of them. At first I think we're in a cave—I can see an opening up ahead and what looks like snow blowing in, which is bizarre. Maddie and I live in Arizona.

This . . . is not Arizona.

I don't think it's a cave, either, as I look around. Everything is super square and the floor under me feels like metal against my skin. I'm sticking slightly to it, like my fingers do when I touch a wet ice cube, and I shudder inwardly. The big cave-room-whatever seems to be pretty empty. There are no lights, but there is a warm fire built up in the middle of the room. There are people sitting near it, though—big people. Basketball player–sized people with enormous shoulders and curling horns sticking up from their heads. Are they really blue or are the shadows playing with my mind? I look at them again, trying to calm myself and logically make sense of what they are. I see tails, and horns. Their skin seems rough and rippled across the breastbone and on the lower arms. One watches Maddie with intense emotion, but most of them are scowling, probably because my sister has only one volume—loud. I see one demon with long hair and thick muscles watching me with a rather creepy intensity, and I pull the blankets closer to my body. This can't be real, can it? If I close my eyes, maybe it'll all go away.

Even as I question my sanity, I make eye contact with another one of the demon-men. His eyes glow light blue, like they're lit from within. It's eerie, and yet his expression isn't cruel. He watches me with a look of concern and empathy, not the skin-crawling interest that the other one does. He crouches near the fire, his inhuman features lit up in shadow, but from what I can see, his chest is bare and he doesn't seem bothered by the cold. How can he not be? I'm freezing and I'm wrapped in a fur.

None of this makes any sense at all.

My sister makes another angry gesture, drawing my attention back to her. One of the scowling males hands her a blanket, and my sister turns and storms back toward me. As she does, I see for the first time that there's a human woman—how did I miss her?—with all the devils. She's average looking except for the weird glowy-blue eyes she has, just like the devils. She wears furs like the men do. Why is she here with them?

Maddie kneels at my side and begins to sign. *You are not going to believe this shit.*

*What?* I sign back.

The other woman comes forward and squats near my sister. Maddie looks pissed that we're interrupted and pauses before she can tell me what's going on. The stranger looks at my sister, and then at me. She begins to speak and I read her lips. *Can she not hear? Is that sign language?*

*Back off,* Maddie tells her, and I can just imagine my sister's bitchy tone. It makes me smile, weirdly enough. Maddie speaks again. *We need a moment.*

The woman's brows draw together and she nods, giving me a fragile smile. She retreats, hugging her fur clothing close to her slim body, and moves to the side of one of the devils, saying something to him. He puts an arm around her shoulders and kisses the top of her head, and I realize that she looked about my size when she knelt, but next to the demon, she looks tiny—

Fingers snap silently in front of my face.

I look over at Maddie. *Focus,* she signs.

*Sorry. I'm freaking out.*

*Me, too.* Her mouth flattens and she thinks for a moment, then continues signing. *Do you remember anything that happened?*

I shake my head. *All I remember is falling asleep watching* Castle, *I think. Then I woke up and we're here and it's silent. What's going on?*

*It sounds ridiculous but . . .* Maddie pauses, then starts to sign again. *I think we've been kidnapped by aliens.*

## Rokan

Even though I know the females are uncomfortable, I cannot help but watch them. They sit in the back of the cave, bundled in furs. That is the only help they will take from us; they want no fire, no food, nothing but to be left alone right now. Kira says we should give them time, but looking at Hassen's and Bek's hard faces, I worry they will not be given time. Already my companions are disappointed that neither female has resonated yet.

It is clear the females are frightened, though. They are silent, shooting furtive glances over at us when they think we are not looking. Their hands move frantically and they give each other worried looks. The big one with the yellow mane will do well here, I think. She is a fighter. She has already bellowed at Kira in a way that would make even Leezh proud. It is the other one—the female with the dark mane—that worries me. She seems fragile compared to the other, and cannot stop shivering. I think of the thick snow outside, the sky-claws that dive from above, the harsh weather, the metlaks, and a hundred other dangers. This is not a world for those that are fragile. Everyone in the tribe knows that; the weak do not last long.

But there is something about her that draws my gaze, endlessly. I cannot stop staring, even though I know it worries them. I think of the human and her dull eyes that do not shine with a healthy khui. There is something about this female that pulls me to her. My chest is silent, and so is my "knowing." If it is not resonance, what is it, then? Maybe it is protectiveness; she still shivers despite the fact that neither of them will approach the life-giving warmth of the fire. I glance at the stew pouch. There is still plenty left. Kira has eaten, and the other hunters avoid it, as we prefer our meat raw. Should I offer the females food? Will they take it?

Hassen makes an impatient noise in his throat and jabs the end of his spear into the fire. "Their teeth are clicking again."

"It's cold," Kira says in her gentle voice. "They don't have khuis to warm them. When they're ready, they'll come join us. Right now I think they need more time to adjust. The kindest thing we can do is leave them alone."

"The kindest thing we can do is drag them to the fire," Hassen snarls and tosses his spear down onto his blankets. "They are too valuable to the tribe to let them freeze out of stubbornness."

I glance over at the females again, then back at the stew. If they will not come to us, perhaps I should give them a peace offering. I get to my feet and pull a small carved bowl from my pack and scoop it into the pot, then cross the cave toward the females. Hassen and Bek make angry noises, but I ignore them, my gaze focused on the two small humans huddled in the blankets. I deliberately make myself as unthreatening as I can, dropping my shoulders and walking slowly. When I get closer, they scoot back against the wall, and so I drop to a crouch and offer the bowl to the dark-haired one.

"Food," I say in the human language. "It is warm."

She gazes at me with frightened eyes, glancing over at the yellow-maned one. At the other's nod, she reaches one hand out, and I hear the rumble of her stomach. A surge of protectiveness moves through me, and I want to do more for this small, frightened female. I want to keep her safe, to show her we are friends. I hold the bowl steady, because I know any movement will terrify her.

Her fingers twitch and then her gaze flicks to something over my shoulder. She shrinks back and the yellow-maned one pushes in front of her, a snarl on her face.

Feet move to my side, and I glance up to see Haeden snarling down at me. "Leave them alone, Rokan." In a lower voice, he murmurs, "You are giving Hassen ideas."

I swallow my annoyance. Haeden means well, but he is protective of his task; he promised his mate he would bring the females back safely, and he is determined to do so. I nod—again, slowly—and set the bowl down on the floor in front of the females, and then unhook my waterskin and leave it as an offering as well. Then I get to my feet in unhurried motions and walk away with Haeden. I do not look back to see if the females pick up the food. I know they will; they have no choice. A pang of sympathy makes me feel uneasy at my role here. Of course they are terrified—if their story is like Kira's, they woke from their furs to this strange place with no explanation. To them, we are monsters. It will take much convincing to get them to accept our help.

And somehow we have to gain their trust and convince them they both need a khui, or else they will die.

"Stay by the fire," Haeden snaps. He picks up his spear and goes to talk to Raahosh, and then the two of them move to stand midway between the females and the fire. Their backs are to the new females and it is clear to all that they are not there to keep the females back, but to keep us from harassing them.

I return to my seat, torn between irritation and resignation. I want to speak to the dark-haired one, to ease her fears, and now I am treated as if I am just as much trouble as Hassen and Bek? I glance over at the two males and they have their heads together, whispering and scowling as they converse. They shoot glances over at Raahosh and Haeden.

Haeden is right to be wary. My "knowing" sense tells me that Hassen and Bek are hatching a plan, though it does not take much to guess that. It is plain on their faces.

And perhaps my action has made things worse.

Casually, I glance back at the bowl I left. It is gone, and so is my skin.

That is something, at least.

"Maybe I should bring more food over," Kira says in a soft, worried voice.

I pull a bone cup out of my bag and offer it to her.

She gives me a grateful look and gets to her feet, then dips it into the stew pouch. "We'll give them tonight to adjust. I can't imagine how terrifying this is. When Nora and Stacy and the others came out of their pods, they had a bunch of humans to help them acclimate. Right now it's just me, and I feel inadequate." She sighs and then taps her temple, near her eyes. "This isn't helping, either."

"The khui?" Aehako guesses.

She nods. "We look different. Probably scary. And I think one of the girls can't hear."

Bek crosses his arms. "A khui will fix that. We need to find a sa-kohtsk to hunt before the females get too weak." Taushen and Hassen nod.

Aehako glances over at Haeden and Raahosh. "I am sure a hunt will be soon."

"It needs to be very soon," Bek continues. "The females will not last long if they shiver inside the warmth of the cave. There are metlaks and sky-claws to think of, as well. This place is dangerous. We must get them khuis and get them to safety."

"You just want them given khuis because you want them to resonate," Aehako muses. "Do not disguise it as your concern for their comfort."

Aehako and Bek start to argue loudly, Aehako with his hand on his mate's shoulder protectively. At my side, Kira sighs and gives me a frustrated look. "I'm thinking it might have been smarter to bring mated hunters along on this trip."

"They are needed by their families," I tell her. My brother's mate's face is drawn and unhappy. "We will get them back safely. That is all that matters."

"Yes, and until then, everyone's going to bicker over the girls until they resonate." She sighs again and gathers her blankets, then gets up from the fire to go visit the females.

As she gets up, Hassen glances over at the spot she's vacated. He tosses a bit of bone into the fire. "You have been silent, Rokan. What does your knowing tell you? Will the females resonate?"

"I sense nothing about the females," I tell him honestly. "Perhaps because they have no khui."

He nods slowly, and then fixes his gaze on me. "It does not matter to me about the yellow-haired one. But the soft one? She is mine." A possessive look glitters in his eyes.

My jaw clenches and I fight back my anger at his bold statement. "Resonance decides, not you."

He narrows his eyes at me and then shrugs his shoulders. "Then you will watch me resonate to her. One way or another, she is mine." He gets to his feet. "And I do not need a 'knowing' sense to realize this."

He leaves to go to the front entrance of the cave, and I am left stewing in my own anger. Why does the thought of him claiming the "soft one" fill me with such rage? She is soft, and gentle, this is true. Someone as bold and blunt as Hassen will storm all over her. Is that why I am angry at the thought?

Or because I want her for myself? I force the idea out of my mind. It is wrong to be possessive of the females. Resonance chooses a mate, not me. I have waited many, many seasons to take a female to my furs, because I am waiting for resonance. I am not like Bek, who had Claire as his pleasure mate before she resonated to Ereven. I want resonance, and resonance only. When I take a female into my arms, I want it to be for forever.

It might be one of these females. It might not. Warrek is almost twice my age and has never resonated. Maybe I will never have a mate.

But that does not mean that I cannot be a friend to these females.

*The soft one? She is mine.*

The deadly words repeat in my mind, and my jaw clenches every time.

# CHAPTER THREE

## Lila

So apparently a lot happened while Maddie and I were unconscious. It seems that we were kidnapped by one kind of alien, who also kidnapped the human woman here. Then the ship crashed and we've been asleep in some sort of stasis for over a year and a half, until another human found the remains of the crashed ship and realized we were still in hibernation in the wall.

It's all a little muddy to me. The aliens here that look like demons? According to Kira's story, they're not the bad guys. She even shows us the frozen corpses in the front half of the crashed ship to back up the "there's more than one kind of alien" story. And even though it's completely crazy, we don't have a choice but to believe her. When she says the part about how she and her friends were taken and examined, and one girl was even given an abortion because the alien captors didn't want her pregnant? I think of my missing cochlear implants and realize it's probably all true.

I'm more than a little horrified by all of it. To think that aliens kidnapped me and examined me and operated on me, all while I was unaware. To think that we've flown halfway across the galaxy and crash-landed, all unaware.

To think that if it hadn't been for a stranger randomly finding the remains of the ship, we might have slept for a lot longer than a year and a half. What if . . . what if no one *ever* came to find us? The thought makes my gurgling stomach even more ill at ease.

Kira and Maddie talk for hours, with Maddie passing along info to me. She's doing her best to remember to sign, but sometimes the conversation gets away from her and I only get a few half-assed hand signals. It's all right. It's a lot to take in and it's been ten years since Maddie had to be my interpreter. And sometimes I think I really don't want to hear more of what they're going to tell us.

Kira seems nice enough. She keeps the others at bay, even though she says one is her husband and she loves him. She says she has a half-alien baby back at "home" and that the reason why her eyes glow is because she has something called a "symbiont"—Maddie spells it out with her hands because there's not an ASL sign for something like that. It's something that lives inside the body and helps it adjust. Kira pauses in her explaining to build up a small fire near us for warmth, and her mate—one of the biggest of the aliens—brings over her blankets. It seems Kira is going to be staying with us tonight. I steal a glance over at the main fire. The alien men are there, and they're all watching us. It's really unnerving.

Maddie taps my arm, and I tear my gaze away from the fire Kira's building. *What do you think?* she signs.

*It sounds like a parasite to me,* I reply, worried. *A parasite and we're the host.*

*Me, too, but what can we do? She says we have to have one. They all have one. Did you see the part where she said there's a poison in the air?* She sniffs dramatically, and I admit I take a deep breath myself. Smells like normal air, if damn cold.

*Do you think they're lying?* I ask, hesitant.

*Does it matter if they are? We're outnumbered, we're not dressed for the situation, and we don't know what's going on. Like, I would think it's a prank except I got close enough and those guys aren't wearing makeup.* Her hands fly as she signs, agitated. She doesn't like this any more than I do, but like she says, we don't have a choice. *Their eyes really are glowing, and there's a lot of damn snow out there, so we're definitely not in Arizona anymore. And Kira says that there are only twelve humans and thirty-something of the blue guys, not including babies. If this place is what she says it is—an ice planet—there are no cities.*

I feel tears threaten. *Well, fuck,* I sign back. *Why couldn't we get stuck on a tropical planet?*

Maddie throws her head back and laughs, and everyone turns in our direction again. This is how we deal with things—Maddie laughs, and I cry. I swipe at my cheeks, because it feels like if I do cry, the tears are going to freeze to my face. I'm so cold. This is awful. I hate all of this. I want to go home, back to my stupid desk job and all the stupid credit card bills I'm behind on. I want to go spend Friday night sitting at the hotel bar watching Maddie sling drinks and pointing out all the drunks. I want to curl up on the sofa and finish watching season two of *Game of Thrones.*

I want a freaking heated blanket.

I touch Maddie's arm to break her out of her hysterical laughter. *I don't like the way they watch us,* I sign to her. *The men.* I feel like a bird in a cage, or like a bird being hunted by a cat.

*Just stay at my side,* she tells me. *I won't let anything happen to you. Big Sis is on alert. Get some sleep for now.*

I give her as much of a smile as I can muster. *All right.* Like that's gonna be easy knowing we're now in "Parasite Planet"? With a bunch of horny blue dudes that look like they want to eat me? Oh sure, I'll just tuck into my frozen blankets and take a nice power nap.

Instead, I sip more of the water from the strange waterskin that the one guy gave us. I avoid the stew—it's so spicy it makes my nose burn. I'm hungry, but I can't bring myself to eat much of it, and Maddie says she doesn't have much of an appetite. She jokes that she can live off her fat for a while, but I need to eat. Funny how I don't feel like eating.

She and Kira start talking again and I gaze over to the other fire. The men there are still watching us. Good lord, they need a hobby. Since we're hidden in the shadows and I'm snug next to my protective sister, I find the courage to look back at them. The men fall into two camps, I think. There are those like Kira's husband and the two guards that look at us as if we're slightly annoying. And then there are the ones that sit around the fire and look at us as if they want to eat us. Gee, and I wonder why I feel uneasy.

The one that left me the water glances over here, and I decide that I need a third category, just for him. Uninterested, Creepers, and him. I'm not sure what he is yet, but he's not giving off the same vibes that the others are. Weirdly enough, I feel like he could be a friend if I was less scared.

Maddie and I shiver all night despite the fire and the fur blankets. I've never felt so cold in my life, and it feels like no matter what I do, I can't get warm.

"It's colder this time of year than usual," Kira says, and I read her lips in the firelight. She's warming her hands at our fire. "And when you get your *coo-ee*, it won't be so bad."

The coo-ee must be the parasite. At least, I think that's the word. It's hard to tell with lip-reading, and half the time I'm guessing what someone is saying. It's not comforting, though. The thought of a parasite keeping me warm? I'd almost prefer to stay cold.

No, actually, scratch that. I'm so tired of being cold. I slept terribly last night, and everything I touched felt like ice. My toes are tingling with numbness, and the thought of leaving the cocoon of furs that keeps me warm is a deal-breaker. I don't know how Kira can stand it. More than that, I don't know how the big guys wander around in summery clothing. Two of them have bare chests and several others wear vests that look as if they wouldn't keep a flea warm. Lots of muscles on display around here.

Today? I take everything they offer. When they offer me hot tea? I take it and drink it, not caring that it has a weird leafy taste to it. When they give me more stew? I eat it all and ignore the fact that my nose runs like a faucet. Last night, in the dreadful, freezing-cold hours that I was supposed to be sleeping, I came to a realization.

Maddie and I are alone here. We're completely at the mercy of these strangers who decided to retrieve us and are now feeding and clothing us. We can try to escape, but how far are we going to get? Just the thought of stepping outside the safety of the wrecked ship and into the fiercely blowing winter winds is enough to make me want to vomit.

And me? I'm completely dependent on Maddie to communicate. I can talk, of course, but I can't hear myself; I can't tell if I'm loud enough or misunderstood. If they're not facing me, I can't see their response. And the aliens? Maddie says that Kira told her that they know our language, but I can't read their lips. They have fangs and they enunciate differently than I'm used to, so that's a bust.

So we're completely dependent on the aliens, and I'm completely dependent on Maddie.

This doesn't make me happy. I'm not the most outgoing person, so I'm happy to let my exuberant sister take the lead. At the same time, I'm terrified. What if we get separated? What if something happens to Maddie? What am I going to do?

Everything just feels dangerous. Last night, as I shivered and clung to Maddie, trying to sleep, I came up with a plan: the Yes Plan.

Do I want to eat this stew? Yes.

Do I want to wear all these nice furs they're handing me? Yes.

Do I want to be friendly with all the new aliens? Yes, yes I do.

I'm not stupid. I know that the happier they are with me, the easier things will be. So right now? I'm going to be easygoing as heck and keep an eye on everything. I haven't told Maddie my plan—mostly because the words *Maddie* and *easygoing* do not belong in the same sentence. But if she thinks I'm safe and protected with these strangers, she'll come around.

Kira holds a boot out to me. "Shoe? Do you want this shoe?" She taps it. "We can adjust it to fit your foot."

I nod at her, Yes Plan in effect.

Hours later, I'm dressed in warm castoffs from one of the supply packs. Since the other human women knew Maddie and I were here in the pods, clothing was sent along for us, and now Maddie and I are fitted into leather tunics, leather leggings, and warm, fleece-lined boots. I have big furry mittens that I wear even inside the cave, and I've had my fill of spicy stew. My nose is stuffed up and I suspect I'm coming down with a cold, but I manage to nap for most of the day. For some reason, most of the big blue dudes left the cave, leaving just Kira, her mate, and one of the others, who remained guarding the entrance. It's relaxing. I'm still anxious and my stomach is in knots, but without the hot, glowing eyes of the others, some of the tension eases.

I wake up when a hand touches my arm and shakes me awake. I sit up in the furs, rubbing my eyes. There, by the fire, the big blue guys have returned and are gesturing excitedly about something to the one that's the leader. They point at us and pick up their packs, but the leader shakes his head and says something that makes one of the hot-eyed ones fling his bag down and go storming off. The others settle in but they don't look pleased.

Maddie takes it all in and then comes and sits next to me in the furs. She pulls her knees up and leans closer to me, her hands moving in small motions. It's almost like we're whispering—not that it matters. They don't understand sign language. But maybe Maddie doesn't want them to know we're talking.

*The angry one is Hassen,* she tells me. *We need to keep an eye on him. He watches you a lot.*

*I know,* I sign back. *It worries me. What happened to make him angry?*

*They are looking for something. A sock? It sounds like* sock, *though I know that is not the right word. They want it for us. I think it carries the parasites. Hassen is angry that Haeden—that is the leader—won't let them hunt tonight. Haeden says to wait for dawn, because we are too vulnerable. So Hassen is throwing a pissy-fit.*

Hassen and Haeden? Gosh, their names sound the same. I don't know how I'm going to keep it all straight in my head. *So they want to go hunt the sock?* I peek out to the front of the crashed ship, where the sky and the snow can be seen—it's dark and the snow is falling heavily. My breath is fogging even in the warmth of the ship's hold. If I leave the fire, it frosts. *I don't want to go out,* I tell Maddie. *I agree with Haeden.*

*Me, too. My ass is frozen.*

I smother a laugh behind my hand and look over at the fire. The one with the nice eyes—the friendly one—is watching me. His mouth curls a bit. Did he hear my laughter? I feel a blush scorching my cheeks and shrink down next to Maddie. *Do you know the names of the others?* I sign back.

*I'm trying to memorize them all,* Maddie signs to me. *I think Kira's husband is named Yayhago, though I might have that wrong. There is one called Raw-hosh but he doesn't seem nice. The one standing by the fire is Beck. That one is Toshen. I think that one is Rowdan but he doesn't say much, even to the others.*

My mind whirls, trying to absorb all these names. They're not easy ones to remember, except maybe Beck, but I don't want to get to know him better. He's one of the ones with the possessive eyes. I look over at the one that interests me. Rowdan.

His name, I will try to remember.

As if he can sense my stare, he looks over and tips his chin at me, a bit of a playful smile on his mouth. His lips stretch into a grin, and then I see nothing but white fangs.

I shudder and look away again.

After another horrible, cold night, I'm more than willing to get this coo-ee thing if it means I'll be warm. This place is awful—it's freezing cold and barren, and by the time even the warmest of food gets to me, it's cooling off. If what they say is true, there's no Burlington Coat Factory around the corner, no McDonald's, no nothing. There's no warm beach to look forward to, or a break in the weather, even. This is an ice planet.

Sometimes I really hope Kira and the others are lying to me. That this is all an elaborate joke, like they do on those TV shows. That we're going to go outside and see a city in the distance, and everyone's going to laugh and hand me hot cocoa. I won't even be mad. I'll just be relieved.

But that doesn't explain why my cochlear implant is gone, and nonconsensual surgery definitely takes the joke too far. So this has to be real.

And that terrifies me.

Maddie seems to be handling things better than me. She's wary and combative with the others, and protective of me, but she doesn't shiver as much, and she sleeps like a log. She doesn't look as if she's living every moment in abject fear.

I'm envious of that. I keep my complaints and my fears to myself, because if Maddie knows I'm silently freaking out, she'll worry about me and go into Mama-Bear Mode. And while I love my sister, I don't know if I want her to smother me with overprotectiveness. Maddie can be awesome, but Maddie can also be too much. I'm glad that she's here, and at the same time, I resent that I'm forced to rely on her again. It's not Maddie's fault that after years of hearing and independence, I'm back to helplessness.

Whoever took my implants is a jerk.

After we eat a quick hot breakfast of leftover stew, the aliens get out their weapons and pack their bags. Kira talks to Maddie for a long moment. I try to follow the conversation but Kira's talking too fast. Maddie nods at her and then comes over to me.

*They want to leave,* she signs. *They know where the sock-thing is and want to go hunt it to get us parasites. They say if we don't get them, we will die, and they worry you're not strong enough as it is.*

That's a tough pill to swallow—that I worry them and look "weak." I'm not much smaller than Kira. I resist the urge to flex my arms and show them the small muscles I've got. I may not be as hulking as the rest of the aliens, but I'm not a wimp. *That's fun,* I sign back to her, because what else can I say? *Can you tell them to go fuck themselves?*

Maddie's eyes brighten. *There's that fighting spirit! Where's it been for the last two days?*

*Hiding and praying this will all go away?*

*Just think of it as camping. As long as they're good to us, this is just like a camping trip, right down to the leeches.*

I make a face at her. *Yuck, thanks for that. You know I hate camping.*

She pats my arm, and then signs, *Suck it up, Buttercup.*

Guess I need to.

Kira waits for us to be done with our conversation and then hands us more furs to put on. I notice the men are wearing fewer wraps than before, which means they're giving them to us. She produces a pair of rough-looking snowshoes and holds them out to Maddie and me.

Oh boy. We're leaving the wreckage of the ship. I'm not sure if I'm excited or terrified. I guess it's too much to hope that the sock-thing we're going after lives in a nice, warm shelter. If so, I just might become its new best friend.

Maddie takes the snowshoes from Kira and hands them to me. *Bundle up,* she gestures as Kira hands over even more furs. *We need to keep you warm, weakling.*

I know my sister's teasing, but it still grates on my nerves. I scowl at her as I take the shoes. She's in such a good mood, and I'm a bit resentful of that. Maddie loves adventure and challenge. I think she's thriving on irritating the big blue guys that look at us like we're treats to be devoured. Me, I just want to be left alone.

Preferably somewhere toasty warm.

I put on the furs that Kira hands over, and it seems like layer after layer, until I probably resemble a stuffed toy more than a human. There are fur chaps that go over my leggings, a fur wrap that goes over my shoulders and then around my torso. Kira produces a belt and ties the wraps against my body, and then comes another layer, and then a heavy cloak. I'm itchy and stiff, and so I don't protest when she bends down and starts to strap the snowshoes to my new fur boots. By the time she's done with me, I look ridiculous. Maddie does, too. I want to joke that we look like a pair of teddy bears heading out for a picnic, but my hands are wrapped in warm, double-lined mittens and so I can't sign.

Kira bundles up once she's satisfied with our clothing, and then we all waddle to the broken end of the spaceship. I'm a little jealous of how well Kira can walk in her snowshoes; it's clear she's had practice. I want to stare at my feet to make sure that every step I take is a solid one, but I need my sight to know what's going on around me. If I stare at my feet, I'll truly be isolated.

We're the last ones in the ship, I realize—the others are outside waiting for us in the pale gray light. I pull my hood down deeper over my face and step forward. The crunch of snow under my shoes can be felt, if not heard, and it comforts me.

Because what I see when I step outside takes my breath away.

I've stared at that sliver of light for the last two days. I know to expect a bleak landscape of snow and wintry skies. Even so, I'm not prepared for just how different everything is. I gaze around me in a mix of horror and wonder.

Rolling, endless hills of white snow cover everything. It's snow as far as the eye can see, heaps and heaps of it. There isn't much in the way of landscape—no trees, no bushes, only a few rocks here and there. Behind the ship, purple, glass-looking mountains climb toward the skies like teeth and cast long shadows over the valley. No wonder it's so bitterly cold—we're in the shadows and the sun never hits us. I look up, squinting to see the sun. The sky is covered with thick clouds, but I spot the suns. Two of them, clustered together like mating fireflies, so small and watery-looking that it's a wonder they give off any light. My heart sinks at the sight of them and I realize I'm never going to feel a warm summer day ever again.

I'd cry but my eyes would crust shut with ice.

The aliens are standing a short distance away, as if waiting to grab me if I topple, but wanting to give me space at the same time. I shiver and make no move to get near them. It's even colder outside of the ship's protective warmth. A hard gust of wind nearly knocks me off my feet and I wobble in my snowshoes. I stagger, staring down at my feet, and then I notice some of the snow isn't all that clean. Dark specks cover patches of the area, and I take a few steps forward, moving around the edge of the ship. Something reddish flashes and I approach it, curious. It looks like an emergency light of some kind, blinking over and over again, embedded into the body of the ship. It must be hot, though, because all of the snow around it is melted clear away. I avoid it and look over. There's a male alien dragging what looks like a corpse of a giant, car-sized creature away. He pulls it by the long, spindly legs and then tosses it onto a snowy heap of what looks like other bodies. I shudder and head back toward the entrance, where my sister will be. I don't want to be alone.

Maddie is standing at the gaping hole in the side of the ship, her lips parted in surprise. I see her mouth something like *oh wow* and she twists and turns, trying to take it all in. Kira moves to her side and then slips past, heading for her husband. I sidle closer to Maddie, who has pushed her hood off and is gazing around her with unbridled interest. I huddle deeper into mine, hating the cold.

That's the Taylor sisters in a nutshell—Maddie staring out into the world with excitement, and me hiding behind her wishing I were somewhere else.

Someone grabs my waist and I squeak in surprise, stumbling backward into my sister. I feel Maddie grab me and try to right me, but I tumble into the snow, landing flat on my back like a turtle.

I close my eyes, embarrassed. Good thing I can't hear them laughing.

A hand taps my shoulder and waits.

I open my eyes a bit and see the nice one—Rowdan—offer me a hand up. His dark blue hand is enormous, and I see three big, thick fingers and a thumb. I stare at it for a moment and then reluctantly place my hand in his. He hefts me back to my feet with ease and tilts his head as if to say, *Are you all right?* I give him a faint smile.

Another one appears—the one with the scary, possessive eyes. Hassen. I watch in surprise as Rowdan steps in front of me and looks as if he's giving Hassen a dressing-down. Hassen gestures at me, a rope in his hands, and then makes a motion for tying the rope at his waist. Was that what he was trying to do? Tie me to him?

I don't like this at all. I try to take another step backward, but that's nearly impossible in snowshoes (as I'm learning). I lose my footing and flop onto my back again. This time, both alien men rush to my side and offer hands, along with Maddie.

I ignore both of them and let Maddie help me up, even though I nearly knock her down in the process. I cling to my sister as both men continue to argue and a third one—the stern-faced leader—arrives and wades into the argument. They gesture at me and Hassen shows his rope and then points at the sky. Rowdan points at me and then at Hassen. The argument continues and then Hassen looks expectantly at the leader.

The leader throws his hands up in disgust and then nods, pointing at me. He gestures to Rowdan and then Maddie. Rowdan's mouth thins and he does not look pleased.

Hassen, however, does. He stalks toward me, that predatory look on his face, and comes to put the rope around my waist. I cling to Maddie's arm, trying not to be scared. This is what the leader wanted, right? There must be a reason for this. It's a safety precaution of some kind, I realize. Like the climbers on

Everest. Except when he starts to tie the other end of the rope to his waist, I panic.

I don't want to be tied to this one. I realize now that's what Rowdan was trying to argue about—he knows I'm scared of Hassen. I guess he lost the argument, because he moves to Maddie's side with his own length of rope.

"No," I squeak out and cling to Maddie. "No! I don't want to be with this one."

Maddie says something back to me, brows furrowed. *You're babbling. It's okay, Lila.*

Oh sure, it's okay for her—she's not going to be strapped to this guy. I shake my head again and then try to rip my gloves off so I can signal to my sister in private that he makes me uncomfortable and I don't like him. But Maddie stops me and shakes her head. *We need to go,* she mouths.

I stare at her.

*I won't let anything happen to you, I promise.*

The itch to extend my middle finger at her heightens, but I ignore it. Am I being ridiculous and babyish by not wanting to be tied to this guy? Maybe, but I'm scared. I'm allowed to be a baby. I look around and everyone's watching me, waiting. There's impatience stamped across more than one face.

I have to remember the Yes Plan.

Shit. I already hate the Yes Plan.

I sigh and put my hands down. This time, when the scary one—Hassen—ties the rope around his waist and points for me to start walking, I do.

Because I guess the only thing worse than being tied to the scary guy would be being left behind.

# CHAPTER FOUR
## Rokan

My "knowing" feeling is rumbling in my chest. Something is about to go wrong. It sets me ill at ease. My feeling is centered around the soft one—Li-lah—but I am not entirely certain of what it is I am feeling. I do not feel she is in danger. I am not resonating to her. And yet . . . I do not like this.

I eye how close she walks to Hassen, and the protective looks he gives her. Is this jealousy, then? Am I envious that he has staked his claim on the same female that intrigues me? Or is it something more? Normally my "knowing" is clear, but this time, it is as muddy as the churned snow at our feet. I want to say something to Haeden, to call off this hunt, but I am torn. Until I know why I am troubled, it is foolish to end the hunt. The humans are already out in the snow, and moving slow. The trek back to the cave would take as long as moving forward, and they need khuis to warm them and heal their bodies. Li-lah needs a khui most of all; as others have pointed out, she is not strong, and the fact that she cannot hear worries everyone. Her hand-words are fine in the cave, but in the wild, when she cannot hear the scream of a sky-claw as it rips through the air, or the growls of metlaks as they emerge from a cave? She is in danger.

Perhaps this is what makes me uneasy. If so, all the more reason to get to the sa-kohtsk and bring it down.

"Are we close to there?" the one at my side says. Mah-dee. "I'm tired and I'm sure Lila is, too."

"Soon," I tell her, and it is clear that my vague answer irritates her.

She snorts and mutters under her breath. "Been saying that for the past hour."

I steal another glance at Li-lah and Hassen. The human's steps are slowing, and as I watch, one corner of her fur cloak falls off her shoulder and drags on the snow behind her. Before she can recover, Hassen scoops it up and tucks it around her body.

And my gut burns once more.

That is what this is, then. It is not my knowing. It is envy that he gets to keep her close and I do not. I am ashamed—Hassen is my friend and a good hunter, if hotheaded. If he resonates to Li-lah, I will be glad for him and their happiness. I have no claim on her. I cannot, because resonance decides. Reluctantly, I tear my gaze from her and point into the distance. "Do you see the trees? The tops have been shorn. That is because the sa-kohtsk was here recently. We will get to those trees and there we will find our prey."

Mah-dee puts a hand to her forehead, squinting into the distance. "Those are *trees*?"

"They are. Do they not look the same in your world?"

She laughs loudly. "No!"

As we walk, I see Li-lah's arms flail and she grabs at Hassen for her balance. I fight the strange envy in my gut at the sight of that, and the sight of his arms going around her.

Then I feel it a moment later—the ground vibrates. A second later, it vibrates again. It is the heavy footfalls of the sa-kohtsk, and it is near. I sling my bow off my shoulder and look over at Haeden. "Our prey is near."

He nods, jogging over to us. "I feel it."

We cluster as a group to discuss the setup of the hunt. One of the hunters will stay behind, all three human females tethered to his waist so they cannot be lifted away by a sky-claw. The worry is still present even though the skies are clear at the moment. They will hide in the safety of the trees while the rest of us bring down the creature. When it is safe, they will be brought forward again. All of this is said in the human language so Mahdee can follow along. I try not to watch Li-lah, but I see her studying our faces as we speak and I wonder what it is she looks for.

I am a selfish male, because I want her hearing to be fixed. I want to speak to her. I want to hear her laugh.

"Can we have weapons?" Mah-dee asks, and gestures at her sister. "Me and Lila?"

Hassen crosses his arms over his chest and scowls down at her. "Why? You will not be hunting."

She flattens her hand and pushes it in front of his face. "Talk to this." Then she turns to Haeden and repeats her question. "Can Lila and I have weapons?"

The look on Hassen's face is incredulous and he pushes Mahdee's hand aside. "I said—"

"You do not decide for the humans, Hassen," Haeden says in a weary voice. Raahosh just rolls his eyes, annoyed with Hassen and the rest of us. "If they will feel safer with blades, we will give them weapons."

"Ha!" Mah-dee says triumphantly and smirks up at Hassen.

"Suck on that, Smurf." She wiggles her fingers at Haeden. "Now gimme a knife."

"Is this wise?" Hassen demands, switching to sa-khui. "We should not arm them!"

"Why? Do you not think you can take them?" Bek counters. He is no happier with Hassen than I am for being selfish with the dark-haired female.

"Hey, speak English," Mah-dee interrupts, frowning. "This is rude!"

Hassen ignores her. "I do not want the females to hurt themselves," he says, and looks at Taushen and Aehako for support. "Remember when the other human females were given their khuis? Some of them fought out of fear. And now you wish to give these two blades? They will not hurt us but they can easily harm themselves."

"He is right," Raahosh says. "My Leezh is strong like this one and she fought hard against the placing of her khui. We do not need to give them weapons."

Haeden considers Raahosh's words, then nods. "It is decided, then. Unless someone feels strongly that we should do otherwise?"

Kira raises a hand, and then sighs. "I'm outvoted, aren't I?"

Aehako grins and presses a kiss to the top of his mate's head. "You are."

"Okay, but you guys break it to them, then." Kira raises her hands. "I absolve myself of this conversation."

"What are you guys talking about?" Mah-dee asks. "Why—" Her mouth opens and she goes silent.

The sa-kohtsk lumbers into view in the distance, all legs and shaggy gray fur. Even from here I can see its four eyes glowing.

Li-lah whimpers.

Mah-dee's gaze remains locked on the creature. "Fuck, that is hideous."

"That is what we are hunting," Haeden says.

"Where's the parasite?" Mah-dee asks.

"Inside," Kira tells her. "We have to kill it and pull them out of the heart."

"Gross."

"Yup."

A snowstorm grows overhead, the skies darkening to an angry gray. A few of the others eye the clouds with worry, and glance over at me. It is well known in the tribe that I am good at understanding the weather, but this particular storm is not what is making me anxious. Even if it is, we must continue.

It is more important to hunt and get the khuis for the females.

The sa-kohtsk is not in a herd, which means it is a young male. It is alone and, because it is young, is swiftly brought down by our group of experienced hunters. Raahosh's arrow hits it in the eye and it tumbles to the ground in a crash and an explosion of snow. The females are hurried forward even as Hassen and Bek pry the rib cage apart, exposing the still-beating heart and the glowing khui threads within.

The women look faint. Mah-dee turns to Li-lah and pulls off her gloves, moving her hands frantically. I watch them, curious to see if I can understand the words. But Li-lah just shrugs. "We do it," she says, words soft and slurred. I am surprised—and strangely pleased—to hear her sweet voice. "There's no going back."

Mah-dee throws her hands up in exasperation. "Fine."

"Are you ready?" calls Raahosh. He looks at me and Taushen. "Keep your spears on alert. The smell of blood will draw metlaks."

"Or sky-claws," Haeden adds.

I nod and ready my bow while Taushen jogs away a short distance to keep watch. Bek and Aehako do so as well, and Kira ushers the females forward. "The sooner we get this done, the better, ladies," I hear her say. "It's starting to snow."

Kira is right—fat, slow flakes are appearing in the air, and within moments, the skies are white with falling snow. I turn and scan the darkening skies, watching for sky-claws. Visibility is decreasing by the moment, and my job grows ever more important. I want to watch the females—Li-lah especially—but I am a hunter and I have my duty to protect. There were shadows hovering on the horizon and I watch to make sure they do not come closer.

I must ignore the swift intake of female breath, the soft whimpers, Kira's encouraging murmurs.

*Focus.*

I want to see her, though. I want to see Li-lah's strange green eyes flooded with comforting, glowing blue. I want to know she is safe and she will be strong. I—

A shadow swoops in the distance, barely visible in the heavily falling snow. I squint, not sure if it is my imagination, and then I see it again, circling closer. "Sky-claw," I warn, raising my arrow higher. "Be alert!"

"Get them up," someone shouts. "Get them protected by the trees."

I glance backward and see Aehako scrambling toward his mate. The two new humans are sprawled on the blood-spattered snow, unconscious. This is normal when one accepts a khui, but they do not have hours to recover. Not with sky-claws in the air. Another shadow flits overhead and I look up. Not just one sky-claw, but three. "Be alert," I shout again, loosing my first arrow when one dips low. "Look to the air! Get the females to safety!"

Out of the corner of my eye, I see Hassen scoop up one of the females and run for the tree line. Bek scrambles past me, and I hear him arguing with Haeden over the other female and who should carry her. I nock another arrow and let it fly, and then I see Raahosh at my side, his bow raised. We loose arrow after arrow. Two hit the thin, veiny wings of the sky-claws and one hits low in the belly. The small wounded one gives a high-pitched scream and whirls away, and then a second breaks off and chases after it. As I watch, the larger one attacks the smaller, and snaps its neck. Before the body can plummet from the air, the victor scoops it up in its claws and carries it away.

That just leaves one. It circles around the sa-kohtsk corpse, and I turn, shooting my last arrow before tossing my bow aside and picking up my spear. It snarls and snaps at Bek, and I rush forward with the other hunters. Taushen's spear slams into the creature's lashing tail, and then it is pinned. Bek, Taushen, Raahosh, and I stab it over and over with our spears, avoiding the dangerous, grasping jaws. Bek's arm is scored by the teeth, but he sidesteps and is out of danger quickly.

Then it is nothing but a corpse, bloody and reeking next to the discarded sa-kohtsk. I pant, wiping blood from my face.

"Is anyone hurt?" Haeden asks, storming forward, his spear in hand. "Do you need a healer?"

Bek rubs his bleeding arm. "There is no healer, so it does not matter. And the wound is not deep."

Haeden hands Bek his waterskin. "They have dirty mouths. Wash it well and see Maylak when we return." He looks around, a frown on his face as he stares out into the driving snow. "Where is Hassen?"

I look as well, but my gaze is seeking someone else, someone with long, dark hair and a pale human face. Mah-dee rests under a tree, unconscious. Kira is at her side, and Aehako protects them both. Li-lah is not with them.

My knowing sense shoots through me with force, and I realize that I have been wrong. I am not jealous of Hassen. It is not because I am envious of him that my sense surges.

*He* is the danger. It is not the storm. It is not the sky-claws. It is Hassen. "He has stolen her," I say aloud. "He has taken Li-lah."

Hassen is going to try to force resonance. The thought fills me with helpless fury, and my hands curl so hard that my bone blade cracks in my grasp.

# CHAPTER FIVE
## Lila

I stifle a yawn and burrow deeper into the blankets. For the first time in what feels like forever, I'm warm. My toes aren't frozen under the furs and I . . . oh.

It's because I have a parasite. The coo-ee. I rub my chest, eyes closed, but I don't feel any different. Just warmer.

I roll onto my back and open my eyes.

A blue face is inches from mine, glowing eyes wide. Fangs jut from the grinning mouth.

I shriek and fling myself backward, desperate to get away. My head cracks into a hard wall and I groan, pressing a hand to the back of my head as I stare in alarm. What the—

Hassen reaches for me and I slap his hand away. I look around me in shock, because I'm not entirely sure where I am. In fact, I have no clue where I am.

It's a cave . . . I think. There's a small fire burning a short distance away in a dugout firepit that is lined with rocks. I'm sitting in a bed of furs, and there's rock under the bed, not metal.

So, I'm not at the ship. Okay. I rub my eyes, trying to think. My memory's a bit blurry but I remember the big, leggy creature that they pried open and the glowing-spaghetti-noodle-things that they handed to me and Maddie. I remember someone cutting me with a knife, at the base of my throat.

My fingers go to my throat. If there was a cut there, it's healed over already. Wow. Either I healed fast or I was asleep for a really long time again. I'm trying not to think about that year and a half I lost in the pods, or the fact that it could have easily ended up being so much more. What if I was in there for longer than I thought? What if I thought it was only a year and a half and it was more like ten or twenty?

I lick my dry lips. I guess it doesn't matter. The moment I saw those twin suns, I knew I was never going home. It could be a hundred years and it wouldn't change anything. I feel a pang of loss for my old life, but I have Maddie. It's always been just the two of us, and as long as I have her, I know I'll be good.

I glance around for my sister, ignoring Hassen's too-intent face and the fact that he's practically crouching over my bed. I don't see Maddie, though. In fact, I don't see anyone. It's just me and Creepster here. "Maddie?" I call out gently. "You here?"

Hassen gestures, and when I look over at him, I realize he's talking. He seems rather pleased with himself, and his tail—yeah, it's weird—thumps on the ground. He sweeps a hand out, indicating the cave.

I have no idea what he just said. His lips move all wrong for proper lip-reading. Not for the first time, I feel completely overwhelmed and isolated, and I reach a hand back to my ear, feeling for the cochlear implant that isn't there.

"Maddie?" I say again. I'm starting to get uneasy.

Hassen says something again. He taps my blanket-covered knee and then pulls out a waterskin, offering it to me.

Where is everyone? I look around the cave again. The fire is very small, with no meat roasting over it. The cave itself is tiny, with me and Hassen squeezed in, and there's no room for more blankets on the floor space. In fact, I get the impression that this is not more than a two-person cave. So why am I here with him?

Maddie wouldn't let this happen.

I slowly get to my feet. Hassen stands also. He's close, but not so close that he's in my personal space—yet. I avoid the eager look on his face, and the waterskin he shoves in my direction. I'm thirsty, but I want answers. I step out of the blankets and try to go around Hassen. The cave entrance is a short distance away, neatly covered with a stretched hide that acts a bit like a tarp.

Hassen steps in front of me and puts his hands up. Even though I can't read his lips, his message is clear. I'm not supposed to leave.

That's when real panic sets in. Have I been kidnapped?

"*Maddie*," I scream, hopefully loud enough to rattle the cave. "*Maddie! Maddie!*" I start to hyperventilate. "*Maddie!*"

He grips my arms and gives me a little shake, as if to calm me.

It has the opposite effect. I'm in full-blown hysteria at this point, screaming my sister's name and pounding my fists against his chest. There's devastation on his alien features as he realizes just how upset I am.

Good. I want him to know how it feels. I slam my fists on his chest again, and when I realize how ineffectual it feels, I fling myself away from him again and throw myself down on the blankets, crying.

This is the worst thing that could have happened to me. I'm

here completely and utterly alone, with a guy who looks at me like he wants to own me.

I don't have a friend on the entire fucking planet. I'm totally alone and I can't even speak to him. I can't hear.

I'm so alone.

My crying jag lasts a few hours, until I'm weak with exhaustion and my eyes feel hot and swollen. I eventually sit up again and look over at Hassen. He's sitting by the fire, and his shoulders are slumped with dejection. He's disappointed? I ignore the twinge of pity I feel, because the jerk freaking kidnapped me. This shit is not right, not at any level.

He looks over at me and the expectant, hopeful look returns to his face. God, he looks so eager to see me. He gets to his feet and brings the waterskin over, offering it to me again.

I want to refuse, but my throat feels like a desert, so I take it and sip cautiously, watching him. He returns to the fire and comes back a moment later with a bowl of stew. I take it, too, because I'm starving and I'm going to have to eat something if I'm going to live.

I certainly don't plan on dying, not now that I've gone through the trouble of getting the parasite. And it doesn't seem like Hassen wants to hurt me, so I just need to endure him until Maddie finds me. I know my sister—she's not going to rest until we're reunited. She's tireless in her efforts to protect me, and I feel a twinge of guilt that I resented the fact that I needed her for the last few days.

Because right now? I'd give anything to see her in the cave with me.

I tip the stew bowl to my mouth, and to my surprise, it's not as spicy as before. Maybe Kira's a bad cook? Or maybe the parasite's changing other things.

Big blue fingers reach out and brush over my jaw, startling me. I gasp and slap his hand away, ignoring the hurt look on his face. I don't care how nice he is; he's not getting into my pants. I'm not going to fall into his arms because he kidnapped me. If he thinks that, he's got another thing coming. Of course, now that he's tried to touch my cheek, everything is taking on a sinister sort of bent. This cave is awful small and has no privacy. I'm going to be alone with him until he takes me back.

After that cheek-touch? It's pretty clear to me what he wants. He wants himself a human wifey.

And I am absolutely not volunteering.

*Come and get me, Maddie. I'm gonna sit right here and wait.*

I glance over at Hassen. He visibly perks up when his gaze meets mine, and I quickly look away again. I don't want him getting the wrong idea.

I eat and pull the fur blankets tight around me again as a shield. I set the bowl and water aside and then huddle in the corner of the cave with my back against the wall, so I can't be surprised by Hassen. His eagerness is almost puppyish the way he watches me, but then again, a puppy wouldn't kidnap a woman. I'm not sure why he thinks stealing a girl will somehow win her heart. It's bizarre.

I also wonder why the others let him get away with it. Don't they care about what happens to me? Aren't humans supposed to be precious to them? It makes me think of Rowdan, the one with the nice, kind eyes. Maybe he's not so kind after all. Maybe this was all part of the plan.

I can't trust anyone.

I spend hours in bed, watching Hassen. I'm no longer crying; now I'm just afraid. Afraid that Hassen's going to get tired of waiting for me to like him. That he's going to decide to touch more than my cheek. I'm alone with a strange, enormous man who clearly doesn't have pure thoughts in his mind, so of course I'm terrified. It doesn't matter that he's treated me kindly so far; I'm waiting for the other shoe to drop.

He tries to talk to me a little. He comes over and is all smiles, talking as he sets up a fresh waterskin in my reach and offers me a little bowl of what looks like trail mix. I take the food and deliberately turn my face away so I don't read his lips. I'm not interested in hearing what he has to say. What's he going to tell me? *Yeah, my bad, I stole you. Hope you're not mad. Wanna make out?*

He seems more and more disappointed in my reaction to him with every hour that passes. When I do bother to look over at him, he has a dejected look on his face and he rubs his chest. The moment our eyes connect, he lights up and looks at me with anticipation. It's weird, but he watches me so expectantly that I keep getting the feeling that he's like a kid waiting for Christmas, and I'm not sure why.

Also? I really, really have to pee and he's not leaving. There's a carved, covered bowl in one small corner of the cave that I can pretty much guess the use of, but there's no privacy and I'm not about to drop trou and squat in front of him.

He waves a hand and says something, but I ignore him. "Go away," I mutter, and pull the blankets tighter around me. How long can the human body wait to pee, I wonder. It would serve him right if I just made a mess wherever, but I don't know how long we're going to be here, and the last thing I want to do is shoot myself in the foot by peeing in my own furs. I squeeze my thighs tight, determined to wait it out.

A short time later, the urge to pee gets worse. I look over at the fire again. It flickers but Hassen's gone . . .

I sit up, surprised. I didn't realize he'd left me here. Immediately I charge out of my blankets and head for the screen over the cave entrance. I pull it back and take a step outside—

—into a howling blizzard. At least, I assume it's howling. It's utterly silent to me, but the snow whips at my face like needles, and the wind is almost enough to knock me over. I sink, knee-deep, into the building snow in front of the cave. Shit. Do I go after him or do I wait for him to come back? I squint at the gray landscape, but I can't see very far and that familiar, bone-numbing cold is returning.

I retreat back into the cave and replace the screen, then use the "toilet." I wash my hands with a bit of water, then sit back down in my furs and wait.

He *is* coming back, isn't he? As much as I don't want to be here with Hassen, I don't know that I'm ready to be abandoned. Where would I go?

To my relief, my captor shows up again a short time later, brandishing an animal that looks like a stretched-out porcupine with a catlike head. He holds it up and says something I don't catch, then gestures at the fire. *Cook it?*

I lie down in the blankets and close my eyes. A response would mean I'm talking to him, and I'm not talking to him. As long as I'm not alone in this blizzard, it's enough, for now. I can ignore him for a while longer.

I silently take mental stock of the supplies I'll need if I'm going to run away. I'm going to need a backup plan for if something bad happens before Maddie comes to save me.

*Freaking come on, Maddie!*

## Rokan

"It's been two days! Why is it no one can find my sister?" The human's voice reverberates in the small cavern we have called home for the last two sunrises.

Raahosh scowls down at Mah-dee, who has her hands on her hips and is glaring right back up at him, unafraid. "Look outside. You can see as well as I can that the storm has covered any tracks."

"So? This is your planet! You're hunters! You should know this place! How many places can he freaking take her? Go get your happy blue ass out in that snow and find her!" Mah-dee gestures at the cave entrance.

I pause in my sharpening of an arrow and glance over to where Mah-dee stalks near the fire, furious. I understand her frustration; it does not change the fact that Li-lah is nowhere to be found, and the storm has covered all traces of footprints that Hassen might have left.

"I have been out in the snow, searching," Raahosh grits out. "We all have. Rokan has been out searching endlessly and only stopped because I made him return. Taushen is out hunting for them even now. We are doing all we can, but we must keep hunters here to protect you and Kira."

"A poor choice of words," Haeden mutters as he comes and sits next to me. He picks up one of the new arrows I have made and watches Mah-dee out of the corner of his eye.

Mah-dee makes an outraged noise. "Protect me? Protect me? I don't even want to fucking be here! Don't do me any fucking favors! I can take care of myself! Just go out there and find my sister, or let me!" Unafraid, she reaches for the knife at his belt. "Give me a freaking weapon and I'll go find her my damn self—"

Haeden makes an annoyed sound.

Raahosh puts a hand over Mah-dee's and stops her before she can draw his blade. "You do not want to do that."

"I'm pretty sure I do," she bites back.

Kira puts a hand to her face and rubs the smooth spot between her brows. "I know we are all stuck in this cave together right now, but can we please pretend we get along? I promise you we're doing all we can, Maddie."

"Mah-dee." Haeden snorts and glances over at me, handing back one of the sharp arrows I have created. "It is a good name. She is always mad."

I do not laugh, though my mouth twitches with the need. "I understand her anger. They are new to this place and her sister has been stolen. She is upset." I am upset, too.

By stealing Li-lah away, Hassen is trying to force resonance. He could be robbing Taushen, Bek, or me of a mate even now. I tell myself it will not work, and that if Hassen was meant to be Li-lah's mate, he would have resonated to her when she received her khui. But then I think of Raahosh and his Leezh. He stole her and they returned nearly a full turn of the moon later, resonance mates. And I think of Har-loh, who was taken by Rukh. When she returned, she was his resonance mate.

I am furious for all the wrong reasons, and I am angry at myself for it.

I should be angry because Hassen has broken tribal law. I

should be angry for Li-lah that he is hiding her away from her sister and from the tribe. I should be angry that his impulsive action will cause us to be many sunrises late in returning to the tribe, and my mother will worry.

But instead, I am angriest that he is trying to choose for Li-lah. Because I want her for myself. It is wrong to feel possessive of a female I barely know, but I want to get to know her, and not as someone else's mate.

"Do you need this many?"

I look over at Haeden, puzzled. "Many?"

He gestures at the pile of arrows I have made from animal bones. "Many arrows."

Ah. I nod absently and run my thumb along the blade-sharp tip of one. "It is my turn in the cave." Three hunters must remain with the human females at all times to protect them, because we are still in metlak territory. This means Aehako, Bek, and Taushen are out hunting for signs of Li-lah and Hassen while I must wait in the cave with Haeden and Raahosh until they return.

It does not matter that I have not slept in the last day. It does not matter that I have spent every minute allowed out in the snows, searching for a hoped-for footprint. I only return when my exhaustion is greater than my strength, and because I must find out if the others have discovered them yet. Each time I return, I am disappointed to hear there is no news. And then because I must rest—according to Haeden and Raahosh—I spend the rest of the time readying my weapons so I can be prepared to go out again.

I will find Li-lah.

I must find Li-lah.

"It's going to be okay," Kira soothes, getting up and putting her arms around Mah-dee before she can pick another fight with Raahosh. "We're going to find her. Hassen will keep her safe."

"I just don't understand," Mah-dee complains, letting Kira lead her back to sit next to the fire. "Why would he steal her? What's the point?"

Kira hesitates, then admits, "Resonance."

Mah-dee's yellow brows draw together. "What?"

"You know, *resonance*." There's an uneasy look on Kira's face and she glances over at me and Haeden. "We explained resonance, didn't we?"

"Um, no, this is the first I'm hearing of it?" Mah-dee tilts her head. "What's resonance?"

Kira's face goes pale, the color draining from her cheeks. She looks over at Haeden and then Raahosh. "Either of you want to handle this?"

"Resonance is for mating," I volunteer when they are both silent. "The khui in your breast picks a mate for you and then you will bear him a kit."

Mah-dee's brows go up slowly. "Do. *What*?"

Kira gives me a little horrified shake of her head. "You know what? I'll handle this, Rokan." She waves a hand at me, indicating I should hush, and then pats Mah-dee's arm. "Okay. So the khui you have in your body has a number of duties. It keeps its host healthy and adapts you to the environment."

"The parasite, right." Mah-dee's face is unyielding. Her arms cross over her chest. "What does this have to do with a mate and a kit? What *is* a kit?"

Kira looks acutely uncomfortable. "So one of the other duties of the khui is to ensure the propagation of the host species. It picks two people that are the most genetically compatible and, um . . ." She puts her hands into two fists and bumps them together.

Mah-dee's low gasp echoes in the cave. "The fuck you say."

"Yeah. It was hard for a lot of us to deal with it at the time, but the good news is that everyone gets along with their mates."

"Not all," Haeden calls out. "Asha and Hemalo hate each other."

Kira waves off Haeden's comments with a frown. "Most," she corrects. "*Most* love their mates. Some just haven't come around yet."

"So, wait." Mah-dee covers her face and sucks in a deep breath, and then looks up. "I'm trying really hard to follow along here. The parasite decides that I need a man and finds me one? So we can bump uglies?"

"Uhg-lees?" I ask, curious. "What is an uhg-lees?"

Both women ignore me. "It is a bit like that," Kira agrees.

"Why does this thing care if I have sex?"

"Propagation of the species," Kira repeats, though I do not grasp what those words mean. She winces when Mah-dee makes a low scream of rage.

"Are you fucking with me? Is this *Twilight*? Am I going to turn the corner and Stephenie Meyer is going to be there?" She gestures over to where Haeden and I sit. "Are they werewolves?"

"Wayr—?" Haeden begins, frowning.

"No, no," Kira assures her with another wave of her hands. "You're panicking."

She waves her hands so much it makes me think of Li-lah. And thinking of Li-lah makes me wonder why the others are not back yet. I stalk to the front of the cave and peer out. The snow is still falling heavily.

"But the parasite wants me to procreate," Mah-dee says in a

flat voice. "And you didn't think to mention that before we got the glowing-spaghetti-noodle-of-doom shoved into our throats?"

"It's not like you had an option," Kira replies, but her voice is growing small in the face of Mah-dee's obvious displeasure. "And really, not everyone resonates."

"Oh? How many of the humans that came here with you haven't resonated?"

Kira bites her lip.

"And they all have babies?"

With a little sigh, Kira clasps her hands in front of her breast. "You're making this worse than it is, Maddie. It's because there are so few females back at the sa-khui tribe cave—"

Mah-dee's head goes down, her chin ducking. A moment later, I realize it is because her brows have gone so far up—what Kira is saying now has upset her. "Excuse me?"

"Few females," Kira repeats, then bites her lip again. "Okay, yeah, this does sound bad."

"You think? I just found out we're on Popsicle Planet with Captain Horny and the Hairy Palm Crew, and you didn't bother to tell me that I get an assigned playmate?"

Haeden frowns and looks over at me as I drop back into my seat and pick up my carving knife again. "What is she saying? Her words are nonsense."

"She is mad," I tell him. "She wants to make her own choices."

"I can hear you two," Mah-dee snaps, looking over at us. "I'm not fucking deaf." And then she bursts into tears.

Kira shoots us an exasperated look and then puts her arms around Mah-dee, rubbing her back. "I'm sorry," Kira says. "You should have known before we gave you the khui, but it doesn't change anything. You have to have it to survive. I promise. It's not an option. It's just a fact of life. And the guys here are nice. They will treat you very well if you resonate, and they won't touch you if you don't. I swear. Your sister is completely and utterly safe with Hassen, no matter how crazy this all seems."

Mah-dee wipes at her cheeks and straightens, nodding. "So, he stole her because he mated to her? Resonated to her? Do I have a brother-in-law now?"

My heart clenches with jealousy at the thought. "Or he is trying to force it," I add, unable to help myself. Haeden shoots me a quieting glare and I fall silent.

"Force it? What do you mean, force it?"

I remain silent. I am just making things worse.

"What do you mean, force it?" Mah-dee asks again, looking at me. "Rokan?"

"The human females resonated to our males quickly," Haeden says, glaring at me for bringing this up. "Hassen took her because he is hoping that if he is the only male she is around, her khui will resonate to him if they are together enough."

"Like a consolation prize?" she shrieks and jumps to her feet. "He wants a consolation prize mating? Are you shitting me?"

"Are all the yellow-maned ones so angry? She reminds me of Leezh." Haeden shoots an accusing glance at Raahosh.

"My mate is much sweeter," Raahosh grumbles, looking just as annoyed with Mah-dee.

"Even when you stole her?" I jab back. "That is not what Leezh says."

Now Raahosh scowls at me. Perhaps if I make everyone in the cave angry, they will send me out to go look for Li-lah. I scoop up my arrows and drop them into my hip-quiver. I am ready. More than ready. "If the hunters have no luck by the morning, we should take Mah-dee back to the tribal cave," I say to the others. "Hassen will bring her back in his own time. I will go find her."

"You will not," Haeden says. "The sky-claws are a great danger and we have two humans to protect. Without Hassen, I need all the hunters."

I stiffen with anger. Li-lah must come first. She is in danger. She . . .

Across from me, Kira rubs her eyes. They are hollow with lack of sleep. Across the cave, Mah-dee is staring out into the cold. They both look exhausted and frail.

I hate that Haeden is right.

Mah-dee and Kira must be protected, and I cannot leave the group until they are safe. My brother's mate has a young kit she must get back to. And Mah-dee cannot stay here in dangerous lands.

I mull this for a few moments, and then nod slowly. I will go back to the tribal cave with them, and then I will seek Li-lah on my own. It gnaws at my gut to think of leaving her here in Hassen's arms, but he will keep her safe until I can come for her.

I have no other choice. I cannot risk the safety of my brother's mate for Li-lah. Not when Li-lah is safe. I will come back for her.

I will not tell them this, though, or they will seek to stop me.

So I tap my forehead. "We should return. My knowing tells me this is what we should do."

Raahosh nods slowly, brows furrowing. "You're sure?"

"I am."

"Then why not wait here?" Kira asks.

I play on her worry for her kit. I do not want to stay here. Li-lah will not be returning, and the sooner I can separate from the group, the sooner I can go find her. "My knowing tells me we should return to the tribe. Already you have been away from family for too long." Each of them is missing someone back at the home caves—Raahosh misses his Leezh, Haeden misses his Jo-see, and Kira cries every night for her young kit that she left at home to make this journey. "I do not think we should stay."

"This is your knowing speaking to you?" Haeden asks.

I nod.

"Your knowing?" Mah-dee spits at me. "What, are you psychic?"

"Actually, kinda?" Kira says.

Mah-dee throws up her hands. "Oh sure. Why not? I'm going to bed."

"You should get some sleep," I call after her retreating back. "For your journey back to the tribal caves."

She gestures at me with one finger, and that puzzles me. Does she think I speak their hand language? I decide to memorize the signal in case I need it to talk to Li-lah. I practice it a few times and then pack my bags for the morning.

My knowing sense is never wrong, and now that I have said it aloud, I know it to be true. We will return to the caves, and when the others are back home, I will quietly slip away and hunt for Li-lah on my own. It is then I will find her.

It will not be right away, but I will find her. I must be patient.

# CHAPTER SIX
## Lila

It's been almost three weeks, and I think I've slept for all of two hours.

I can't relax. Not stuck here alone with Hassen. Not with him hovering constantly, offering me food and watching me like he's waiting for something to happen. I still haven't figured it out.

He's nice enough, I guess, for a guy that kidnapped me away from everyone else. Yet the fact remains that I can't help but resent him for taking me away from the others and dumping me here. I can't talk to my sister, and I don't want to talk to him, which leaves me with a lot of free time to plot how to escape.

I've got it all figured out, too.

Hassen leaves the cave regularly to go hunting, and it's not like I'm tied up. Maybe he's arrogant enough to assume that I won't ever try to leave? Or maybe he knows that if I leave, he'll just come get me? Whatever it is, I'm not guarded, and for long stretches of time, I'm by myself. This gives me time to catch furtive naps, pack my bag, and hide away the spicy trail mix he keeps trying to feed me. My snowshoes are nowhere to be found, so I've spent the last few days stuffing my boots with extra fur that I've been ripping off one of my blankets. I don't have a knife, but when Hassen leaves, I take one of the bones and sharpen the tip against one of the rocks by the fire until it's almost a shiv. Almost.

I've had a lot of time to consider where I'm going to go, too. I've seen some survival shows on television, so I know water and shelter are the most important things. Water's pretty much handled, though I know you're not supposed to eat snow because it lowers your body temperature or something. I'm not sure that applies to me with my new space heater of a parasite, but that's not my biggest worry. It's shelter. With the coo-ee in my chest, I can withstand the terrible cold a bit longer, but that doesn't mean I'll be able to handle it for a long period of time. I'll need shelter, which means I need someplace safe to go that Hassen won't find me. I'm not exactly sure where that is yet, but I'll know more when I see scenery. I'm thinking trees, maybe a nice snowy forest, something where it'll be easy to gather foodstuffs.

From there, I don't know where I'll go. I don't know where the big blue guys live, or if I even want to head in that direction. What if they're all like Hassen? I want Maddie, but late at night, when I'm alone with my thoughts, I worry. I worry they won't let me find Maddie. What if they separated us deliberately? What if this is some weird devil-guy ritual to separate women until we fall in love with our captors or something?

Because I'm pretty sure Hassen isn't looking for a charades partner.

That's why I need to leave. Because even though it's crazy-stupid to trek out into the wild on my own, it feels even more crazy-stupid to stay and just hope he remains a gentleman the whole time. I'm not that dumb. He's got all the power and I have none, not even a knife.

Like it or not, I've got to ditch my zero and become my own hero.

Hassen returns to the cave about midmorning, like he always does. He brings in a freshly caught kill, like he always does, and finishes butchering it by the fire. Then he stokes the flames higher so he can cook my portion.

I go and sit across from the fire with him because I want to watch how he makes it. I need to know how to make a fire if I'm going to survive. Actually, I need to know how to do an overwhelming list of things, but I'm trying not to worry about that. One thing at a time.

Hassen is poking at the coals with a stick—no, wait, a bone, a really long, curved one—and when he stirs them up, he then crumbles something that looks like dried poop and pushes it into the coals. He leans down to blow on them, and when he looks up, our eyes make contact. Crap.

I see a smug smile curve his mouth and it bugs me, because now he's going to think he's wearing me down. So arrogant. He feeds a few more bits of the springy, pale wood to the fire, then washes his hands before returning to butchering his kill. I'm glad I have a strong stomach, because the sight of him hacking at that poor critter makes it tough to have an appetite.

He pulls a juicy (ugh) bit free and I'm pretty sure he's going to offer it to me again. I've noticed that he eats his meat raw and it wigs me out a little. Instead of handing it to me, though, he leans over and tries to feed it to me.

I slap his hand away.

The chunk of meat goes flying across the cave.

We stare at each other, shocked. My heart thunders in my chest, terrified. What's he going to do now that I've lashed out at him? Is he going to hit me back? Hold me down and force-feed me?

His eyes narrow in my direction, and it takes everything I have to remain still. Hassen slowly gets to his feet and picks up the meat, then tosses it into the fire. The look on his face is stony, and my heart is beating a mile a minute.

This can't go on.

I can't keep slapping at him. And he's not taking the hint.

I need to go. Now. Tonight. Soon. ASAP.

Hassen is sullen as he sets up the stew pouch tripod over the fire and adds a handful of snow, and then dumps in the meat he's been cutting up. He gives me a resentful, why-can't-you-see-how-generous-I-am look and then storms back out of the cave. I've clearly put him in a bad mood.

*Time to go,* my brain reminds me. *Time to effing go.*

I hesitate.

I'm scared.

If I go out there, it could be a death sentence. What if Maddie never finds me? What if I freeze to death? What if I can't make a fire or find anything to eat or a million other things that can go wrong do?

But what if I stay? Am I going to be stuck with just Hassen for the rest of my life? Is this the alien version of that story about the girl that lives in a secret room in the basement? Can I live utterly dependent on the jerk that stole me for the rest of my days and be okay with that?

What if the others are just over the next ridge and I haven't even realized it?

I'll never know unless I try. If worst comes to worst, Hassen will find me again and drag me back. Actually, worst comes to worst, I'll turn into a human Popsicle. I guess there's a sliding scale of "worst" after all. But either way, I can't stay. I return to my blankets and pull out the bone shiv I've sharpened, and grab my bag. I shove my feet into my boots hurriedly and lace them tight.

I move to the front of the cave and peer out. There's only a very light snow falling, and the skies are a lighter gray than the dismal, stormy gray they were yesterday. That's improvement, I suppose. I look around for Hassen, but he's trudging away in the distance, his back to me. Out to hunt more food maybe, or get more fuel.

Now's my chance.

I sling my bag over my shoulder and step forward. Without snowshoes, I sink to my knees, and gasp. It's cold out here, colder than I expected. I rush back into the cave, grab one of the blankets and wrap it around my shoulders, and then race back out again.

The first thing I need to do is get out of sight. I stagger through the deep snow, my feet sinking with every step, and head around the wall of the cliff until I can't see Hassen any longer. That means he can't see me, either. I'm that much closer to freedom now. And I picture Hassen's angry face when he realizes I'm gone and it makes me pick up the pace.

My gloved hand grips the cliff wall as I push forward, my shiv in the other. I stagger with each step but I continue forward, because I'm not going back. I'm not going to sit on my butt and wait for him to decide that I'm not an agreeable enough captive. If I'm on my own, I'm on my own.

The cliff gives way to a ridge, and I climb up it. In the distance, I can see pink, fluttery things waving against the snow, and what looks like a stream. It's not frozen, which is strange. But there's landscape in that direction instead of the endless white hills back where I was, so it's a good way to head. I tug my hood down tighter around my face, because the cold is chapping my skin, and head onward.

I walk for maybe a half hour, putting distance between myself and Hassen's cave, before the worst happens. I'm high on the ridge, looking down on the valley below. I need to get down fast, because I'm visible up here and I need to hide from Hassen. I take a step on the downward slope. The snow beneath my feet gives with a crackle of ice and then I'm tumbling forward. I land on my ass, flop onto my side, and then roll, roll, roll all the way down the snowy side of the ridge before it ends abruptly.

Then I go flying the last ten feet and land on my belly in the snow below.

The breath whooshes out of my lungs and I lie on the snow, on my stomach, trying desperately to catch my breath and get rid of the dizziness swimming in my head. Wasn't expecting that.

I'm not expecting the hand that grabs the heel of my boot, either, and hauls me forward.

Shit. He found me.

I slam a hand into the snowy ground, frustrated, as I'm dragged backward. I twist and turn around to glare at Hassen . . .

Except it's not Hassen.

It's a yeti.

I think.

My eyes go wide and I stare at the creature. It's so weird. From the back, it looks like a dirty teddy bear with a long, shaggy tail and no ears. The fur is a matted, filthy grayish-yellow, and it smells *so* bad. Like wet dog times ten. I can't see its face as it drags me behind it, but the hand that grips my boot is three-fingered and looks almost human. It's so strange. I'm too shocked to be frightened.

There are other people here? Yeti people?

The yeti-thing turns, looking off to the side, and I see an enormous, round eye. It glows blue, just like Hassen and all the other blue aliens. As I watch, the creature throws its head back and its mouth works, like it's calling or crying or something. I don't think it's a word.

The yeti pauses, does the call again, and then waits.

A few moments later, another shadow appears and I look over to see another yeti, just like the first.

Shit.

I look around for my shiv, but it's nowhere to be found. If I had a few minutes to dig around in the loose snow, maybe I could find it. But something tells me I won't get that chance.

The one dragging me forward starts walking again, and I lift my head so I'm not scraped raw along the ice. The new one walks next to it, and they ignore me—for now. Is it because I didn't scream? I'm still too afraid to make a noise.

The new one looks back at me and then touches the other's arm. They've realized I'm awake and looking back at them, I think. I freeze in place, terrified, as both look back at me. What do I do now?

One squats next to me and I can tell by its spread legs it's clearly male. Eesh. Its face is matted with dirty fur and there's a puckered scar where the other eye should be. It looks at the other, makes a small gesture with its hands, and then reaches out to touch my hair.

I remain still and the other makes a noise with its mouth, then a gesture with its hands.

Are they . . . talking? Do these things sign to each other? I raise my hand and make a greeting gesture in ASL. *Hello, nice to meet you.* They won't understand it, but I feel like I need to say . . . something?

Their weird, fishlike glowing eyes focus on my hands. One makes a gesture similar to mine, then tilts its head back and makes another noise that I can't hear. The other moves a hand to its face, almost like a scratch, but even that looks like a sign of some kind to me. I try to repeat the motion.

They both cock their heads and, for a moment, remind me of dogs.

Then they look at each other and purse their small, round mouths, their hands moving in what seem like crude signals—or scratching at fleas. Then the one grabs my boot again and continues dragging me.

I'm not sure if this is worse or better than being Hassen's cave candy. All I know is that I've traded one captor for another.

## Rokan

We leave with a protesting, angry human who wants to stay to find her sister. Even Kira has no sympathy for Mah-dee's frustration, because she wants to return home to her kit. The journey back is long and takes many days. Mah-dee fights the entire way, until even Kira's sympathetic demeanor cracks and she snaps at her.

We all hurry, making good time, and when we return, the tribe streams out to meet us, overjoyed. Mah-dee is angry and makes a great fuss, and I feign an easiness I do not feel. If I am to get away from the others, they must not suspect that every step away from Li-lah is torture. So I smile and joke with the rest, my gaze on the distant hills we have just left behind.

The moment the others turn to go back to the caves, I shoulder my bag and quietly head away. Now is my chance.

Now Mah-dee is safe, and I can go find her sister without endangering the safety of the others.

"Wait! Where are you going?" Taushen calls, racing up to my side.

I do not stop. Already too much time has passed. "To find Li-lah."

"You are? But we will set out in the morning with a group."

"No. Everyone should stay. I will find her. It is my task."

He frowns, jogging after me. "What about Mah-dee? She will want to come with you."

"She will slow me down. She needs to stay." I look at him. "Tell the others there is no need for a hunting party. My knowing is telling me that I will find Li-lah. It tells me I must do this alone. You are needed here to hunt."

Taushen frowns. "I want to come with you, then."

I mull this idea, but my knowing does not respond. No, Taushen will not find her. I will. My knowing sense grows stronger every time I think of her.

My "knowing" about Li-lah's rescue does not include others . . . just Li-lah and me. Every time I mentally add Taushen or Mahdee to the idea, it feels wrong. "It will be just me, Taushen. Tell the others where I have gone so no one worries, but she is mine to find. Everything I am tells me this."

He protests for a bit longer, but when I do not give in, he returns home, dejected. He will try to console Mah-dee, a thankless task if ever there was one.

I take to the trails to try and find where Hassen is hiding with his human prize. Without the humans to slow my steps, I can race as fast as possible through the snowy valleys of my home lands. I know these trails, and I am fast. By myself, it only takes a handful of days to return to the edges of the mountains.

Hassen will still be close to the strange sky-cave. With a human in tow, and one as fragile as Li-lah, he will not go far. That means he is still in metlak territory, and she is in danger of the ever-present sky-claws that have descended upon the land. I want to stomp a boot on his stubborn head for taking her from the protection of the others.

And I want to do more to him if he's convinced her khui to resonate. I am a calm, rational male most of the time, but when I picture Hassen with Li-lah, I am filled with anger. I know my friend has taken her because he so desperately wants a mate, but it does not mean I will not throttle him when I find him.

So I hunt for him. I follow each snow-covered, twisting trail through the mountain passes, looking for hunter caves. He will take her to one of those, because they are filled with supplies, and he will need to keep her comfortable. I know every rock on this side of the mountains, so it is just a matter of finding them before he moves her. He knows someone will be searching for them, so he will take her to the spot we are least likely to find her. And he will do his best to keep her hidden from us, even if it means moving her from place to place until she finally resonates to him.

I have to find her before then.

A day of searching passes. Then another. And another. My body is tired, but I do not give up hope.

Li-lah is waiting for me, I know it. With every sunrise, I feel my knowing sense grow stronger. I will rescue her soon. It is what keeps me going even when my tail goes limp with exhaustion. But every cave I check? There are no signs of Hassen or Li-lah, so I move forward.

It is after many days of searching when I see a set of footprints in fresh snow—large footprints.

Hassen's footprints.

My heart pounds at the sight and I race forward, following the trail. They lead around into one of the shallow canyons near the mountains and I follow it in—and nearly collide face to face with a tired-looking Hassen.

My frustration boils over at the sight of him, and I fling down my pack before he can even greet me. My head lowers and I charge, ramming my horns into his gut and sending him sprawling.

"Rokan!" he snarls. "Stop!"

Before he can get to his feet, I am on him again. I slam him back to the ground and my fist crashes into his jaw. The rage and frustration inside me are so great I can practically feel my khui humming with the force of my emotions. I raise my fist again, only to be flung off of Hassen. I skid backward into the snow and pick myself up, ready to charge at him again.

"Just wait, Rokan," Hassen growls at me.

"Take me to her," I tell him, fists clenched at my side.

He touches his jaw, and there is blood at the corner of his mouth. He spits into the snow and then glares at me. "Let me speak."

"There is nothing to say. You stole Li-lah. You *took* her. She is not yours to steal away—"

"She is gone." He grabs his spear from where it was discarded in the snow. "Which I tried to say, if you had let me speak."

I ignore his sullen words and straighten, frowning. "What do you mean, she is gone?"

"I mean she left. I had her safe and comfortable in a cave, and when I got back, she was gone." He looks angry. Good. Now he knows what I have felt ever since he stole her.

But his words do not make sense. Li-lah is soft and fragile, and she does not know this place. "Did metlaks take her? Do—"

"No. She took a pack and food supplies. She stole some of the furs from the cave. She decided to leave." He sounds disgruntled. "It seems that wandering in the snow is preferable to letting me care for her."

I bark a short, hard laugh. "Good."

"Why is that good?" His expression is full of bitterness. "I would care for her. I would make her my mate." He rubs his chest. "But she hates me."

I feel a burst of pleasure at his words. Li-lah may be small and weak, but she is not too weak to push away Hassen. "Where did she go?"

He shrugs. "She laid a clever trail. Her footsteps end abruptly and I can find no trace of more of them. I have been out looking for her." He gives me a sour look. "You can help me look, now that you are here."

I smile. I cannot help it. In all of my tortured thoughts of Hassen and Li-lah for the last several hands of days, I never expected this. "You should return to the tribe home. I will find her." I tap my chest. "My knowing tells me this."

His eyes narrow and he gives me a curious look, dusting the snow off his furs. "I am surprised you, of all the tribe, are the one to attack me. When you hit me, I thought it was Bek." He rubs his chest. "Or does your knowing say something to you about Li-lah? Does it tell you who she will resonate to?"

"It does not tell me she will resonate to you." His face falls and I feel a surge of pity for my friend. So I add, "It does not tell me she will resonate to me, either."

Hassen sighs and leans over to pick up his discarded pack. "I know you say that you will find her, but I will not leave until I know she is safe. Even if she hates me, I still care for her. I am responsible for her safety."

I nod. Li-lah's safety is greater than my pride, or his. We are united on this. "We will cover more ground if we split up. Shall we agree to meet in a few days to check back with each other? So we are not searching endlessly?"

He agrees, and we make plans. There is one hunter cave larger than the others and more central. It is also farther away from metlak territory, and we agree to meet there in a hand of days and regroup.

I retrieve my own pack and set off in a different direction than him. We must find Li-lah before she is hurt or attacked. Until I have her seated safely in front of a fire, I will not relax.

And the pleasure I feel at the thought of Li-lah running from Hassen?

I will savor *that* when she is safe.

# CHAPTER SEVEN
## Lila

I'm not sure the one-eyed yeti knows what to do with me.

I've been with the yeti people for two long days now. At least, I'm pretty sure it's been two days. It's hard to tell because they stay in caves and don't use fire. There's light pouring in from the cave entrance up above—the yeti cave is more like a deep pit or a hole than a regular cave, and anyone that wants to leave has to climb out. Other than the sunlight at the top, the cave is shadowy and dark. I guess their big, glowing eyes are enough for them to see by in the dark. Me, not so much. And because I can't see—and can't hear—I've spent the last two days in a state of simultaneous fear and calm.

It's weird, but it's almost like I've been captured by animals at the zoo after wandering into their pen. I get the impression the yeti don't want to hurt me, but I also get the impression that if I make a wrong move, they're absolutely going to snap me like a twig.

There are at least twenty of them in this ice cave. Some are young, and some are old. Some are small and female, with a baby furball sucking at a breast. Some are much bigger and a lot more aggressive. They stalk through the cave, trying to establish dominance, and making the others quiver in front of them. Every now and then, the males fight—a brutal, clawing fight with fangs that leaves the defeated one bloody and torn up. And when they look over at me? I do my best to look small and helpless.

They do communicate, though. Their gestures aren't quite like American Sign Language, but I've noticed them give the same subtle hand signal when handing a female a root to eat. One or two have offered me the same roots, but it's always males offering, and I worry that if I accept, I'm going to become Wife #2 or something scary. So I don't answer and just hug my furs tighter to my body. It's only when they leave the roots behind that I grab one and chew on it. It tastes terrible but I'm low on options.

Really, really low on options.

I haven't tried to escape, mostly because there are always a bunch of the male yeti pacing around the cave, and they scare the crap out of me. They're constantly acting like ragebeasts, and I'm afraid that if I don't get away fast enough, they'll dismember me like one is doing to his most recent kill. It seems that the females get roots and the males get whatever it is they decide to kill that day? I watch as one pulls apart a kill and then stuffs a handful of innards into its round, gaping mouth.

Ugh.

I'm waiting for a plan. I don't have one yet, but I'm sure one will come to me. Because I can't stay here. They smell, and I'm cold, and I don't think I've slept since they grabbed me. Did I think I was in danger with Hassen before?

Boy, I had *no* idea.

The yeti male that's eating looks over at me. It's the one-eyed yeti that initially grabbed me. We make eye contact and I mentally cringe, dropping my gaze. The last thing I want is their attention, especially that one's. He hovers a lot and seems to think I belong to him. Or that we're friends. It's impossible to tell with these guys.

He gets up and I cringe. I wish I had my shiv. Or my pack. Or anything.

I wish Maddie was here.

He comes and squats right in front of me, and the stink of unwashed dog hits me like a truck. He makes a subtle hand gesture that I've seen him make several times before, always aimed at me. Does that mean *friend*? *Property*? What?

Before I can attempt to figure it out, my one-eyed buddy holds out a length of intestine toward me.

Is that supposed to be a meal?

Horrified, I grab one of the terrible roots I've been holding on to and start chewing. Maybe if he thinks I'm already eating, he won't push intestine on me. Because if he makes me eat that? Well, I'm not sure how these things are going to react to a puke-fest. I carefully avert my gaze and wait for him to leave.

Seconds pass. He remains seated near me and my skin prickles uncomfortably. Is he just going to wait? Like, forever?

A shadow passes in front of the cave entrance, blotting out the light for a moment. I look over automatically and see a hint of blue.

Hassen? I hold my breath, because at this point, I might even consider that guy a hero if he shows up and gets me away from here.

The blue shadow disappears and the yeti standing near me gives up and shuffles away a few feet to finish his dinner. I continue to stare at the cave entrance up above, hoping someone's come to rescue me. I gaze up for so long that my neck starts to get a crick in it, then I see a small movement again.

There, a hint of horn. Someone *is* there.

My heart hammers in my chest and I press a hand over it, both excited and relieved all at once. I don't know how Hassen's going to extract me from this place, but I'm confident if anyone can, it's one of the big blue aliens.

Then the alien peers out from the edge of the cave, just long enough for me to see his face.

It's not Hassen after all.

It's Rowdan. The one with the kind eyes and the hint of a smile.

My heart beats even faster, and a surge of joy rushes through me. Oh. This is wonderful. I press my fingers to my lips, because I feel like laughing and I don't know how the yeti will like that.

The one-eyed yeti makes the hand signal at me again, head cocked.

This time, I ignore it. I don't need to talk to him. Rowdan's here to save me—from both Hassen and these walking rugs. I look up at his hiding spot and grin as he puts a finger to his lips, indicating silence. He sees me, too. I give a slight nod in response. Quiet. Got it.

My heart, however, isn't paying attention. It's weird, because my chest is practically vibrating, and my pulse feels so loud and frenetic that I can feel it all through my body, like a rumbling purr.

How strange.

## Rokan

Resonance.

It has terrible timing. And yet it is wonderful.

I gaze down at Li-lah's dirty, pale face in the metlak cave. My breast is humming a loud, possessive song at the sight of her. My knowing is vibrating all through my body.

This is what has nagged at me for endless days. This is why I feel so possessive of Li-lah. This is why the thought of Hassen touching her enrages me. This is why she did not resonate to him.

She is mine.

*Mine.*

The thought fills me with unspeakable joy, and utter terror. She is surrounded by metlaks. The creatures are known for their wildness and brutality. They can change moods in the blink of an eye and I have seen them tear their own young limb from limb. She is not safe.

I have found her. My khui has found hers. But I must get her away from here.

I rub my breast, the hum of resonance song so loud I worry that the metlaks will hear it. I must retreat from the cave for now, or I risk giving away my position. My entire body clenches in a silent cry at the thought of leaving her, but I must. I take a few cautious steps away, smoothing my tracks in the snow with a branch so none see I have been here. I hurry to the shadows of a nearby cliff and dump my pack out, looking for answers. I have three knives, sixteen arrows, my bow, and rations. I have a waterskin, fire-making supplies, and . . . and many, many metlaks standing between me and my mate.

The thought staggers me and I grip the cliff wall to support myself.

A mate. I have a mate. Beautiful, fragile Li-lah is *mine*. My khui sings louder at the thought, until the noise is echoing in my ears and feels so strong that I am surprised I am not shaking the snow off the mountain peaks with the force of my song.

I realize, almost as an afterthought, that my cock is hard and aching. Resonance has well and truly gripped me.

Now, however, I must focus on rescuing my mate, not on how my cock aches to be buried in her cunt. Or how warm it made me feel to see her eyes light up with pleasure when she saw me.

*Focus.*

I stare down at my supplies. Normally when I run into metlaks out in the wild, it is never more than one or two, and they are easily dispatched or scared away. I have never had to confront them in their burrow. I think of Li-lah, at the bottom of the metlak den, and reach for my arrows. Metlaks do not like fire. If I can find a way to bring fire to them, I can chase them out. I gather my supplies and shove them back into my pack, thinking. What if I wrap something around the head of each arrow? It will weigh it off balance but it does not need to go far, just to drop into the den and flush them out. Maybe fur? Dvisti fur? But how will I get it to stick? I think, then change directions, heading for the pink, swaying trees on the next ridge. If I cut through the slippery outer skin, the inner part of the tree is sticky with sap that burns. I can use it. I will destroy my cache of arrows, but it does not matter.

As long as I can save my Li-lah, I will do anything.

It takes longer than I would like to prepare my arrows. They are a clumpy, sticky mess by the time I have coated the front half of each one in sap and then covered it in tufts of dvisti fur from one of my boots. I build a fire and tuck one of the coals into a small bowl, shielding it with my hands as I slowly approach the cave. The twin suns are heading toward the horizon, which means the metlaks will be in their cave. They do not hunt at night. The sky-claws, however, are another matter.

One problem at a time, I tell myself.

I manage to creep near to the entrance of the metlak den without being spotted. Carefully, I set down my sputtering coal and add bits of tinder to it, then blow on it to make the fire go higher. With cautious, careful motions, I pull my bow free and ready an arrow. I point the tip down in the cavern, considering where to shoot first. Not directly down into the cave, in case Li-lah has moved from her hiding spot. I will not endanger her. I will shoot the ice walls first, and let my arrow tumble to the cave floor below. The first arrow can provide me light, enough to see where my next should go.

I suck in a breath, picture Li-lah's pale, frightened face, and then steady my hands. I will not fail her. My khui hums a throbbing song now that we are close to the cave again, making it hard to concentrate. I cannot think about Li-lah. Not right now. So I concentrate on my plan. I must be ready to leap away at any moment when the metlaks stream out. I do not need an entire tribe of enraged metlaks in front of me, and me with nothing but sticky arrows.

But I must do this. I dare not leave my Li-lah in their hands overnight. I tip my arrow, holding it against the flickering coal of fire. It sputters and hisses, then lights up, the fire streaming down the body of the arrow. It moves very close to where I hold the arrow, flame licking at my fingers. I ignore the searing, burning pain, gripping my bow and aiming for the cave wall.

I let my arrow fly.

There is nothing but silence. I do not have time to worry if it has gone out. I light another and raise it to shoot when I hear the first angry hoots of the metlaks below. I let the second arrow fly, and then a third. There is the sound of hands climbing the icy cave walls and then I grab my weapons and quickly scale the cliff, just out of sight.

I cling to the cliff wall, two full body lengths above the entrance to their den, and look down below as the metlaks pour from their cave. They scream and race out into the night, terrified by the flames on my arrows. I watch, anxious, as more and more crawl forth. Then the stream of bodies lessens to one or two. Then just one. Some race into the valley, but braver ones are lingering. I have to get Li-lah, and now is the time. I swing back down to the ground and land with a thud, then toss my bow to the ground, exchanging it for a knife. I grip it between my teeth and use my hands and feet to climb down the steep walls of the metlak burrow. My arrows still sputter with fire, though one has gone out. The others will not last much longer.

There, in the corner, hiding under furs with frightened eyes, is my mate.

I rush forward and take her by the arm. The action startles her, and her entire body shivers with a jolt of fear, her eyes snapping open. She gasps when she sees my face, and then her hands fling around my neck. "Rowdan," she whispers.

I take my knife from my mouth to speak. "I am here for you, Li-lah," I tell her, tossing it aside and stroking her hair away from her face. She is filthy and smells like metlak, but she is beautiful to me. "Can you hold on to my neck?"

"I can't see your mouth," she mumbles, and pats at my chest. The frantic look in her eyes just grows worse. "Can't see your mouth to read what you're saying. You have to help me."

"I wish I knew your hand signals," I mutter, but haul her to her feet anyhow. We can communicate later. I take one of her hands and put it at my neck, and then try to drag the other arm around my throat, hoping she gets the idea.

She does—both her arms go around my neck from the back and then she's choking me with how tight her grip is. I feel her small body shivering with fear, even as our khuis hum and their songs blend. I ignore the surge of excitement that the press of her form against mine brings, and hike her legs around my waist. Time to climb out. I grab my knife again and put it between my teeth, and then take to the walls.

Li-lah makes small, frightened whimpers as I climb. I do not blame her—my handholds are poorly chosen and we sway back and forth as the ice crumbles, but my goal is speed. We must get out before the metlaks return.

Amazingly, we manage to break free from the cave to the surface just as the first metlak regains its bravery. It screams an angry challenge at me, but does not approach. Li-lah clings to me, chokingly tight, even as I scoop my pack and discarded bow from the snow. I consider lighting another arrow, but Li-lah is whimpering and scared. I grab my nearly extinguished coal and fling it—bowl and all—at the metlak lurking nearby. It scampers away, hooting a warning, and I haul Li-lah higher on my back and then race into the hills.

I will not stop until I get to a hunter cave and she is safe.

## Lila

It's so cold. I feel like all I do now is complain about the weather, but being in the yeti cave hasn't prepared me for being out in the snow again at night. It's dark out, but the twin moons (yep, there are two of them, too) are gleaming bright on the snow and I can see around us. The yeti have disappeared, and Rowdan's taking me up one ridge and then down another. On and on he goes, powering through knee-high snow like it's nothing. His tail has wrapped protectively around one of my thighs, but I don't point out just how, um, impolitely it's gripping me.

After rescuing my ass? He can put his tail anywhere he wants.

I squeeze my thighs tighter around his waist, blushing at my own thoughts. I'm clinging to him from behind, piggyback style, and every time his tail moves, it rubs against my butt. Add that to the fact that my chest won't stop with the weird purring—and he's doing it, too—and I figure all this movement and vibration must be why I'm feeling so horny. Or maybe it's adrenaline after my rescue.

Whatever it is? It's kind of awkward. I didn't think I could be attracted to the aliens—they look like devils with horns and fangs, and they're massive. But there's no denying that my body's definitely paying attention to his right now.

Which makes for a really uncomfortable rescue.

Not that Rowdan is noticing. He's charging ahead, ignoring the cold, his hands holding my thighs and keeping me pinned against him. I can feel my teeth starting to chatter. "Are we going to be someplace warm soon?" I call out, even though I hate that I'm wimping out. "I'm really cold."

Silence. Of course there's silence. I can't hear him. I hate this; I hate how isolated I am without my hearing, and I itch to touch the small bald spot behind my ear where my cochlear implant used to be. Nothing I can do about it, though. I'm comforted a little when one of his big hands reaches up to pat one of mine where I cling to the collar of his shirt. God, he's warm. He's like a big space heater. I press my body a little closer to his at the thought.

A short time later, he heads toward a rocky tumble in the distance, near the cliffs. He pats my hand again, as if trying to say something to me. What it is, I don't know. This entire planet seems to be snow and rock, snow and rock. Right now? We just found more rock, so I'm not sure if I should get excited.

But then he eases me down off his back and I drop, hip-deep, into the snow. He turns and looks at me, mouth moving, but I can't tell what he's saying. I shake my head at him and he takes off his shirt and then tugs it over my head and the furs I'm bundled in.

And I should protest. I really should. But it's warm and smells like sweat and spices and, okay, I get a little more turned on. I hold it against my body, frowning at him. Isn't he cold? Because he's, like, half-naked. And, like, really, really built. He's got a six-pack going down that lean, hard torso of his, and he even has hard, ridged obliques. They disappear into the waistband of his pants and I try not to be disappointed about that. He gestures behind him and then gestures back at me.

"I should stay here?" I guess aloud.

He nods and then pulls a new knife from his belt and hands it to me.

Oh, okay. Well, at least we're getting somewhere now. I clutch it in my hand and watch as he disappears behind the tumble of rocks with his pack. There's a cave back there, I think. Has to be.

A moment later, a dark brown something the size of a cat streaks past my feet, and I hop backward, screaming silently. What the fuck?

Rowdan appears again, giving me a thumbs-up. He pats my shoulder and then takes my hand, pulling me along with him. Oh. He was checking the cave to make sure it was safe, I guess.

I follow close behind, and when he ducks into a black, jagged hole in the side of the cliff, I swallow my fear and let him lead me forward. After all, he wouldn't steal me away from the yeti just to let a bear eat me, right?

Once inside, he releases my hand and then pats my arm and moves away.

Shit. I don't know if that's *stay here* or *move to the left* or what. "I'm going to stay here," I call out.

He pats my hand again and then there's nothing but darkness. I resist the urge to squeeze my eyes shut out of fear, because blocking out the world right now won't do me any good. I need to be brave, and I need to find out what's going on. The stay in the yeti cave has opened my eyes to just how much shit I'm in, and I need to start paying attention.

A spark flares in the darkness, illuminating Rowdan's face in shadow before disappearing. God, he really looked like a devil just then. I ignore the shiver that creeps down my spine—and the quiver low in my belly—and watch, waiting for another spark. It comes a moment later, and then Rowdan's face lights up again. He's bending over a firepit, blowing on a little mound of tinder. After a tense second, it catches, and I watch his big hands move as he feeds more bits to the flame.

In what seems like no time, there's a fire. A sigh of relief escapes me.

He looks up, eyes gleaming in the firelight at me, and for some reason, it feels like my weird purring strengthens. Rowdan gestures that I should join him. I move forward and hand him back his knife, then sit down next to him by the fire. I ignore the fangs that show when his mouth curls into another faint smile, because I know he's got kind eyes. The fangs don't mean anything.

I smile back.

My chest vibrates a little louder, and I'm getting embarrassed because it's practically jiggling my boobs at this point with the force of it. "I think my coo-ee is cold," I tell him. Maybe this is the parasite version of teeth chattering.

He just smiles and continues to feed the fire.

For some reason, I appreciate that he's quiet. He knows I won't understand anything he tries to tell me without a lot of effort, and he's not trying to talk around me like I'm a problem. It's like he knows I can't hear him, and he's okay with waiting to talk. And for some reason, that's awfully comforting.

I settle in by the fire. Man, I love fire. I stretch my hands toward it to warm up for what feels like the first time in days. The awful tension that's lingered in my body for the last week—first from Hassen and then from the yeti—is draining out of me. No matter what happens now, I know I'm safe. My eyelids get heavy, and I find myself nodding off by the fire after mere moments.

Warm arms go around me, and that same, friendly hand taps my arm. It's like he's telling me *I've got you.* And a moment later, I'm lifted into the air like a princess in a fairy tale and carried in his arms. He sets me down on what feels like the most decadent pile of furs ever, and then gives my arm another pat.

I'm pretty sure that pat means *go to sleep now.* And I do.

# CHAPTER EIGHT
## Rokan

I watch her sleep, scarcely able to believe that she is truly here. She is safe, and she resonates to me. Even in her sleep, I hear the hum of the song in her breast, and my chest is filled with a joyous ache.

To think that I have a mate. To think that all this time, my knowing has been sending me signals. It is why I have been so obsessed with her, why the thought of anyone else touching her fills me with rage. She is mine to protect and mine to care for. Eventually, when she allows it, she will also be mine to touch.

I am eager for that day, but I will be patient. So much has happened that I cannot expect her to fling herself into my arms, no matter how greatly I desire it. My body aches with wanting her, but there is such happiness in my heart that it does not matter. The body can wait.

For now, there is much to be done. The hunter cave we have retreated to is well supplied, but I do not like how close we are to the metlak den. We will not be able to stay here for long. While we are here, though, I must take care of my mate.

I break into a grin at the thought. My mate. Mine.

I must focus. The only thing that matters now is getting my mate safely out of metlak territory. She must rest, and I will prepare our supplies. Then we will meet Hassen at the central cave and journey back together. I ignore the vicious pleasure I feel, imagining his expression when he realizes she resonated to me. I should feel pity for him; he wants a mate badly, and yet over and over again, he is not chosen. When he returns to the tribe, he will be punished for risking Li-lah, and he will not even have her to show for it.

Hassen will not be envied. Vektal will punish him for breaking tribe rules, but the true punishment comes from losing Li-lah.

She turns in her sleep, facing the cave wall, and I can no longer see her face. Time to work, then. I must take stock of the food supplies in the cave, cut new furs to fit her small frame, make snowshoes, replenish my arrows, and a dozen other small tasks that will eat away at the waking hours. I do not have time to sit and watch my mate sleep.

My mate. Another idiotic grin creases my face as I pick up a knife to sharpen it. This is the best day ever.

By the time Li-lah begins to stir, I have made a thick, hearty stew from dried meat and some spices. I have hung a second pouch on the tripod and have water warming there. She is dirty and smells of metlak after spending days in their cave, and I suspect she will want to wash. I have my spare tunic out for her to wear, and fresh furs. I have cut leather strips out of one of the hides in the cave and have begun to string a snowshoe for her out of curved bones. And I keep a watch on the entrance of the cave, just in case a metlak ignores the signs of a sa-khui hunter and comes hunting for her.

I must always be at the ready.

At the far end of the cave, Li-lah sits up and rubs her face. Her dark mane is tousled and spills over her shoulder. There is a smudge of dirt over one cheek, and when she touches her face, she leaves another.

And I am stunned at how beautiful she is.

My khui sings a loud song of agreement, reminding me that it would like for me to mate with her. My body reacts to her nearness and I pull a fur over my lap, so she does not see my stiff cock and get frightened.

The look on her face turns from soft and sleepy to wary as her gaze focuses on me. Even though I rescued her, she does not trust me. I am not surprised, though I feel a small twinge of anger at Hassen for this. It is because of his actions that she does not trust. I will have to show her that I mean no harm.

I slowly pull one of my knives free from the sheath at my belt and then move to set it on the floor between us, then gesture for her to take it. She feels stronger with a knife, so I will give it back to her.

Li-lah scrambles forward and snatches it, then retreats back to the furs with it in her hand. My khui hums alongside hers, the sound nearly overwhelming in the small cave. She gazes at me with a troubled expression.

"I am not like Hassen," I tell her, turning toward the fire and stoking it, just to give my hands something to do. "I will not push you."

"I can't see your mouth," she says in a small, breathless voice. "Can't tell what you are saying. Can't hear you."

I look over.

She taps her ear and makes a gesture with her hands, indicating that she cannot hear. Does she read my mouth to see words? Her khui has not fixed whatever the problem is with her hearing, then. I nod, then remember the hand gestures her sister was fond of making, and try one out, extending my middle finger at her. This is the signal Mah-dee used to acknowledge someone's words.

Li-lah's little breathless laugh fills the cave, and my balls tighten against my groin in response. "Did you just flip me the bird?"

I try to make sense of her words. "Is this not a signal?" I make sure to face her and I watch her brows furrow as she stares at my mouth. It seems unfair to speak words if she cannot hear them. I need to learn her hand gestures.

So I decide to try another tactic. I lean over the fire and fill my traveling bowl with stew, then wipe the underside clean and offer it to her.

She blinks and watches me.

I gesture at the bowl, then touch my mouth, indicating she should eat.

A smile bursts over her face, startling in its beauty. I am in awe. Mah-dee is attractive enough in a plump, healthy human way, but Li-lah? She takes my breath from my body. When her lips curve, I feel a sense of completeness that I have never felt before.

How my mother would laugh to see me so fascinated by a human. She has teased me since the humans arrived, wondering why I did not chase them like Aehako did his Kira. Now I know—I was waiting for Li-lah.

She makes a gesture and murmurs a small "thank you." Ah. I make the gesture back, and she smiles again. Her happiness feels like a prize I have won, and I am determined to keep her smiling. I watch as she takes a bite of the food and then goes to lick her fingers. But she wrinkles her nose and sets the bowl down, a look of distress on her face.

Her hands fly in another gesture and then she makes a brushing motion with her fingers. Ah. She is dirty and she does not like it. I tap my fire-poking stick on the second pouch I have hanging. "Water," I say, then realize I do not know how to gesture it. I think for a moment, then make a washing indication.

"Water?" she asks, and I nod. She then makes a gesture, putting three fingers near her mouth and tapping. "This is water."

She is teaching me her words. Pleasure rushes through me and I repeat the motion, trying to get it as close to her gesture as possible given that I have fewer fingers than her. I mentally repeat it over and over again, determined to learn. I want to communicate with her in the way she is comfortable with. If she cannot use spoken words, I will not, either.

Li-lah washes her hands in the warm water and then looks at me. I tap my cheek and make a splashing gesture, because her face is still dirty. She nods and rubs the warm water on her face and then dunks her hands again, making sure they are clean. She pulls her hands from the water and flicks them to get rid of moisture, and I take the pouch from the fire and go to toss it. She will want new, fresh water to finish bathing once she is done eating.

By the time I have filled the pouch with more snow, melted it, and then filled it again until there is a decent level of water for warming, Li-lah is curled up in her blankets and eating. She watches me, but her shoulders seem a bit more relaxed and the knife rests on her leg. She will come to trust me, but it will take time.

I am a patient male; I am willing to give her all the time she needs.

She finishes the food with a little sigh and I look over in her direction. Her gaze meets mine and I make the *water* sign, tapping my spread fingers near my mouth. Is she thirsty? My signal gets a smile from her and she nods, then hands the bowl back to me. I give her my waterskin and watch as she drinks. She will need more water for drinking, more water for bathing, and she will need to make water and relieve herself. I know that the humans like privacy for their bodies, and they are much shyer than the sa-khui. I do not want her to feel pressured, so I gesture at the bowl in the corner of the cave that is set aside for such actions, and then point at her. Then I point at the water I have warming over the fire, and make the washing motion. I point at myself and indicate I am going to leave the cave for a time. I should check my traps anyhow.

Li-lah nods at me and makes a flurry of gestures with her hands, then pauses, a bashful smile on her face. "I guess we're not quite there yet. I'll wait here, yes." And she points at the floor.

I nod and pick up my bow and spear, wrap a fur around my shoulders, and then head out, making sure to secure the screen over the cave entrance. My khui is humming a protest; it does not want me to leave her. My cock throbs with need, and I grit my teeth as I plunge into the snow.

Perhaps I am not as patient as I think I am, because as I walk away from the cave to check my traps, I picture Li-lah naked and in the furs with me, her arms welcoming.

I wish we were already there.

## Lila

Rowdan is possibly the nicest alien I've met so far, I think as I hurriedly strip off my clothing to give myself a sponge bath. He's trying to take care of me like Hassen, but unlike with Hassen,

I'm not getting a weird vibe from him. With Hassen, every time he handed me food or a drink, I could almost feel a mental tally going on, like "If I get her to eat four more times, then she will want to be my girl." With Rowdan, I don't get that feeling at all. He seems nice. I might be biased because he's not overbearing, but yeah, I like him.

My furry garments still reek of yeti cave and the stink is getting to be too much. I toss them into a pile and the smell lessens a bit. I don't know how long he's going to be gone, so I decide I need to hustle. There's no soap, so I settle for splashing the warm water on my skin and rubbing with the torn scraps of my sleep shirt to get the worst of the grime off. I give my greasy hair a quick rinse, too. By the time I feel clean and can no longer smell the yeti on my skin, the water's almost gone and I'm shivering despite the warmth of the cave.

I glance down at my discarded furs and realize I don't have anything else to wear. That's depressing. I debate putting them back on, but I can't bring myself to do it. I'm probably going to send the wrong signals if Rowdan comes back and I'm nude, but actually, I don't think he would view that as an invitation like Hassen would.

I'm about to climb into bed naked when I realize there's a fresh tunic on the ground near the bed furs, neatly folded. I pick it up, studying it. It's clearly hand-stitched with a deep, open collar that has laces and fur-trimmed sleeves. There's a hint of darker, decorative fur at the hem, and I brush a hand over it, curious. The stitches are jagged but seem to be patterned, like a design. It's clear that a lot of work and love went into this—did he leave it for me or did he make it for me?

I pull it over my head and choke back a laugh. This was

definitely not made for a human physique. The collar hangs open practically to my navel, and the sleeves flop well past my hands, the furry hem calf-length. It must be thigh-length on him, I decide, and roll up the sleeves. By the time I lace the collar high enough for decency, the screen over the front of the cave moves and Rowdan peeks in. The look in his eyes is questioning.

I nod and gesture for him to come in.

He enters and sets his weapons down, then secures the screen. I climb back into bed, where it's nice and warm, and pull the covers over my lap. Now that he's back, my breast feels all weird and vibratey again, which is so strange. I like seeing him return, though. Something about him fills me with pleasure, and I press my thighs together, only to realize that I'm wet and slick between them.

Um.

I hitch the blankets closer against my body, silently willing my nipples to stop pricking. Wow, inappropriate timing much, body? I have no idea why I'm responding like this. I mean, I like him, but I don't know if I like him enough to think about grabbing his horns and . . .

A shiver rockets through me. Okay, maybe I do like him enough to think things like that. Which is weird. Maybe I'm purring because I'm happy. I tap my breast and look at him. "What is this?"

He says something, and then taps his own chest.

I shake my head. I didn't catch that.

He repeats it three times more, and each time, I still don't get it. The fourth time, he frowns and thinks, then says, "Song?"

Okay, I get that part, I guess. It must be part of the coo-ee thing. "Coo-ee song?"

He nods, smiling.

I smile back. I don't even mind the flashes of fangs he's showing now. They're like his horns and his tail—they make him different, but it doesn't mean he's a monster. I pat the front of the tunic, and I'm pleased when he makes the *thank you* sign in ASL. I'm the one that should be saying thank you, but the meaning is clear, and I'm happy he's trying to communicate with me. My thighs tingle again and I squeeze them tight, resisting the urge to slide my hands between my legs. I feel super awkward and flushed, like the dweeby virgin I am. I'm twenty-two, and most girls my age have had at least one lover to call their own, but I've always been a lot shyer than most. I can barely even remember the last time a guy kissed me. Sitting here in front of a half-dressed alien that's making me get wet between my legs for absolutely no reason at all? I'm totally feeling every minute, every hour, every second of my virginity.

Especially when he comes and sits down across from me. I can't seem to stop blushing. He looks at me with a focused intensity that tells me that I'm probably not the only one full of super horny feels, which is even more awkward. He takes one of the furry pillows and sets it in his lap, and then walks his fingers across it and then points at me. What's he asking?

I gesture for him to show me again.

He points at me, and then does the walking motion again, and then says something. Oh. *Hassen*, he's saying. He wants to know why I left.

I purse my lips, trying to think of the best way to describe how I felt. There's no way a hand gesture is going to adequately convey things, and he only knows a handful of signs. "He made me feel unsafe. Too watched. Like he wanted me to be his wife or something. I worried he was going to stop asking and start demanding." I sign the words as well as speak them, just because it's comforting.

The look on his face grows thunderous with anger, and he shifts in his seat, as if just the idea of Hassen being pushy is making him antsy. He picks up the knife I've left lying on the ground and puts it back in my hand, handle first. He thinks for a minute with his hands in the air, as if trying to come up with the right gesture. Then he clenches a fist and nods. *Safe,* he mouths, then points at himself.

If this were Hassen? I'd totally laugh at the thought of him declaring himself safe. But this is Rowdan. He's just different in every way. "I know, Rowdan. And thank you."

His lips twitch. *Rowdan*, he mouths.

"Rowdan," I repeat helpfully. "Is that not your name?" I tap at my breast. "Lila." Then I reach forward and tap on his chest. "Rowdan."

And oh boy, I shouldn't have touched him. His skin is velvety soft under my fingertips, and I have to fight the urge to touch him again. The purring vibration in my chest increases and my nipples get all tight again. Jeez. Mental note to self—no more alien touching. That way lies danger.

But if he notices how unsettled I am, he doesn't say anything. He taps my shoulder and I watch his tongue move as he mouths my name. *Li-lah.* Then he taps himself and mouths his own name.

It looks like *Rowdan* to me. I say his name again.

He shakes his head.

"I'm sorry," I blurt aloud. "Lip-reading is an imprecise science because a lot of it depends on how the mouth moves with the tongue and I'm not getting the nuances. I—"

I go quiet as he takes my hand in his and presses my fingers to his mouth. He's warm. Holy heck, he's so freaking warm. My fingers—which are always a little cold here on this icy planet—feel like they're rubbing against a velvety heating pad. Gosh. I could touch him all over.

And then, of course, I blush at the thought and press my thighs tight together once more.

His mouth moves, and I realize he's saying his name. This is important to him, then, that I get his name right. Okay. I focus on his mouth and how it moves under my fingers, but all I can think about are his surprisingly soft lips brushing against my fingertips. I could almost swear he's purring, or maybe I'm just purring hard enough that I can feel it all through him.

Except now he's waiting.

Yeah, I got nothing. I realize I wasn't even thinking about his name, just how he felt. "Again, but slower?"

He does it again, and oh my God, it feels like he's kissing my fingers. *Stop it, Lila,* I chide myself. *Focus.* So I concentrate on each syllable. *Ro* is the first part, but when he comes to the second part, I realize there's no tongue flick against the teeth that would be there for a *d* sound. I try again a moment later. "Ro-kan?"

He nods and then his mouth stretches into a grin, and I feel it move against my fingers. I smile back, delighted. I feel so good touching him. Then he goes extremely still.

And I realize that we've both been silent, not communicating, and my fingers are still on his mouth. Boy, less than a day and I've already made things awkward with Rowdan—sorry, Rokan. I snatch my hand away, shove it under the blankets after rubbing a half-assed *sorry* sign in front of my chest, and turn from him. I'm so embarrassed—

He grabs my hand, forcing me to look at him. The look on his face isn't weird or too intense, like Hassen. Now that he has my attention, he drops my hand and makes the circle motion on his chest, and looks at me, questioning.

Oh. "That's 'sorry.' I'm sorry I touched you."

His brows go ever so slightly down and he nods slowly. I notice for the first time that his face has thick ridges over the brows that lead to his horns. It's interesting. There are so many things I want to ask about but I feel strangled by my inability to pick up the nuances of conversation.

Maybe Rokan feels the same. Because he taps my shoulder to get my attention and then points at the knife. His hand moves slightly and then he looks at me, a question in his gaze. He wants to know the sign for it.

He wants to be able to communicate with me.

I'm filled with warmth, and I settle in and gesture.

# CHAPTER NINE
## Rokan

**THREE DAYS LATER**

*Out?* Li-lah signals to me, a question on her face as she rises from her furs. *You out?*

*Hunt,* I signal back. *Food.*

Her brows draw together and she frowns, as if displeased with this answer. *Food?* She gestures at the smoked meat by the fire.

*Food. Travel.* I sign the words, wishing I knew how to communicate better with her. *You, me, travel. Food.* It's the best way I know to communicate that we are going to need additional supplies. It is not a lie, though I feel guilty telling her that this is the reason why I must leave the cave this day. Because it is the truth, but not all of it. I gesture at her and then indicate that she should stay, and I will go.

She looks vaguely unhappy but then nods and moves back to her blankets. Her long, slim legs curl under her, flashing under the hem of the tunic before she pulls the blankets over her body.

I smother my groan, biting my lips closed. I do not want her to see my mouth moving and wonder what it is I say.

Instead, I just nod at her and leave the cave behind.

Being with Li-lah is better than I have ever dreamed, and somehow very difficult. I want to spend every moment with her; I watch her small movements, the way she moves her long hair over her shoulder with a graceful sweep, the tiny smile that plays on her lips when I do a sign badly, all of these things. I could watch her all day. Sometimes I watch her sleep, just because she is a craving in my gut. I love the faint, almost nervous sound of her laugh, and her rushed words that can be very loud or very quiet, because she cannot hear herself. I love the way her hands move as she talks. And I am doing my best to learn her words because there are so many things I wish to say to her.

I am also doing my best to fight resonance.

It is not as easy as I had hoped.

My heart, my mind, and my body? They all want her. When she sleeps, it takes everything I have not to join her in the furs. When she smiles, my entire body reacts. When she says my name in that soft way, I feel my sac tighten and my tail flicks in response. I have felt desire before, and it has always been something quickly taken care of with my hand in a private moment.

But in the small cave, there are not many private moments. And I do not want my hand. I want Li-lah.

If she is as affected as I am, she does not show it. She seems easy and relaxed, and her smile is always bright when she sees me. When her khui hums, she will rub her chest, but has not said more about it.

She does not know what it means to resonate. Mah-dee was quite upset when she found out, so it is likely that Li-lah does not grasp what her khui is telling her. Humans do not resonate, so I cannot expect her to come into my arms right away. Either way, I have vowed that I will not touch Li-lah until she asks me to.

And then I worry she will never ask.

It is one reason why I must leave the cave, and do so quickly. I need time alone to take my cock in hand. I cannot run and hunt with my cock standing upright, and I cannot remain in the cave with her all day and not be overwhelmed with need.

I must be patient.

I must.

I will not lose Li-lah's smiles, her trust, for anything.

I head out into the snow, down a safe distance from the cave. When the entrance is no longer in sight, I sling my bow over my shoulder and tear at the lacings holding up my loincloth. My stiff, aching cock is freed to the cool air and I take it in hand. Li-lah's face is in my thoughts as I stroke myself quick and hard. This is not about pleasure. This is about relief.

Even so, it feels like a betrayal to do so. My body is Li-lah's now.

I return to the cave a short time later, and I feel no more at peace than I did when I left. The time spent with my hand was short, and brought only a moment's relief. Only resonance will cure the ache in my body, but I will not pressure Li-lah. I will simply make do until she is ready. And I feel another stab of resentment for Hassen for making her even more frightened of us than she needs to be.

She will not trust me when I tell her that we need to find him and let him know that she is safe. As much as it pains me, finding Hassen is the right thing to do. I know Hassen well, and I know he will not stop in his searching until he finds her. He will feel responsible for her safety. I must let him know she is safe, and then we will travel back to the home caverns together.

I am not sure how he will react when he finds out I have resonated to Li-lah.

That is something we will need to deal with, but not now. For now, I must speak to my mate. The thought makes my chest hum pleasantly. My mate. As I enter the cave, she is there, curled up in blankets near the fire. She sits up at the sight of me, pushing her long, dirty hair off her face, and gives me the greeting gesture. I am struck by how beautiful and fragile my mate is. Was there ever a male as lucky as I am to mate such a lovely female? It makes me want to protect her even more.

While I was out, I hunted, and I bring my small quill-beast to the fire. She prefers her meat charred instead of full of fresh blood, so it will be skinned and go on a skewer. She will need a lot of meat for the walking we will do. As much as I would like to stay here alone with her and wait for her to welcome me to her furs, we cannot.

I skin the quill-beast and spit it over the fire, turning it so it does not burn on one side. I keep a watchful eye on her, in case she wants to hand-talk. I do not want to miss a word. But she is silent, her gaze on the fire. I decide to stay busy, then, melting snow for drinking water and flipping over the quill-beast hide to pluck the thorns it carries on its back and feed them into the fire.

"Rokan?" Her soft voice sends a shiver up my spine.

My body reacts, my sac tightening, and I clench a fist, trying to control myself. I would close my eyes, but I cannot, because I must see her. So I force a smile to my face and nod. I make the *talk* hand-word she has taught me to indicate I am listening.

She begins to gesture, and then sighs aloud. "You won't know the words. Are you okay? You seem tense." She moves her hands, pulling back in a gesture that must be the hand-talk. "Jittery."

I do not know what *jih-tree* means, but she is right that I am tense. I think about my response. "It is resonance," I tell her, and put a hand over my heart and then tap it, indicating the thrumming song that sings out of my breast even now. Hers is doing the same. "And it is more." I try to think of the right hand-speak words. "Tomorrow we travel." I put my fingers on the ground to indicate legs, and walk them, then point at her. "You. Me. Travel." I point outside, then try to gesture something that communicates the suns coming up over the mountains. "Morning."

Her big eyes are thoughtful as she watches me, then nods. "We're leaving?"

Relieved, I nod.

To my surprise, she smiles. "Maddie? My sister?" She makes another hand signal. "This one means 'sister.'" Her eyes light up. "You're taking me to her?"

She has misunderstood, and the excitement in her eyes dies when I shake my head. I am frustrated she has ignored my mention of resonance. Does it not bother her like it does me? It consumes my every moment. A darker thought occurs to me—does she ignore it because she does not like the idea of resonating to me? I am filled with despair. Reluctantly, I tap my breast and then drum my fingers over my heart, trying to signal the song it makes for her.

Li-lah just furrows her brows slightly and then shakes her head. "Maddie?" she asks again.

I bite back my sorrow. Perhaps in time she will come to care for me. "Hassen," I correct. "We travel to Hassen."

She recoils, jerking back from the fire. "What?" She remembers herself a moment later and then makes the same incredulous hand gesture.

It takes me a few moments and a lot of hand-waving before I can successfully communicate to her that Hassen is hunting her, and will not stop until he finds her. *Hassen home,* I signal. *Li-lah home. Rokan home.*

Her expression grows sad again. "My home is across the stars," she whispers, her eyes growing shiny.

Her unhappiness pierces my gut. I sign a new answer. *Li-lah go Rokan home.*

At this, she nods and the look in her eyes is wary. *Rokan no Li-lah Hassen?*

It takes her gesturing this twice before I realize what she is saying. Am I giving her back to him?

"No!" I make the gesture quickly, and relief crosses her face. Even if I wanted to, I could not. She is my resonance mate. I tap my breast and then point at hers. "Resonance decides."

She tilts her head and then gives a small shake. "So tomorrow we travel?" She gestures *sunup*, then *walking*, then points at me.

I nod, though my heart is sinking. Again, she changes the subject. Is she not even curious what resonance means? Why does she not ask? Does she not wish to be my mate? Does she want to go back to Hassen after all? That cannot be, can it? I think of Leezh and Raahosh, and how their bickering is teasing between them. I think of Asha and the mate she hates. My heart feels as if it is being crushed in my chest.

"Rokan?" Li-lah looks at me with concerned eyes.

I nod. "Tomorrow."

She smiles again, then gestures at the water warming over the fire. *Drink? Wash?*

If she wishes to wash, I will just melt more water. I make the *yes* signal, and then reach into my pack. While I was out earlier, I found soapberries and gathered them for her. I pull out the small pouch and offer it to her.

Li-lah takes it and studies the bag, then looks at me. She opens it and pulls a berry out, then sniffs it. *Good?* her hand signal asks.

I nod absently, concentrating on the fire and willing my khui to stop singing.

A moment later she spits, and I look up in time to see her wiping her tongue with the back of her hand. She makes a horrified face.

I laugh. I cannot help it. *Good, wash,* I sign. *Not good eat.*

"Now you tell me," she mutters. She wrinkles her nose and hands the bag back to me. "I don't know how to wash with berries."

Do they not have such things on her world? I try to think of what the other humans have mentioned, but I have not paid much attention to their tales of their old home. Now I wish I had. I take a handful of berries from her and close my fist around them, letting the juice drip into foam. I gesture at her hair with my other hand, and make the *water* signal.

Her face lights up. *Yes,* she signs, and then moves to the water warming over the fire. She unhooks the pouch, and looks over at me. When I nod, she bends over and half pours, half dips her long mane in the water, working it through until it is wet. I watch this with some fascination, and when she reaches for the berries, I hold my hand out to her.

Li-lah's fingers brush over my palm in a caress. My cock surges to life and I grit my teeth. My khui sings even louder, the song urgent and full of need. I hear hers respond but she ignores it, lathering her fingers and then working the berry juice into her hair. Her eyes close and there is a look of utter pleasure on her face. A breathless little moan escapes her.

It is too much.

I jolt to my feet, the need to leave the cave overwhelming. Actually, I do not wish to leave at all. I wish to take her by the hand and lead her to the furs, where we can discover each other's bodies. I wish to bury my cock in the warmth of her cunt.

But since I can do none of those things, I must leave and take myself in hand again.

## Lila

I open my eyes and watch as Rokan stumbles out of the cave. My hands are in my soapy hair, so I can't sign to him and ask what's wrong. Not that I need to. I can guess based off of the enormous erection that's tenting the front of his pants.

And that makes me feel both good and bad.

Maybe it's the constant purring in my chest that's acting like a low-grade vibrator (granted, a vibrator in the wrong spot, but still), and maybe it's the fact that I'm sharing close quarters with a guy that I find sexy in a rather bizarre, horned-and-tailed sort of way. Whatever it is, landing on this ice planet has turned me into a different woman. I never really thought about sex too much before. Now, I can't stop thinking about it. And I can't stop thinking about it with Rokan. I've imagined dozens of scenarios between us in the last few days. Maybe I lick my fingers and then he decides to have a taste. Maybe he wakes up in the middle of the night and slides into bed with me and I don't say no. Maybe I show him the ASL gesture for *sex*?

Maybe I moan on purpose when I start washing my hair.

I mean, it does feel good to lather up and get rid of some of the grease in my hair. Definitely moan-worthy. But a tiny, naughty part of me wanted to see how he'd react.

And he bolted, so I guess that's a reaction, even if it wasn't the one I particularly wanted. Then again, I'm not entirely sure what I want. I'm troubled by the fact that we're going to leave tomorrow and go find Hassen. He's the last person I want to find, but I understand what Rokan is saying—Hassen's still out there searching for me. And while a small, petty part of me is glad he's having a rough time, I know that Rokan's a good, caring guy, and he's going to want his buddy to be safe. Or something.

One thing's for sure—I never purred for Hassen like I do for Rokan.

I rinse the berry lather out of my hair with the last of the water, and I feel a hundred times cleaner. Rokan's not back, so I toss the used water out into the snow, then hurry back into the cave to sit by the fire and thaw the frost off my wet hair. I finger-comb it and hum to myself, waiting for him to return. My body is flushed and my nipples feel incredibly tight. I'm pretty sure if I put my hand down my pants, I'd be wet.

And I don't know what to do.

Masturbation seems the most likely response, but that feels like a slippery slope—what if getting myself off only makes things worse? I've been trying to figure out why I'm constantly amped up around Rokan. At first I thought it was because of the coo-ee, but I wasn't turned on when around Hassen. The opposite, really. And Kira didn't seem like she was in a constant state of ecstasy. So the coo-ee can't be like Spanish fly, can it?

It's only around Rokan that I'm constantly aroused. Maybe he just does it for me. They say when you know, you know. Maybe my body just knows he's gonna be everything my virgin mind has been dreaming of.

I've been scared to make the first move, imagining that he'll look at me like I'm crazy. He's always been so careful of me. *Friend,* he calls himself, and uses the gesture.

Yeah, well, maybe I'm tired of being friends. Because it's clear from his reaction—and mine—that something is going on between us, and I'm intrigued enough to want to know more.

I consider how I'm going to broach the subject as I wait for my hair to dry—the right signals to use, the right way to approach things. When he returns, though, his face is troubled and he has another fresh kill that he sets down near the fire.

*Food?* I sign. I'm still full from the last critter.

He nods and points at the flat rocks surrounding the fire, then gestures at the smoke rising from the coals. Ah. We're going to smoke it. Then he makes the travel gesture and begins to gut the creature.

I wrinkle my nose in distaste as he dresses the kill. There are innards coming out and blood on his hands and a focused, determined look on his face. All right, maybe now is not the time to talk about flirting.

And if we're traveling tomorrow? It might not be the time, either. Not if we're heading toward my good buddy Hassen.

I'll be patient and wait, then. And if I stare a little hard at his broad shoulders while he works? Well, no one would blame a girl.

I dream all kinds of impossibly dirty things about Rokan. Dirty things involving tails, horns, his fangs, and lots of kissing. I'm disappointed when I wake up, because I want to go back to those dreams. But I force myself to sit up and greet the day.

The fire's nearly out and Rokan's already moving about the cave, packing things and cleaning up. I want to help, but I feel like I'll just be in the way, so I sit patiently and wait for him to notice me.

He finishes rolling up a fur and then looks over in my direction. His entire face lights up and the grin he gives me is staggering. Whew. It just got hot in here. I resist the urge to fan myself and smile back, then greet him with a small wave.

*Eat,* he signs. *Drink. Then travel.*

I take the food he offers me and quickly scarf the smoked meat down while he finishes straightening the last of the cave. He hands me boots, and when I stand, he immediately starts packing the bedding. By the time he's done, I've got my first layer of warm furs on over my clothes, and he stops to help me with the next few layers, like I'm a little kid. It'd be funny if it wasn't so frustrating. I want to be able to take care of myself. I feel like I'm dependent on everyone and it's tough. I know I'm capable of so much more.

Rokan finishes bundling me in the furs and helps me strap on the snowshoes he's made for me. I'm given the scabbard to my knife, and I tie it to the outermost belt on my layers upon layers of fur garments. My hood is on, gloves are on, and snowshoes are on. I look like a stuffed animal, and I'm ready to go find Hassen, because after we find him, we go to my sister.

Then Rokan holds out a rope, and I blink at it in surprise. *What is that for?*

He gestures, indicating that he wants to tie it around my waist. Another belt? I hold still and let him, and then my eyebrows go up when he immediately ties the other end around his own waist, leaving a lead-line of just a few feet between us.

Why? I wasn't a fan of being tied to Hassen, and that led to him kidnapping me. This . . . isn't some bizarre courting ritual, is it? "I need to ask about this," I say aloud, then point at the rope. I sign *why* to him, because I don't understand. Is the snow that deep? Or does it have nothing to do with snow at all?

He hesitates, then puts his hands together and makes something that looks like flapping wings.

"A bird?" I ask, then realize they might not have the same thing here. "Wings? Something with wings?" When he nods, I try to think where he's going with this. Not being able to truly communicate means we do a lot of charades and this is one that I can't quite follow along with. "Why rope for birds?"

Rokan gestures again. The "bird" he makes with his hands swoops down, and then he points at me, and then makes a chomping motion with one hand.

Cold prickles go down my spine. I start to gesture, then realize he won't know what I'm asking, and just blurt it out. "How big is this bird?"

He points at one end of the cave, then behind me. I turn and he's pointing at the wall several feet in the distance. The cave is at least fifteen feet long.

Okay, what the *fuck*.

A memory flashes through my mind, of the aliens standing outside the crashed spaceship, one tossing an enormous dead creature atop a pile of others. That was just before I was tethered to Hassen.

Are . . . those the birds? If so, oh my God.

My panic must show on my face, because he pats my arm to

reassure me and gestures at the rope. *No Li-lah,* he indicates. *No bird Li-lah. No eat.*

I guess that's comforting. Sort of. The rope will ensure that the gigantic car-sized bird doesn't eat me? Is that supposed to make me feel better? Because I'm still trying to wrap my head around that. "I'm scared," I admit, and spread my hands in the sign. "Real scared."

To my surprise, Rokan cups my cheek. He points at me. Then at the rope. Then he clenches his fists and does his best to puff his shoulders up, as if trying to seem bigger. I think he's telling me that he's got me. No matter what happens, he's got me and will keep me safe.

It's a sweet message, but I'm a little fixed on that brief cheek touch. His skin felt so soft and hot against my own, and it's made me purr even louder.

I nod slowly, my eyes flicking to his lips before meeting his gaze again.

Rokan, though? He's still watching my mouth. His hand rests on my shoulder, perilously close to touching my cheek again, and we're standing inches apart. Is he . . . is he going to lean forward and kiss me? Every inch of my body comes alive at the thought.

But he only gives me a gentle smile and pats my shoulder, like we're bros or something.

I want to scream with frustration, but it wouldn't be satisfying since I can't hear it. I settle for clenching my fists and scrunching my face when he turns his back.

Then we're off into the snow, nothing but a few feet of rope separating us. He walks slowly, letting me set the pace, and I move to his side instead of at his back. I glance up at the sky, worried.

Rokan taps my shoulder and, when I look over, gestures at his belt, then points at my hand. Do I want to hold on to him?

I do, but instead of grabbing his belt, I take his hand. Mine's mittened, so I can't feel his skin against mine, but I can imagine it.

He seems surprised at my response, but then a look of pleasure moves over his features, and I start purring hard all over again. I feel a blush staining my cheeks and ignore it, squeezing his hand. *Okay?*

Rokan nods and squeezes my hand back.

That makes me feel a little better. Plus, now I have something else to focus on other than being eaten, like how big his hand is compared to mine. Thinking silly, romantic thoughts about a space alien is better than worrying about being bird food.

# CHAPTER TEN
## Rokan

Traveling with Li-lah fills me with joy and terror all at once. I hold her small hand in mine and we take careful steps through the deep snow, because she must tread carefully with the bulky snowshoes. She is silent, her ability to talk hampered by the fact that her hand is in mine, but it does not feel lonely. It feels wonderful, and the suns are out, the weather mild, as if the suns are smiling down upon our journey.

It would be pleasant if it were not for the shadows of sky-claws in the distance, and the spear I grip in my other hand. The female tethered to me is the greatest prize, and I must do everything I can to protect her. I am tempted to throw her over my shoulder and carry her down through the valley and over the other side of the cliffs, into less dangerous territory. Anything to get her closer to safety. But I will not risk angering her or frightening her, not when the risk could be minimal. We traveled with Kira and no sky-claws came close to our party. Perhaps my larger body next to Li-lah's will make us look like intimidating prey.

Haeden's mate, Jo-see, was snatched, but Jo-see is also the tiniest of the humans. Li-lah is much taller.

Perhaps I worry over nothing.

We pause at midday to eat and rest our feet. She's shivering and her waterskin is frozen solid. I hand her mine; I keep it under my wraps to let my body heat thaw it. She takes a few sips but refuses the meat I offer her. *Cold,* she signals, and tucks her hands close against her body.

And then I have something new to worry over. Perhaps sky-claws are not the biggest danger to traveling with a human. Perhaps I am not tending to her as I should. The cave I am to meet Hassen at is but a brief hike of hard travel away from where we are. We can make it there in one day, but it is clear to me that humans do not walk as fast as sa-khui.

There is a hunter cave not far from here, a smaller one. I will take her there instead, and we will take two days to get to Hassen. He will hopefully wait to hear from me before setting out again.

We rest for a short time longer, and then I get to my feet, offering her my hand. I make the *travel* motion with my fingers and gesture at a distant cliff. On the other side of that is a hot stream and the hunter cave. It will not be much farther.

She nods and hauls herself to her feet, wobbling on her snowshoes. She gives me an apologetic look and lifts her hands to signal, then frowns at her gloves. Li-lah starts to pull them off but I shake my head and gesture at the faraway cliff again. We can talk later.

With her hand in mine, we walk some more. Her steps seem slower than before, and I know she is tired. I turn to ask her if she would rather be carried, when my knowing sense rushes through me, sending a chill through my body. A moment later, I see a shadow out of the corner of my eye.

It covers us in darkness before there is even time to think. All I see is a gaping mouth, reaching claws, and teeth—so many teeth—as the sky-claw flings itself down from the sky and heads straight for my Li-lah.

I do not even think; I react. I shove Li-lah aside and hoist my spear into the air, bracing my legs for the inevitable impact.

I feel it a moment later; the spear jolts in my arms, then snaps into a thousand brittle shards even as the jaws close over me and I am flung backward. Hot liquid rushes over me—blood and the sticky filth of the creature's mouth. The sky-claw screams in my ears, even as I hear the faint, high-pitched cry of Li-lah's voice. My legs throb and my bones ache, but I am alive and whole.

I am also in the creature's mouth.

The thing screams in pain again and I feel the aching grind of jagged teeth against my plated lower arms. I grunt in pain as the tongue moves and the teeth dig into my skin. It is trying to chew me or work me free from its mouth, and my arm is trapped between rows of fangs. My spear is gone, nothing but a slick, broken handle remaining. I use my other arm to feel along my belt, looking for one of the many knives I carry. All the while, the sky-claw tries to move its jaws and my arm feels dangerously close to snapping in its grip.

In the distance, muffled, I hear Li-lah screaming my name. She does not sound close; did the rope snap? Did the creature hurt her? Worry over my mate fuels my body, and I move faster.

I must get free to protect her.

My fingers close around one of my belt knives; it is a small one, because I gave the larger one to Li-lah. I pull it free and slam it into the creature's rough tongue. It sinks deep and I feel the sky-claw shiver in response. Over and over, I stab it. *Die now. Die now! You are keeping me from my mate!*

The knife cracks in my grip, the broken handle stabbing into my palm. The shock of it jerks me free from the bloodthirst clouding my mind. I stop, realizing that the mouth I am stuck in is no longer trying to chew me—the teeth digging into my arm have stopped moving. I can still hear Li-lah's terrified cries outside, though. I try to move, but my head is stuck—the back points of my horns are buried in the roof of the creature's mouth. It takes some pushing before my head is freed, and then my arm is freed. I crawl out of the sky-claw's widely gaping mouth on hands and knees, exhausted and bloody.

Li-lah. I must find her. Must protect her. I struggle to get to my feet. My arm throbs painfully and my entire body feels sore. There's a stabbing pain in my tail and one under my ribs, but I ignore them, searching the red-bathed snow for my mate.

There she is, her back to me. Her knife is in her hand and she's sobbing openly and staring at something in the distance. The broken cord of the rope tether drags behind her in the snow like the tail she does not have.

"Li-lah," I call wearily. I just want to hold her close and see for myself that she's safe. She does not turn, and then I feel foolish. I have forgotten. I stagger toward her and touch her shoulder.

She gasps and turns, brandishing the knife. Her eyes are wide and wet as she looks me over. There is a large scrape on her smooth human forehead and a purpling bruise on her cheekbone.

I did this?

"Li-lah," I murmur, horrified. I shoved her out of the way to protect her, never dreaming that I would have harmed her. She must have landed on a rock. Shame and loathing fill me, and I reach out to touch a knuckle to her cheek. "My poor mate."

She sobs and flings her arms around me, squeezing my waist.

I stiffen, because I am covered in gore and drool from the sky-claw, but she still clings to me. She wants me to comfort her, even though I have hurt her. I am a terrible mate, but she is safe. The realization of it strikes me and I stagger at the thought, dropping to my knees. I press my face against her fur-covered breast, feeling the hum of her khui as it matches its song to mine.

Li-lah is safe. Safe.

Safe.

"Rokan," she sobs, her soft voice broken. She pats my shoulder over and over. "Rokan. Rokan."

I hold her for a moment longer, then reluctantly get back to my feet. All of the energy has drained from my body and it feels like effort to hold my horns high and to flick my tail. Her face is filthy and so are her furs, but that can be fixed.

I can never fix the fact that I have hurt her. Just seeing the bruise on her pale cheek is enough to sicken me. *Sorry,* I sign, and then brush a knuckle over her cheek.

She makes a gesture I don't recognize. "Blood," she says aloud, and repeats the gesture. "There's blood everywhere. Are you hurt? Are you okay? That was the thing you were worried about, wasn't it?"

I nod slowly, a strange calm overtaking my body. I give her the *I am well* hand-talk gesture, and then run my other hand over her arms and legs, checking to make sure she is not wounded in a place I cannot see. She is far more important than me. I am a strong warrior and hunter; I have been wounded in the past and worked through it.

But Li-lah? Li-lah is my fragile, precious mate. No harm must come to her.

When I am satisfied that she is healthy other than the terrible bruise on her face, I take her by the hand, and then stop. She is tired, and it is my duty to take care of her.

I will carry her the rest of the way.

## Lila

When Rokan signals that he wants to carry me, I'm pretty sure he's crazy. I sniff, ignoring the hiccups that are mixing with the purring in my chest. The guy just got half-eaten by a pterodactyl-looking thing with a wingspan the size of a bus and he wants to carry *me*?

I resist the urge to fling my arms around him again. I'm just so damn relieved that he's okay. That he's whole and alive and smiling at me. I'm shaking with the aftermath of an adrenaline spike, and I'm mad. I had hearing for ten years and I didn't realize how much I'd come to rely on it until some asshole aliens stole it from me again. I should have known something was off when he turned around. Instead, I had no clue until he flung me to the ground, face-first. I smacked into a rock, and when I hit, my first thought was shock that he'd hurt me. I was utterly crushed because I thought I'd been all wrong about him. Then I looked up just in time to see the awful beast swallow him and his spear.

I think I screamed. A lot. Rokan and the creature skidded several feet away, flinging snow everywhere. There was blood all over the place and the creature was thrashing, and I could see one of Rokan's legs sticking out of its mouth, and no one was getting up.

I didn't know what to do.

I still don't know what to do.

Over and over, this place keeps making me feel like a helpless, hand-wringing princess in need of a rescue. And I am really not a fan of that.

Starting now, I'm going to be a self-rescuing princess. "I can walk," I tell him, and take a step forward. My knees buckle, and my entire body starts shaking. I'm on the verge of crying, again. It's shock. Of course it is. I just watched the guy I have a crush on get eaten by a flying monster.

He scoops me up into his arms like I'm nothing, and carries me just like the princess I didn't want to be.

Okay, starting *tomorrow* I'll be a self-rescuing princess. That sounds good. Today, I'll shiver and be a wimp for a little longer. I'll burrow in the hero's arms and let him take care of me.

Just until tomorrow.

Rokan doesn't carry me for long. Just like he pointed out, we head for the distant cliff and there, tucked away in the rock wall, is another small cave. This entire planet seems to be nothing but snow, rock, and more snow, so I guess it's not surprising that there are a bunch of caves. He sets me gently on my feet, and instead of making me wait outside the cave this time, he puts my knife in my hand, grips his last knife in his own hand, and we go into the cave together.

It's completely dark and I can't hear a thing, so I'm relieved when he gives my arm a gentle pat and steers me toward the cave wall. I wait there, and a few moments later, there's a spark of fire in the firepit. I wait patiently as he builds the fire and then sits up, indicating that I can come join him.

I move to sit next to him and watch as he sets up his cooking tripod over the fire and takes the pouch to go collect snow. "I can do that," I say aloud, and then sign it when he looks in my direction.

He shakes his head and gestures that I should stay sitting by the fire. I do so, but it's irking me a little. Is this a control thing? Is this how he handles the trauma of being nearly eaten? Because I'm all shaky and freaked out, and he's completely chill. It's weird. You'd think I was the one that got eaten by the way he's acting.

Rokan puts the pouch over the fire and peels his furs off, then helps me peel mine. He seems to take more care over my appearance than his, examining my hurt cheek over and over again with a distressed look on his broad face.

*It's okay,* I sign.

He shakes his head. *No okay.*

*You nearly got eaten,* I want to scream at him. How does he not understand how much this affects me? If he gets eaten, I'm lost. I won't find Hassen, or my sister, or anyone. I won't know how to feed myself or build the fire or anything.

I won't have anyone that will make me purr or smile at me. I won't have a big alien with curling horns, a glorious chest, and who tries so hard to learn American Sign Language because he's desperate to talk to me. I won't have anyone that tries to make me smile even when I want to cry, or anyone that will fuss over my stupid bruise after he nearly got eaten.

I don't know why or how Rokan became so important to me, but he did, and I have to fight the urge to fling my arms around him again. Instead, I clasp my hands tight and sit by the fire, my mouth pursed in frustration.

I watch as he tugs off the last of his tattered, bloodstained furs and reveals his bare chest. He's just as dirty underneath all the layers, which is kinda surprising. I guess the creature chewed him good. Just thinking about that makes me a little ill.

He leans over the water pouch to see if it's melted, and then gets out the dipper from his bag and offers it to me.

Is he serious? *Are you serious?* I sign, even though I know he doesn't get it. Then, because he's waiting, I sign something he will recognize. *You. Wash.*

He scowls at me and pushes the dipper in my direction again, then gestures, *Drink*.

Why is he trying to take care of me? I'm not the one that was nearly eaten by a monster. I resist the urge to slap the dipper out of his hand, because the water shouldn't be wasted. I'm frustrated, though. Here I am worried about him and he wants to take care of me? That's nonsense.

It's clear from the stubborn look on his face that we're not going to get anywhere if I put up a fuss, though. So I take the dipper, drink it as fast as I can, and then offer it back to him.

He sets it down and then indicates that I should sit. When I do, he immediately comes over and kneels in front of me. I watch in surprise as he pulls my boots off, because I'm not sure where this is going.

Then he starts to rub my feet.

I jerk away from him, and he looks up in surprise at the same time. I must have made a noise when he touched me. My chest is purring like no tomorrow and I'm feeling all hot and bothered just from that brief brush of his fingers over my feet. This feels wildly inappropriate, though, especially given he's still covered in blood after saving my life. *No,* I sign. *You wash.*

The look on his face is devastated, like he's done something wrong. He shakes his head and tries to take my foot in his hand again. It's clear he wants to take care of me. It's sweet, but it's also awfully out of place at the moment. I shake my head again and touch his arm. "Rokan. I'm fine. Really. Please go wash and take care of yourself. I'm worried about you and it would make me feel better to see you take care of yourself." I push a lock of his long, dirty hair back off his face.

He stills, eyes closing, as if my touch is the best thing he's ever felt.

That hot flutter returns to my belly and I have the strangest urge to run my hands all over his half-naked body, filth and all. Man, I have been just the *horniest* lately. It's not like me. There must be something about Rokan that gets me all fired up. But I'm pretty okay with that? I mean, I really like him. There's something about his attentiveness and his sweet personality that charms me, for all that he's built like the Hulk's blue brother.

Then he opens his eyes again and gives me another heated look that makes my toes curl.

*Wash,* I sign again. Because it's easier to push him away than to unpack what I'm feeling right now.

Rokan nods, a flicker of disappointment on his face. He turns away and heads to the fire, and I wonder if I've hurt his feelings, somehow, because I didn't encourage him? Was I supposed to?

And if I did, what happens then? I'm not experienced. What if things are different with aliens than they are with humans? What if me hitting on him and letting him know I'm interested means we're married or some craziness?

I rub my forehead. When did this all get so complicated? I wish Maddie were here. She'd know what to do. After all, my sister's a bigger girl, and she's confident as all get-out. Me, I'm the shy, awkward one.

I look over at Rokan.

And then I blink. Hard.

While I was busy moping, he's been stripping down. Gone are his leggings and the only thing he's wearing is a rather small breechcloth. The sides of his ass are visible, and he's just as blue and taut and oh-so-bitable—sigh—there as he is everywhere else. His tail flicks back and forth, long and graceful, even if there's a slight bend at the end of it that wasn't there before. His entire torso is covered in grime and there are smears of blood going down the broad muscles of his back.

Sure, he's been shirtless before, but he's never been quite so close to naked. And I can't stop staring.

I watch in fascination as he leans over the fire to dip the washcloth into the pouch of warm water. The cave is small and tight-quartered, and that means his ass is within grabbing reach, if I was a grabby sort of girl. Seeing him like this? It definitely makes my fingers itch and makes me want, so desperately, to be a lot braver than I am. Maddie would grab. Maddie would let him know just how interested she is.

Not for the first time in my life, I wish I was more like Maddie.

Then he straightens, his back still to me, and begins to wash his chest with broad strokes. I bite my lip because it'd be creepy for me to move to the other side of the cave just so I could get a better view, right? But I really, really want to. I want to watch his big hand trail over wet muscles. The purring in my chest seems to be throbbing in time with my aroused pulse, and the urge to slide my hand between my legs is overwhelming.

This is so, so wrong and yet so right.

I clamp my legs together and clasp my hands on my knees, as

if that will help slow my arousal. As if that will make me stop thinking terribly dirty thoughts, like *Is he going to take that breechcloth off?* Or *What's alien equipment look like?* Or *Is his skin that furry-feeling-soft on his inner thighs as it is on his arms?*

Oblivious to my attention, Rokan continues bathing, swiping the cloth up and down his arms, getting the worst of the gunk off his skin. He dips it over and over again, trying to clean his skin off. There's a large spot on one big, flexing shoulder, and as I watch, he misses it. And then misses it again.

God, it's like it's taunting me with its presence.

If it was me bathing him? I'd totally get that spot. My fingers itch at the thought, because how bold would that be? But he moves the cloth over his arm again, and misses it once more.

Argh.

Rokan glances back at me and makes the water signal. If he notices the way I'm devouring his backside with my eyes? He doesn't say anything. If anything, he's a little stiff and awkward as he takes the dirty water to the front of the cave to toss out into the snow.

I notice as he walks past that there's an old blood smear on his tail, too. God, this really is a travesty of bathing, isn't it? I should help out.

I really should.

Just as a friend, of course.

A friend would totally point out to a friend that they were missing a spot on their big, brawny shoulders. It has nothing to do with the insistent, hollow ache between my thighs.

When he walks back in a moment later, water crystallized on his skin like a glossy coating, he's carrying the water pouch full of snow directly in front of his crotch. No wonder he was walking stiff and awkward a moment ago—he's trying to hide his erection from me again.

I press my fingers to my lips, watching as he puts the snow over the fire and crosses his arms impatiently. He's got his back to me. That's something Rokan never does, because he wants to be able to see my hand gestures. He's always so very careful about that.

But right now? Back to me, and won't turn around.

That needy feeling pulses between my legs again, and I squeeze my thighs tight.

Should I say something? Do something? It's clear he's as attracted to me as I am to him. I'm just terrified of being turned away. What if he has a lady alien waiting at home for him? That would be devastating.

I chew on my lip, full of indecision, as he tests the melting snow, then dunks his cloth again and begins to wash once more. His movements are quick and hurried, and he's missing the dirty spot on his shoulder with every brusque swipe.

Gah.

I can't let this go on.

*Courage, Lila. He likes you, too. Remember that.* I suck in a breath and get to my feet. My entire body feels like it's trembling. Of course, that might be because I'm purring so hard. I'm surprised he hasn't commented on it. It has to be noisy, doesn't it?

The frost covering his body is melting, leaving little taunting rivulets all over his skin as he washes. Naturally, that one spot that's driving me crazy seems to be spared, because of course it is. It's the universe telling me to step in.

I'm on my feet; I just need to move forward. I can do this. He's not repulsed by humans; the hard-on he's doing his best to hide from me tells me that. But then I falter—what if there's another reason he's not acting? Because he's, like, married or something?

Crap.

Crap crap crap.

For some reason, the thought of that hurts. I'll never know unless I ask, though. So I suck up my courage and take a step forward, touching him on his arm. "Rokan."

He jerks around, glowing eyes wide with surprise. His gaze meets mine and I feel a charge of electricity shoot through me.

No going back now.

I make the *wash* signal and then hold my hand out.

He puts the scrap of cloth into my palm. I can feel his gaze on me, even if I won't quite meet his eyes. I'm blushing. There's heat in my cheeks, just like the heat between my legs that's driving me to distraction.

"You missed a spot," I mumble aloud and dip the cloth. The water's still cold and slushy, having not had enough time to melt yet, but it doesn't seem to bother him. I indicate that he should turn, and he does, presenting me with his broad back.

And I take another steeling breath before I put the wet cloth against his skin.

He's so warm. So hard and covered with muscle. It's like being this close just puts everything into overdrive. I can feel my chest purring wildly, and I really want to scrub him, all business, and show that I'm not affected. But I can't. My hand trails over one broad shoulder with the cloth, and I watch in fascination as the water sluices down his back. In the flickering light of the fire, he's all blue shadow, and I'm dying to touch him.

So I do. My fingers graze over his shoulder blades, and he stiffens, but doesn't move. His tail flicks against my leg, then stills, as if he's afraid of scaring me off. Like that'll happen. I'm in this deep. Might as well get a little pleasure out of things, right?

I trace his muscles with my hands, feeling along his back. He's soft to touch, like velvet pulled over slabs of muscle. It's such a strange feeling, but a pleasant one, too. Along his spine, he has the bony, plated ridges like he does along his brow and his arms. I let my fingers explore those before dipping to the small of his back, where the water droplets seem to be gathering.

I bet I could pull the tiny breechcloth off of him in no time.

The naughty thought enters my mind and won't leave once it's there. I don't act on it, though—it's taking all my courage to touch him like this. I don't know what I'd do with him naked, but my mind has a few ideas. Filthy, filthy mind.

He turns slowly, and I can't quite lift my head to face him. Instead, I focus on the fact that now my fingers are skimming over the flat planes of his belly instead of his back. He's just as taut here, without an inch of flab to cover the six-pack I'm tracing. Below, right in my line of sight, is the tented front of his breechcloth and it seems a lot bigger than I realized. Whoa. Okay. Alien equipment is definitely larger than human equipment. The sight of it makes my mouth dry, even as it makes me purr harder.

All right, the parasite I got is definitely a horndog of a parasite. I wonder if everyone's is like that. Though I have to admit mine has excellent taste. I trail my fingers up that six-pack, and over his chest, he has the same hard plating. I place my hand over it, fascinated by the texture—

And I feel him purring underneath my hand.

I look up, startled. He's purring, too? I didn't realize because I couldn't hear it, but I wonder if he's been purring all along like I have. The look on Rokan's face is utterly intense as he gazes down at me. It seems possessive and full of longing all at once, and it makes me shiver.

"I don't know what this means," I whisper aloud.

He lifts a hand to gesture, and then hesitates, as if trying to think of the right words.

That's when I notice his arm is wounded.

# CHAPTER ELEVEN
## Rokan

I remain utterly still as Li-lah makes small fussing noises over the scratches on my arm, dabbing at them with the cloth. They are not deep and will heal in a day. My ribs and tail hurt worse, but even those can be ignored.

My cock aches the most of all, and that one cannot be ignored. Not with her standing this close and her small hands on my body.

This is the moment I have dreamed of—my mate touching me, the perfume of her cunt filling the air with her need. Her hand on my chest, feeling me resonate to her. It is everything I have ever wanted—

—until she said she did not understand what the resonance meant.

It is like a knife in the gut to remember that she does not know what resonance means. She does not grasp how important it is, how life-changing. How my world has changed to focus entirely upon her. It is such an important part of my people and our lives that I cannot comprehend that she does not know of it.

No wonder she has not approached me. It is both relief and

frustration to realize that. My mate does not know that she is my mate.

I let her touch and prod the wound on my arm until she is satisfied, though the look on her face is charmingly distressed for such a small scratch. I must think. If she does not realize we are mates, then I must woo her, like human males woo their females. I must show her affection to win her. I cannot assume she will come to my furs unless she feels what I feel.

Her gaze meets mine, and it takes everything I have not to cup her lovely face in my hands, to touch her like she touches me. When she offers me the washcloth back, I get an idea. I make the *wash* gesture like she did, and then indicate she should turn around.

Just as she did to me.

She presses her fingers to her mouth, and I wait. I am asking much from her. After a moment, she pulls her hair over her shoulder and presents her back to me. Her hands move to her throat and she starts to undo the laces on her clothing.

Need rages through me and it takes everything I have not to grab her tunic by the collar and rip it from her body. I force myself to wait. Her fingers are trembling and she is moving slow, but then she tugs at the tunic and it slips around her shoulders, revealing pale human skin.

A groan escapes me, but she doesn't turn. She stands before me, shy, her khui singing loudly to mine. *I must woo her,* I remind myself. I take the cloth and gently brush it over her bared skin, even though she is soft and clean. If she was brave enough to touch me, I will touch her back.

Her trembling stops, and as I continue to smooth the cloth over her skin, bathing her, she relaxes. The tension leaves her shoulders and they drop, and she tilts her head to the side, her hair sliding over her shoulder. She is enjoying my touch, and the thought fills me with joy. I want to press my mouth to that soft skin, to taste her, but I will go slow. I must go slow.

Then she drops the rest of the tunic to her waist, and I drop the cloth I am holding, stunned at the sight of her. The gentle curve of Li-lah's back is the most beautiful thing I have ever seen.

Until she turns toward me.

And the breath whooshes from my throat.

She gives me a shy look and starts to sign, then drops her hands. "I . . . I want to see your face if you say something," Li-lah tells me. "It's awful quiet on the other side."

Of course. I lift my hands, then drop them. I do not have hand-words for how beautiful she is. How the sight of her bared teats makes me nearly lose control. How I am both filled with pleasure that she is my mate, and frustrated that my body sings so loudly for hers that it takes all of my control not to push her down into the furs. But I do not know these hand-words, so I signal *yes*, and then step forward to close the distance between us.

I feel her small body tremble as I come closer. Like this, the top of her head goes to the center of my chest. She is fragile, my Li-lah, yet I would not change a thing about her, because she is mine and she is perfect. I lean closer, and the light scent of her fills my nostrils. I close my eyes to savor it, the smell as delicate as she is. I want to rub my face against her skin and breathe it in.

"Could you . . . could you please kiss me?"

Her small voice catches my attention. I open my eyes and she is looking up at me, her head tilted back. She looks flushed and breathless, and her gaze flicks to my mouth and then to my eyes.

I am filled with a mixture of excitement and horror—the humans kiss with their mouths, but I do not know how to do this. I will not be good at it, I fear, and I want to impress her.

*Yes,* I sign, and then hunch down, holding her shoulders and studying her face. I will need to aim my mouth carefully at hers, and with our size difference, I must squat a bit. I consider her mouth, then lean forward and press my lips against hers with a smacking noise. There. A kiss. I pull back to see if she is pleased.

Her brows furrow together, and then a small giggle escapes her. She claps a hand to her mouth, her shoulders shaking.

*Yes?* I sign again. Did I do well? She is so pleased she is smiling?

But as more giggles and snorts peal out of her, she starts to wipe her eyes, her shoulders moving with the force of her laughter.

"I'm sorry," she says, trying to catch her breath even as more tears stream down her cheeks. "It's just that that was so terrible." And she snort-laughs again.

I stiffen, doing my best not to scowl. She asked for a kiss. I tap at my chest and then sign *no*, then make a kissing face to tell her I am new to it.

She just howls with more laughter. "Sorry," she gasps. "Sorry, sorry."

My irritation fades, and instead, I find myself smiling. Her amusement is adorable, and this is the happiest I have seen her since she was pulled from the cave wall. I make the signal for *again?* just to tease her, and she giggles even more, clutching her sides.

This leaves her pink-tipped teats bare and shivering with her laughter. I am not displeased by this at all. My fingers ache to explore her, but I will settle for her smiles now.

"Sorry," she breathes again, and makes a signal. "I guess you guys don't kiss?"

I shrug. We are learning much from humans, but I do not have the hand-words for this, either. Again, I am frustrated by the fact that I can only speak bits and pieces to her. I have so many things

I wish to say. How did Vektal get around this with his mate, Shorshie?

Then I remember—the elders' cave. The one with the talking walls. It teaches languages. It will know how I can communicate with my Li-lah.

I will take her there. I grab her and hug her close, excited.

She stiffens in my arms, surprised by my touch. A small "oh" escapes her.

Another groan rips from my throat at the feel of her skin against mine. She is soft all over, except the tiny pink nipples that drag against my chest. My Li-lah is rounded and sweet in my grasp, and my cock throbs with the need to claim her.

"I guess you guys hug," she murmurs against my chest, and she does not push away. I am glad; she feels right in my arms. She belongs there. I stroke her hair, her arms, her shoulders, anywhere I can touch her without frightening her.

I want to lick her pale skin and taste her. Everywhere.

Her hands smooth up my sides and then she pulls back, looking up at me. "Do you want to try kissing again? I promise I won't laugh this time. I was just surprised."

I nod quickly. I want it more than anything.

She gives me a shy smile. "Okay. Why don't you sit and I'll stand this time? Even us out a bit."

I edge backward and drop onto the large, smooth rock she was using as a seat earlier. I spread my legs and gesture that she should come forward.

Li-lah bites her lip and her hands go to her teats, covering them.

I frown. Why does she hide herself? As she moves forward, I take one of her hands and pull it away from her breast, shaking my head. Is she ashamed? There is no need; she is lovely, and I will not touch her if she does not ask for my touch. There is no need to hide away.

"Right. I guess that seems silly." She drops her hands and then puts them on my shoulders, closing the distance between us. From this angle, her teats are close to my face, but I ignore them, looking up into her eyes instead. "Now, I'm no expert at this, either. I think I've kissed maybe one guy in my life."

This pleases me. I like that she is mine and mine alone. I give her hand-speak word for *good.*

She laughs again and gives a small shake of her head. "You won't be saying that after I give you my own lousy attempt at kissing."

Nothing she does could be "lousy." I do not need my knowing to understand this. She is perfect in every way.

But then she moves and sits on my knee, and our faces are level. Her fingers brush over my cheek, and I go still.

I hold my breath, lest I move wrong and frighten her before she places her mouth on mine. I need her to kiss me. I need it more than anything. The throbbing song of our khuis fills the cave, and as she leans in, she presses her teats to my chest. Her small hands cup my jaw, and she lowers her mouth to mine.

Her lips are soft as they brush over my mouth. I should not be surprised; humans are soft all over. But I am surprised when her little tongue slips out and brushes over the seam of my mouth. I jerk backward, astonished. That small touch of her tongue nearly made me lose control. My cock aches like stone, and I am breathing hard.

"Sorry," she says again, but there is a smile on her face that says her apology is a lie. "That is what kissing is. It's mouth pressing, but it's also tongues. Did you not know that?"

I shrug again, my skin prickling with awareness of her. I should have guessed that tongues were involved, but I thought humans pressed mouths together and blew air into each other's mouths. I thought it was something that would make sense when I had a mate.

I am a fool. I smack my own forehead. Of course tongues are used. Tongues are for pleasuring. It can go in a mouth as easily as a cunt, I suppose. I have done neither, but the other hunters talk about how to please a female. It seems I should have listened more. I am making a muck of resonance. My mate does not understand it, and when she tries to show me affection, I am surprised.

I am a terrible mate.

"Ready to try again?" she asks, caressing my cheek to get my attention.

That small touch makes me suck in a breath, and I close my eyes, because I am close to spending my seed. I take a few moments to compose myself, and when I open my eyes again, she is frowning down at me as if something is wrong.

Afraid that I have worried her into stopping, I place a hand at the back of her head and pull her against me for another kiss. Our lips meet and mash again, and she makes a small, surprised noise, but she does not pull away. Instead, her lips work against mine, caressing, and I pay attention. I will let her lead in this. When her lips brush against mine in a light movement, I kiss her back. When her tongue flicks against my mouth, I part my lips so she can taste me.

In the next moment, her tongue brushes against mine, and I am lost. A kiss with tongue is like nothing I have ever experienced before. Her mouth is hot and slick, and her tongue is smooth, so smooth. She rubs it against mine and a little moan of surprise escapes her, which makes my cock throb in response. She does not stop once her tongue touches mine, though. She keeps kissing me, her tongue dancing and playing against mine with delicate, teasing brushes. In this, I let her lead as well. Not because I do not want to take charge—but because I am stunned at how much I am feeling at the moment. Over and over again, we kiss, tongues locking and playing, until I am breathless and a mere touch away from losing control.

She pulls away, her lips wet and swollen, and gives me a dazed look. "That was . . . wow."

*Yes,* I signal.

Her gaze flicks to my hands and she laughs, then wraps her arms around my neck and snuggles close against me. I am surprised she has come to my arms, but pleased. I put my arms around her, feeling her soft skin against mine. She shivers, and I realize she is cold. That is why she is so eager for my touch. Of course.

I pick her up and take her to the corner of the cave. There are furs rolled up and stored, and as I set her gently on her feet, I indicate that I am going to make her a bed. She nods and crosses her arms over her chest again, shivering once more.

I feel like a fool. My mate is cold and here I am playing at kisses. I should be taking care of her. I quickly undo the furs and shake them out, then layer them until they form a thick nest. Once it is done, I gesture at it and she slips under the blankets.

Before I can get up to stoke the fire, her small hand catches mine. She peels back the blankets and pats the bed. "Just to snuggle?"

I do not know what *snuh-gull* is, but I can guess. She does not want to do more than what we have done, because she is not experienced. And even though her khui is singing as loudly as mine, I understand. I am just happy she wants me at her side.

I move under the furs with her, and her arms go around me, her breasts pressing against my side again. I put my arms around her, my chest singing with happiness.

"I guess I have an alien boyfriend now," she muses as she presses her cold hands against my side. "That's different."

If *boy-friend* is the human word for *mate*, then yes, yes she does have one.

I make Li-lah rest all afternoon and throughout the evening. There is a cache nearby and I raid it for a small kill—a frozen hopper—before throwing a layer of snow atop it and returning the marker. I keep the fire stoked and make a stew for my mate, and she teaches me more hand-talk. There are so many words it makes my head dizzy, but I do my best to learn them all. I have so much to say to her.

We practice more kissing as well. There is more tongue, more sighs, and my cock is so stiff and aches so badly I feel it will snap off. But Li-lah seems content with kissing and hugging, and so I will be, too. She falls asleep in my arms and I remain there for hours, afraid to leave and lose the moment.

Morning comes too early. I am pleased that Li-lah's bruise has faded from her cheek. My own aches have lessened, as well, my khui hard at work. Li-lah yawns and burrows back under the covers as I clean up our cave. We must meet Hassen today. He will be waiting, and he needs to know he should return home.

He will also need to tell the others that Li-lah and I are safe, but we are not going home yet. We must go to the elders' cave, so I can learn her words. And I am not sending her back with him. She stays with me. I have not told her yet, but I think she will want this, too.

As if my thoughts have summoned her, Li-lah peers over my shoulder, pressing her cheek to my arm. She yawns and watches me tie the pack closed. "I need one of those." When I look over at her, she clarifies. "A pack. A survival kit. I want to learn how to take care of myself in case anything should happen to you."

I rock back on my heels, shaken by this thought. She is right. What if something should happen to me while we are traveling? She will be helpless and alone, and unable to hear the creatures that could hunt her. I nod quickly and make sure that one of the two knives I have left is for her. Tonight, when we rest, I will make her a bag of her own supplies. After we visit the elders' cave and we can talk in more than a few short sentences, I will teach her how to hunt and how to build fire. She is smart and will learn quickly.

And it will give me an excuse to keep her to myself for just a little longer.

We eat a cold meal, drink a bit of meltwater, and then I finish packing up the cave while Li-lah puts on her many layers of fur. My outer furs are filthy and I pack them in my bag for cleaning when we set up camp again. The day looks to be sunny and warm enough that I will not need them. Then we strap on Li-lah's snowshoes and go, hand in hand, out in the snow once more, our waists tethered together. I pull her a little closer and stay mindful of the skies, in case more sky-claws emerge.

But the weather is warm, the suns bright, and the sky-claws are nowhere in sight.

By midmorning, I see Hassen's tracks in the snow. His trail goes down into the next valley, heading south toward the tribal cave. I tap Li-lah's arm and point the tracks out to her.

"My buddy?" she asks in a dry voice.

*No,* I sign, confused. *Hassen.* Does she worry someone else is out here?

But she only gives an amused little snort and holds on to my arm a little tighter.

We round a curve and there, in the distance, is a hunter in furs with two spears strapped to his back. I recognize the stance and call out to him, raising an arm. "Ho!"

He turns and raises a hand halfway before pausing. I can tell the moment he sees Li-lah next to me, because he lowers his head and races toward us, plowing through the snow like a charging dvisti buck. There is a look of joy on his face as he nears, and it fades as he approaches and sees Li-lah's hand on my arm.

"You found her," he says, steps slowing as he approaches. "She is unharmed?"

"Unharmed and well," I agree. His gaze devours her, and I ignore the stab of possessiveness I feel. She is mine. He cannot take her from me this time.

Li-lah scoots closer to me, her grip tightening. I pat her gloved hand to comfort her, and my khui immediately grows louder, the song reverberating through my chest and joined by hers a moment later.

Hassen's expression turns to one of devastation. His shoulders slump as he looks from Li-lah to me. "Resonance," he says, and there is much heaviness in his voice. "You are lucky, my friend."

I nod. There is no point in berating him. He is defeated. I have what he wants more than anything. He turns away, his back to us, and I feel a pang of sorrow for my friend and tribemate. To want something so badly, only to have it slip out of your grasp, it is difficult. "It will happen for you someday," I tell him, and

I feel a little echo in my chest that tells me my knowing is confirming this. "There is Mah-dee, and Farli will be of age soon. Perhaps—"

"Mah-dee hates me. And Farli is like a little sister. Who is left? Esha? She is but four turns of the season old. One of the new kits? Perhaps I will be an old, withered elder before my female's breast resonates to me." He snorts. "It will be that long before Vektal forgives me for betraying the tribe rules. I shall be a lonely old male with no one but Bek and Warrek to understand my sorrow."

I ignore his bitter words. "It will be sooner. Do not give up hope."

He sighs heavily, staring off into the distance even as Li-lah gives me a concerned look. She cannot hear our conversation, and I feel guilty that we talk around her.

He rubs his face, and his tail flicks angrily in the snow before he stands. "All I have ever wanted is a mate and family. I thought for sure . . ." He shakes his head and then puts a hand on my shoulder, the one opposite of Li-lah. "If I am not her mate, I am glad it is you, my friend. You are a good male and a good hunter. You will make her happy." He looks over at Li-lah. "She hated every moment with me, you know. She would not speak."

"She speaks with her hands," I tell him, and make a few of the gestures that Li-lah has shown me. *Water. Good. Yes.* "It is not fair to talk when she cannot hear the words, so we must make the words with our hands."

Li-lah looks between me and Hassen, a frown on her face as she tries to decipher our conversation. She begins to pull off her gloves but I stop her. I will explain more later. For now, I must send Hassen on his way. "Because she has hand-speak, I must learn her words to talk to her. She does not understand resonance."

Hassen gives me an incredulous look. "Not understand resonance?"

"It is true. She knows her breast sings but does not understand."

He crosses his arms over his chest. "Take her to your furs and show her, then."

I ignore the flash of anger that moves through me at his words. "When you have a mate, you will understand why I will not do that."

He flinches. "Your words are not kind."

"Neither are yours." I step protectively in front of my mate. "I know my female. I know what is best for her, not you. And I am going to take her to the elders' cave so I may learn her hand-speak and talk to her."

Hassen nods slowly, though the look on his face is hard. This is a day of many disappointments for him. "So you will leave me to return to the tribe, alone, and tell them of my shame?"

"The only shame is your own. Li-lah did not resonate to you. There is no shame in that. And you knew that stealing her would have consequences."

"I just hoped . . ." He sighs and looks at her again. "I was so sure. I thought if I got her alone with me, her khui would sing to mine. It felt like she was the one."

I do not argue. I know that feeling. But standing here with Li-lah at my side, I know he is wrong. She is mine. "Tell them we will return home once resonance is satisfied and I have learned Li-lah's hand-talk. We will be back before the brutal season."

"So long?" He looks surprised. "That is at least a full cycle of the moons, maybe two."

"I will teach her how to take care of herself," I tell him. "She wants to learn how to make fire, to cook, to hunt. It will take time to teach her these things, and the elders' cave cannot do so." I do not tell him that I want to give Li-lah as much time as possible to come to grips with the fact that I am her mate.

It is obvious from her time with Hassen—and the frustrated look she is giving me now—that she does not like to be surprised.

He rubs his chin, and then nods. "It is an easy trail back to the tribal cave from here, once we are out of metlak and sky-claw territory. Are you well prepared?"

"I need a spear and knives," I tell him. "And trail rations if you have extra."

He nods and reaches behind him, pulling his heavy spears free from his pack, then hands them both to me. "I have my sling and extra knives. Take what you need."

"Thank you, my friend."

Hassen looks over at Li-lah, then at me. "Her sister, the angry one. She will not be pleased to see me come back alone."

"She will have to wait." I set my pack down next to Hassen's so we can share goods.

"Are you guys finished bro-ing down so someone can tell me what's going on?" Li-lah says, crossing her arms. "Because this crap is getting really old."

Hassen grunts. "You talk to your mate. I will go through the supplies."

I walk away to talk to Li-lah, and as I do, I hear him mutter something under his breath about Mah-dee not being the only "angry" one.

# CHAPTER TWELVE
## Lila

I watch Hassen leave and feel a little bit of trepidation. The plan has changed, and I'm not entirely sure I know what's going on. The guys talked for a while, and Hassen kept a respectful distance, which I appreciate. In fact, it almost feels like he's not interested in me at all, which is a real turnabout from before. Then they swapped gear, and Rokan tried to explain with his hands what was going on.

Two different journeys, he explained to me. Which, okay, obvious considering that Hassen is now walking away without his spears and Rokan is gesturing in a completely different direction for us. I didn't understand the rest of what he was trying to tell me, and I think Rokan's as frustrated over that as I am. So when he gestures off into the snow-covered hills again instead of in the direction that Hassen is heading, I plant my feet. "What's going on?" I ask, and sign the words at the same time. I know he won't be able to keep up, but I'm frustrated with everyone talking around me. "I thought the plan was that we get together with Hassen and then go home. Your home, not my home."

I'm trying not to think about my home or the fact that I'll

never see it again. That life completely changed in the blink of an eye, leaving me helpless and unable to hear once more. That I'm stranded on an ice planet with no one but my sister, and even she's far away. If I think about all that, I'll start crying and I might never stop. Right now I'm just doing my best to roll with the punches.

Rokan gestures at Hassen's disappearing form, then at me. He thinks for a moment, makes the *travel* sign with his hands, then points at the rolling hills before us. Then does the *fire* sign, then *sleep*.

"I have no idea what that means," I tell him, frustrated.

He does it again, and adds in a sign for *speak*, and then points at himself.

"Still not getting it."

Rokan gestures at himself again, points at me, signs *speak*, and then points at himself and then in the direction he wants to head.

He wants to talk to me, but only in that direction? I don't understand what's changed, unless . . .

Is it because he's my alien boyfriend now? Does this have something to do with courting? Is that why we're not going with Hassen? I mean, I don't like Hassen, but I'm also pretty sure Rokan told me my sister was in that direction, and not the one he wants to lead me in. "I really wish we could communicate."

Rokan gets excited at my words, nodding and gesturing. He takes my bare hand in his and puts it to his mouth, then starts to speak. He wants me to understand his words, but at his touch, a fiery bolt of sensation rushes through me and I gasp. The purring goes up a notch and my entire body tingles in response. He reacts the same way, his eyes getting that sleepy-lust look that I saw last night after we'd started kissing.

Then he gives himself a small shake and focuses. He taps the hand on his mouth and then says something. He wants me to read his lips. *Okay, Lila, focus.*

I ignore the flash of fangs and concentrate on how he's moving his lips and tongue. The aliens slur a lot of human words, so I have to concentrate that much more. It's distracting, though, because the first word he keeps saying makes his tongue press against the backs of my fingers, sending tingles all through me again. He repeats it, and I start to sound out the word. "Luh . . . lord . . . love?" A sweet tingle rushes through me. "Love?"

He shakes his head.

Oh. I shouldn't be disappointed in that. I mean, we just started "dating" or whatever it is blue ice-people do. It's a bit early to be throwing around the *l* word, but it doesn't mean I'm not stupidly sad that I misread things.

I concentrate again. "Lord . . . lord . . . lorn, no, wait. Learn?"

He nods excitedly, makes the *talk* hand sign, and then gestures in that direction.

"Learn to talk? There?" I gaze out in the snow but I don't see anything there except more snow.

But Rokan grins, looking so pleased with himself, and repeats the words, then gestures at himself, then at me.

"Oh. You want to learn to talk to me?"

His quick nod of affirmation makes my nipples hard and warm pleasure rushes through me. "Really? We can learn to talk better if we go there?" When he nods again, I look back where Hassen is disappearing, then back at Rokan. "But what about my sister?"

Rokan's eager expression falls and he grows solemn. He points at Hassen, then picks up his bag and looks at me.

He wants me to choose. One direction will take me back to

my sister. The other direction will somehow magically enable me to talk to Rokan in a way that he's excited about.

I'm torn. Duty tells me I should go back to Maddie. She's probably worried sick about me, imagining her fragile little sister out here with the big bad aliens. And really, she has every right to be. She's always looked after me, stood up for me when no one else would, and fought a lot of my battles for me.

But then there's Rokan. Rokan, who makes me feel turned on and alive, who will teach me how to take care of myself. Who is excited about the thought of being able to really talk to me. Like that's a special gift.

Really, it's the communication thing that makes me point to the hills, not to Hassen. Because if we go back to the tribe cave, no one can talk to me but Maddie and maybe the humans, provided I can read their lips. But if there's a way to get around the language barrier, I want to go for it.

And possibly spend a bit more alone time with my alien boyfriend. Is it weird to pick him over my sister? I wonder if I'm not thinking straight.

But then he puts his hand out for mine, a smile on his handsome blue face, and I feel a giddy surge in my breast as I start purring again. Maybe it's wrong, but it feels pretty right, at the moment.

Rokan is visibly less tense by early afternoon. When I ask him why, he points at the sky and indicates that there will be no more giant people-eating birds. That's a selling point as far as I'm concerned. The tether is untied, and Rokan lashes both spears to his pack instead of carrying one.

The rest of the day is almost pleasant, or it would be if it weren't for the fact that it's bitterly cold and there's deep snow as far as the eye can see. By the time Rokan finds our next cave to stop at, my face feels chapped and my feet throb all the way up to my knees from all the hiking with the snowshoes. I rest, exhausted, on the only stool in the cave while Rokan builds a fire. Tomorrow, I'm going to watch him and learn how, I promise myself. Tomorrow sounds like a good day for that. I'm so tired that my eyes start closing before food is even ready. At some point, I must nod off, because when I wake up, I'm curled up in the furs by myself. I go back to sleep, too tired to even wake up for dinner.

I wake up several hours later with my arm draped over a warm male chest, my bare toes pressed against a warm, velvety leg. My breast is rumbling with the usual Rokan-related purr, and I sleepily slide my fingers over the center of his chest to check if he's doing the same.

He is. His hand covers mine the moment I move, and I'm filled with an affectionate warmth and, okay, that same aroused feeling I've been carrying around for days now. I stroke my fingers lightly over his chest, my head resting in the crook of his arm.

Rokan lifts a hand and taps my breast, then gestures toward his mouth in the firelit shadows. *Eat?* His eyes glow a soft blue in the low light.

I am hungry, but I'm also warm and snuggled up against the world's biggest, most delectable alien. So I don't exactly feel like moving. I shift against him, and one of my thighs is draped over his leg. I have to fight the insane urge to start rubbing up against that rock-hard muscle, because once I start? I don't know that I'll be able to stop. For now, I just want to touch him. My hand slides over his breast again, feeling our linked purrs.

And then I remember I forgot to ask him if he was married.

I jolt upright.

He sits up, eyes wild, and reaches beside the bed, pulling out a knife. His body goes on alert and he tenses, looking around the cave for danger, and then back at me with a confused expression. *Okay?* he gestures.

Whoops. I nod and pat his chest again, trying to calm him. I'm not in trouble or anything, just worried I'm creeping on some other alien lady's guy.

Rokan relaxes, glancing around one last time before setting the knife aside and then rubbing his ridged forehead, his expression saying *don't ever scare me like that again* even if the words aren't spoken aloud.

It's kind of cute to see his worry. "As long as you guys don't have snakes, I think we're good." I slide back toward him, tucking my legs under me. "I should be safe with you anyhow, right?"

He takes my hand and pulls it to his mouth, kissing my knuckles.

Well, dang. My panties aren't safe with him around, that's for sure. Not that I've had any since waking up on the ice planet. I've been going commando under his long tunic and leggings for the last few days, and while it's definitely rather bare feeling, it also makes me hyperaware of just how much being around Rokan turns me on. Right now, we're seated facing each other, and I realize that this is the first night I've slept fully dressed while around him.

I kind of wish I wasn't. I also wish I was brave enough to boldly shuck my pants, but I'm not. Instead, I just sit there, like a dummy, while he brushes his mouth over my knuckles.

Maybe he senses my shyness. He smiles at me, fangs peeping out from under the stretch of his lips, and then moves my hand from his mouth down to his chest. He presses my fingers against his breast, and I can feel him purring again. It must mean something to him, something he really wants to communicate with me. I wish I knew what.

"Please, please tell me you're not married," I whisper. "Otherwise this is going to get super weird."

He cocks his head, then indicates he doesn't understand.

"Is there a girl at home for you?" The words rush out of my mouth, and I feel a sick sense of horror and worry the moment they erupt. Like I've gone over the edge. Like I've broken the spell of being with him and now reality's going to creep in. "Someone you share your, um, cave with?"

His lips twitch and he shakes his head, then gestures at me. I think that's supposed to mean I'm his choice? Or he's staying with me? Or I guess if I want to be paranoid, there are a million ways to read this. But I have to know. "No one and only love at home? No babies?"

He frowns at me slightly and shakes his head, then leans forward and taps right on my purring chest.

Okay, he's choosing me. Or saying that there's no one but me. That's sweet. I give him a nervous smile. "All right, then."

We gaze at each other for a long, electric moment, silent. I wonder if he's waiting for me to make the first move. If so, it might be a while. I'm not sure I'm brave enough.

I start to pull away, and then stop. What's stopping me from touching him? This is a different world, with different rules. No one's here to tell me to be a good girl, or that I'm too shy or mousy for guys to look at. There's no one here but me and Rokan and he looks at me like I'm the world to him.

So I let my fingers glide down the ridges on his belly, toward his navel. And I watch him respond to my touch.

He sucks in a breath and I feel it against my fingers, feel the shiver that racks his body.

I feel the need to keep talking, even though I'm not brave enough to make eye contact and see his reactions. He has to understand me, why I'm so skittish, I guess. "This is hard for me," I tell him. "I'm not very . . . not very confident. It's the cochlear implants, even though they're amazing. *Were* amazing." I frown to myself, thinking of how hard it's been without them. But other than being upset for the first few days, I'm getting by without them. Rokan helps, a lot. Knowing that he doesn't act like it's a burden to try and communicate with me really makes me feel normal. I need that. I crave that. "So, yeah. Implants. I always felt like such a weird kid with them, like I wasn't normal. You know how it is when you're a teenager and you think you're the most awful, geeky thing ever, even if you're not? That was me. Maybe because for the first twelve years of my life, I was that weird deaf kid and I didn't have a lot of friends. Maddie made everyone be nice to me, but if she wasn't there, no one talked to me. And even after I got the implant, that feeling never went away. I guess on the inside I'm still that sad, lonely kid."

Annnnd now I'm verbally barfing my history at him. God. If ever there was a way to scare off a guy, it's this moment, I suppose. I can't help myself, though, just like I can't help stroking those lower abdominal muscles over and over again, tracing my fingers over the part where his platey chest ridges move to smooth abdomen.

I can't seem to stop talking, either. "So I haven't ever dated much. And it's kinda, well, catching, I guess. It's like the moment the dating pool senses that you're out, you're completely out. I've dated all of two guys ever. I had a boyfriend in eighth grade for a week, and then at my first job, I went out with a guy on two dates, until he started asking questions about my implant and if I could take it off. And that hurt my feelings and I never went out with him again, because I felt all weird and awkward all over again. So that was the extent of my dating history. Except now, I guess, I'm here with you."

I peek up, positive that he's going to be looking at me like I'm a crazy person. Like he wants to run away and be anywhere but here. But when my gaze meets his, I feel scorched by the heat in his eyes. There's no irritation there, no shame. No annoyance or wishing I would shut up.

Instead, he looks fierce. Possessive.

And utterly hungry for me.

I shiver, even though I'm not cold. My fingers find his belly button, and I trace around it, then flutter at going lower. And I look up at him again to see his reaction.

The hunger in his gaze seems to intensify. He grabs me in his arms and pulls me against him, and then I'm straddling his knee after all, except this time we're sitting up in bed instead of lying down, and I'm pressed up against him. My hand goes to his chest even as one strong arm wraps tight around my back. His other hand cups the back of my head and he pulls me against him in a kiss.

Not a gentle kiss. Not a timid kiss.

It's a scorching, fierce kiss, and it feels like a branding. A claiming. A "there's no one but you, Lila" sort of kiss. And it leaves me breathless. His tongue glides into my mouth and then I can't think at all—I'm surprised each time he kisses me that it has ridges, and those ridges do all kinds of weird, crazy things to my insides. Each time he strokes his tongue against mine, I'm this much closer to shucking my pants.

Instead, maybe I should shuck his.

The thought is a tantalizing one, and I let my hand trail down his chest as we kiss. It feels both naughty and utterly powerful to think about taking charge like this, but now that the idea is in my head, I can't let it go. I want to touch him. I need to touch him.

I really, really need to find out if he has ridges down there like he has on his tongue. Or even a penis. Actually, I'm pretty sure it's a penis, because the bulge in his breechcloth is hard to mistake.

But when I slide my hand down and drag my fingers over his length to outline it, I feel more than I expected. There's the thick, ridged (yep, called it) outline of his cock that's so big and hard it's practically like stroking an extra-large water bottle. Then there's the soft sac of his balls underneath, but when my fingers circle him at the base, I run into something hard and almost . . . bony. Right above his cock.

I'm so startled by this new discovery that I jerk my hand away and break the kiss.

He doesn't realize that I'm freaking out. His hand fists in my hair and he buries his face against my neck, taking in my scent. His breathing is rapid, and when he shifts me against him, I can feel his purr matching to mine. I start to melt against him all over again.

But . . .

I bite my lip and tap his shoulder. "Rokan?"

He pulls back, gazing at me. There is worry in his eyes, and a question. And I try to think of the best way to broach the subject. I mean, I haven't really had a lot of experience with human penises, but I know they do *not* come with extras. How do I tell him I need to check the goods for myself to make sure I want to move forward?

Not that I'm ready to have sex, of course. It's too early for that. But, like, now that I know there's something lurking under there?

I have *got* to know what it is.

"Can . . . can I look at you?" I ask him. I feel terribly shy and incredibly bold all at once. "Just to, you know . . ." *See things? Make sure there aren't any deal-breakers under there? No barbs, pinchers, or things I don't have holes for?*

He gestures at his body, giving me permission. Oh, so he's not going to do it for me? All right, then. Time to be brave and take what I want. I hesitate, then put my hand on his lower stomach again.

Rokan's loincloth seems to be a simple affair. It's a long length of leather with a thick belt to hold it up. It also looks like if I undo the belt ties, the entire thing will just fall off. Breathless, I'm acutely aware of his big hand moving up and down my back, his knuckles rubbing lightly against me through my clothes, and the big thigh that I'm perched on. I have this insane urge to rub up against him, but before we go any further, I've got to see the goods.

I pick at the knot, biting my lip, and then it's free. I tug on the belt, and the leather falls, but remains tented over his cock. I see I'm going to have to unwrap him like a present.

When I hesitate again, his hand slides under the back of my tunic and he begins to rub my lower back, stroking his knuckles in a gentle caress that seems a thousand times more intimate than it was a moment ago. And because the touch is arousing and comforting at the same time, I take the edge of his loincloth and pull it down, exposing him to my gaze.

All right.

That's . . . a lot of dick.

My hand hovers over him, because wow. He's fully erect,

the head of his cock straining toward me. It's a darker shade of blue than the rest of him, and the head is shiny and wet. There are ridges going down the length, starting under the base of the crown and heading all the way to his smooth groin. I guess they don't have body hair.

Instead, he's got a big blunt horn. Or something. It protrudes above his cock, about as long as one of my fingers, and about as thick. It doesn't look scary . . . ? Just weirdly inhuman and out of place. I study everything for a long moment, wondering if I should touch, and then wondering why I'm so chicken about it. He wants me to touch him. The moment my hand hovers closer, he sucks in a breath. When I don't make a move, he exhales slowly. His hand has stopped moving on my back, and I'm acutely aware of him.

As he breathes, his cock moves, and I resist the urge to measure him, because he seems really large. I mean, he's a big guy already so I shouldn't be surprised that his equipment is big, but . . . wow. I'm pretty sure that's gonna be a tight squeeze. I flex my fingers, hovering my hand closer, and as I do, a pearl of liquid beads on the head of his cock and then slides downward.

That's fascinating and really sexy. My thighs clench and I realize I'm wet, too, just from staring at him. There's a throb deep between my legs and I feel all hot and breathless, and I haven't even touched him. I let my hand hesitate in midair a moment longer, and then gently drag my fingers from the base of his cock all the way to the head. I want to feel those ridges.

Actually, I want to feel all of him.

A shudder moves through him and I look up to see his head has tilted back, his eyes closing. His face looks both strained and sensual at the same time. All that just from one small touch? I feel powerful. I let my fingers trace his length again, enjoying his visual response, the way his entire body shudders again. I explore him with my hand, using touch to learn his length, the ridges along the shaft of his cock, and the slippery feel of the moisture beading on the head. If his skin is normally warm, it's scorching right here, and touching him makes me aroused and breathless. I slide my fingers along the underside of his cock, brushing along his balls. He's hairless here, and the skin is soft and delicate. It's fascinating. I move my hand upward, and brush a finger along the hornlike protrusion, and his entire body jerks in response.

His hand grabs mine, stopping me.

I look up into his eyes, and I can see his mouth moving as he pants, his chest heaving. There's a fine sheen of sweat on his face and he gives a small shake of his head.

"Too much?" I guess aloud.

He nods and clenches a fist, then flings his fingers out, miming an explosion.

I giggle a little at that. "Maybe you should learn to control yourself." I make the sign for *control*, just to be a tease. "Control."

His brows go up and there's a sexy look of challenge on his face. His arm goes around me a little tighter, and I suck in a breath, wondering if I've said too much.

But he only pulls me in for a kiss, and I wrap my arms around his neck, closing my eyes and losing myself to the firm caress of his mouth against mine and the way he works his tongue. Lord, that ridged tongue. I'm kind of addicted to it.

His knuckles rub gently at the base of my spine again, and then I feel his other hand go to the front of my pants.

My eyes fly open again. He presses a little kiss to my lips, sucking lightly on my lower one before releasing it. That challenging expression is still on his face, a mixture of mischief and determination.

And I feel the leather tie that holds my pants come undone.

I get where this is going now. I teased him about his control, and now he's going to test mine. I gaze at him, shocked and more than a little aroused. It seems like if I tease him, he's going to give me equal measure. The thought is both thrilling and a little scandalous, and I squirm against him.

His hand pauses at my stomach, and then moves away. In the shadows of the cave, I see him make the thumbs-up sign. He's asking me if it's too much.

God, he's the sweetest. I lean in and kiss him on the mouth.

Just because I'm terrified doesn't mean I don't want him to touch me.

Rokan rubs his nose against mine in an affectionate nuzzle, and then his hand returns to my belly, under my tunic. It rests there for a moment, and then I feel him tug at my pants strings again.

I remain still.

A moment later, I feel the ties give. My pants go loose at my waist, the leather dropping a few inches.

I don't move. Heck, I don't even know if I'm breathing.

He nuzzles my nose again, and at the same moment, his hand pushes into my pants. I gasp, because it feels like the tension in my body is so great that I might explode. I'm purring up a storm, too, and that just adds to the overwhelming sensations.

But then he kisses me again, his mouth gently claiming mine, and I let him conquer my mouth, even though my entire focus is on the hand that rests just above my pussy. He was completely smooth—is he going to think I'm hairy and gross? Do girls in his tribe have that weird bone thing and is he going to find it strange that I don't? Should I be quite this wet? Am I—

Everything stops when his fingers move.

I press my forehead to his bumpy one, gasping, and gazing right into his glowing eyes as his hand begins to explore me in a place that no one's ever touched but me. He touches the curls of my sex, and I feel him petting it, stroking me like he would a cat. It'd almost be funny, except I feel ready to break into a thousand pieces already, I'm so tense.

Then his hand pushes lower, and one of his big fingers traces the seam of my pussy. Oh my God, I can tell I'm so wet and hot right now, because my pussy seems to just slide apart the moment he touches me. It's like my body's saying, *Yes, come right on in*. And it feels amazing. I'm pretty sure I'm whimpering, not that I can hear it. It doesn't matter—I'm locked in to Rokan and his wonderful, intense gaze, which holds mine even as his hands hold me. It's like as long as he's looking at me, I'm safe. He's got me, and he won't let things get out of control. He won't let me get scared or overwhelmed.

Looking into his eyes, I know everything's handled. I feel like I can let go, because he'll be there to make everything all right.

He tilts his head just a little, his mouth capturing mine again in just the barest of kisses, more affectionate than passionate. All the while, his fingers are exploring me inside my pants. He strokes my pussy again, moving deeper, and then he lets one finger move through my wet folds, rubbing me everywhere. He pauses at the opening to my core, his finger lightly tapping over that spot, and God, I'm so wet and aroused. I want to cry out with disappointment when he doesn't go any farther than that, just goes back to lightly stroking me and petting me. His fingers start to move upward, and I rock hopefully against him. Maybe he'll find my clit and rub it instead.

A moment later, he does. His callused fingertips graze that perfect spot and I grab a double fistful of his hair, sucking in my breath. That was almost too much.

Rokan pauses, and his mouth brushes over mine again, our breath mingling like our purring. He taps the spot with his finger, and a cry wrenches from my throat. I tug on his hair, and press my mouth to his, my tongue seeking him out. There's so much going on inside me, I need to let it out. I need more—more petting, more kissing, more rubbing, more everything. I need him to get me off.

Here I told myself we were just going to do kissing for a while, and right now I'm about ready to grind on his leg if he doesn't start touching me again.

But his mouth captures mine, and then he sucks lightly on my tongue, even as his finger rubs against my clit again. I whimper, rocking my hips back and forth as he teases my clit. "Please," I breathe against his mouth when he breaks the kiss. "Please, I need more."

He nods, the look in his eyes so sexy and full of promise that I feel my pulse flutter deep in my belly. His fingers stroke me again, rubbing my clit, and I moan, then cry out when he doesn't follow up with more clit-petting. Instead, he rubs lower, moving down to my entrance, and he pushes the tip of one big finger inside me. All the sensations in my body feel like they're changing with that one move, and my belly suddenly feels hollow and aching, like I need to be filled. I push against his hand and kiss him again, frantic.

Rokan's mouth slams against mine, even as his finger pushes deeper into me. It feels tight and weird for a moment, and then he thrusts deep inside me, and I'm moaning against his tongue because it feels so good. He rocks his finger into me again, hard, and then repeats it, and I'm riding his hand and kissing him with all I've got as the orgasm that's been flirting at the edges barrels to the forefront. A few more thrusts of his fingers and then I gasp as my thighs seem to lock up, my muscles tightening as pleasure rips through me. I cling to him, choking for breath as he continues to finger me even as I come, pushing into my wet heat over and over again.

I've never come so hard, not when I've touched myself. Having him get me off like that feels like everything's been amplified, and it's terrifying and wondrous and feels amazing.

After what seems like forever, my muscles unlock and I melt against him, drooping with the aftermath of my orgasm. It's like it's sucked all the strength out of my body and left this spent, noodle-boned girl in its place. He kisses my face over and over again, his mouth still frantic, his body still tense.

I wonder if he's come.

I rest my head on his shoulder, mindful of his big horns, which arch around his skull, and reach down to see if he's still hard. He catches my hand before I can touch his cock, and then guides me there. He wraps my fingers around his length, and then his hand covers mine, and he gives a hard pump.

Oh. He's going to use me to get off. I should be appalled . . . instead, I'm rather titillated. He wants my touch, not his. I like that.

After a few hard strokes, I feel his entire body shudder, and then his head leans forward and he bites—bites!—the shoulder of my tunic. Warm liquid spatters my hand, clenched in his. He's coming, lost in his own pleasure moment, and I wish it were brighter in the cave so I could watch his every expression. Instead, I just stroke his hair with one hand, gently squeeze his cock with my other, and wait for him.

He recovers, releases my hand, and then uses a soft bit of fur to clean our hands off. I'm a little sad when he gets up, and I curl up in the blankets that he's left because I'm too boneless to move. I watch, dopey with endorphins, as he puts more water on over the fire.

So that just happened. I went to third base with my alien boyfriend. I could officially be the easiest Earth chick on this planet. My sister would probably be mortified. It's only been a few days since I met Rokan. I should go slower, take things gradually and let us get to know each other, but I can't keep my hands off of him. After years of being content with my virginity, I am now officially "fast."

But I can't find it in me to give a crap. I watch Rokan by the fire, his tight blue ass bare, tail swishing, and feel rather pleased with myself.

# CHAPTER THIRTEEN
## Rokan

This is the best day.

I thought, perhaps, that the day I felt resonance would be the best day. But now I know that it is this day, with my mate sleepy and sated, and the scent of her cunt still on my fingers.

I am ravenous for her. Resonance has not been sated, and will not be sated until she is with my kit. Until then, we will starve for each other's touch. Already I could take her body to mine and fill her with my aching cock, and it has been but a moment since I left her. I poke at the coals, warming a bit of hot tea. I am not thirsty, but I want to have it prepared in case my mate wakes and needs a drink. I must anticipate her every need.

I look over at the nest of furs. Her eyes are closed and she is on her back, her tunic bunched at her waist. Her legs are slightly parted and I can see the undone laces of her leggings. It would not take much to push them down to her knees and to bury my mouth in her warm flesh, to taste her until she fills my mouth with her juices. I lift my fingers to my nose. They are still perfumed with her scent. I want to wear it forever. I want to lick it off my hand and taste it.

Instead, I add a few leaves to the tea and stir it, then hunch down by the fire to wait it out.

I see now why the others are so wild for their human mates. I was pleased for my friends when they mated. I was amused when my brother, ever the flirt, resonated to his Kira and now watches her constantly with a besotted expression.

Now I understand.

With Li-lah in my life, everything has changed. My priority is her. My happiness is hers. When I return home, I will move my small bed of furs out of my parents' cave and ask the chief for a home to share with my mate, so we may start our family.

My desires have changed—now I will crave Li-lah's hand, her sighs, her everything, in order to bring myself to come. Even my seed has changed with Li-lah. Instead of thin and slick like before, it is now thick and milky. All that I am is changing for her.

I welcome it.

Just thinking about my mate makes me turn back around to look at her again. She is soft in the furs, one hand pillowed on a pale cheek. My cock is stiff with need again, and I think of the way her small fingers curled around my shaft, her grip holding me tight as I stroked myself.

Tea can wait.

I stalk over to the bed, sit down gently on my knees to Li-lah's side, and tap her arm. I always let her know my presence because she cannot hear me. I do not want to scare her by looming over her. I cannot imagine what it is like to live in silence; it only emphasizes how strong my mate is.

Her eyes open and she gives me a shy, sleepy smile. "Oh. Hi there."

I lean over and kiss her, and she makes a happy little sound in her throat. Then I slide down her body and move those tantalizing leggings lower, revealing the tiny thatch of mane between her thighs and the soft folds it covers. Her scent fills my nose and I groan aloud, then begin to kiss her belly.

I feel her quiver. She shifts, and I take the opportunity to tug her pants down to her knees, just as I pictured.

"Oh," she breathes. Her hands smooth down the front of her tunic and then she reaches for me. "Oh . . ."

I pull one leg of her pants off, then the other. Now she is delightfully bare. I take one delicate ankle and run my mouth over it.

"Oh," she breathes again, the sound low and throaty.

I kiss my way down her leg, toward her cunt.

"Oh." Her moan fills the cave as I taste her. *"Oh . . ."*

*My mate,* I think with fierce, possessive joy as her flavor dances on my tongue. My perfect mate.

Her hands fist in the furs beside her thighs, and I feel her entire body quiver when I drag my tongue over her slick folds. She is hot, sweet, and wet here, and I explore her with my mouth, seeing which flicks of my tongue make her cry out, and which make her suck in a breath.

Li-lah's hips rise to meet my mouth, and I put a hand on her thigh to hold her still, so I may lap at her cunt over and over again.

"Oh, wait," she breathes.

I raise my head, curious. Did I do something wrong?

"No," she cries out a moment later. Her hand goes back to the top of my head and she pushes me back down. "I didn't mean it. You're doing great." Her head flops back onto the furs. "Thumbs up."

I chuckle and go back to my task. My tongue circles around the small bud of her third nipple. It seems to be the most sensitive, so I focus on it. Her aching whimpers fuel me, and I eagerly lick her until she's crying out my name, her entire body shuddering in response to my tongue.

Perfect.

Everything about my mate is perfect. This moment? Her taste on my lips? Her soft thighs pressing against my ears as she comes?

Perfect.

I wake my Li-lah up in the morning with a kiss to her brow, and then many kisses to her cunt. Her soft squeals and moans from last night haunt my dreams, and I must have my fill of her before I can travel. Once I have made her cry out twice, she releases the double handfuls she has of my hair and uses her hand on my cock so I may come, too.

I think we shall wake like this from now on, every morning. It is a very pleasant way to greet the day.

We bathe, eat, and then bundle our furs. I pack our things while Li-lah braids her hair and sips at the tea I push on her. It will be several days' walk to the elders' cave, going slow so I do not exhaust my Li-lah. Sky-claws do not hunt this far away from the mountains, so we can take our time and enjoy the journey.

We will go even slower than usual, as well, because I must start teaching Li-lah. Just as she has taught me her hand-words, I must now teach her to care for herself, like she has suggested. She knows less about how to survive than my youngest brother, Sessah, who is not yet two hands of age.

I will give her the same lessons that patient, quiet Warrek gave to me, lessons that he gives to my younger brother even now. I must do them all with hand-speak and with her fingers touching my mouth if that does not work. It is important that she learn.

So I take one of the furs we have on the bed and set it on the ground. She looks over at me, sipping her tea, and her eyebrows go up when I gesture that she should come sit by me. A bright flush touches her cheeks and she begins to breathe heavy, and I feel my cock surge in response. Does she think I will taste her, even now?

Of course I like that idea, but I shake my head. I must focus on other things. I pat the fur. It is one of the thicker hides, and not waterproof like mine, but it will do for now. I flip it over to the leather side, and then gesture at my bag.

Her brows wrinkle and she puts aside her tea. "Bed?" she asks, making a hand-talk.

I shake my head and point at my pack, and say the word. Then I pull out several leather cords and pack a few things into the center of the fur—rations, an extra skin for water, the empty stew pouch. I put them in the center, then swiftly roll the bundle and tie it on each end. I loop the straps in the knots that will allow me to create a shoulder harness. It is not the same as my own pack, but an easy-to-make carryall that young kits are shown when they are not strong enough to carry a regular pack.

Her eyes widen with recognition. "You made me a backpack?"

I unroll it immediately and then offer her the straps.

"Oh. I guess I'm making the bag, right?"

I nod.

"All right, show me how to start? Where does this strap go?" Her eyes light up with enthusiasm and she smiles at me. "Don't go easy on me, either."

It takes some time and much patience, but I show her how to make the bundle, to form the knots that create shoulder straps, how to cinch it when it is on her shoulders so it does not dig. She looks pleased with her creation and even more pleased when I hand her one of the spears. If she is to be a hunter, we cannot hold hands as we walk. She must be ready to look for tracks, to flush out game, to be on the alert for predators.

We leave a short time later, after I show her how to put the cave back in order for the next visitor. It has snowed overnight, and Li-lah's steps are plodding over the drifts. It will be a slow journey today, but that means we can make camp and go to our furs that much sooner.

I am . . . very eager for that.

As a hunter alone, I could make the journey to the elders' cave in a day or so. With Li-lah at my side, it takes five days in total. Every step of every day is spent teaching her. I show her how to hold her knife, and how to throw a spear. I point out tracks to her as we walk, and describe the animals they belong to. We gather soapberries and fire fuel as we travel. I show her what to look for in our surroundings—signs of danger, changes in the weather, places where the snowdrifts hide caches of stored meat. I show her how to approach the hot streams and to chase away the face-eaters that dwell on the shores, waiting to prey on anything that moves near. There is no time to stop and show her how to build snares, or traps, but I manage to hunt fresh meat every day, and every night, after she builds a fire, I show her how to cut it open without spilling the innards and spoiling the meat.

It is a lot for her to learn, and by the time we stop for the day at a hunter cave, she is exhausted, her strength ebbing. But she must learn, so I insist she build a fire when every instinct in my body urges me to take care of her and to do it for her. I show her how to melt the snow when all I want to do is hold her and let her relax against me. I show her how to slice up a fresh kill and how to scrape the hide for curing.

She falls into the furs each night, exhausted. There is very little kissing these nights, and she falls asleep in my arms and slumbers until dawn. I tell myself I am patient, but my body craves more of hers. I want the taste of her cunt on my tongue. She is a craving, and I need more of her. My khui's song grows stronger in its distress, and I wonder that Li-lah does not feel the same aching need I do.

Perhaps when she truly knows what resonance is, she will understand. Then we will come together as we should. Until then, I will teach her how to survive, just as she asks.

And though I am aching with need, I enjoy having Li-lah at my side. Every moment with her is such intense pleasure that I feel full of joy and wonder at the world. Every smile makes me smile. Every hand-talk sign I learn brings me that much closer to being able to truly speak to her. Every brush of her hand over mine reminds me that she is my mate, and she is everything I have ever wanted.

It is early on the fifth day of our journey when the elders' cave comes into view in the distance. I recognize the large, smooth, snow-covered mound, so out of place amongst the jagged stone cliffs. It is here that the walls talk and will teach me how to speak to my Li-lah.

I point it out to her, eager to begin.

## Lila

Maybe it's that I'm tired, or maybe it's that I'm not really expecting to see another spaceship, but I don't recognize the big, snow-covered mound for what it is until we get to the entrance and I realize it's not a cave, but a spacecraft. The door is rounded, a metal ramp leading up out of the snow and into what looks like an opening.

I retreat a few steps, clutching my spear, and look over at Rokan.

He's giving me a boyish grin of excitement.

Okay, he doesn't look freaked out. Me, I'm still trying to wrap my head around what this means. "This is a spaceship?"

His brows go down, a close alien approximation of a frown of concentration, and then he makes the *cave* gesture.

I want to point out that this is most definitely not a cave, but maybe there's no word for *spaceship* in his language. The man wears fur pants and carries a spear, so I'm guessing that there's not a ton of technology in his culture. Plus he's been heading us in this direction because he said something would help us learn to speak to each other. I haven't been able to figure out what he meant by that.

I never really thought it would be a spaceship. And I don't know how that's going to help, but I'm worried.

I pull my spear a little tighter to my body, feeling more comfortable with it in my grip. I point at the open entrance. "Are we going in there?"

Rokan nods.

"Whose ship is that?" I ask. Is there another group of aliens I'm unaware of? Is there more going on? I rub my forehead, frustrated at the gaping holes in my communication. For all I know, he's been leading me back to the bad guys and I had no clue.

But as soon as that idea crosses my mind, I dismiss it. Rokan wouldn't do that. I trust him. He's good to me, and sweet. That isn't it. I'm still confused, though.

Rokan thinks for a moment, and then makes a few gestures

that I don't follow. He signs *people*, but I don't know what people he's referring to.

He points at the entrance and then makes the *talk* sign.

"Are there people in there?" I rest my spear on my shoulder and make the *people* sign. "Other aliens? Other humans?" Is that who is going to teach him sign language? Are we going to go talk to them?

He shrugs, and I'm just more confused. So we didn't come here looking for people? What did we come looking for?

My worry must show on my face. He moves toward me and takes my hand in his, then squeezes it. He's asking me to trust him. I gaze up into his alien face, with its ridged brows, fangs, big curling horns, and glowing blue eyes. If I can trust a guy that looks like a demon to save me from car-sized man-eating pterodactyls, I guess I can trust him a few more steps into a spaceship, right?

I put my hand in his and nod. "Lead on."

We take a few steps inside the ship and, well, I'm not really sure what to think. The first room we enter is immense, and reminds me a bit of a warehouse or a large garage. The walls are dark and covered in ice in some parts, but the center of the floor has a few logs, sitting stones, and pillows gathered around a burned-out firepit. There are rolls of blankets and woven baskets tucked into one corner, and spears resting against a wall with flickering, lighted panels. It kinda reminds me of one of the hunter caves. Which is also strange. "Does someone live here?"

He makes a *yes* gesture, and then a moment later shakes his head and points back out of the cave. So someone does live here, but maybe not right now? Or used to live here and doesn't anymore?

There's a set of double doors off to the far side of the broken-down hangar, and another large door that's permanently jammed half-open. Rokan is watching me, so I pull off my snowshoes, shake off my boots, and look around.

Wires hang from the ceiling, and the floor seems like lightweight metal. As I walk across, it feels a bit uneven in some spots, and there's a long hairline crack running from one wall all the way down the middle of the floor. Several of the panels aren't lit, and it's clear that whoever's spaceship this is, it hasn't been very functional for a long time. I glance back at Rokan and he's got his spear put aside and is crouching near the firepit, sweeping out ash and prepping a new fire. We must be safe, then. If I was in any sort of danger, he'd be shadowing me, weapon in hand.

I relax a little and head for the propped-open door, peering inside. It leads down a long hall filled with many doors. The debris is bad here, wall panels crumpled and the ceiling half-collapsed. Living quarters of the old spaceship maybe? The only thing I know about spaceships comes from television, so I'm just guessing. There's a lot of dust and broken bits, though, so it's clear to me that this area isn't seeing much use by whoever lives here. I step over the crate-sized rounded boulder that's holding the door open and head into the hall, but turn back after a few steps. If the floor felt uneven in the big room, it feels shaky in this area, and every door that's open looks like it leads to more wreckage. It's disappointing. I head back into the main hangar and over to the double doors. They slide open as I approach, like department store doors. Kinda a neat trick. Here, the hallway is clean of debris and well lit, and looks less derelict than the other end. These are the current living quarters, I'm guessing. While the place is empty and gives me a bit of the creeps, it's at least seemingly in order. There are several doors along the hall, and I move to the first one, trying to figure it out. There's no door handle, and it doesn't open for me when I approach. Curious, I move down to the next one, but get the same response. Huh. Maybe someone locked up? I head back to the main portion of the hangar.

Rokan gets to his feet, a broad smile on his face as he approaches me.

It's hard not to feel warm and pleased at the sight of his happiness, and I smile back, though I'm confused. I gesture at the fire. *Me fire?*

# CHAPTER FOURTEEN
## Rokan

The smile my mate is giving me is sweet but bewildered. She does not know what this place is. I am a little disappointed, because I thought she would be like Har-loh. Har-loh is very comfortable here in the strangeness of the elders' cave. She takes apart the walls and makes them talk to her. Even Shorshie and the other humans can make the walls talk. My Li-lah just looks at me, then moves to the fire and waits, expecting another lesson.

Perhaps they do not have caves like this where she comes from? Is her tribe very different than Shorshie's tribe?

I need to talk to her desperately. I feel the ache rising in my chest. I need to be able to speak to her like I need air. I rub my jaw and return to the fire as she sets up the tripod and looks at me, a question in her eyes.

I do not visit the elders' cave often. Though I am friendly with Har-loh and Rukh, our paths do not cross much. I had no human mate before now and received the human words when the others did. I do not know how to make the walls obey. I do not know what Har-loh says to the walls to make them do things.

I tilt my head back and pause, then try talking to the elders. "I wish to speak to my mate."

Silence. The walls do not answer.

I scratch my chin and think. The voice in the walls has a name. I have heard Har-loh say it before. I struggle to remember it. *Cu-hor?* No, wait. *Pew-hor?* It sounds right. "*Pew-hor*, speak to me."

*Pew-hor* does not respond.

Li-lah tilts her head at me. "Who are you talking to?"

I gesture at the cave and say the name again.

She watches my lips move, her brows furrowing. "Pu-hur? Wait, 'computer'? There is a computer here?" She makes an unfamiliar gesture.

I repeat it. That does not wake the walls, either, so I try her name for it. "*Com-pew-hor*, I wish to speak to my mate."

"I do not understand your question," the walls call out in sa-khui. "Please restate your question."

"I wish to speak to my mate," I tell it again, eager. It is talking to me now.

"Who are you talking to?" Li-lah asks, a wary look on her face. She glances behind her. "Is someone else here?"

I take her hand and squeeze it in mine. I do not know the words yet. But I shall very soon, and then I will explain it all to her. I kiss her knuckles, and then speak to the *com-pew-hor* again. "*Com-pew-hor*, I wish to learn my mate's language."

"Assisting with languages is one of the many functions of this unit. Do you know the name of the language you wish to study?"

"Hand-speak," I say proudly, and kiss my mate's knuckles again.

There is a quiet pause, and then the walls speak again. "This system does not recognize that language. Please specify: What is the planet of origin for the language you wish to learn?"

I frown, rubbing my mate's knuckles. *Plah-net? Or-gen?* "I wish to learn hand-speak," I say again. "I do not know what else to call it."

"Tell me what's going on," Li-lah says, worry on her face as she stares up at me. "This is freaking me out. If you're not talking to me, who are you talking to?"

I make a frustrated sound and stare at the walls. "I wish to learn hand-speak. My mate cannot hear sounds and I wish to speak to her."

The smooth voice speaks again. "I am hearing two languages. Would you like for this computer to switch to Human English for the default language?"

"Yes? I want to learn hand-speak. My mate cannot hear mouth-speak. She does not hear sounds."

There is another pause. "Is one in your party hearing *dis-ay-buhld*?"

I try not to snarl, because it will alarm Li-lah. "I do not know this word."

"I am sorry, but I do not understand your response."

I make a strangled sound of frustration.

"I am sorry, but I do not understand your response," the walls repeat. "Please be more specific."

"My mate cannot hear you," I grit out. "I need to learn her hand-talk."

"Is one in your party hearing *dis-ay-buhld*?" it asks again.

"She is not hearing," I agree, uncertain if that is what it is asking. Why does it not talk with normal sa-khui words?

"Would you like a *vis-yoo-all ter-muh-nal* for *in-puht* of commands?" it asks.

I do not understand. But telling it this again will get me nowhere. "Yes?" I say again, warily. I worry I will have to return to the home cave and retrieve Har-loh and her mate to make the walls talk properly.

Off to the side, a portion of the cave wall flickers. Scribbles of light appear and wiggle across the stone. It means nothing to me, but Li-lah makes a strangled sound and jumps to her feet, ripping her hands out of mine.

Curious, I follow her.

## Lila

There's a computer here.

I mean, of course there's a computer here. This is a spaceship, right? There are lights in the walls and technological-looking stuff, so it makes sense that there's a computer system running things. The words scrolling across the wall look a lot like a command prompt if a girl ever saw one, but it's not in a language I recognize. Is this who Rokan's been talking to for the last few minutes? I've been racking my brain, trying to understand if he was talking to someone through an intercom, or to me, or what it was.

But it makes sense that there's a computer here, and he's giving it verbal cues. He must have let it know that I need to type, and now it's responding. I touch the wall where the words are appearing. I don't see a keyboard, and I don't know the language.

"Ask it to type in English," I tell him, my gaze flicking between the wall and his face. I don't want to miss anything.

He tilts his head back again and says something, lips moving.

A moment later, the words on the wall change.

Greetings. We will use Human English as the default setting until otherwise notified. Do you wish a terminal to enter your answers? If so, press the button at the base of the screen and a touch-sensitive input pad will be made available.

I drop to my knees and run my hands along the wall, excited. There's a tiny hole that feels like it might be where the button in question used to go, but it's also broken. I shove my finger in there anyhow and hammer at it.

Something moves and there's a hint of air that wafts over my face, then a black pad half ejects from the wall, and then gets stuck. Rokan grabs his knife, but I wave a hand at him to call him off before he can stab it. I need this thing. It's about the size of a book, and very flat—kind of like an iPad. I smooth a finger across the surface, just in case it acts like one, too.

At my touch, it lights up and several circles appear, each one with a letter of the alphabet in it. It doesn't look like they're in order like a QWERTY keyboard, but I can use this.

I press my fingers to my lips, thinking, and then type. where am i

There's no punctuation or capital letters on the thing, but the computer screen responds a moment later, filling with numerals and a word that I don't understand. All right, space coordinates help me none. I stare at the math formula on the screen and try a different tactic.

visual map of area

It shows me a picture of the nearby hills. Again, not super helpful. I keep typing.

geographical map

continental map

The screen changes again, and this time I see continents. The world looks like nothing I've ever seen before. There's a massive body of water off to the left of the continent I'm on, dotted with islands and what look like big floating chunks of ice. Actually, most of what I'm looking at seems like an ice floe. There's not really much green between the two massive ice caps that I can see, and the three continents on the screen all seem to be just as icy as this one, even after I ask the computer to show me the equator.

We *are* at the equator. Well, that's depressing. I think for a moment and type again.

location of earth relative to current location

A star map appears, galaxies zooming past before a tiny arrow pinpoints a small spot on the pinwheel of the Milky Way. Just seeing that makes me sick, and I have to fight back a sob of grief.

If I needed a slap in the face to remind me that I'm never going to get home? I just got one.

Rokan touches my cheek with a gentle finger, turning me to look at him. There's concern in his eyes, and his tail is lashing in the corner of my vision. He's agitated. Probably worried about me. He rubs my arm and there's a question on his face.

"I'm okay," I tell him, and manage a smile even as I make the thumbs-up gesture.

He points at my hand, then at himself, then at the screen full of words.

Right. We came here to learn a language. I flex my fingers and start typing again.

can you teach languages

Words quickly flit across the screen.

This ship's artificial intelligence is programmed with over twenty-two thousand common languages. Do you wish to receive a linguistic upload?

Now we're getting somewhere! i need my companion to learn asl american sign language

The computer thinks for a moment, then words fill the screen again. I do not recognize that language in my database. Did you mean Aslaanti?

This thing has twenty-two thousand languages and it doesn't have the one I need? I'm utterly crushed. I bite my lip and look at Rokan. Maybe it knows it under a different name. Or . . . I look around the old ship and I get a new idea. how long has this ship been on this planet

Emergency landing occurred 289 years ago. Please note that when this system references "years," they are calculated based upon the orbit of this planet versus the planet Earth.

Okay, yeah. It wouldn't know sign language. If the years here are anything like Earth years, sign language hadn't even been invented yet. Well, shit. I set the terminal pad down and walk away, because I need to think. I rub my fingers on my temples.

Rokan is there at my side a moment later. He takes my hand in his and then puts it to his chest, so I can feel his purring. The worry in his eyes is heartbreaking. He knows something is wrong.

I move forward and he wraps me in his arms, bear-hugging me. It feels good to be held. I close my eyes, feeling the purr of his chest against my cheek, and wishing I knew what it sounded like. I really wanted to talk to him, an honest-to-goodness conversation with no confusion. I wanted to not be the only one that knew sign language—well, other than Maddie, who isn't here. I wanted us to really be companions, instead of me just being a burden.

I really, really hate being a burden. Bad enough that I'm dependent on him for food, shelter, and everything else. I wanted us to be equals about something.

I shouldn't be upset. I'm teaching him sign language slowly, and our communication gets better every day. I just got my hopes up. That's all. I slide my hands up and down his broad, warm back, and smile to myself. I can teach him.

Then my eyes pop open as a new idea occurs to me.

I pat his chest to let him know I'm okay, then race back to the computer and pick up the keypad again. I mentally try to compose my question, and then type. if there is a language in your database can you teach it to someone

I can perform a onetime linguistic upload through an ocular light wave. It connects with the synapses in the brain tissue and refracts to carry the information to the cerebral cortex.

I flex my hands and read that twice, trying to understand. So it sounds like a laser beam shoots the info into someone's head. Okay. That sounds freaking ridiculous. But it also sounds like it has potential. if i teach you my language can you teach it to my companion

Any information processed by this artificial intelligence can be transferred to a recipient.

so i can make a word bank and you can send that to his brain

Query: word bank?

a list of words and the translations

Affirmative.

I pump a fist, excited. Then I think for a moment and type again. it is a visual language can i input visuals

Visuals are an acceptable format.

how do we get started

Simply let me know when you wish to record your visuals and we will begin.

I'm excited. It's a daunting task, but it's doable. We take a day or two and I feed all the sign language I can possibly think of to the computer, and then it turns around and dumps the information into Rokan's brain. There are so many signs that I'm mentally cringing a little trying to think of how I'm going to remember them all. What's the best way to go about this? The alphabet, of course, but after that? I can start with common signs, or try to go alphabetically. I type again. **do you have a dictionary or a list of words i can use as a starting point**

**Accessing a dictionary of English words and definitions. Where would you like them displayed?**

I turn to Rokan, beaming with excitement.

## Rokan

The cave's voice does not know Li-lah's hand-speak. I am shocked and angry at this, until Li-lah explains to me with small, soothing pats of her hands that she will teach it, like she has been teaching me. She will tell it each gesture for every word she can think of. Then it will in turn give me the language and I will be able to speak to her.

It will take many days, but she is determined to do so. She gives me a quick kiss, turns to the wall, and begins her work.

My Li-lah is so clever. I am humbled by her quick mind. She has solved this problem without my help, and as I watch her talk to the flashing words and move her hands, I am filled with pride.

My mate is wise.

My task, then, will be to make sure that she is comfortable. I pull one of the big, square pillows over to her place by the wall. I make sure her waterskin is full, and melt more fresh snow for her. I will have food ready.

I stay close to the cave, the entrance always in my sight, and gather fuel for the fire. I unroll the furs and make a warm, cozy nest for us. I make tea for her. All the while, Li-lah sits in the corner of the room and gestures and talks to the wall.

After several hours, her waterskin is drained, and I switch hers with mine. Her voice begins to crack and grow scratchy, and as the night goes on, she continues. Her gestures grow slower and she gives a raspy yawn.

That is enough, I decide.

I get up from the lonely fire and move to Li-lah's side, approaching in her line of vision. She glances over at me, finishes the hand-speak gesture, and then pauses to take a sip of her nearly empty waterskin. Before she can say anything, I scoop her into my arms and take her to the fire.

"Hey," she protests, her voice dry and hoarse. "I'm not done."

I ignore her words. In my eyes, she is done. She has no voice left, and she is drooping. This will not do. She is my mate and it is my job to take care of her. I set her down by the fire in the nest of furs, and she rubs her face with her hands.

"Five more minutes—"

Her words die when I put my hands on her shoulders and begin to rub them. Instead, she moans, closing her eyes. My cock immediately responds, and my khui hums louder now that I am touching her. "How did you know my neck was hurting?" she muses aloud. "Never mind, you can tell me once you've learned sign language."

I nod to myself. I will tell her so many things when I have learned her words.

She sighs and leans back against my hands, and I continue to rub her shoulders, pleased that I can do this small thing for her. I want to ask her so many questions, but she needs to rest.

"Didn't realize how many words there were in the stupid English language until now," she murmurs. "Did you know—"

I press a finger to her lips to silence her. She needs to save her voice. Already it sounds dry and raspy enough to pain me.

Li-lah nods, and I rub her shoulders and back for a while longer, then get her a cup of tea. I watch her until she finishes it, then feed her small bits of trail rations until I am satisfied she has eaten enough. She starts to get up, gesturing at the wall that is waiting for her, but I shake my head and give her a stern look. I make the *stay* gesture and point at the furs.

She nods and lies back down, too tired to argue. She rests on her belly, propping her chin up with her hands. "Will you rub my back some more?"

Nothing would give me more pleasure. I move to the furs and press a kiss to the top of her small, hornless human head with its soft mane. It has been days since I had her on my tongue, and I am a selfish hunter because I crave her taste. She is tired, but perhaps I can give her pleasure. I move my fingers over the shoulder of her tunic and then tap it to let her know I want her to remove it. Will she be shy or will she take it off?

My khui rumbles low with pleasure when she sits up long enough to take her tunic off and then lies back down again, presenting me with the slim line of her bare back. Seeing her like this reminds me how fragile my Li-lah is. I must always be careful of her. I am much larger than she is, my hands capable of spanning her rib cage. How my khui has chosen someone so delicate for me, I do not know, but I will have no other.

I slide my hands up and down her soft back, and she makes another sleepy sound of pleasure. She doesn't move as I stroke her, kneading aching muscles. This has been a tiring journey for her—from the mountains to the elders' cave. In addition to the walking, I have been forcing her to learn tracking and gathering. No wonder she is exhausted and the muscles in her back are taut with tension. I should rub her every night until she's moaning with pleasure.

That thought makes my sac tighten, and I close my eyes to compose myself. Resonance must be fulfilled soon, because every day it becomes that much more difficult to resist her.

Soon, we will talk, and she will realize what it is that connects us. I can be patient for a bit longer, especially as I have seen how hard she is working to be able to teach me her words.

As if her mind is connected to mine, she murmurs, "I can't wait to be able to talk to you. Really talk and not wonder what the other is trying to say."

I feel the same. I lean in and brush my mouth over the soft skin of her shoulder in a gentle caress. Perhaps she is not too tired to let me put my mouth on her cunt and lick her—

She rolls over onto her back, gazing up at me with soft, hooded eyes. Her teats are in full view, and she does not try to hide them or cover them like before, and that fills me with pleasure. She is growing used to being naked around me, and I like that. Li-lah reaches up with one hand and traces my mouth. "I wonder what you sound like."

Her words seem sad to me, and so I kiss her palm to distract her. It does not matter what I sound like. I sound like *hers*. I *am* hers.

Li-lah gives a little moan as my fangs scrape over her skin. She moves her hands to my chest then, smoothing over me and touching me everywhere she can. I lie down next to her, propping my body up carefully on one elbow at her side so I do not crush her smaller body under mine. I am filled with need for my mate. I want to kiss her everywhere, to put my mouth on every bit of her skin and taste her with my tongue. I want to lap up her juices until she's crying out.

"I've never felt this way about anyone," she says to me, and reaches for my long braid. She plays with the tip of it for a moment, and then locks eyes with me. "Have you?"

The question makes me sad and frustrated—if she understood resonance, she would not ask. She would know that she is my mate, my other half. There is no way I could feel like this for another. She would know I have waited my entire life for her. But I cannot say these things to her yet because I do not have the words. I take her hand in mine and kiss her knuckles, and then hold it against my heart.

Her soft smile is beautiful enough to make my tail flick, a tremor rushing through my body. "I'm addicted to you, too."

She is wrong; she is not as addicted as me. If she was, she would understand the agony I silently endure while I wait for her to understand what it is to be my mate. She would know how hard it is to hold her and wait, endlessly, for the signal that says she is ready to be mine in all ways. She would know the mix of joy and despair I feel every morning when I wake up and she is mine and I have not claimed her yet.

"Oh," she whispers, and her fingers reach for my tail, flicking on the furs beside her. "Look at your poor tail—it's healing crooked." Li-lah runs her fingers down the length of it, where the bones now lie bent after the sky-claw attack. The bruises have faded and the pain is gone, but it does not lie straight as it did before. "You have a kink in your tail." And she strokes it again.

Her fingers on my tail are more than a male can bear. I have never had mine stroked before, and I did not realize until now that it is just as sensitive as my spur. The groan that I have been fighting erupts from me and I press my head against her stomach, needing desperately to touch her but wanting her approval first.

"Eek, watch the horns," she says, and I lift my head carefully. When our eyes lock, she bites her lip playfully and traces a finger around the pink tip of her teat. "If you're going to put your head down, maybe over here?" And she licks her lips suggestively.

A possessive snarl rises in my throat at the sight. I am the luckiest male alive because she is mine. I bend down and kiss her soft, pink mouth gently. Then I move farther down and kiss her soft, pink teats until she is panting and clinging to my horns.

After that, I tug down her leggings and kiss her soft, pink cunt until her juices flood over my tongue and she is exhausted from crying out.

My own pleasure can wait for another day. Just being able to do this for her? For now, it is enough.

# CHAPTER FIFTEEN

## Lila

It takes three long days to go through as many words as the computer spits at me. Three. Looooong. Days. Not every word in the dictionary goes into the Ice Planet Sign Language (or IPSL, as I've been jokingly calling it). There's not going to be any need for Rokan to know the sign for *book*, for example, or *turkey*. That speeds things along, but it's still achingly slow progress to feed each word and gesture into the computer.

I lose my voice at the end of each evening, and Rokan pampers me with tea and cuddling (and okay, lots of making out) until I drowse off in the furs. When I wake up each morning, my throat is better, which is pretty impressive. I've never recovered that fast from a sore throat before, but I'll take it. Maybe my body knows how badly I want this to be done.

During the day, Rokan has to go out hunting, so I have to close the doors to the ship for my safety. I can't hear him knocking, and I don't trust the computer to know to let him in, so I force myself to get up and stretch—and check for him—on a regular basis. He always returns with fresh meat, more fuel for the fire, and many, many kisses for his tired alien girlfriend.

Even if the work is exhausting, the company is excellent.

It's on day three that I get through the letter *z*. There aren't that many *z* words that apply to our situation. *Zip?* Maybe. *Zoom?* Probably not. *Zero?* Sure. *Zoo?* Nah. I pick through the list of words and then, suddenly, there aren't any more to go through.

Wow. I'm done.

I sit back, rubbing my neck, and stare up at the screen, trying to think if I missed anything. I got the alphabet. I got numbers. I even added some slang as I remembered it. Is it . . . is it time?

It almost feels like it's my birthday.

I bolt from my seat and rush to the doors that lead outside. I fling them open and step out onto the snow-covered ramp, looking for my mate. Sure enough, he's heading back toward the ship with a large kill slung over one shoulder. It's amazing that he always seems to know just when I'm ready to take a break, because whenever I look for him, he's right there. It's like he knows.

I wave for him to come, and when his gaze lands on me, a smile crosses his face. He's breathtaking when he grins, and I feel my purring rev up as he jogs a little faster toward me. I'm practically bouncing with excitement when he gets to the door. *It's ready,* I sign, and then point at the computer terminal on the wall.

His brow furrows until I point, and then he lights up. With a broad grin, he dumps his kill by the door. Clearly it's not as important as the language stuff. He takes my hand and we dash to the computer like children, excited. I'm practically shaking with anticipation, which is silly, but it's suddenly become super important to me that we be able to communicate at every level.

He speaks, and I watch his mouth move, holding his hand tightly. He waits a moment, and then speaks again, and then squeezes my fingers. A red dot lights up on the floor and I look at it curiously before glancing up at Rokan. He gestures at the spot on the ground and then points at his eye, then does the *talk* sign. Okay, I remember the computer saying something about ocular download or something, so that must be why he's gesturing at his eye. I'm a little confused by the *sleep* gesture he makes next, but maybe he'll need a nap afterward? The thought makes me antsy—I'm eager to let all the words I've been storing spill out of me—but he knows this system better than I do.

Rokan lifts my hand to his mouth and kisses my knuckles, then gestures that I should stay in place. He moves to the red glowing dot on the floor and says something to the computer. A mechanical arm emerges from the ceiling, and I'm so busy staring at it in surprise that I don't realize what it's doing until a laser-beam shoots right into Rokan's face and he collapses.

"Rokan!" I don't realize I'm screaming his name until my throat aches with the force of my cry. I fling myself at him, cradling his head in my lap and patting his cheek. "Rokan?" I say again, trying to wake him. He's out cold, his big alien body sprawled on the floor. His poor, crooked tail is limp, and I feel like bursting into tears. "I really hope this is what you meant by 'sleep,'" I tell him, stroking his velvety cheek. I look over at the computer screen set into the wall but there doesn't seem to be anything out of the ordinary going on. Meanwhile, the mechanical laser arm tucks itself neatly into the ceiling and disappears as if it were never there.

I pat Rokan's cheek again, but he's still out. Worried, I chew on my lip, thinking. I should get up and ask the computer a question, but I don't want to leave my man's side. "Computer," I call out, and hope it can hear me. "Rokan is unconscious. If this is normal after the procedure you just did, please flash the screen green." It's the only thing that I can think of, my head spinning with frantic thoughts.

A moment later, the screen flashes green.

I exhale with relief and stroke Rokan's cheek again. Thank God. "Computer, can you flash blue on the screen if he's going to be unconscious for less than an hour, and red if he's going to be out for more than an hour?"

Red flashes on the screen.

Drat. I gaze down at Rokan's gorgeous, sleeping face. I want to curl up next to him and put my head on his chest and just wait. But the fire is nothing but coals, and there's a big limp carcass of a hairy pony-looking thing by the door that will go bad if the meat isn't smoked, and we're low on water. Rokan's been teaching me how to take care of myself. I guess now's a good time to start doing so.

I gently set his head on the floor, mindful of his horns, and retrieve one of the pillows and a fur blanket. I carry them over to him and fix him up as best I can, tucking the pillow under his head and making him comfortable. Then I straighten and look over at the dead animal by the entrance.

Yum, yum, dinner.

In a way, it's comforting that there's so much work to do, because then I can't obsess over Rokan. There's the fire to be constantly nurtured—not too low to give off any heat, but not so high to burn the meat that's smoking on the stones. There's water to be melted, and since I just butchered an animal about the size of myself, lots and lots of handwashing, which means more snow to melt. I'm careful not to put too much fuel on the fire, because I'm not entirely sure how long Rokan will be out. I close the doors to the ship just in case of predators, because I won't be able to hear them. I scrape the big, bloody, sticky hide until I've gotten the worst bits off of it, then roll it up like Rokan has shown me, tie it with leather cords, and put it off in a corner for more processing later. I'm sticky and gross with both sweat and blood by the time that's done, so I bathe and then it's time to melt more snow.

All of this keeps my mind off of worrying over my alien boyfriend. For a while, anyhow. By the time I can relax enough to bathe, I worry that he's been asleep for far too long. Maybe we fried his brain instead of teaching him a language? Maybe he gave the computer the wrong command? Maybe he's never going to wake up?

The thought fills me with so much grief that the breath escapes my lungs. I clench my nails into my palms to center myself, then shake the horrible idea off. That's not going to happen. Rokan, he . . . well, he's *mine.*

I'm not the least bit ashamed to be possessive over him. He's handsome, sexy, fit, smart, funny, and a really good kisser now that he's gotten the hang of it. I'll happily claw out the eyes of any alien chick that tries to take him from me, too. My chest purrs in agreement.

Something touches my foot, and I yelp, stumbling backward.

Strong arms go around me before I can fall into the fire, and a crouching Rokan is grinning up at me, his arms locked around my waist. His tail flicks against my foot again.

He's awake!

I fling my arms around him and pull him close, which means I'm hugging a lot of horn and the back of his head. That's all right, though. I don't care as long as he's fine. His hands smooth along my back and he nuzzles against my breast, sending jittery little shocks of pleasure through my body. He's always a little amorous when he wakes up, and I'm tempted to shuck my tunic and fling him down onto the floor and have a little bit of playtime, myself.

But I have to know.

I step backward, mindful of the nearby fire, and study his face. "Are you okay?"

*My head hurts,* he signs, a sheepish grin on his face.

My heart stops in my chest. The casual way he made those gestures, without pausing to think . . . it's too much. I burst into tears.

Rokan pulls me against him, stroking my hair.

"Sorry," I mumble. Then I realize I don't have to speak out into the silence to be heard. I pull back and look up at him, then gesture, *You learned the language? Everything is all right?*

He nods and begins to do a series of signs that are so beautiful it makes me want to weep. *I am still a little slow, but I see your hand-words and know them now. I am glad.*

*We can really talk now.* I can't stop smiling. *Now we can say all the things we have been wanting to say for days and didn't have the words.*

*You worked very hard for this. I am glad for your efforts.*

It's weird—I've been waiting forever to blab at him and now I'm feeling all shy and awkward. I can tell from the expression on his face that he is, too. It's like we've been communicating, but not as well as we could. Now we have the chance to say whatever we want, and I'm a little intimidated about where to start. *Well, anything you want to get off your chest?*

He thinks for a long moment, his face solemn. Then he looks at me and begins to sign again. *You are perfect. I would change nothing about you. And I am glad that you are mine. I have waited many days to say that to you.* He stops for a moment, thinking, and then continues. *I want to say it again. You are perfect.*

I burst into tears again. He thinks I'm perfect? Even after having to get his head lasered just to talk to me? I feel so loved. I throw my arms around his neck and tackle him, sending us both tumbling to the floor. I press kisses to his face, my purring breast matched against his. Rokan tenderly cups my jaw and kisses me back, and I feel more cherished and adored than I ever have.

I'm dangerously close to falling for this guy—if I haven't already. I mean, I've never met a man that makes me purr. He's so thoughtful, and wonderful, and he's never made me feel like I'm less because I can't hear him. He acts like it's been his problem that he can't hear *me*, and not the other way around. Maybe that's why he makes me purr.

I break the kiss and stroke his cheek, fascinated by him all over again. I love the way he looks at me when we kiss, those glowing eyes all sleepy and sexy and yet utterly focused on me. Like he's waiting for me to tell him what I want to do next.

Or like he's waiting for me to give him permission to do whatever *he* wants. I shiver, thinking of the times he's woken me up from half-sleep by tugging down my pants and then licking me until I'm writhing in the furs. He's never taken it further than that, though, and I wonder if he's waiting for me.

Has he been waiting for me to say something to him?

There are so many things I haven't even cracked the surface of. Now, I can get some answers. And right now, answers are more important than kissing. Well, sort of. I force myself to ignore the hungry looks he's giving me. Answers first, then kissing. *What are your people called?*

He thinks for a moment. *I do not have the hand-words for this.*

*Can you sound it out for me? With the alphabet?*

He nods and then starts to spell. *S-A-C-W-E-E.*

"Sacwee?" I say aloud.

He makes a *kinda* gesture with his hand. *Very close.*

*What does it mean?*

*It means people of the cwee.*

*And your people? They come from here?*

*This cave,* he agrees. *Like you came from a cave.*

The ship had mentioned an emergency landing. All right, so Rokan's people aren't natives any more than me and Maddie are. They had a crash landing and never left. That's rather depressing. Just another gaping hole in the "rescue" plan, not that I really expected there to be a rescue. *I see. And you are the people of the cwee. What is a cwee?*

He taps his chest. *It is the thing that lives inside you.*

*The glowing thing? The parasite?*

He pauses over the word "parasite." *It is helpful. It makes you strong.*

*And makes me purr, I guess?*

*Purr? I do not know this word.*

*The rumble in my chest.*

Recognition dawns on his face and he grins, the sexy, heated look returning to his face. *It is because of me that you rumble. That is resonate.*

Resonate? I ponder this. That can't be the right sign. Or maybe he is mistaking it for something else? I sign to him, *I don't understand. You are making me purr?*

*You resonate to me. I resonate to you.* There's pride and hunger in his face as he signs the words to me. *You are my mate.*

Whoa. What? He just made the joined-fingers sign indicating we're mated . . . as in a married couple? *Could you repeat that?*

He does. *You are my mate. We resonate. Now that we have hand-words, I can teach you about resonate.* He leans forward and taps my breast. *Your cwee chooses a mate for you. It finds you the male that is perfect for you, and you resonate to him. I resonate to you; you resonate to me. We are mates.*

My eyes widen. This entire time, I've thought he was my boyfriend and I'm his wife? *So it's decided? Just like that?*

*Just like that,* he agrees, a pleased expression on his face. *I have been waiting for you to understand so we can mate*—this time he uses the *sex* version of the *mate* sign—*and then we will return to the tribe cave and start our family.*

I am stunned into silence at this. For a long moment, I can think of nothing to say. Then I have to ask, *Family? Babies?*

*Yes. Resonate always brings babies. It is the reason for resonate. Mate and baby.*

Okay, so my parasite has decided that I get a husband and kids and I get no say in this? I'm not sure I'm ready to take care of a baby or be a mom—I'm still learning to take care of myself on this planet. *What about birth control?*

*I do not understand.*

Oh God. I rub my forehead, trying to think. I keep circling back to the resonate part. The parasite chooses a mate for me? Is that why Hassen stole me? He was trying to get me to choose him? I think back to all the expectant looks he constantly shot me. No wonder he was so hands off when we saw him again. I thought it was baffling—but welcome—at the time. Now I know the truth—he didn't look at me because I was off the market.

And all this affection for Rokan? This lust? This need for him?

It's not mine at all. It belongs to the parasite. None of what we have is real.

None of it.

That *really* hurts.

# CHAPTER SIXTEEN
## Rokan

The look on my Li-lah's face is alarming. She looks broken. Like Asha did when her kit died in her arms. Her expression looks as if she has lost something that means much to her. I go through our conversation, trying to follow why it would upset her so. We spoke of resonance and kits. *Do you not wish to resonate to me?* I ask her, my own heart hurting.

*Does it matter?* she signs back rapidly. *It does not sound like I have a choice.*

*Resonance always picks the right mate, the best mate. We will be happy together.*

*Because it's forcing us,* she signs, and then begins to cry. *None of this is real.*

Her sorrow hurts me. I hate that she weeps. I hate that this pains her. I would give anything to make it go away. *It is real. Why do you say it is not?*

*Because you wouldn't like me if this thing weren't forcing you to.* She taps her breast. *It's pulling our strings like we're puppets. What we feel between us isn't real if it's pushing us together.* She swipes angrily at her cheeks. *I should have known it was too good to be true. That you were too good to be true.*

I reach out and capture her hands to get her attention. The words she is saying are upsetting and make no sense. When she glares up at me, I sign to her. *You and I are mates. Just because resonance is what brings us together does not change what I feel for you. You have always been mine.*

She shakes her head. *That's a lie. You only wanted me after you started purring.*

*I came for you even before that happened.*

Her brows go down and she looks frustrated. *I thought everyone was out looking for me.*

*No,* I sign. *I sent the others back. I knew I would find you.*

Now she looks even more confused. *What do you mean, you knew?*

I shrug. *I knew. I just knew. I always know.*

*What do you mean, you always know? Why are you not making any sense?* She puts her hands to her face and speaks in a low voice. "Why is it that now that we can sign, you make even less sense than before?"

I ignore her frustration. She is misunderstanding. It happens with the humans, who choose their mates differently than we do. Patiently, I keep signing. *I know things. I sense things before they happen.*

She gives a little moan of frustration. *So now you're psychic in addition to my fated mate?*

I do not know if psychic is good or bad. Or even what it is. *I have always known things. And I knew when I saw you that you were to be my mate. It is why I feel so strongly for you.*

Li-lah signs back angrily. *No, you feel strongly for me because I am your mate. If there was no khui, you would feel nothing for me. How would you feel if we hadn't resonated?*

*That does not make sense.*

*How does it not make sense?*

*Because you are mine. Of course we resonated.*

She throws her hands up in the air, then signs, *I give up. I don't want to talk about this anymore. I need time to think.*

*Are you angry that you are my mate?*

*I am angry that it's making me care for you!*

*Why?*

*Because I can't tell if what I feel is real or if it's all pretend because it wants us to sleep together.*

*It does not want us to sleep. It wants us to mate. Afterward, we can sleep.*

Her eyes narrow at me. *Conversation done. I'm not talking to you anymore.*

*Why not?*

*I need time to figure out my feelings.* She gestures in a *done* motion and then storms to her feet, moving to the fireside.

I watch her go, confused by her reaction. What did I say that was so bad? Is being my mate and having my kits such a terrible thing? She has enjoyed my kisses and my mouth until now. Now she acts as if this is upsetting.

I do not understand. Li-lah has always been soft and welcoming in my arms before. Why would she think anything has changed? She has and will always be my mate. It does not matter if we resonated or not.

She is mine.

Li-lah does not want me in her furs that night. I ignore the stab of betrayal I feel and make my own bed. My anger at being pushed out gives way to helpless frustration when I hear her quiet crying in the dark. She is clearly upset by whatever she has learned. My attempts to hand-talk to her are ignored and she will not look at me.

She is being stubborn, my mate. And until she will talk to me, I can do nothing about it.

I do not sleep at all that night. My body aches for hers, and my heart aches to comfort her and make her tears stop. She will not let me, so I wait in quiet agony for her to fall asleep. When her breathing finally evens out, I still cannot rest. I spend the evening keeping the fire burning, because she does not have my warm body to curl up against, and she will be cold.

In the morning, Li-lah is composed. She sips her tea, and then looks me in the eye. She sets down her teacup and begins to sign.

*I have made a decision,* she tells me.

*I am listening.*

*I know that you think what we have is real, but I am not convinced. I need time to think about whether or not this is me that's attracted to you, or whether it's the khui.*

I say nothing. She does not realize the two are intertwined. If she was not perfect for me in every way, my khui would never have resonated. That is why she did not respond to Hassen; he was not right for her. But I understand her frustration. She thinks time will help, but I know better. *Time will only make the hunger greater,* I tell her. *Your body will crave mine. You will want to mate.* She makes a face, and I continue. *That is not arrogance;*

*that is how resonance works. Do you not feel a great need for me already?*

Even though it is shadowy in the cave, I can tell her cheeks are heating. She has an embarrassed look on her lovely face. *I am not going to answer that.*

*Your khui will make you ache for me,* I sign to her, deciding to be bold. *I have tasted the sweet dew between your thighs and I know this is true. Just like the thought of your hand on my skin makes my cock ache. These are truths, no matter if you choose to believe them or not. But I will wait for you.*

She raises her hands to sign, then drops them. She does not know what to say.

That is fine. I know what I wish to tell her. *You are my heart, always. I can wait for you to realize that.*

Li-lah licks her lips, the tiny gesture sending an ache through my body. *Well,* she signs, *until I decide, what do we do?*

*We continue as we have,* I tell her. *I will teach you how to hunt and to build traps. Whether or not you choose to remain at my side, you must be able to take care of yourself.*

She nods, a smile curving her mouth for the first time in many long hours. *I would like that.*

## Lila

Over the next few days, I slowly come to the realization that Rokan isn't wrong about most of the things he's told me.

Is it wonderful to be able to speak to him? To really speak to him? Absolutely.

Do I crave him like I crave chocolate when I'm PMS-ing? God, yes.

Has anything changed about how I feel? Nope.

Is he pushing me? Nope. In fact, he's not acting any differently at all, other than when he's happy, he doesn't reach out to touch me like he used to. And I'm sad that I find myself missing it. I keep wanting to grab his flicking, crooked tail when we are sitting near the fire at night and pet it, but I force myself not to.

But do I want to touch him because I like him? Or because the khui inside me thinks we should be soulmates? That's the part I keep getting stuck on. Is it my choice or is it just the parasite messing with me? And if it is just the parasite, how am I going to feel after the "need" it's shoving down my throat is fulfilled? Will I wake up one day and be completely blah about Rokan? That worries me, too. Because right now I like him so much and he makes me feel so good that I'm terrified of losing that.

I'm paralyzed with indecision.

I've been reading up on the computer for the last few days about this whole "resonance" thing, too. Rokan wasn't lying about it, which doesn't surprise me—I don't know that he's capable of lying. He's right that it's a sort of supercharged forced mating, and with my khui (the spelling according to the computer) resonating, I'm in a constant state of amped-up ovulation and will be until he puts a baby inside me. It's a species propagation instinct, apparently, and it works for all intelligent life with a khui, humans included.

So that's fun.

I'm not griping about my partner, of course. If I had to pick someone, I'd pick Rokan. He's sexy, smart, understanding, and kind. I just . . . I liked the way things were. Now everything's changing and I don't know what to do. I feel terrified of picking the wrong path. Which is funny, because half the time I don't feel like there's even a path to pick.

I need a sign. And not in one of those woo-woo ways that Rokan claims he can sense. I need a real, honest-to-goodness sign that Rokan really is my mate, and that we're more than just compatible genetically. I need to know that what I feel is real, and what he feels for me won't fade the moment I'm pregnant.

Rokan's been a saint, of course. He's given me space and acted as if nothing's changed, which I appreciate and yet makes me even crazier. Sometimes I just want him to grab me and show me that it's not just the khui compelling him. That he wants me for me.

And then I think of him telling me that *I am perfect*, and I want to stick my hand down my pants and relieve some of the overwhelming need I feel.

But I'd rather have him do it.

Instead, he takes me hunting. And fishing. And we build traps. We keep the elders' cave (as he calls it) as our home base and take to the snowy hills every day to continue my education. For now, we're staying here. Maybe I should be upset that he's not taking me back to my sister, but my thoughts are so consumed with Rokan and this thing between us that I haven't thought about Maddie much, and that makes me feel guilty. I know she has to be worried sick.

I'm a bad sister.

This morning, Rokan is quiet. Normally he greets me with a morning cup of tea and we go over the things he wants to teach me that day, like I'm his apprentice. It's another thing that drives me crazy—it's like he's able to turn off the whole need thing and talk about setting snare traps and fish cages while I keep watching his hands and picturing him doing naughty things with his fingers. Half the time he has to repeat his signs because I'm distracted. But today? Today he's not chatty.

*Tea?* I ask, sitting down next to him by the fire. *Then we go out and check traps?*

He thinks for a moment, and then shakes his head. *Not today.*

*What do you mean, not today?*

*Today we shall stay in the cave. I do not like how the weather feels.*

I look past him and squint at the open doorway. Sunlight pours in, and the snow that normally piles around the entrance is melty-looking. *The weather? It's sunny!*

He nods and fills my teacup, then holds it out to me. *It is. But I do not like the way it feels.*

I roll my eyes and take my drink from him, blowing on it. More of this psychic stuff? Seriously? That's what got us into this in the first place, isn't it? If it wasn't for him having a "feeling," he wouldn't have come after me. Is he trying to convince me that there's more to his "feeling"?

I take a few sips of my tea and then set the cup down so I can talk. *What about the traps we set yesterday? You said we had to check them first thing.*

Rokan shrugs. *They will be empty, then. I do not care.*

*But we worked so hard.*

*Sometimes we work very hard for nothing. Such is the way of the hunter.*

*Okay, well, that's crap. This is the best weather we have seen in days. You said yourself the traps would be full this morning, and we're just going to let all that meat go to waste? I hate that. It doesn't make sense to me. One of the things you've taught me is that nothing goes to waste. Except now because you don't like the sunlight, we're going to let a bunch of meat go to waste? I don't get that.*

He rubs his chest, gazing at me thoughtfully. Then he nods. *Very well. We will go. I do not like it, but we will go.*

*Why?* I ask. *Why don't you like it?*

He shrugs. *I do not know.*

*Great answer,* I think to myself, but I'm just being bitter because he used to greet me with kisses and affection, and now he just hands me a cup of tea and talks about hating the weather. It's just another thing I've ruined, I guess. Frustrated, I turn to my pack and pull out my hunting gear. Dressing for the weather—even with the sun out—takes time, and it'll get my mind off of how distracted he is this morning.

By the time I finish layering my clothing on, my tea is cold. I slug it down quickly and then head to Rokan's side so he can finish tying my outer layer of furs onto my body. It used to be one of my favorite parts of traveling, because he'd pull me against him with the pretense of bundling me up, and steal a kiss or two. Now he's all business, and it makes me sad. I know I told him I wanted time to figure stuff out, but I also miss his kisses.

Or my khui does. I still haven't figured out which it is yet.

He's in a serious mood today, quickly prepping me and demonstrating the knots this time so I can do it myself in the future. That's depressing. I remind myself that this is what I wanted. I asked him to give me space.

I just didn't expect so much space, I guess. Or I didn't expect to care so much.

He puts on his own gear, grabs his spear and his bow, and puts his knives in their sheaths. I have a spear and my one knife, and the sight of all his weapons surprises me a little. The sunlight really is bothering him. Wow. I consider following his advice and staying in, but then what are we going to do? Sit around in the crashed ship and stare at each other while not talking?

That might be more torture than I can stand. Plus, I think of the small animals that might be trapped in our snares, and I don't like the thought of letting them suffer longer than they have to. And that sunlight looks inviting. I do believe it's one of the first sunny days I've seen here since I've arrived—most days are just overcast.

That decides it, then.

The day is warm—well, for an ice planet—and beautiful. The breezes are mild, and the snow on the ground is bright and pristine. It reflects the sunlight, and I worry about snow blindness. Rokan smudges some mud under his eyes and then my own, and I guess that'll take care of things. Then we're heading down the trails, following paths that I'm getting to know pretty well. I recognize this rock, that cliff, this little cluster of flimsy trees. It's such a nice day I almost don't mind that Rokan is silent, his hands quiet.

Almost.

Our first set of snares is empty, but the second one has a fat, wriggling weasel-like creature with hind legs like a long, gangly rabbit. A hopper, he calls it, and then waits for me to put it out of its misery. Today, I only cry a little as I grab it by the scruff and cut its throat with my blade. It's meat, and it will keep us fed and warm, and I can't look at it as anything other than that. Every day of hunting makes it a little easier, though I worry I'm too softhearted to be able to do this. I'd rather cuddle the thing than kill it, but cuddling it doesn't put food on the fire. This next part is my least favorite—field-dressing the kill so I can travel without the guts and the blood ruining the pelt. I cut it open, remove the offal and bury it, then drain it of the majority of blood before tying it to my belt. It's already crusting up with ice, and in an hour, it'll be frozen solid, its khui going dark.

Then it's time to move on to the next set of snare traps. We have at least a dozen set over what feels like miles of trails. I clean my hands off with snow and get to my feet with Rokan's help. *Lead on,* I tell him.

He nods and then gazes up at the distant cliffs, a frown on his face.

I tap his arm to get his attention and sign, *What is it?*

*Just my feeling.*

*Should we go back?*

Rokan gazes down at me for a long moment, then up at the cliffs. *No,* he eventually decides. *But let us hurry. Maybe there is bad weather coming in.*

I give the sunny skies a skeptical look but pick up the pace when we start walking.

Our paths take us into one of the many valleys tucked between the jagged cliffs and hot streams. The landscape may be snowy, yet it's anything but bare around here. There's rock everywhere you look, and clusters of trees and bushes. Reeds stick up from the banks of the sulfurous-smelling streams, and in the distance, there are the jagged purple mountains that protrude like teeth. It's very pretty, even if it's not particularly warm. I like seeing what the world has to offer, though; I prefer being out here than sitting by a fire and waiting for Rokan to return. Maybe I'm more of an outdoorswoman than I thought. I'm kind of proud of this, I realize, as I trek along behind Rokan into the valley, mindful of the cliffs with their overhanging icicles.

I'm lost in my own musings when Rokan grabs me by the shoulders and shoves me up against the cliff wall. The rock bites into my back through my furs, and I yelp. "What the fuck?"

The look on his face is intense, his eyes a startlingly vivid blue. *Know that you have my heart,* he signs to me, and then presses his body against mine, shoving me even farther against the rocks. What the heck—

Then I feel a purring. It's not my khui; it's doing the same low rumble it always does, and this one feels bigger. I can't peer over Rokan's shoulders, because he's got me shoved hard against the cliff wall, his arms a protective cage over my head. He's gazing down at me, unblinking, and there's such an intense look on his face that it nearly takes my breath away.

The purring continues and I realize it's coming from the ground—and the cliff wall behind me. Oh God. Earthquake? I peer over Rokan's arms just in time to see a sheet of snow and ice cascading over the lip of the cliff.

An avalanche.

I scream as the world goes dark and shakes around us. Rokan's body jolts over mine, but he never moves. The moment seems to last forever, and it feels like the world is collapsing. I cling to the front of his tunic, terrified.

All I can think is that he didn't like the weather. He didn't like how today felt. I should have listened. He knew. Somehow, he knew, and he pushed me out of the way before anything bad would happen. Just like with the birds—

I gasp, because I realize that he's done this more than once. Maybe this "feeling" isn't all wishful thinking after all. "I'm sorry, Rokan," I whisper to him, patting his chest.

He's silent.

In fact, he's really, really quiet, no touch, no comforting hand gestures, nothing.

My skin prickles. I give a little tug to his tunic to get his attention. His eyes are closed, so I can't see their comforting glow. In fact, it's pretty dark all around us, and tight. I'm starting to feel claustrophobic. "Rokan?"

He groans and his head lolls to one side. Snow rains forward, splattering my face. Then he collapses against me, crushing me to the cave wall.

The panicky feeling rushes over me, and I try to wriggle out from under him, but there's snow everywhere, taller than I am. I push at his arm, trying to see around him, but all I can see is Rokan's big body and even more snow.

His lips move, and then he staggers to the side, and I can breathe. Fresh air rushes in. He gestures above him, indicating with slow, halting movements that I should climb. I'm too panicked to argue; I use his tunic as a ladder and climb over his shoulders and out onto the snow.

The entire valley's changed, I realize as I crawl forward. There's a fresh layer of at least ten feet of snow, and it's a miracle we survived. We would have been buried if it weren't for Rokan and his "feeling." I stare out at the new landscape, utterly chilled.

I turn around when I realize Rokan hasn't followed me, and I crawl back over to the hole against the cliff wall. He's still there, his big body pressed against the rock and mostly buried in snow. His head has lolled forward again, and I see nothing but horns and dark, messy black hair.

"Rokan?" I call out.

If he answers, I can't tell. After a moment, he doesn't move, so I tap one of his horns. When he doesn't respond to that, I pull on one of them and tug his head back.

His eyes have rolled back in his head. As I watch, a rivulet of blood trickles from one side of his temple and trails down his cheek.

A new feeling of panic rushes over me. "Rokan!" I release his horns and then start digging frantically. He's been hurt, and I need to get him out of there. He can't stay here—what if another avalanche is coming? As I dig, I frantically try to think what causes avalanches. Is it melting snow? Is it because today is too warm? Or is it that there's too much snow? I burrow through armfuls of snow, calling his name over and over again.

Eventually, he jerks awake, and his head lolls back again. I nearly get stabbed with one of his big horns and I scramble to the side, caressing his face. "Are you okay?"

He tries to raise a hand to sign to me, but his movements are slow.

"I'm going to get you out," I promise him, trying not to freak out. I dig farther, pulling the snow away from his back and shoulders. My hands feel like ice but I ignore it, because I have to be strong right now. This is no time to be a wimpy human. Something's wrong with Rokan and all I can think, over and over again, is that I should have listened.

*Know that you have my heart.*

I bite back the sob that threatens and sniff hard. I'll cry later, when he's safe back at the ship and drinking a hot cup of tea. Until then, I have to keep my shit together.

I continue to scoop the snow with my hands. If it takes all damn day, I'm going to dig him out. As I dig farther down, though, I see a lot of broken icicles mixed in with the snow behind his back. There's one chunk the size of my fist near his shoulder, and it's got blood on it. Did it hit him on the way down? I move closer to him and tug on his horn, tapping his cheek. He woozily leans back, blinking up at me. It's clear he can't focus. I peer into his eyes—his pupils aren't like mine, so it's hard to tell if one is dilated or not, but I bet he's concussed. *Can you get up?* I sign. *I can't carry you. You're too big.*

He reaches out and touches my cheek, then signs, *You okay?*

I nod and tug at his arm. "I'm fine, but you've got to get up,

Rokan. You can't stay here. We need to get you back to the ship—the elders' cave."

Rokan lifts one arm and then the other, and tries to pull himself free from the hole. He's buried up to his waist in snow, and the spot that I vacated against him just filled in with more. I keep digging as he tries to slowly move his body free. It's not a fast process, and he has to keep stopping, his eyes drifting shut. I tap him on the cheek, over and over again, trying to keep him awake. If he's got a concussion, he can't sleep.

If we have any hope of getting back to the ship, he can't sleep.

After what feels like an eternity, Rokan is finally out of the hole. He rolls onto his back and sprawls on the snow, exhausted. I crawl over to his side and brush my fingers gently over his scalp, looking for the wound while he rests. It's not hard to find—there's an enormous lump on the very top of his head, and when I touch it, my fingers come away bloody.

My poor Rokan.

He reaches up and touches my cheek, then gestures, *You okay?*

I want to cry. *I'm fine,* I sign back. *Can you walk?*

*I . . . try.* His hand flops back down to the ground, as if he's too tired to say any more than that. It's like a dagger in my heart, and I hold my breath as he struggles to sit up.

After a few moments of this, it's clear to me that he's not going to be able to stand without help. I move to his side and loop his arm over my shoulder and try to help him stand; it's like trying to lift a dozen sandbags at once. My back and legs protest at the strain, but I refuse to give up. With a lot of wobbling and effort, I'm able to finally help Rokan to his feet. He hangs on to my shoulders and nearly drags me to the ground.

This isn't going to work, either. It has to, though. "Come on," I whisper aloud. "We're going to get you home."

We take two steps, and then Rokan topples forward, slumping back to the ground and spilling me with him.

I roll away, wiping snow off my face, and turn back toward him, frantic. "Rokan!"

*You okay?* he asks me with a slow hand sign.

I want to scream in frustration. He's the one that's hurt, not me, and the awful, wonderful man is worried about me and only me. Even now, he's trying to protect me.

I need a new plan. I pull off one of my outer layers of warm furs and wrap his head to stop any bleeding. "You're going to be fine," I tell him aloud. "Let's wrap up your head and get you comfortable, and then I'm going to go look for something to help us out, okay? Maybe a nice sled or something." Oh sure, because sleds just grow on trees. I don't know what else to do, though.

I can't carry him. I can't leave him here.

I *won't* leave him here.

He grips my hand in his and pulls my fingers to his mouth for a kiss. *You're cold,* he signs sleepily, his eyes closing.

The hot tears I've been fighting come rushing forward. I sob into the air and stroke a hand down his cheek. Right now? In this moment? I could care less if it's the khui making me have feelings for him or if it's the real deal. All I know is that I love him and he's in serious danger.

*I love you,* I sign, but his eyes are closed; he won't see it. *I love you and I'm going to fix this, I promise.* "Then I'm going to be your mate," I whisper. I lean in and kiss his mouth, swiping at my icy tears. He's falling asleep again, and I don't know what to do. I can't leave him here alone and defenseless.

I'm not going to give up, though.

I get to my feet and grab the shoulders of his tunic. All right. We're not more than a few miles from the ship. Hopefully. I'll just have to drag him to safety. I hold on tight and tug with all my might.

Rokan moves an inch. Maybe two.

"Come on," I snarl. "Move!"

But it's impossible. I try again, and again, but his shoulders only lift. I can't move the rest of him; he's too heavy. He probably has at least two hundred pounds on me and I'm not exactly a powerlifter.

I can't move him. I want to, but I can't.

Desperate, I look around the valley. Maybe there's bushes or trees or something I can cut down to act as a sled. But all I see around me is a blanket of white. There are a few trees at the far end of the valley, but then I'd have to somehow make it all the way there with him to chop them down, and I can't even move him three feet.

I won't leave his side, either. Not with him unconscious and bleeding. I picture the big birds swooping from the sky and shudder. "I'm not leaving you," I whisper, fitting my body against his side. "You're mine and I'm staying here until we can walk out together."

I press my head against his chest, feeling the low, gentle purr of his khui to mine. They say there're no atheists in foxholes and I can relate to that. Right now? I'd give anything to have Rokan healthy and smiling at me. I don't care if the khui is manipulating me or my emotions—all I know is that I love the guy and I want what we had before I pushed him away. I'll take manipulated love, if that's what it takes to give me Rokan.

He's everything I want. I'll take him any way I can have him.

I don't know how long we lie there in the snow. It's silent, and my world consists of feeling his chest rise up and down with slow, steady breaths. In a way, I suppose it's good that the weather's nice, because at least it's not snowing on us. Instead, the suns are cheerfully warm, almost hatefully so.

All I can think about is how he didn't want to go out today.

*Know that you have my heart.*

I wipe my tears off my cheeks before they can hit his tunic, because I don't want to leave an icy spot. *Oh, Rokan. Wake up and let's go home and I can show you how much you mean to me.*

The gentle rise and fall of his chest is my only answer.

I run my hand over his breast, and as I do, a shadow falls over us. Before I can process this, I smell it. Wet dog.

I sit up, gasping as a yeti gazes down at us. It's a tall adult male, and as it squats next to Rokan, the stink grows worse. It gazes down at him, and then looks over at me.

The face is scarred, one of the eyes missing.

It's the same one-eyed yeti from before.

# CHAPTER SEVENTEEN
## Lila

I hold my breath as the creature looks down at Rokan's unconscious body. My hand goes to my belt, where my knife is sheathed. If he so much as makes one wrong move . . .

The yeti looks at me and makes a hand sign. It's a small, subtle movement, one that might not be noticed by anyone . . . except for someone that has learned to talk with her hands.

Oh. He's asking me something.

He makes the hand sign again, and it jars a memory. It's a sign that I recognize—one that he did before, when he handed me the intestines and tried to feed me. I don't know what it means, though.

The yeti leans over Rokan, sniffs hard, and then looks at me. He shuffles closer to Rokan's head, then leans in and sniffs again, his nostrils flaring. Maybe he smells the blood? I bite my lip, worried.

He smacks a big hand on Rokan's chest, and then makes the signal again.

Is he asking if Rokan is mine?

I nod, then I realize he might not understand what that

means. So I make the sign back to him, trying to repeat the subtle finger movements.

He grunts at me, and then gets to his feet. I rise also, uneasy. What now?

To my surprise, he reaches over and grabs Rokan by one arm, slinging him over his hairy shoulder as if my big blue alien weighs nothing. I follow behind as he starts to walk away. I don't know where he's going, but even a cave full of these things might be safer than leaving Rokan bleeding out in the open.

Then I remember the length of intestine this one tried to feed me, and I shudder. Maybe not.

I keep my knife ready as I struggle to follow behind the yeti. My snowshoes are gone, lost in the avalanche, so I stumble through the heavy, soft snow more than I walk, but I'm determined to stay with them. This thing seems to know where it is going, and he's got my man. Falling behind is not an option.

The yeti goes to the far end of the valley and heads for one of the rocky walls. I squint up, worried, as he begins to climb, Rokan still unconscious and slung over the thing's shoulders. Where is he going? The valley walls are steep, almost sheer, and at the top there's nothing except more snow.

As I watch, though, he gets about halfway up and then disappears behind a rock.

I gasp and climb after them, terrified. Where did they go?

I get a few feet up when the yeti's head appears from within the rock and he makes a beckoning gesture. It takes me a few minutes to climb after them, my legs and arms screaming a protest, but when I get closer, I see there's a human-sized fissure in the rock wall. It's practically invisible to the naked eye, and hidden behind another rocky outcropping. The yeti makes another *come* gesture, and disappears inside it again.

It's a cave.

Cautious, I pull my knife out and follow the creature inside. My heart is hammering, but I have no choice—he has Rokan, and I won't leave him behind. The entrance to the cave is narrow and not much taller than I am, which makes me worry that the rest of the cave is not much bigger. I don't think I'll be able to handle close quarters with the stink of the yeti. Claustrophobia at the tight squeeze threatens to overwhelm me, but I clench my knife and force myself to ignore it.

Rokan is my focus. Only him.

For a weird moment, it feels as if the cave is getting hotter. I step forward into the darkness, the feeling of isolation growing. If there's something dangerous in here, I can't hear it. I can't smell anything but the wet-dog scent of the yeti, and I can't see anything.

I'm going in on faith alone.

A wave of moist, damp heat hits me, and then I see light. Strange, flickering whitish-gray lights. It's not fire, or the heart of a volcano. I don't know what it is, actually. The yeti appears again and gestures me forward, and I follow.

The small cave passage opens up, and then I'm in wonderland.

I suck in a breath, in awe at the sight before me.

It's a massive cave. Well, sort of. It's more like a hollowed-out beehive, with ridges and layers along the edges of the cave but not much in the way of flooring. It looks like a fissure in the rock that has broken open.

I gaze up, because there're plants crawling all up the walls of this strange, hot cave. Tier after tier of rock is laden with bright green leaves, blue splashes of color, and red berries that drip from thick vines. The cave ceiling climbs high, and at the top, the bright lights flicker and flutter, but remain constant. The lights are coming from a piece of the alien ship, broken and wedged into the rock so high above that I'd never be able to reach it. I don't know what it's doing here, but there are lit-up panels in varying colors, and chunks of debris are scattered on the cliffs amongst the plants, giving them light.

I look down, and at the bottom of the cave there's a bubbling, bright blue spring, the edges of the pool striated with color. This must be where the heat and the moisture are coming from. I step forward, awed.

This is the most beautiful place I've ever been. Everywhere, there's bright color—greens and blues mix with reds, and it's all plant life. This isn't the washed-out pink of the trees outside, or the endless white. This is an explosion of greenery that's somehow found a toehold on this frozen planet, and I am amazed. Somehow this little piece of the ship in this perfect spot has created an enormous cave greenhouse full of blooming plants. Light floral scents mix with the wet-dog scent, and I look around for the yeti—and for Rokan.

My man's laid out on a rocky ledge off to one side, and I move closer to him, kneeling. He's breathing evenly. I search for the yeti, but there's so much to see that I'm overwhelmed. There, in the leaves at the edges of the hive, the yeti is climbing the thick vines. He grabs a few bright red fruits and shoves a handful of the gleaming green leaves into his mouth, chewing hard. Okay, so he's having himself dinner. I guess I can't blame him. This place is as safe as any, I guess.

I touch Rokan's cheek, but he's still unconscious. Should I try to move him somewhere safer? I worry if he rolls over, he'll fall off the ledge. Not that there's a lot of room to move him, of course. The plants are hogging all the space, growing riotously in every possible inch.

The yeti lands on the ledge next to me, making me jerk back in surprise. He shoves the red fruits at me, and I grab at them before they can roll off the edge. Each one is the size of a cantaloupe, the rind hard. I make a gesture at myself, asking if he wants me to eat them. God, they look amazing. My mouth waters at the thought of melon. It's been so long since I ate anything but meat.

He continues to chew, his mouth open and showing me glances of the green double-mouthful he has. Gross. Then he makes the same signal he always does, looking at me expectantly.

The gift of the fruit suddenly has a double-edged meaning. What if I take it and he thinks we're now mates? That I'm choosing him over Rokan? Even if they smell incredible, I can't eat them. I put them aside and point at Rokan, and make the signal over him.

If yeti can look disappointed, this one does. He tilts his head and makes a face—or a sound—with his mouth and then continues chewing.

I remain silent, one hand tight on the knife, and the other on Rokan's sleeve.

The yeti watches me for a moment longer, still chewing. Then it turns to Rokan and pulls the bandage off his head, sniffing. I watch, not sure what else to do. It doesn't act like it's going to hurt him . . . but I remember how unpredictable they are.

He sniffs again at the spot on Rokan's head where he's wounded. I can see the blood crusting in Rokan's thick hair, and my heart aches. This is all my fault.

I'm so lost in that thought that I almost miss the part where the yeti spits out the mouthful of greens he's got in his cheeks and slaps them directly onto Rokan's wound. Oh. Oh my God. I make a gagging noise, and the creature looks over at me, a bit of chewed greenery still dribbling from his mouth. I put a hand over my lips. Silence is probably best. I think this might be the yeti version of healing. In a way, it's kind of sweet.

The yeti pulls the last of the greens from his mouth and pats them over the wound, then crawls back out along the vines to get another mouthful. He returns a few moments later without fruit for me, and spits another round of the disgusting poultice onto poor Rokan's head.

Then he looks at me expectantly.

Er. I'm not sure what he wants. I put the leather wrap back on Rokan's head, careful not to disturb the wound. I'd thank him, but I don't know the yeti signal for it.

It seems my yeti friend is a one-trick pony, though. He makes the *mate* (at least, I'm pretty sure it's *mate*) symbol again and watches me.

Yeah, I'm not changing my mind. I pat Rokan's shoulder. This one's my mate. I almost feel bad for turning him down—not that I want to be a yeti-bride, but he's been so sweet and helpful.

In response, the yeti bares his teeth, and I feel a rush of hot, fetid breath hit my face as he screams at me. He snatches the big fruits and hops away, climbing up the vines. I watch him go, shocked. A few moments later, he disappears out of the cave, and then it's just me and Rokan.

Okay, that was a little scary. So much for feeling sorry for the darn thing.

I clutch my knife close, ready to defend my mate. All is quiet, though, and after a few minutes, I begin to wonder if the creature is truly gone. I'm still surprised he showed up after all this time. Maybe he's been following me, waiting for the right moment to try and convince me to be his mate?

Great, I have a yeti stalker. Totally what every girl dreams of.

When more time passes, though, and the yeti doesn't come back, I relax. My stomach growls and I eye all the greenery near me. Maybe I should try eating something. I get to my feet and move along the ledge, looking for fruit that's in reach. There's a big yellowish-orange fruit overhead nearby, so heavy that the vines are bowing with the weight of it. I carefully pull it free and sniff it. It smells like peaches, but the rind is smooth and hard. I return to my spot next to Rokan, brushing my fingers over his hand as I do so. I just want to touch him, to know he's there.

It takes a little time to peel the fruit, and the interior has a hard, springy white rind that's at least two fingers thick, and tastes bitter and awful. I cut all the way down to the pit, only to find that it's not a pit at all, but a soft, smooth center that reminds me of avocado. It tastes like a cross between spinach and watermelon, which is a weird flavor, but it's so fresh and light that I eat every bite of it and lick the rinds.

Then there's nothing to do but sit back and wait for Rokan to wake up, or the yeti to return. I take his big hand and place it in my lap. His tail is so still, and that bothers me, so I reach over and gently drape it over my legs, running my fingers lightly along the length of it.

It makes me feel better just to touch him. Less alone.

*Please wake up.*

## Rokan

My head throbs and aches behind my eyes. It is worse than the time that I, as a kit, stole my father's fermented sah-sah and drank it all by myself. I am a little sore all over, my mouth dry, but it is my head that pains me the worst. I open my eyes, squinting, but all I see is a mixture of blinding color. I close them again, rubbing a hand over my eyes. It is very warm, and my entire body feels damp with sweat and uncomfortable.

As I do, I realize there are soft, gentle hands petting my tail. "Li-lah?" Then I feel stupid for speaking aloud, because she will not hear me. I force myself to open my eyes again and peer over at her.

Her face is blurry but I can tell she is smiling. Her fingers touch my face, stroking it. *How do you feel?* she signs. *Are you okay?*

*Hurts,* I sign back. My limbs feel heavy and tired. I want to close my eyes because the colors are making my head ache even more, but then I cannot see my sweet mate. *Where are we?*

*Cave,* she signs. *Rest. Have some water.*

She pushes something against my mouth—her waterskin. I take several sips and then lie back again. My memories of how we got here are fuzzy; I do not recall walking back to a cave after the rumbling avalanche. I do not recall all these strange colors, either. I cover my eyes, because they are hurting me.

"Rest, Rokan," Li-lah says in that sweet, soft voice of hers. "We are safe. There is food and water, and I'll watch over you. We're fine." Her hands clasp one of mine before I can start signing a response. A moment later, I feel her mouth press against my knuckles, and my khui reacts, humming loudly.

I have so many things I need to say to her, but the pressure in my head is making it difficult to think. I am tired, and she is nearby and safe. Nothing else matters. Her small hands grip my larger one, and I hold her tight. As long as I can feel my mate's hands on me, I can relax. She is safe.

I tumble back into sleep.

I sleep fitfully, half awake and half in dreams. My Li-lah is always there, her touch comforting, but there are things that do not seem right. It is hot, and I sweat so much that I want to pull off my clothing, but I dare not. It could be fever tricking me. I do not smell smoke, which means there is no fire, yet I constantly thirst and can feel my mane is soaked. Li-lah gives me water and cool, tart things to eat, and insists I sleep more. That she is watching over me, and I am safe. There is food and water and we are protected from the cold. There is nothing to worry over.

And I am proud of her, because my mate is smart and clever. So proud. No male could ask for a better mate than mine. Or more lovely. Or more pleasant, or kind. Truly, I am the luckiest of the sa-khui to have my Li-lah, and she fills my dreams with her smiles and her soft skin. When she feeds me sweet, juicy things, I imagine they are her cunt, and I always crave more.

After several sleeps, I wake up to find that my head does not fill with pain when I open my eyes, and that the ache behind my brow is dull instead of piercing. I slowly sit up, squinting as I look around. My Li-lah is curled up next to me, my tail in her hand. We have no furs, and she is stripped down to the barest layer of her clothing. She wears only a small band of leather around her teats, and a short skirt covering her hips. Much of her pale skin is exposed, and my cock responds to the sight. I trail my fingers down her arm, then pull back when I remember that she does not want that, not until she decides if she will heed her khui.

Her eyes open at my touch, and a smile curves her mouth. The sight of her fills me with warmth. *How is your head?* she signs, sitting up.

*Better. Are you hurt?* I think of the rumbling snow, the aching, awful sensation I had in my "feeling" that told me she was in danger. I grab her and pull her against my chest, stroking her hair. My relief that she is safe—that her small, fragile human body is whole—overwhelms me.

Her hand pats my arm. "Rokan, I'm okay. Really. Let me go."

Reluctantly, I do so. I want to hold her for days and know she is safe in my arms.

She does not pull away, though. Instead, her hands go to my head and she tugs at a wrap. She pulls it free of my sweaty hair and then a strange scent fills the air. "Looks better," she murmurs to herself, even as her teats press in front of my face and it takes all of my power not to pull the band of leather down her front and bury my face in the valley there.

Li-lah brushes her fingers over a spot on my head and I wince, because it's sensitive there. I touch it myself, and when I pull away, my hand is covered in green sludge. What is this? I sniff it and the odd scent is coming from this.

"Don't eat that," she warns quickly, grabbing my wrist. "You do not want to know where it came from."

As if I would eat this? It smells terrible. I give a small shake of my head and wipe my hand on my tunic, frowning.

*How do you feel?*

*Hot. Sweaty. I want to bathe.*

*Good luck getting to the water,* she signs back with a grin. *It's a bit of a climb. That might have to wait a few days until you're steady on your feet.*

Her words are strange, and I study my surroundings for the first time since waking. The colors are still here. I was not sure if they were part of my dream, but the green that overflows from the cave walls is not fading now that I am awake. What is this place?

*It's a garden,* she says. *I have so much to tell you!* Li-lah reaches forward to cup my face, radiating happiness. Her smile does not fade, and in the next moment, she presses her mouth to mine. Hot, sweet lips brush over mine and then her tongue dips into my eager, waiting mouth. The taste of her is stunning, and I hold tightly on to her as she kisses me. I have missed this.

My khui rumbles agreement in my chest, and the need to possess her grows with each breath. Our kiss grows more intense with every moment that passes. I let her flick her tongue against mine, but when she goes to pull away, I hold her close and suck on her lower lip until she is moaning, her teats rubbing against my chest, her hands buried in my sweaty hair.

Does this mean she will take me as her mate now? Her little tongue is as eager for me as I am for her, and I can smell the hot scent of her need amongst the fragrances of the plants. If she will let me, I will lay her down here in this cave and make her mine. My breechcloth feels tight at the thought of pushing deep inside her, and I break the kiss and close my eyes, afraid I will lose control.

Her soft little moan in my ear makes me break into a sweat. "Oh, Rokan. I thought I lost you."

I pull back and study her face. I see no fear or anger there, only need. Even though it pains me to release her, I need my hands to speak. *I am yours. I will always be by your side.*

To my horror, her eyes well with tears. *Yes, but I didn't listen. I didn't know what you meant when you said you weren't feeling good about the weather. I should have listened. About everything.*

I shake my head. *You did not understand. Not many do.*

*But I'm your mate. I should understand. You've always done your best to understand me. I'm a jerk and I should have tried harder.*

My mate? Fierce joy surges through me. I cup her face and

stroke the tears from her cheeks, pressing a kiss to her soft mouth before signing again. *You accept you are my mate?*

*I nearly lost you in the avalanche. It made me realize that I don't care what makes me feel this way. I just love you and want to be with you. Do you still love me?*

*You always have my heart.*

Her teary smile is beautiful. *You have mine, too.*

I want to make sure she understands what it means to accept me as her mate. *My people mate for life, Li-lah. Resonance will bring us together for a kit, and we must stay together until it is created.*

But not all stay together afterward. It is not common, but it has happened, and I think of Raahosh's miserable parents, and of Asha and Hemalo. I will not wish her misery if she does not want to stay with me.

So I add, *If you will not have me, I will not force you to stay.*

She shakes her head fiercely. *I'm not sure I'm ready for a baby, but I do know that I'm not losing you. If there's a baby, we'll be parents together. I love you. And next time you have a bad feeling about the weather, make me listen to you.*

Her words warm me. *Then let us mate. I will make you mine now.*

She giggles and shakes her head, looking amused at my suggestion. *Now is not the time. You still need to rest and get your strength back. Plus, your head is covered in someone else's chewed goop.*

I touch my head, even as she puts the leather bandage back over my wound. I wait patiently until she is done, and then ask, *Someone else? Who is here?*

*Long story.* She puts a hand on my shoulder. *One that can be told later. You should rest.*

I sign to her, *I am not tired. I would rather touch my mate.*

Her eyes gleam at that and her hand slides from my shoulder to my chest, slowly. Very slowly. *Maybe you let your mate touch you?* That enticing hand leaves my belly, and I almost groan aloud with disappointment. She presses her hand on my shoulder again. *Lie back down.*

Let my mate touch me? The idea fills me with pleasure, and yet pleasing her is one of my greatest joys. *If you will not let me touch you now, I will touch you double when it is my turn.*

*That sounds like a deal to me. Now, are you going to lie back?*

I do so, and her fingers tug at the laces of my tunic. I am suddenly eager to remove it—not only because it is sweaty, but because I want her hands on me. It does not matter that this strange cave is stiflingly hot, because my Li-lah is wearing very little, and when she touches me, I feel her bare skin rub against mine.

I suddenly do not mind the heat at all.

She finishes with the laces on my chest and then tugs at my tunic. I lift my arms so she can help me take it off, and just that small motion makes me tired. Perhaps she is right and I need to rest for longer. *I do not like being so weak,* I tell her.

*I am here,* she signs to me. *I will take care of you.* There's a naughty gleam in her eyes as she gives me the hand-speak, and then her fingers go to my belt.

I lie back again, watching her as she undoes my belt and then loosens my breechcloth. One hand strays up my belly, her fingers tracing the outline of my muscles, and my cock jerks in response. That small movement does not escape her notice. Her gaze moves lower, and she peels back my breechcloth to reveal my cock, hard and aching, the head covered with thick droplets of seed.

She makes a pleased sound in her throat that causes my tail to twitch, then gazes up at me. The look in her eyes is as hot as the air around us, and as I watch, her hand curls around the length of my cock.

The breath hisses from between my teeth. I cannot look away as she drags her fingers up and down my length, feeling the ridges and learning the texture. Her fingers trace a large vein along my shaft, and then she lowers, and her mouth slicks against my cock-head.

My hands flex, helpless. I want to grab a handful of her silky mane and rub her face along my cock. I want to pull her away and kiss that soft, slick mouth. I want her to take me into her mouth in the shocking way she is suggesting.

I am full of want.

"I've never done this before," she murmurs, glancing up at me. "So tap me on the shoulder if I do something you don't like, all right?"

Do something I will not like? Impossible. But I force myself to nod, my gaze locked on her. I could not look away if sky-claws descended in the next moment. My gaze is on Li-lah and only Li-lah as she drags her teasing fingers over my length again, her mouth hovering ever closer.

Then she licks a bead of wetness off the tip of my cock, and I feel that small graze of her tongue all the way through my body. "You taste nice," she whispers, and her breath skitters over my sensitive skin. "I might have to do this more often."

My groan of need is swallowed as her lips close over the head of my cock. I watch as she pulls me deeper into her mouth, her tongue dragging along my length. I have never felt anything so good. I want to touch her, to bury my hands in her hair, but I also do not want to distract her from her task. Not when she is licking and sucking on every bit of my cock.

My khui is thrumming loudly, its song matching hers, and I

can feel the gentle vibrations of it through her mouth and her tongue as she sucks on my length. Her fingers tease at my spur, exploring it even as she licks me.

I have to close my eyes. If I do not, I will spill right into her mouth and on that lovely pink tongue, which is even now tracing teasing circles on the head of my cock. I picture that and am nearly undone. I clench my fists and press one to my forehead, forcing myself not to touch her. Let her work her mouth over my cock, and I shall gladly endure all that she will offer to me.

But my mate is tricky. I am so focused on her mouth dragging over my length that I am not paying attention to her hands. She takes the end of my tail, and before I can realize what she is doing, she strokes it with her fingers, just like she has stroked my spur.

My eyes fly open. I watch as she lifts her mouth from my cock to lick the end of my tail.

And it is just as sensitive as my spur. My entire body jerks in response. I put a hand on her shoulder to stop her, to warn her to pull away because I am about to lose control.

Li-lah looks up at me, and when I give a small shake of my head and begin to gesture, the look on her face grows naughty. Her mouth descends on my cock again and she sucks, hard.

And I come. All over her tongue and her lips, in her hot, sucking mouth. It is stunning. The breath has been stolen from my lungs, just as my heart has been stolen from my chest.

I am not worthy of such a perfect mate.

# CHAPTER EIGHTEEN

## Lila

Even though Rokan seems to be doing better, I make him "relax" in the garden cave for an extra two days. At least, that's the idea. He needs to rest and rebuild his strength. I'm not entirely sure the man knows how to relax, actually. I try to tire him out with blow jobs (which, okay, are a lot more fun than I expected) and back rubs. He does his best to try and help out—building me new snowshoes out of some of the thicker, reedier dead vines, re-stitching torn leathers, and even climbing down to the pool of water below our cozy ledge so he can bathe.

His inability to stay in bed is driving me crazy, but I suppose he can't help it. I'm the same way. There's no need for a fire here in this cave—it's too humid and warm. It reminds me a bit of a sauna, which is pretty darn nice in my opinion, even if Rokan complains about the heat. I guess it's more "human" temperature than sa-khui. Since there's no fire, there's no need to melt water, and the vines have provided plenty of food for us. There are all kinds of fruits and melons, and a few tuberous-looking plants that taste starchy and awful raw, but will probably be pretty good cooked. Rokan likes the fruit but is puzzled by it; he's never had it before. It makes me wonder about this little cave. If these plants aren't familiar to him, did they come on the spaceship with his ancestors and spill from the broken part of the ship wedged into the ice and stone above us? Is that why they only grow here? Or is it that this fissure just happens to be warm enough to allow these plants to flourish when everything is icy outside? Either way, they add a bit of variety to our diet, and I'm careful to ration them out, saving the seeds when I can.

My one-eyed friend hasn't returned. I can't say I'm sad, because I think of his possessive gestures toward me, and his constant attempts to get me to ditch Rokan. But he did save my mate, so I'm still grateful. I want to leave enough fruit for him, too, in case he comes back. Rokan doesn't believe me at first when I say the creature—a metlak, he calls it—signed to me. He doesn't think they're intelligent. Maybe they're not at our level, but it's clear that the yeti knew a lot more than Rokan gives him credit for. I don't argue the point, though. I'm kind of hoping the yeti doesn't show up ever again. Maybe he'll go home and find a nice Mrs. Yeti to fulfill his furry dreams. I'm just not the girl for him.

On day three of our stay in the garden cave, Rokan's head no longer hurts him, and it's time to go back to the elders' cave. I'm a little torn—our cave here is so pretty and warm, and I love the fruit. But Rokan is uncomfortably hot, and all of our things are still at the elders' cave. Plus, the ledges here are narrow, which means it's difficult for me to sleep next to Rokan without fear of someone rolling off the ledge and into the pool far below.

And it's clear to me that Rokan is very eager for us to have sex. And the elders' cave seems like the best place for that, with our nice, clean furs, a toasty fire, and lots of room to roll around.

Okay, I'm pretty eager for that, too, I admit. We've done a lot of playing around and I've explored every inch of Rokan with my mouth over the last few days because he's been "recovering" but I'm eager to become his in all ways. We'll return to the elders' cave for a day or two, gather our things, and then head to the tribal cave to meet back up with the rest of the group.

For some reason, I'm nervous about that.

If Rokan senses my nervousness, he doesn't comment on it. He helps me dress to go back out in the snow, shaking his head over my wet braids, which are sure to ice up, and my furs, which are probably going to do the same after being in the damp heat of the cave for several days. He scowls when he finds that I've loaded my pack down with fresh fruit from the laden vines, declaring it to be too heavy for my "small human body" to carry, and shoulders it himself. Then he holds my new, flimsy snowshoes while we climb carefully out of the cave and back into the blast of wintry chill that is the valley outside. There's a herd of pony-type creatures nearby, but we have no spears, only our bone knives. They will wait for another time, Rokan tells me.

Then we get to the valley floor and I put on my snowshoes. Rokan secures the hood of my cloak, fussing over me, and then frowns down at my face. *You look unhappy. What troubles you, my mate?*

*I'm just thinking.*

*About?*

*The future? What happens next for us?* I've spent so long thinking about only one day ahead that it's weird to stop and realize that I don't have a big plan for what comes next.

He leans down to press a kiss to my forehead, then signs, *We will get our gear at the elders' cave and then I will put a kit in your belly.* His eyes gleam hot at the thought.

The look he's shooting me makes me all squirmy, even if his words are a little, well, blunt. Of course he's focused on resonance and us coming together. I admit it's eating up my thoughts, too, and all of my dreams have been rather filthy as of late. *I mean when we go to your tribal cave,* I tell him. *I worry what it's going to be like.*

*Everyone will be happy you are home and safe,* he tells me. *As for what it will be like, there will be a celebration with much singing and my father's favorite sah-sah. My brother Aehako will be very loud and boisterous, to the amusement of his mate. My mother will try to feed you all the time. And I will try to steal you away into my furs all the time.* His tail curls around my leg, pressing against my thigh like a dirty promise. *Though we will have to move out of my mother's cave first.*

I giggle at that. *You still live at home with Mom and Dad? How old are you?*

He shrugs. *There is not much room in the caves. Hunters who are not mated remain with their parents or live together. Private caves are saved for families.*

Oh. I don't know how I feel about that. I think of spending the next few years living in the back of someone else's cave, and a sinking feeling curls in my belly. *Where do we fall?*

*Fall?*

*Will we get our own cave?*

*Yes.* He touches my flat stomach. *I will fill this, and we will make a new cave together with many kits.*

Eek. So much talk about filling me. I'd be appalled at the crudeness of his words if I wasn't so turned on at the thought.

He leans in and rubs his nose against mine. *Also, I am ten hands old. How old are you?*

That makes me sputter. *Your hands or my hands?*

*My hands, of course,* he tells me with an arrogant tilt to his head. *They have the right number of fingers.*

*You're forty? Holy crap, Rokan! That's old!*

*Is it?* He looks amused. *I thought we were of an age.*

*I'm twenty-two!*

His brows furrow. *So young. How long do humans live?*

*I don't know. Seventy or eighty years?*

He looks alarmed at that. *My mother is a hundred brutal seasons old.* He reaches out and taps my breast. *You are lucky you have a khui, then. It will keep you healthy for much longer than your human world would. My people live to be very old. Vadren has seen a hundred and sixty-two brutal seasons and is still agile on the hunt.*

I gawk at him. Holy crap. A hundred and sixty-two years old. I guess forty isn't that old for his people after all. Rokan doesn't seem forty. Like he said, it's almost like we're the same age. *How old are your brothers?*

*Aehako is twenty-seven. He is young, but he is a good hunter. He has a mate and a kit. My other brother, Sessah, is two and a half hands of age.*

His hundred-year-old mom has a kid that's ten? This is crazy. Maybe they hit maturity and just stop aging for a long, long time. Who knows? I remember Aehako from our "rescue" party and he looks to be the same age as Rokan, not fifteen years younger. I guess that between twenty and, say, eighty, there's not a lot of difference to these people.

So strange.

*What about language?* I ask him, confessing the other part that's worrying me. *I won't be able to talk to anyone.*

He frowns. *You will. The others will go to the elders' cave and learn the hand-talk language.*

And get their brains lasered? I worry he's wrong about that. *How do you know?*

*Because when Vektal's mate and her companions arrived, they could not speak our language. We learned their language in the elders' cave and they learned ours. How would this be any different?*

He makes it sound so simple, but I still feel uneasy. Until I got my cochlear implant, I always felt isolated, with Maddie translating for me when someone absolutely had to talk to me. I was limited in who I could talk to, and it was awful. I've been fine, for the most part, without my implant, yet I worry about being isolated all over again. But Rokan wouldn't lie to me.

Then again, I wonder if Rokan realizes how self-centered some people can be? How easy it is to just talk over someone? *I just don't want to be left out,* I tell him. *Or a burden.*

He looks shocked at the thought, as if it has never crossed his mind. *Why would you be a burden?*

*Because I can't hear when they talk to me?*

He scowls. *You have many words to say. It is not your fault they do not know hand-speak yet. It is easy to learn, so there is no excuse for them to not welcome you as part of the tribe.*

*Sweet man. And this is why I love you.*

His eyes gleam with arousal. *Save your love words for when we are by the fire, or I am going to throw you down in the snow and put my cock in your cunt even now.* The look on his face makes it seem like he thinks that's a pretty damn good idea at the moment.

Eeep. I feel a hot blush stinging my cheeks. I'm pretty sure that if we mated right here, we'd scare off the ponies. Plus, I'm thinking about my yeti stalker. *Let's go back to the cave, all right? So you can romance your woman properly.*

He takes my hand in his and we set off for the elders' cave.

The walk back to the elders' cave seems laughably short, compared to how yawning a distance it seemed when Rokan was unconscious. We make it there in no time, and I have to admit that I'm glad to see the smooth, snow-covered dome of the place as it rises into view. There's a storm picking up—because of course there is—and a light snow is falling from the skies. We've gathered a bit of fuel—mostly dried pony poop—during our walk, but I hope there's enough fuel back at the ship itself so we can stay in tonight and relax.

And then I feel my cheeks heat up, because of course I'm not thinking about relaxing. I'm thinking about sex with Rokan. Sliding under the furs together, bodies bare, and just doing it. Finally sealing the deal. Letting him get me pregnant. I've never even had sex, much less had a guy come inside me without protection, and I'm nervous and excited about it. My chest has been purring a mile a minute all day long, and Rokan's been sending me heated looks all day, so I know he's thinking about the same thing.

When we approach the doors to the elders' cave, though, I'm surprised to see new, fresh footprints churning the snow at the entrance.

Rokan points them out the same time I see them. *Someone is here,* he tells me.

*Who? Someone in your tribe?*

*Or the metlak you found.* He steps forward, knife out, gesturing that I should wait behind him.

Oh crap, I hadn't even thought about the metlak. I pull out my own knife, hoping it's not my "buddy" from before. Something tells me he wouldn't be happy to see Rokan again. "Be careful," I whisper as he goes in.

I stay at the bottom of the ramp, worried, as he disappears inside. It's probably just his tribemates coming to check up on us, considering we've been gone for a while. Surely that's it.

Impatient, I wait for him to come and give me the signal that it's safe to go in. As each moment ticks past, I get a little more anxious. What's taking so long? Is he all right in there or is there a fight going on that I'm unable to hear? Is something happening?

Just when I think I can't stand it any longer, a stout figure appears out of the shadows and bursts through the door and down the ramp. The fur hood is pushed back and then I see bright blonde hair and a beaming, round face.

It's Maddie.

I shove my dagger into its sheath and then jog forward as best as I can in my snowshoes, my arms going wide. "Maddie!" My sister's bangs are overgrown and hang down in her face, almost obscuring the bright, new khui-blue of her eyes. Her face looks thinner, but the grin is totally my sister and she looks healthy and whole, and just as barbaric as I do.

As she gets closer, I fling my arms around her and weep tears of joy into her tangled hair. It's been so long since I've seen her, and so much has happened. I knew she was safe, and I knew she was nearby, but seeing her brings it all to the forefront, and I can't help but cry a little.

Okay, maybe a lot. But it's a good cry.

Maddie pulls back and studies my face, her eyes bright and shiny with her own emotions, and then takes a step back. She checks me over as if making sure that I'm in one piece and not mistreated. Typical Maddie—she's always been my protector. Then she smiles and signs, *Good lord, look at you!*

*Well, look at you,* I sign back. *You look like one of them!*

*You're one to talk! Your eyes are so creepy!*

*Oh, like yours are any better?* I laugh, because of course we've both got glowing, creepy eyes now. It's part of the khui-thing. I don't even mind that she says it, because seeing her eyes with no whites? That's throwing me off, as well. She looks strange to me, so of course I look strange to her. It'll take some getting used to.

She flips me off and then I can't stop laughing. I hug her again, and it just feels so good to have my sister at my side. It's like a little piece of home has settled in and made everything on the ice planet click. It doesn't matter where I'm at. If Rokan is at my side and my sister is here?

This is home just like anywhere else. I can be happy in this strange new world.

# CHAPTER NINETEEN
## Lila

*What are you doing here?* I ask my sister, once the initial surprise of her arrival has worn off. She looks healthy—a little disheveled maybe, and she's possibly lost some weight, but otherwise? She looks great. And she's so very happy to see me, which makes me feel guilty.

Because my first instinct at seeing that my sister is here? Disappointment. Now Rokan and I don't have privacy to fulfill our resonance. It makes me a bad sister, because while I'm thrilled to see Maddie, I'm also frustrated that her timing is so terrible. Couldn't she have shown up tomorrow? Tomorrow, I would have been ecstatic to see her.

Then again, I suppose it's good that she didn't show up while we were under the blankets and wrapped around each other. I should count my blessings.

She gestures, and I force myself to pay attention. *Farli and I slipped out yesterday,* she said. *This place isn't far from the cave, so we figured we'd jaunt over here and say hello.*

*Slipped out?* I ask. That sounds a little ominous.

*Yeah. We're not being held prisoner, of course, but the tribe seemed to think we should give you guys some space.* She rolls her eyes. *They don't seem to realize you're my sister and we need each other.*

Her words fill me with guilt. I have missed her, but there's been so much going on. My sister, in her typical headstrong fashion, has ignored the advice of the tribe—good advice, too—and decided to come find me on her own. I ignore the stab of frustration I feel. Maddie loves me and has my best interests at heart. She worries about me.

How could she possibly know that I've been doing just fine without her? That I've been enjoying the freedom Rokan and I have to go hunt and do as we like? That his lessons on how to take care of myself have been empowering and I feel stronger and more capable every day? That I was about to suggest to him that we stay in the elders' cave for another week or so, because I'm not ready to join the tribe?

But Maddie wouldn't know any of that. To her, I'm the scared, weepy little sister. I always have been.

I just smile and squeeze her hands briefly.

She gives me a chiding look and signs again. *Of course, then we got here and you weren't here. Where did you guys go?*

*It's a long story,* I tell her, gesturing at the ship and indicating we should go inside. *Rokan got hurt and we had to stay in a cave for a few days while his head got better. I—*

She grabs my hands and stops me from signing. *Are you all right? Do we need to talk?*

I'm puzzled by the serious, worried look on her face. *I'm fine. Are you all right?*

She waves off my concerns. *The tribe is nice, if a little overly helpful and* Brady Bunch. *I mean, are you okay? First that caveman Hassen stole you, and then he comes back without you, and I thought I was going to lose my shit on all of them. But then Hassen says you resonated to Rokan and you're his mate? Without even asking? That's bullshit. Do we need to run?* The look on her face is deadly earnest. *I have some food on me, and weapons. You say the word and we'll blow this joint. We can figure out how to survive together. You don't have to be anyone's little wife.*

"Little wife"? What the hell? *I love Rokan,* I tell her.

*No, that's the resonance talking,* she says with a roll of her eyes. *They told me all about that. It doesn't give you a choice. It's forcing you to think that you love him because it wants you to have his babies. You don't have to fall for this shit, I promise. We'll find a way to break resonance.*

*I'm not falling for anything. It doesn't matter if it was my choice or not. Maybe it wasn't at first, but I love him now. I want to be with him. He's good to me. You'll like him, too. He's wonderful.*

Maddie looks skeptical. *So wonderful he stole you from the first guy?*

*No, he rescued me. Big difference.*

*Whatever. Did he get you pregnant?*

Now I'm getting annoyed at my sister. She means well, but she has all the subtlety of a hurricane and doesn't seem to grasp that I can be in love with Rokan. All she sees is that the sa-khui are the enemy. *Not yet, and that's a personal question.*

There's hurt on her face. *I'm your sister,* she signs with rough, jerky movements, upset. *What am I supposed to think when you get kidnapped and you're staying away with a guy until he knocks you up? How am I supposed to handle that?* Her fists clench, and then she keeps signing. *I know we're stuck here for now, but we can escape, I promise. You don't have to stay with him. You—*

I put my hands over hers, calming her frantic signing. "I love him," I tell her. "We're together. That's all there is."

There's a flash of hurt on her face, and she nods slowly. She pulls her hands from mine. *Okay. We'll do it your way for now.*

*Thank you.* Hurricane Maddie's wrath has been averted for now. I gesture at the entrance to the ship. *Let's go join the others?*

Maddie's silent as we enter the ship, and she keeps a protective arm on my waist. I don't shrug it off, but it irks me a little. I can take care of myself, but she's acting like I need help to go up a snowy ramp. Really? Suddenly, it feels as if there's a massive gulf between us—she wants me to be scared little Lila, I think, because it lets her be Big Bad Maddie. But I don't need a protector.

I can take care of myself, and it makes me feel strong. I'm capable. But I don't need my sister to be my protector anymore, and I wonder how that will make her feel.

When we get inside the ship, Rokan is there, arms crossed, and talking to a girl. She's about a foot taller than I am and all lean, gangly arms and legs. Her chest is just as flat as Rokan's, but her features are like a delicate female version of his. Her long black hair is braided into an intricate series of loops decorated with colored bands, and her horns are a dainty version of his big, arching ones.

I can't stop staring at her. She's the first female alien I've seen, and I had no idea she'd look so different. It's fascinating to see the big, strong features of the sa-khui on a delicate female face, and as Rokan says something, she laughs, chattering at him, and for a moment, she looks really, really young. She's a teenager.

Holy cow, she's a huge teenager. That shouldn't be surprising, given that all the aliens are enormous, but I'm still surprised.

She looks over at me and smiles eagerly. To my surprise, she begins to sign. *Hello, I'm Farli.* She spells out her name with careful precision.

*You learned sign language?* I ask, surprised.

Her smile falters and she looks over at Maddie. My sister signs, *Farli wanted to learn how to say hello to you, so I taught her. That's all she knows so far.*

*I told her she can learn the hand-speak from the elders' cave,* Rokan adds. *She is eager to learn.*

Maddie looks over at Rokan's gestures, a frown on her face. She gives me a curious look.

*I taught the computer sign language,* I tell her. *And then I had it teach him so we could talk.*

*Oh. Guess you've been busy.*

I laugh at that and gesture, *Busy is an understatement. A little.*

Rokan approaches me, his movements easy and fluid, and I can feel myself purring as he moves close to me. For a moment, I think he's going to sweep me into his arms, princess-style, and I start blushing. But he only touches my cheek, and then signs, *Since we have visitors, I will go to the nearby cache and get fresh meat so there will be enough to eat.*

*They have food,* I point out. *And you're still recovering. How is your head?*

*My head is fine. And it will give me something to do. I will not be gone long.* He gives me a sheepish look and touches my cheek again. *Do you understand?*

I think I do. Our sexy little rendezvous we were planning has been interrupted by my sister and her friend. It's just an excuse so he can retreat for a bit while they chatter my hands off. *Go,* I tell him. *I'll start a fire.*

*I will bring back more fuel.* He gives me a light, tender kiss full of promise and looks into my eyes, then sighs heavily and heads out the door.

I watch him leave, my body aching and my nipples tight under my tunic. Man, our visitors really do have the worst timing. I turn back to my sister and Farli.

*Did we chase him off?* Maddie asks, a skeptical look on her face.

"Just us for now," I say aloud and sign as well. "He's going to get food."

The cave—funny how I'm starting to think of the crashed ship as a cave now—interior is more messy than when we left it, and I attribute that to Maddie, who's a bit of a slob. The fire's down to nothing but coals, and so I move to it and begin to stoke it higher, feeding it fuel. Within moments, I've got a cheery, roaring fire once more, and I set up the tripod and put on some tea.

I sit down and Maddie's looking at me as if I've grown a second head. *What?* I ask.

*How did you do that?*

*I've been learning how to take care of myself,* I tell her. *I can hunt and trap now, too. I'm not great at either yet, but I'm getting better every day.*

She blinks. *Oh.*

*This isn't like home. I've been trying to learn everything I can. Have you?*

*I learned that if I show up at the fire every morning, someone will feed me. Does that count?*

I snort and look over at Farli, who is watching our hands move with a fascinated expression. *We should include her in the conversation. I know what it's like to be excluded.*

*Of course. She's going to want to learn the language. Everyone back at the tribal cave has been trying to learn some basics so they can talk to you. I've been teaching them the easy stuff but there's a lot to cover.*

I have to blink back sudden tears. That's so sweet and unexpected. *They have? They're learning sign language to talk to me?*

She nods. *They're very excited to meet you. The ladies are really nice. There aren't very many alien girls, though. Two older women, two about our age, and Farli here. All the other women are human.*

I remember Rokan saying something about that and nod absently. I glance over at the entrance, but no sign of my mate. I rub my purring chest. Weird to say *mate* and have it be no big deal. It feels right. Natural.

*I wasn't lying, you know,* Maddie says. *If you want to get away, I'll go with you. It doesn't matter where we go as long as we're together. We can wait for Farli to be distracted and take the packs and get out of here. Rokan's gone right now so it's perfect timing.*

I stare at my sister. Does she not believe me when I say I'm happy? *I'm not leaving Rokan. He's my mate and I love him.* In fact, I'd be loving on him right now if she hadn't shown up today. *Maddie, this is our home now.*

*It doesn't have to be! There are two crashed ships we've seen so far! It doesn't mean there aren't more! We can try to find a way home—*

*I don't* want *to go home.* Signing it to her feels brutal. Angry. *Why do you think I hate it here?*

*Because I do!* She slams her hands on her chest. *How can you like this place? My ass freezes every damn day! There are no real toilets! No phones! No showers! No cheese! No French fries! No nothing, Lila! We're giving up everything!*

*So we give up some foods and beach vacations. I have gained so much—*

*You're deaf again, Lila! How can you sit there and tell me you prefer this?*

I flinch at her words. Farli's gaze moves between us, back and forth, an uneasy expression on her face.

*I'm sorry,* Maddie signs when I'm silent. *You know I didn't mean it—*

*I am deaf,* I reply. *You think I haven't noticed?* My sister makes an unhappy expression and I shake my head, continuing on. *But you know what else I've noticed? It doesn't change who I am. I can talk to you. I can talk to Rokan. I'm just as capable as anyone else on this planet. It's not holding me back, Maddie. You may think it's awful, but I feel like I can accept my deafness for the first time in my life. It doesn't change who I am. I'm the same person, whether I have the implant or not. It doesn't define me.*

*I know, Lila. I know that. You know I love you.*

*I love you, too, Maddie, but I love being here. I love Rokan. I love all of this and it feels exciting to me. I want to keep learning and growing stronger. And I'm sorry if you don't like it here, but that doesn't mean I want to leave. There is nothing back on Earth that holds a candle to what I've got with Rokan. Nothing.*

I drop my hands, done.

Maddie's mouth trembles, and she nods slowly. *Okay. I guess we'll have to agree to disagree.* She gets up from her seat by the fire and flounces away. She storms into the double doors that lead to the other end of the ship and disappears from sight.

I watch her go, sad. I hate that this is coming between us. Maddie's miserable, it's clear. She's never been a big fan of the cold, and maybe she doesn't get along very well with the tribe. I don't know what it is. But even if we had a choice, I'd choose to stay here with Rokan. Even now, I'm antsy at him being gone so long.

Farli waves a hand to get my attention. I give her a small smile. That had to be awkward to witness. "Sorry about that."

She points to the computer screen, which is still showing the map I left up a few days ago, and says something. I think she wants to learn sign language.

"Sure," I tell her. Might as well. It's going to be a bit before my sister returns from wherever she stomped off to, and someone has to be here to catch Farli when she passes out.

## Rokan

I am slow to arrive at the cache. It feels as if my strength is at a low ebb, but at least my head does not ache. I take my time, choosing my steps carefully as I walk, because my mate would be very upset if I were to get hurt. And then I cannot help but grin to myself. My mate. Li-lah is my mate. She has accepted me. All we need is a quiet moment and I will claim her as mine.

With Farli and Li-lah's sister Mah-dee here, that quiet moment has been delayed, and my aching cock does not want to wait another moment to take her. Now that I am so close to fulfilling resonance, my body craves it even more. I do not want to take myself in hand again, though. Not when she is so close and willing.

When I return to the cave, my Li-lah sits near the fire, alone.

Farli is spread out on the furs, unconscious, and Mah-dee is nowhere to be seen. Li-lah's eyes are red but she smiles at my return.

*What has happened?*

*My sister is angry,* she tells me.

That one is always angry, but I do not say it aloud. *What can I do to help?*

Li-lah gets up and comes to my side and wraps her arms around me, pressing her cheek to my chest. "You just be you and love me like you do."

I stroke her hair. I can do that.

It is an oddly quiet afternoon. Li-lah is not very talkative, preferring to lose herself in work. She insists I keep up her lessons, and so I correct her as she scrapes the skin of the quill-beast I have brought for food. She makes a stew of half the meat, letting the rest thaw on stones for me and Farli, who prefer our food raw.

Mah-dee eventually emerges from her hiding place, her mouth a firm, unhappy line. She hugs Li-lah and joins us by the fire but it is clear that she is not pleased. Farli wakes a short time later, and eagerly begins to sign at my mate, trying out the new language. She chatters with her hands enough to distract all of us, and the evening is filled with Farli's questions and Li-lah's thoughtful answers.

Farli fills us in on what is going on with the tribe since we left. Shorshie and Vektal's baby, Talie, has her first tooth. Claire's belly has seemingly grown double in size overnight. Leezh is carrying another kit. Jo-see and Haeden spend most of their time in their bed together, much to the amusement of the tribe.

And Hassen? Hassen has been given a mild exile. He does not have welcome furs in any of the caves, until the snows are too brutal for him to go out and hunt. Vektal has gone soft on him and given him a light punishment. Farli tells me that Hassen's sadness and remorse are so great that it is difficult to punish him more. What can be harder on him than losing Li-lah?

I do not know if I agree, but I suspect there are other reasons that my chief would not send Hassen away completely. Exile did not work on Raahosh, anyhow, because his stubborn mate simply tried to follow him. I will ask Vektal about it, though. I am still angry that Hassen did such a dangerous thing to my Li-lah. There must be some punishment.

But those are thoughts for another day. Tonight my attention is on my mate. Even though Mah-dee is silent, speaking with Farli lightens Li-lah's heart. I can tell by her quick, light movements and the way her eyes sparkle. By the time she begins to yawn, her sweet smile has returned.

*Sleep,* I declare after Li-lah yawns four times in a row. *There will still be words to be said in the morning and we must travel back to the tribal caves. They will be looking for both of you,* I say to Farli and Mah-dee.

Farli rolls her eyes. *I know how to take care of myself!*

*Yes, but your mother is like mine, and mine still fusses over me at my great age.*

Farli snorts, but then my Li-lah yawns again, and sleeping furs are unrolled near the fire. I make one bed for myself and Li-lah, ignoring Mah-dee's raised brows. Surely she has to know that I will sleep with her sister in my arms? We are mated. That is how it is done.

Li-lah's cheeks are bright red in the glow of the firelight, but she climbs into the furs next to me. I start to pull off my tunic, but Li-lah makes a squeak of alarm and Mah-dee's eyes are wide. Ah. Humans and their strange modesty. Very well. I lie down and tuck my mate against my chest. Her khui is humming a loud song in tune with mine, so loud that I wonder that Mah-dee and Farli can even sleep.

As for me, her teats push up against my chest and she fits so perfectly in my arms that my cock remains stiff and aching for long hours after the others have drifted to sleep. I am too aware of my mate's body, her sweet scent.

How very close we were to mating and fulfilling resonance, only to be denied by Mah-dee and Farli's arrival.

Tomorrow, I decide. Tomorrow, I take my mate to my home and I will claim her as mine.

I wake Li-lah early the next morning and she sits up in the furs, her hair a wild nest atop her head. She yawns hugely and then a surprised expression crosses her face. She puts a finger in her ear and wiggles it.

*What is it?* I ask.

She shakes her head after a moment. *My ears popped and I thought I heard something. It's my imagination. There's nothing now.* Her hand goes to her hair and she smooths it, a shy expression on her face as she glances over at her sleeping sister before looking back to me. *When do we leave?*

*After you eat. There is no reason for us to stay longer.*

She licks her lips and then signs, *I wish there was. I wish we were here by ourselves.* And her khui hums louder, the look in her eyes telling me exactly what she is thinking.

I bite back a groan, because my body is responding to hers. My cock always rises in the morning, but with Li-lah at my side?

It will be aching for many hours now. *There are private caves here,* I tell her. *We will go to one of them, quietly, and I will lick your cunt until you quiver—*

She grabs my hands, blushing, and looks over to where Farli and Mah-dee sleep. *I want that,* she signs after a moment. *But not with them right here.*

*Then tonight, when we are in the privacy of our own cave.* I vow I will lick her cunt for hours. I want to bury my tongue inside her and taste every fold and then I will bury my cock inside her. And we will resonate. It will be glorious.

Li-lah nods up at me. *Tonight. We just have to make it through today.*

And then my sly mate strokes my tail, a wicked expression on her face.

Today? Today will be very long.

With Farli and Mah-dee to keep us company, the day goes by quickly, even if the travel does not. I carry both my pack and Li-lah's, and Farli carries Mah-dee's. The two humans are slow to move over the snow, and it is late when the familiar cliffs that house the tribal caves come into view. I see old Vaza guarding the entrance, and along the path, there are neat rows of small, growing plants—Tee-fah-nee's work.

"Ho!" Vaza calls out as we approach, raising his spear.

"Ho!" I call back, and Farli races ahead, sprinting despite the heavy packs she carries.

Li-lah's hand slips into mine, and I can feel her nervousness. This is frightening to her, because she worries she will not be able to communicate. I want to pull her close and snarl at anyone that will dare to make her uncomfortable. My mate is perfect. If they cannot understand her, they are the ones with the problem, not her.

I need not worry, though. A moment later, people begin to pour out of the cave, all eager to greet the newest tribemate. My brother Sessah races forward, and I grab him just as he flings himself at Lilah and me. I swing him in the air, grinning. "Little brother, do not knock down my mate!"

"I want to say hello," he calls out, waving happily at Li-lah. He makes a new gesture, one that makes my heart swell with pride. *Welcome home,* he signs to Li-lah, and then looks at me. "Did I do it right?"

I rumple his messy hair and set him down. "You did well."

Li-lah smiles and signs a greeting back to him, looking at me. *Your brother?*

I nod. *The little one. He is full of energy.*

*I see that.* The worried look on her face has faded, and when Sessah reaches for her hand, she gives me a look of amusement and lets him lead her forward.

Others swarm around us, and then there are humans calling out with excitement to meet Li-lah. Meh-gan, Claire, and Mar-layn give her hugs in greeting, while Leezh is trying to remember her signs and Shorshie laughs at her efforts. Tee-fah-nee, Jo-see, and No-rah greet my female and then my Li-lah is being swept away on a sea of well-meaning people eager to say hello. I watch her go, amused at how Sessah clings to her hand and how, even now, someone is trying to hand her a kit to hold. How did my mate ever think she would not fit in?

Off to the side, I see a flash of yellow mane, and Mah-dee hangs back from the group, a sad expression on her face. Out of the entire tribe, she does not look pleased that her sister is so welcomed. Is she jealous?

Vektal appears a moment later, striding away from the crowd and heading toward me. He raises a hand in greeting, his daughter, Talie, tucked against his chest. The kit has grown bigger with every day, and right now, she is batting a hand against her father's face, smacking his chin over and over again while making gurgling kit noises. "Glad to see you back, my friend. You have brought your mate home?"

I clasp him on the arm in greeting. "I have. I think Shorshie and the humans have carried her away."

He nods. "The moment she came into sight, Georgie handed me my daughter." He grins at the child in his arms and pretends to bite the little hand thumping on his chin, which makes Talie howl with laughter. "We were about to send hunters out after you, since Mah-dee and Farli disappeared to go find you."

"We were out hunting and were delayed. I took a blow to the head and Li-lah nursed me."

My chief looks concerned. "Have the healer check your wounds."

"I am better," I tell him, but I shall. I will not risk my health, because I must be at Li-lah's side, always. "Hassen told you that we resonated?"

He nods, distracted by Talie's tiny smacking hand as she swats at his nose. "He was not himself when he returned. He apologized, and offered to leave the tribe forever. I gave him exile, but not a harsh one." Vektal glances over at me. "He should suffer for his misdeed, but the truth is, we need him for the upcoming brutal season. It will be upon us soon and the storage caves are not full. You know as well as I do that he is a strong hunter. One of the strongest. Am I punishing all of us if I send him away?"

I say nothing. He is clearly unhappy with his decision, and I understand. Hassen is a friend and a good tribemate. He is impulsive, perhaps, but I do not sense bad in him. And Vektal is right—if there is a choice between feeding the tribe or exiling Hassen, the tribe must take priority. "You are my chief and I abide by your decision."

He grunts and Talie smacks his mouth again. "And Li-lah?" he asks. "Will she be frightened? If he approaches her again, I have told him he will be permanently exiled."

"He no longer wants Li-lah," I tell him. In this, I am confident. "He wants resonance, not her. When he found out that I was Li-lah's mate, I could see he was defeated. He will leave her alone. As for my mate, if she is scared of him, she will show him her knife. She is fierce when she needs to be."

Vektal nods, pleased. "A fierce female is a good one." No doubt he thinks of his own Shorshie.

I watch Mah-dee trail behind the others, and glance over at my chief again. "What about Mah-dee? Should we worry that Hassen will take her and try to force resonance on her?"

Vektal snorts at that. "You have not been at the cave, so you have not seen it. Mah-dee and Hassen hate each other. She snarls at him and he is determined to avoid her. There is no spark between those two."

"Mmm." My feeling pricks, telling me there might be something there. I think of Haeden and his Jo-see, who bickered and fought until resonance. Now they are so hungry for each other they cannot be pried from their furs. "Has Mah-dee shown preference to any of the males?"

Vektal shakes his head and switches arms, and Talie immediately starts to smack the other side of his face, babbling. "She has not. There is hope she will resonate, but it might take time, like Jo-see and Tee-fah-nee."

I nod. "My mate and I will need a cave of our own, and privacy.

I know that Mah-dee should come and stay with us because she is family, but my Li-lah is shy. She will not feel comfortable if her sister is near when we mate."

The look he gives me is full of understanding. "Resonance has not been fulfilled yet?"

"Not yet." I try to keep the heaviness out of my voice. "But soon."

"Is she fighting it?"

I shake my head. "Her sister has poor timing."

Vektal laughs, and Talie whacks him on the nose and giggles. "You will have a private cave, my friend. Your mother has already taken over one of the storage rooms and prepared it for your mate's arrival. As for her sister"—he thinks for a moment—"Asha can cave with her."

"Asha?" I am surprised. "Then—"

He nods slowly. "It is broken between them. Hemalo beds with the hunters."

I think of quiet, gentle Hemalo. He is not a hunter, and once, many turns of the seasons ago, he loved Asha. "I am sad for him."

"Sometimes resonance is a curse," Vektal says. "And sometimes, it is the greatest gift." He pulls his daughter close and gives her a smacking kiss, which makes Talie giggle all over again. "The sooner you claim your mate, the sooner you will know this for yourself."

# CHAPTER TWENTY
## Lila

Even though I'm deaf, the signs of a party are obvious. Skins of strong-smelling drink are passed around, and someone's face is contorting in an ecstatic rendition of what must surely be singing. Farli is racing around, painting bright circles and dots on people's exposed skin, and yet another woman hands me a fat blue baby, beaming at me.

It's sensory overload, but the best kind.

All my worry about coming to the tribal cave was for nothing. These people are warm and friendly, and everyone has been trying to sign some sort of greeting to me. They really want me to feel welcome, and it's so sweet I could cry. My poor Rokan has been pulled away by his chief, and now he sits talking to another woman in the corner of the room. Maddie has drifted toward my side to interpret, and she winces when someone staggers past, a skin in hand, yelling something up at the ceiling that I can't hear as someone else plays a drum.

*You should be glad you can't hear this,* Maddie signs. *These people are nice but they are terrible singers. Just awful.*

I giggle and rock the baby in my arms. It's so stinking cute, with little nubby horns, pale blue skin, and a wee little tail. The mother—a quiet redhead—just smiles at me, content to hang out and let me admire her baby. I hand him back after a few minutes and turn to Maddie. *I don't remember her name.*

*Harlow,* she spells out.

"Thank you, Harlow," I say aloud.

Harlow says something long and involved, but I can't catch all of it, and look to my sister.

*She is heading out to the ship tomorrow, she says, to get the language. She says it's very clever of you to teach the computer. Says she's working on a broken medical machine, and if she gets it fixed, maybe she can have it look at your ears.*

"Thank you, but I'm good either way," I say aloud to Harlow.

*You sure?* she mouths, her brows going up.

I shrug. "I'm fine either way."

She grins and gets up, and as she does, I catch a glimpse of a few people frolicking naked in the nearby pool located at the center of the cave. Okay, that's a lot of nudity—both male and female, human and sa-khui. I blink rapidly and turn away.

*Yeah,* Maddie signs. *In addition to the singing? They are also not shy. But hey, bonus. There's a bath.*

*Might be a while before I get brave enough to do that,* I tell her.

*You and me both. Gonna be a long time before I go native.* Maddie nods her head toward the corner, where Rokan is now being fussed over by both his mother and the other woman. *Did you meet the in-laws?*

*I did,* I tell her. *Very briefly.* I'd been expecting an old crone and instead was surprised to see that Rokan's mother, Sevvah, has gray hair, but her face is youthful and her smile bright. She's the same pale blue as Aehako, and Rokan's the darker shade like his father. When the party first started, Sevvah hovered over me for a time, patting my stomach and then pinching my cheek, making it obvious that she's super excited to get more grandchildren. She got pulled away with Sessah, and right now she's busy splitting her time between fussing over Rokan and dishing out food. Rokan's dad is apparently the one in charge of the booze, and everyone keeps heading over to his corner of the cave. They seem like a nice family, though.

As I look over to my mate, I watch as Sevvah pinches Rokan's cheek, and I stifle a giggle. Imagine getting your cheek pinched at the age of forty. Mothers are mothers wherever you go, I suppose. I look over at Maddie. *Should we get something to eat?*

She makes a face. *More stew? I'm so sick of it I could puke.*

*Oh. I have some fruit. You want some? It doesn't taste like regular fruit, but it's still pretty good.*

Maddie's eyes go wide. "You what?" She's so startled that she speaks aloud, and two or three human girls also turn to look at us.

"Um, I have fruit? It's in my bag." I glance around at the other women, curious. "Found a whole cave of it."

Two other humans immediately pile into the small group near the fire, and one, I think, is the chief's wife. She says something to me, and I look over at Maddie.

*She wants to know if it's real fruit.*

I nod slowly. "I ate a lot of it. Do you guys not have fruit?"

*Not that I've seen,* Maddie signs, and talks to the woman for a moment. *Georgie says that the plants they can eat consist of something like a potato. I've tried it, and it sucks. Where's your bag?*

*I think Sessah ran off with it?*

Maddie turns to Georgie and they speak, and then Georgie charges to her feet with a speed that astonishes me. A few other humans gather, and by the time Sessah returns with my pack, there are no fewer than ten eager humans crowded near me, most holding babies.

I open the bag and pull out one of the big reddish fruits, and every mouth rounds into a little "oh." I can't hear it, but it's funny to watch. "This one is sour," I say as I hand it over to the closest set of hands. "A bit like cherry. This one is kind of like spinach mixed with melon." I pull out the next and hand it over. "And these sweet little berries taste, well, kind of like berries. They're a little squished after being in my bag, I'm afraid." I pull them out, passing the "little berries" around to the others. They're actually about golf ball–sized, but compared to the other fruits? They're tiny. "I have a few more in the bag, too."

It looks like everyone starts talking at once, and it's clear they're excited. Maddie begins to sign. *They want to know where you got these.*

"There's a cave," I say aloud. "In a little valley close to the elders' cave. It's about halfway up the cliffs and you can't see it from the ground, but when you go inside, it's full of all these plants and it's warm like a sauna. It's almost like a greenhouse." As I watch, a pretty black woman claps her hands and says something to Maddie.

*She wants to know if you can take her. She's their gardener.*

"I can, but give me a few days? In the meantime, you guys can have this stuff. I'm kind of fruited out at the moment."

The fruits are snatched up eagerly and a few girls come over to give me a hug, which is surprising. You'd think it was Christmas the way they're acting.

*They're super excited,* Maddie says, an envious look on her face. *You're now the most popular girl in the cave.*

*I am? It's just fruit.*

*You know they're worried about food shortages, right? Everyone's out hunting like crazy to try and have enough food for the winter.*

*Wait, winter? It's not winter right now?*

Maddie shakes her head slowly. *This is summer.*

*Oh God.*

*So yeah, the fruit is great. They are going to love you even more.* My sister gives me a smile that doesn't quite reach her eyes. *And here you were worried about fitting in.*

I shrug, feeling awkward. This isn't like Maddie. She's normally so assertive and right now she seems . . . lost? My poor sister. This has been hard on her. She hasn't had a Rokan to lean on through all this. She's been alone, except for me, and I haven't even been here. I've been with Rokan.

My body fills with warmth at the thought of him, and I peek over at the corner, where he's been ensconced with a few of his tribemates for the last while.

Our eyes meet from across the busy cave, and I feel an electric pulse race through me. It's like he was thinking about me in the same moment, or his psychic sense told him I was thinking about him. And in that moment, I wish we were back in one of the other caves, alone. Everyone is nice, but I really just want to crawl into Rokan's arms and kiss him until the suns come up.

We stare at each other for a long moment, and then he gets to his feet. His movements are slow, sinuous, and I get all hot and bothered just watching the man freaking stand up. God, he's sexy.

He's all mine, too. I feel the need to fan myself.

Then he starts walking toward me. He says something to his mother, hovering nearby, and she smiles and turns away. It feels as if the entire room is watching us as Rokan steadily approaches me across the crowded cavern. My breath catches in my throat, and my chest is purring like it's got a motor in it.

I get to my feet, drawn by his intense gaze.

*It is time,* he signs as he comes to my side. And before I can ask exactly what he means—though I have my suspicions—he picks me up and tosses me over his shoulder like I'm a girl in one of those caveman movies.

And okay, it's hot as hell. I'm so aroused at that quick, decisive action that I'm practically squirming. Everyone's going to know what we're leaving the party to do and I kind of don't care. I want my mate. I want my Rokan.

Everything else can wait.

## Rokan

I have been a patient male. I have let my mother fuss over me. I have let the healer check over my wounds. I have watched as my mate has been handed every kit in the tribe and introduced to all of the humans. I have endured the envious looks Vaza and Taushen are sending in my direction. Hassen is not here, but his name is mentioned several times. It is a small tribe and gossip flows freely, but I will endure it all for my mate. I want her to enjoy her celebration.

But when her eyes meet mine over the crowd and she has that soft look on her face that tells me her breast is resonating as hard as mine? I am no longer patient.

It is time to claim what is mine.

I get to my feet and push my way through the group to her side. I hear a few muffled chuckles from the gathered tribe as I scoop my mate up, but they are lost amongst the cheer that rises as I storm away with her over my shoulder. They are ready for us to consummate our resonance, just like I am. They want our happiness.

I want that, too.

My mother has told me about the cave she prepared for us. One of the new storage caves—a smaller one, but that does not matter to me—has been cleared out and readied for our return. I head down the long, winding passageway that was recently opened and there, off to one side, is our cave. A decorated screen leans against the entrance, waiting for us.

I duck to enter the cave, a hand on my mate's back to ensure she is not scraped by the low rocks. I set her down gently in the room and then move to the entrance. The screen fits perfectly over it. Now, we have privacy. Now, no one will disturb us. We will climb into bed and mate until we grow too hungry to stay in bed any longer.

And then we will eat and return to bed. My cock aches with pleasure at the thought. I do not plan on letting Li-lah out of my furs for several days. Not until we are both utterly sated.

"It's dark," Li-lah whispers. "I can't see your hands."

I feel a stab of shame at her words. Of course I should build a fire. I touch her cheek to let her know I hear her words and then kneel beside the cold firepit. In a few moments, I have built a small blaze and there's a relieved smile on my mate's pretty face.

"Is this our home?" she asks, glancing around the cave.

I nod. *Do you like it? The furs are mine, and if you need*

*anything—pillows, blankets—I shall make it for you. Whatever you need, I will provide.* I want her to be happy here, with me.

She bites her lip and looks around. She gets to her feet and I watch as she explores the cave. There is not much to see, and I worry it will not be enough to please my mate. Her hands move over a covered basket, then she touches a decorative leather hanging my mother has thoughtfully put up. My weapons are stacked neatly in an alcove, and there are extra bowls, skins, and other items the tribe has donated to make our home. Li-lah turns and looks at me, and there is a soft smile on her face. "I like it."

*It is enough for you?*

She moves to my side and puts her hands on me, stroking my chest. "I love it, because I am here with you. You are all I need."

A groan escapes me, because seeing her smile fills me with lightness. She is my happiness. *My heart,* I sign to her. *You are my heart.*

*I know,* she signs back, *and I'm not going anywhere.* Then she slides her hands down my arms and whispers, "Are we in private here? Do we have to worry about being interrupted? Or someone hearing us?" She bites her lip and gives me an awkward look; all the while, her hand rubs my forearm.

Just that small touch is making my cock ache unbearably.

*Do you see the screen?* I point at it. *Over the entrance to our cave?*

She nods.

*As long as it is in front of our cave, no one will interrupt us. Behind it, we do not exist.*

Her eyes widen in surprise and she peers at the entryway. *Are you sure?*

*It is a tradition honored by my people.*

*Then they will know what we're doing in here?*

*My heart, of course they know.* I take her small hand and press it to my chest, where my khui sings loudly to hers. *The moment we resonated, they knew we would be joining. No one denies resonance for long.*

*So obvious.* Her hands return to my chest after she signs. "I guess there's no hiding it."

I shake my head slowly. *I do not wish to hide it. I want everyone to know you are mine. I am the luckiest of my people.*

Her fingers fidget on my breast. *So we should just do it?*

She is not sure? I would be amused if my body did not ache so badly for hers. *That is my choice, yes.*

Her chuckle makes me ache. "I just, I've never done this before, you know?"

*I have not, either. In that, we are both new.*

Li-lah makes a face. *I almost wish that wasn't the case.*

I go very still. *You would wish another female has touched me?*

"No! God, no. I just wish I knew what I was doing right now. I feel like such a dork." Her hands move over my shoulder and caress my arm. "I think I'd kill another woman if she tried to even look at you twice."

Her words fill me with pride. *We do not need experience. I know what to do. My cock goes inside your cunt.*

Li-lah's small hands cover mine and she giggles. "It's so weird seeing you sign such dirty things to me. And yes, I know how babies are made, thanks for the lesson. I just mean I don't know any of the nuances. How to make you feel amazing. How to get you to make me feel amazing." She gazes up at me. "I want us to be really good at this so we can do it often."

*We shall,* I declare. *I will not rest until you have come, even if it takes the entire evening. My cock shall wait until your cunt is dripping and ready.*

She makes a soft little noise and glances over at the entrance of our cave. Is she still shy about that? I kiss her forehead and move to one of the large baskets of dried fire-making materials and carry it across the cave, then shove it in behind the screen, further wedging it into place. There. Now no one will be able to come in even if they should attempt it. I look over at my mate for her approval.

*Sorry. I'm being weird, aren't I? It's just that I can't hear if anyone walks in on us.*

*No one will walk in,* I assure her.

*I just don't want anyone to see me, bare-ass naked.*

*They will see my bare ass, not yours, if we are doing things right.*

She giggles at that, and the sound is sweet. *You do know there is more than one position, yes?*

I frown. *How do you know?*

*Because I've read books! And seen stuff on TV! Haven't you seen other people do it?*

I shrug. *My parents are always under their furs. I do not go look to see who is on top.*

Li-lah's laughter peals through the cave. *Thank goodness for that! We can go easy for now and learn the basics before we toss some weird stuff in, I guess.* She grins and slides over to me, reaching for my tail. "That means you get to be on top."

Of course I will be on top. I want to ask how else it is done, but her fingers encircle the base of my tail and she strokes it gently. My body breaks out into shivers, and I bury my hands in her hair, losing myself in her scent and the feel of her body against mine.

"I guess at some point I should get you naked, right?" Her

voice is a soft whisper that feels like a caress of her hand down my skin. "Get things rolling?"

I nod, rubbing my face against her mane. The thought of my mate pulling my leathers off fills me with pleasure, and I think of our touches before, when she slowly peeled back my clothing to gaze at my cock. It felt hard and aching then; today it throbs with even greater need.

"Naked it is," she murmurs, and then she pulls on my knife belt and unties the knot, letting it drop to the ground. Her hands go to the laces at my neck, and she loosens them and then pulls on the hem of my tunic, dragging it up my chest. She cannot reach the rest of the way, so I finish for her, yanking it over my head and horns and then dropping it onto the cave floor.

*Pants next?* I suggest. My cock is aching to be free of its confines.

"I'm deciding." She studies me for a moment, as if choosing what to pull off next, and then drops to her knees, tugging on my boot. I am amused by her choice. Is she savoring her undressing of me? I shall do the same to her when it is my turn. She wears a great many more layers than I do, so it shall be an exercise in patience.

I obediently lift one leg as she pulls my boot free, and then the other when she moves to that. Then I am in nothing but my leggings and breechcloth. My body feels tense with anticipation, and as I watch, she licks her lips and remains on her knees, gazing up at me.

That small little flick of her tongue is nearly my undoing. It makes me think of the last time her mouth has gone over my cock, and I nearly come in my breechcloth at the image. Resonance has filled my mind with nothing but thoughts of her, her mouth, her teats, her soft skin. I am useless until she is done with me, and gladly so. If the cave were to collapse around us, I would not leave my furs until she was done with me. That is how badly I want this, and how badly I want her.

Her attention goes to the waist of my breechcloth. "I remember how to do this," she whispers, and slides a hand up and down the hard length of my cock before undoing the next set of ties. Then the leather falls down my legs and to the floor, and my leggings follow a moment later, pooling at my ankles.

Li-lah sucks in a breath and her hands go to my hips, holding me there and just staring. "The sight of you always overwhelms me," she murmurs. "In a good way, though. I scarcely know where to touch you first."

Then her fingertips graze the head of my cock, and I nearly lose control. If I am going to last long enough to please my mate, I must take over. Before she can touch me again, I put my fingers to her chin and pull her attention back to me. *My turn,* I tell her.

She nods, getting to her feet. I can tell she is feeling shy; her movements are fidgety and she cannot remain still. I do not understand why. Have I not kissed her most private spots? Have I not dipped my tongue into her cunt and tasted her sweetness before? There is no need to be bashful now.

I shall simply have to kiss the shyness out of her.

I step out of the last of my clothes and sit down on the large rock near the fire, then pat my knee, inviting her into my embrace. Li-lah slides into my arms and starts to put her hands on my shoulders. I stop her, clasping her smaller hands in my bigger one, and pull her against me for a kiss. Her lips part under mine in surprise, and then she moans against my tongue as I lick inside her mouth, tasting her sweetness. With her in my arms, I can feel the vibrations of her khui resonating in time to mine, and her thigh is very close to my erect cock. If she had no leggings on, I could prop her up on my thighs, pull her legs apart, and bury myself deep.

I groan into the kiss, picturing that, slicking my tongue between those soft lips and thrusting deep, as my cock aches to do.

She clings to me, her mouth greedily accepting my tongue, and as we kiss, I tug at her clothes. The home caves are warmer than out in the wild, and she is only wearing a tunic, a fur wrap, and leggings. All are easy enough to remove. My hands work on her clothing as I kiss her, removing the wrap first, and then loosening the ties on her tunic until I can slip it over her head. Li-lah is so lost in my kisses that she makes a small sound of regret when I break the kiss long enough to pull her tunic off her body. Underneath, she is wearing her leather band over her teats. *More* clothing. Always more clothing with her. I want to see her naked, to weigh her teats in my hands and feel the tips harden against my touch.

Her mouth goes back to mine, her kisses hungry and eager. I move my hand along the band and find a knot at the back. It is easily undone, and then her teats are bare and lovely. My fingers skim her skin and she is so soft here, softer than the backs of her knees, or the sweet dip of her neck.

Li-lah moans at my touch and her hips rock against my thigh. I pull her tighter against me, fitting her hips against my cock until I can feel my length pressing against her. She still wears her leggings, but they will be gone soon, and then we will be skin to skin.

Her small teats brush against my chest and her arms wrap around my neck as she rubs her body against mine. Another harsh groan escapes me, and I cannot take any more; I must have her under me.

I hold Li-lah pressed against me and stand, moving to our furs. Cradling her close, I lower our bodies until she is underneath me in the furs. Her legs wrap around my waist and it takes everything I have not to rip the last of her leathers from her body and plunge deep into her.

I must be calm. Controlled. I must give my mate pleasure first. And I know what she likes—I know what makes her cry out and writhe as if she is being pulled apart. She likes kisses on her teats, but she likes kisses on her cunt even more.

She makes a soft, mewing sound when I tear my mouth from hers, but I am determined. I want my mate's sweet flavor on my tongue, and I want it *now.* I kiss her lovely skin, moving downward over chest and belly, even as my fingers work at the knot at her leggings. I pull them down her thighs, and as I do, the hot, needy scent of her arousal fills my senses.

My mate. She is soaking wet for me.

A growl rises in my throat and I jerk her leggings off, then push her thighs wide.

"Rokan," she breathes, and I can hear the anticipation in her voice. Her hands go to my horns and she holds them tight.

I remain still, waiting to see if she is going to steer me away from her cunt, but she pushes me down toward her thighs, a silent encouragement even as she arches up off the furs. Already, she is wriggling with anticipation, her breathing coming sharp and rapid.

"You don't have to do that if you don't want to," she tells me, just as my tongue is about to drag through the soft, slick folds of her cunt and lap up her taste.

Not want to?

Licking her is my *favorite*. Not want to? It is what I want more than anything. I could stay with my tongue buried between her legs for hours and never get my fill.

I want to protest that yes, I do want this, but it is better to just show her. I slide one finger up and down her folds, dragging through her juices. At her whimper, I lean in and put my mouth over her third nipple. Her gasp of excitement and the way her fingers tighten around my horns? Those are delicious, but not as delicious as her taste. I explore her at my leisure now, dragging my tongue over her folds in slow, methodical motions. I know what she likes best, but I am going to tease her first. I deliberately avoid her third nipple, because it is the part that makes her crazy when it is licked. Instead, I nudge a knuckle against the entrance to her cunt even as I brush kisses over her wet folds.

One hand smacks my horn, and then the breath hisses from her lungs. "Oh God," I hear her murmur, and then one leg jerks as I let the tip of my tongue graze her flesh. Her knee moves, and she's wiggling again, so I grab her leg and fit my shoulder under it, pinning her movements and allowing myself free rein to her slick, delicious heat.

This? This is much better.

My tongue dips deep, seeking the center of her heat, and she cries out my name again when I taste her. I can feel her cunt tighten around my tongue as I push it into her again. Her little cries grow stronger and her juices sweeter with every thrust of my tongue. I can feel her thighs quivering on my shoulders, her fingers tight on my horns.

I grind my cock against the furs as I lick her, over and over again, her hips rocking against my face. I want to do this forever, but my body aches to claim hers, to fulfill resonance. I lift my head and she immediately presses a hand down on the top of my mane, trying to push me back into place.

"So close," she breathes. "Please, Rokan—"

I will not fail my mate. I push a finger into her wet warmth and immediately her cunt tightens and quivers around it. I stroke it in and out, her moans fueling my need, and my mouth descends on her third nipple, the aching little bud that has been waiting for my attentions. Her cries become heated, her hand pulling on my hair as she rocks against my mouth. I lick her nipple over and over again, her desperation becoming my own. I need her release, need to feel her milking my finger with her cunt, need to fill my mouth with the taste of her.

She is everything.

A small cry, and then I feel a burst of fresh wetness on my tongue. Her thighs clamp on my shoulders and her cunt ripples tightly around my finger, clenching over and over again as she comes. I lick her with renewed urgency, not stopping even as she quakes with release. My own need for her is overtaking my senses; even if I wanted to stop, I could not. Over and over, I hungrily lap up her juices, burying my mouth and tongue in her sweet folds. My finger thrusts into her again and again, until she's quivering with a new release and crying my name out.

It is still not enough. I need more.

I tear my face away from her sweetness, gently nipping her thigh before I sit up. My cock aches to be buried inside her, and I am desperately close to losing control. I press a hand to my brow, trying to recover. *Patience. Calm. Let your mate catch her breath and then you can claim her—*

Li-lah makes a satisfied little moan, still sprawled in the blankets. She rubs her foot on my thigh. "Where did you go, Rokan?"

Already she misses me. I miss her warm, soft body, too. My body shivers with the need to retain control, and I give myself a hard shake before lying back down on the furs next to her. I touch her cheek and then begin to caress her once more, peppering her neck and shoulder with kisses.

She hooks a leg at my hips and pulls me against her in silent encouragement.

*More?* I ask, signing to her.

Li-lah nods and her hand steals to my cock, her fingers grazing over my spur.

A splash of liquid erupts from my cock and I jerk her hand away, pinning it to the furs. I give her a small shake of my head. More touches, more exploring from her fingers, and I will paint her belly with my seed. Tonight, I want to be inside her.

"Close to losing control?" she whispers, curious. She wriggles under me, deliberately dragging the tips of her teats against my chest. "Poor baby."

I groan silently, closing my eyes for strength.

Her little heel digs into my backside and I feel her shift against me, opening her thighs. "Claim your mate, Rokan," she whispers. "I'm ready for you."

My beautiful, perfect mate.

I can maintain control no longer. I slide between her legs, settling my weight against her. I fit my cock at her entrance, ready to thrust deep. She is tight, though, and I rub the head with her slick juices to ease the fit. As I do, she digs her little fingernails into my arms, encouraging me with breathless little pants.

My mate. My resonance.

Mine.

With a hiss, I push forward. My cock sinks deep, my body

claiming hers. Her cunt is like a fist, clenching me tighter than my own hand, and the feeling is like nothing I have ever experienced. I close my eyes, savoring this moment. Mine. Mine now.

Li-lah's gasp makes me freeze. It penetrates the pleasurable haze clouding my thoughts, and I force myself to go still. Have I hurt her? Agony lances through me at the thought—she is my mate and the reason I breathe. To hurt her is unthinkable. I brush a finger over her cheek in a silent question, and when she opens her eyes, I sign, *Okay?*

"Oh my God, what was that?" Her hand slides to where our bodies are joined, and I feel her fingers moving, tracing my spur. "I think the earth just moved."

I frown, looking around. An earth-shake? Now? I did not feel it, but I was too lost in the wet clench of Li-lah's body.

"Figure of speech," she says, breathless, and her fingers move against my spur again. "With this, you rub up against me really nice." She gives a little sigh that sounds like pleasure, and then drags her fingers through her folds and rubs my spur and her little hard bud. "Do it again?"

She wants more? Nothing would give me greater pleasure. With one hand on her hip, I thrust again.

Li-lah throws her head back, crying out. Her hand moves to her cunt again and she rubs my spur as I rock into her again. "Feels so good," she tells me. "Incredible. I didn't dream—" Her words die in her throat and her mouth forms an O as another wave of pleasure overtakes her.

Fascinated by her response, I press my fingers to her folds and stroke forward again. This time, I feel it as she does—when I move, my spur drags along the sensitive side of her third nipple. She cries out as I touch her, and I feel her cunt clamp around my cock, sucking me deeper.

My control is gone.

I pump into her, thrusting my cock into her tight, sweet warmth. She clings to me, moaning as our bodies rock together. I can feel her cunt rippling in response each time I push into her, until my name rips out of her throat and she stiffens, lost in another release.

The sight of her, the feel of her body clasping mine? The loud, triumphant song of our khuis? My own release explodes out of me with enough force that stars swim before my eyes, and my entire body shudders. Dimly, I can hear Li-lah breathing my name, her thighs quivering as they clasp me against her. My seed empties into her, and it feels as if I am coming forever, and I press my forehead to hers as pleasure overtakes us.

We are one, Li-lah and I. Forever.

# CHAPTER TWENTY-ONE

## Lila

I'm pretty sure Rokan has ground me so hard into the blankets with our lovemaking that I have tufts of fur up my butt. I'm also pretty sure I'm deliriously happy.

My toes curling, I wrap my arms and legs around him, pinning his big body against mine. I never want him to let go.

Sweaty and sticky with lovemaking, he nuzzles my face and holds me tight against him. It seems we're on the same wavelength with that. With his arms around me, he can't sign to me, but talking is unimportant at the moment. I don't need it. I don't need anything but his skin pressed to mine, his cock deep inside me, and his spur sending jolts through my body every time he so much as shifts.

I shiver. That spur, man. Someone should have warned me. That thing can turn a girl's brains to mush.

He presses a kiss to my neck and I yawn, sleepy and pleased.

My ears pop, and for a moment, it almost sounds hollow in the cave. Almost. It might be my imagination, though. I put a finger in my ear and rub it, frowning.

Rokan sits up, gazing down at me with concern. *Are your ears bothering you? Do you need the healer?*

I sigh with disappointment as his skin leaves mine. So much for skipping signing and just snuggling. *No, I'm fine. My ears just popped.*

*Is your hearing coming back?*

*I don't think so. Why would it?*

*The female with the flame-colored hair—Har-loh. She says she has a growth in her brain and her khui fixed it.*

Oh. Did she? I make a mental note to ask about it but not right now. In the morning. Or the day after. Whenever. I'm more interested in getting my mate to press his big, yummy chest against mine again. *Does it matter to you if I can hear?*

*Of course not. You are perfect as you are.* He looks indignant that I would suggest otherwise.

I smile up at him and trace my fingers along one rock-hard pectoral, feeling the ridges that cover his breastbone and how they graduate to smooth, suede-like skin. "I'm okay if it never comes back," I tell him. "As long as I have you, you'll keep me safe."

*I will be at your side, always,* he signs, a solemn look on his face.

"Promise?"

He taps his chest. *My feeling tells me it is so. You will not come to harm as long as I am here.*

Somehow, I knew he'd say that. And somehow, I believe him. Who better to keep me safe than the guy with the sixth sense? I rub my fingers over one of his rock-hard nipples. "Then come over here and protect me with that big, sweaty body of yours."

Rokan's eyes gleam as he moves to cover me again.

Time to resonate, again.

# Maddie

I stare out at the celebrating tribe, not paying attention to the people that dance past with a skin of sah-sah or the woman that pulls her top down to breastfeed not one but two blue babies. I ignore the exclamations over the fruit that they've managed to savor all damn night, and I sure as shit ignore when they start singing again.

Everyone's so damn happy. Everyone but me.

Me? I'm struggling.

In the space of the last month or so, I've gone from confident, independent bartender to lost, lonely captive torn from my sister. I've gone back to my old role as Lila's protector only to be ousted from that role the moment she returned, freaking hand in hand and lovey-dovey with an alien. She's mated. She's happy. She wants to stay.

And me?

I'm just kind of here.

Alone.

I've got no one anymore. It's clear that Lila doesn't need me. Everyone in the tribe already adores her and they can barely tolerate me. Not that I blame them—I wasn't exactly Miss Pleasant to be around while my sister was gone. I was worried about her, and I took it out on everyone else, even the women who have gone out of their way to be nice to me.

They don't understand what it's like to be so alone, even in a sea of people. Everyone here's part of a family. There are happy women with babies, and men utterly devoted to their ladies. As I look over, the chief—Vektal—is tossing his baby daughter into the air and giving her exaggerated kisses just to make Talie laugh. And boy, does that baby laugh. It'd be adorable if it didn't make me feel so sour inside. He's got a wife and a baby. All of the humans here have someone. Even my sister—scared, timid little Lila—has returned utterly confident in herself and in love with Rokan.

I've been forgotten. I sigh and stare out at the entrance of the cave. Sometimes I wonder what would happen if I just up and left. Would they hunt me down like they hunted for Lila? Or would they be all "good riddance" and not care because I've been a bitch?

Glowing eyes stare back at me, and a big, bulky form emerges from the shadows of the cave entrance, spear in hand, a dead animal in the other.

It's Hassen. The one that stole my sister. The one that decided he wanted a mate so much he'd just up and fucking steal her.

Him? He can kiss my fat ass.

Though the look he's giving me right now? That tells me he'd enjoy that far too much. That he'd do more than just kiss it if I bared it for his inspection.

And for some reason, I find myself prickling with arousal at the thought of Hassen folding his big body down to give my plump ass a kiss. Which is all kinds of wrong. He's exiled. He's a dick. He wanted my sister. None of these put him on the "Ice Planet's Most Desirable Bachelors" list.

I jerk my gaze back around to the fire, scowling.

Totally not gonna keep picturing him with his mouth on my ass. Biting one of my rounded cheeks. Dragging his fingers over my body and exploring the fact that I have no tail.

I give my face a hard slap to bring me back to reality. Like a hate-fuck will make everything better? It'd just make things a whole hell of a lot messier.

Nearby, Farli gives me a startled look. "Are you all right?"

"Just distracted," I tell her. Farli's a good kid, and the closest thing I have to a buddy here, for all that she's like fifteen years old. Right now? She's my ride or die, because, well, I don't have anyone else. Even my sister, Lila, is off in a corner somewhere, making out with her new hubby. I can't even be mad about that—she's so happy and she is such a wonderful person that she deserves every bit of joy. I'm thrilled for her.

I'm a little jealous of her radiant happiness, sure, but still thrilled for her.

Even though I shouldn't, I peek over my shoulder back at the cave entrance again. Just in case Hassen is still there. But he's not, and I ignore the little stab of disappointment I feel.

The last thing I need is to get involved with the bad boy of the ice planet.

# BONUS EPILOGUE

## TO THE FRUIT CAVE

# Lila

Rokan tests the light pack on my shoulders, checking the straps. Then he ties it at my waist, fussing, and frowns to himself.

*Too heavy?* he signs.

*It's fine,* I sign back, amused at his actions. I'm feeling strong and capable, and I can certainly carry a lightweight pack on my shoulders for travel. There's nothing in there but some rations and empty waterskins for filling up with snow later. We have a few additional empty packs that are folded up with the intention of filling them with fruit from the cave we discovered. Rokan tells me that we'll build a sled when we get ready to come back, but for the first part of the journey out, we're walking.

We're standing at the front entrance to the main cave. Weak sunlight pours in, offering a bit of brightness to the otherwise gloomy interior of the cave system. There's a scent of fire from a dozen hearths, and it masks the other smells around, like food and people. Since my hearing was taken from me again, I've noticed that scents are more predominant, something I appreciate. But it might not be a good thing living in such close quarters with everyone else.

It's a little strange to think that we just got "home" and now we're going out again. I thought we'd rest for a while now that we've arrived, but some of the others approached us about going out to visit the fruit cave once more so we can show them where it's at. I don't want to be apart from Rokan so I suggested we go together.

It's not like me to volunteer for something like this, but I'm embracing my new fearless side.

Well, not *completely* fearless. Just slightly more independent. The last few weeks have shown me that my entire world can be turned upside down, I can return to the deaf state that was past, and I can still thrive. Maybe it's a little strange, but I'm feeling pretty high on myself.

It's probably the resonance, though.

Rokan adjusts the leather belt at my waist that ties my pack there. *Better?*

It wasn't bad before, but I nod, smiling at him. We're still resonating. Despite days of making love, my khui still vibrates in my chest, and I know if I reach out and touch his breast, I'll feel his doing the same drumming, humming rhythm mine is. Resonance makes us need each other. It makes me want to be constantly at his side, day and night. It makes me reach out and take his hand constantly.

It makes me want to pull his leather leggings down and rub my face all over his cock.

I blush at my own thoughts, distracted, and almost miss that he's signing at me.

*. . . back or front?* Rokan asks, his long, blue hands elegant as they move. His eyes are heated, as if he's somehow guessed my thoughts.

My mind is still on his cock. Is he asking about sex? *Right now?*

*No, when we travel.*

Lips pursed, I blink at him. *You want to have sex when we travel? In front of the others?*

Rokan's mouth parts and then he moves forward and cups my face, tilting my head up so he can kiss me hard. I cling to him, loving this affection, this greedy hunger. If he wants to have sex when we travel, I'm actually considering it, because right now my khui is thrumming in time with my pulse, and my pulse seems to have set up shop between my thighs . . .

He taps my cheek and I open my eyes. His smile is easy and sends a fresh curl of heat through my belly. *I was asking if you want to walk at the front of the group or the back.*

Oh. Well, now I feel silly. *At the back,* I sign. *If we're at the front it will make me uncomfortable because they'll be behind us but I can't see what's happening.*

Rokan nods. *Makes sense. We can guide from the back. It is not a problem.* He tips my chin up and kisses me again, and I keep my eyes open. When he pulls back, he adds, *And if you like, I will take you from the front or back later.*

*Back,* I tell him. *I like back.*

*I do, too.* That heat is back in his eyes. He pauses in his signing, distracted at something over my shoulder. His tail flicks back and forth and he gently pulls me against him, turning me.

Haeden stands behind me, his mouth moving so quick I can't read his lips. He looks at Rokan and then gestures back at the caves behind him. His gaze slides to me and I can almost see the color drain from his face. His hands lift and he fumbles with a few signs, flustered.

"It's okay," I say aloud, and make the sign at the same time. "I don't expect everyone to know signing overnight."

Normally I'd be a little offended at someone talking behind my back, but I'm in a cheery mood and I know this is new for so many of them—and the fact that they're trying so very hard to learn eases a lot of frustration.

Rokan moves forward so he can sign to me. *He is apologizing that they cannot come with us. His mate is feeling unwell this morning and he does not wish to push her.* He pauses and then adds, *He also asks that we bring some of the melon back for his mate because she has mentioned it many times. Many, many times.*

I grin at him and turn back to Haeden, who is watching Rokan's hands move with a bit of wonder. "We will of course bring melon back for Josie."

Haeden's grim face lights up in a grin. He puts his hand to his mouth in the gesture for *thank you*. He thinks for a moment, then indicates the same to Rokan and heads off, trotting back toward his cave. His tail is almost wagging, and I can tell from his steps that he's in a good mood.

Glancing back at my mate, Rokan is watching Haeden go, a look of amusement on his face. *I have never seen him like that,* he tells me.

*Like what?*

*Happy. He is very happy with Josie.* Since spellings mean nothing to his people, we have bastardized *J-S-E* into a single, somewhat fluid gesture to mean "Josie."

*I'm glad for him,* I say, and I mean it. Rokan has told me about Haeden and his troubled past, and about Josie, too, and I've seen the way he looks at her in the few days since we've been back. They've mostly kept to their cave, but when they emerge, they're very obviously deeply in love. I had a brief conversation with Josie, who was very excited at the prospect of going to the fruit cave and learning sign language so she could speak with me. Our children will be born close together, and she wishes to be good friends. I like the thought.

Honestly, everyone in the tribe seems kind and pleasant, with two notable exceptions—Hassen and my sister. Hassen could fall off a cliff for all I care, but I do worry about Maddie. Things haven't been quite the same between us since I got back.

I don't think she wants me to be in love with Rokan. I don't think she wants me to enjoy being here. I think she wants me to rail against my fate and fall behind her so she can protect me from the world like she did when I was little. But things are different now, and I love Maddie . . . but I also love Rokan. And I love feeling strong and capable and I might never go back to scared Lila.

Maddie doesn't know how to deal with that, and it's hard for me because my sister's always been my best friend and my biggest supporter. She wants me to be happy . . . just not here.

I'm hoping that with time she'll come around. I've already said my goodbyes this morning, and things were strained. We'll return soon enough, and maybe after a bit more time passes, Maddie won't look at me with betrayal every time I smile.

Just because she hates it here doesn't mean I have to.

# Rokan

Being mated is . . . different.

I have never considered myself an angry sort, or the kind to rage and bluster. I leave that to Bek and to Hassen. Yet as we travel and I hear conversations floating on the wind from the four in front of us and I know Li-lah cannot hear them and is being left out?

Anger fills my belly.

Salukh and his mate take up the front, followed by Ereven and his mate a few steps behind. We walk a few paces behind both couples. I like both of them. They are good hunters and their mates are pleasant and easygoing. Tee-fah-nee is excited to see the plants, and I think Claire just wants to get away from the cave for a bit. Our pace is brisk so we can make good time and get to a hunter cave later tonight, one large enough that we can all fit comfortably.

But with the brisk pace, it means there is not a lot of time to pause. My mate keeps up, but she pants, and it is clear the other females are struggling. Claire says something breathless and Teefah-nee laughs and another spear of frustration lodges in my gut.

Li-lah waves a hand at me to get my attention, and I turn to her.

*You look mad,* she signs, and makes a face, mimicking mine. *Are you upset about something?*

I wonder how much to tell her. Part of me wants to protect her from anything that might hurt her feelings, yet at the same time, she deserves to know what goes on. *They are speaking,* I finally offer. *And I do not like it because you cannot hear it.*

To my surprise, she smiles. *You are sweet.*

*Why is that sweet?*

*Because you are upset for me.*

*I do not like that you are being left out.*

*I do not like it, either.* She thinks for a moment, glancing up at the others, then back at me. *But what is the solution? Should they be silent because I cannot hear them? That seems foolish.*

*True.* I pause, then add, *But that does not mean I have to like it.*

She giggles. Now that we are around the others, I am noticing that her spoken voice sounds slightly different than the others, as if she is speaking in a different part of her mouth or throat. She cannot hear herself and it affects how she speaks, she has told me. Sometimes it sounds as if she swallows her words.

I decide I like the way she sounds better than anything.

*Look at it this way,* she tells me, her graceful hands moving. *We have a language they cannot speak. We could be saying dirty things to each other and they would not know.*

My khui sings louder in my chest at her words. *Are you thinking about mating? Because I am thinking about mating.*

Her skin is pink from the cold, but she makes the face I associate with her cheeks coloring. *It is because we resonate.* Her gesture for *resonance* is her hand trembling over her heart, a perfect representation of it. *But . . . yes.*

And she giggles again.

My smile grows. I love her happiness. Everything about Lilah fills me with joy. Just looking at her brings me so much pleasure, knowing that she is safe, and content . . . and mine. I do not mind walking at the back, I decide, because it is as if I am in my own world with my mate at my side.

So I slow my steps and gesture at the two suns in the sky. *The day is early yet. We can slow down. They will not go ahead without us, and I would rather talk.*

Her answering grin is bright, her eyes sparkling, and my knowing feeling flares in my chest. This female has my kit inside her. Right now. I know this like I know my own heartbeat, and emotion floods through me. I stare at her, full of wonder.

To think that I have a mate—my other half, my everything—and now a kit on the way? It feels like too much joy for one person to contain. My throat grows suspiciously tight and I find it difficult to concentrate on walking. I want to stop and laugh. I want to stop and clutch Li-lah to my chest. I want to fling myself down into the snow and wave my arms and legs in it like a kit, just to work some of this emotion out of my body. Will our kit be a boy? A girl? My "knowing" tells me nothing yet, but I am content to wait.

*You all right?* Li-lah signs to me, a curious look on her face.

My attention is drawn back to her. *Sorry,* I sign. *I was distracted.*

*By thoughts of what to say to me? Dirty thoughts?*

I chuckle when she touches the corners of her mouth in the

sign for *laughing*. I will tell her about the kit later, I decide, when she has time to sit down and consider everything. She might need a moment. She might weep. She might throw herself into my arms and I want to be able to hold her for as long as she requires.

Later, I decide. I will tell her later.

# Lila

Even though I was excited for traveling this time, I find that it's not as much fun as expected. The morning's pace is bruising, and when we slow down in the afternoon, I find I'm staring at the backs of the others more than anything. Rokan tries to keep up the conversation, but sometimes we have to climb up a rocky hill or watch for snowdrifts, and then there is no time for signing. It makes things very isolated, and I'm left alone with my thoughts.

They're not bad thoughts, though. Instead of fretting over my sister, Maddie, I think about the future. Rokan and I will have a cave to ourselves, and I wonder how I can make it cozier and feel more like a home. I think of soft furs and wall hangings and a thick, plush nest big enough for the two of us. Maybe it's silly to get excited over having a cave to live in, but Rokan and his people are happy and I think I can be happy without a cell phone and the internet and the conveniences of modern life. I glance over at Rokan as we walk, and he's watching me, that melting, adoring expression on his face.

Oh, yes, I can definitely give up a lot of things for someone who looks at me like that. Perhaps I'm giving up more than others, but that's just life. I handled the lack of my hearing in the past, and I can handle it again now.

When twilight falls, we head for a hunter cave, and I'm a little less pleased to find that it's hard to see inside. It's dark and shadowy, and Rokan steers me to a seat by the fire with small touches, and a hand on my shoulder tells me I should sit while the others get to work. Someone builds a fire and I can vaguely feel the air moving behind me, which tells me that others are busy in the back of the cave, but it's isolated and lonely without hands or mouths to see.

But then the fire is going and Tiffany smiles at me from across the flames. Rokan sits at my side, brushing my hand with his, and then pulls out a dead animal to skin. It looks half-frozen, judging from the stiffness, and I recall stopping by a pit earlier to pull out meat. It's a little unnerving to watch someone yank a dead body from a cache in the snow and realize that's going to be your dinner, but I remind myself that it's no different from a refrigerator.

It's just coming with its own packaging. Sorta.

Claire sits in front of me next to my legs and I look over at her in surprise. She hesitates, her hands in the air as if she wants to sign something to me but can't remember the words. Embarrassment is written on her face.

"I can read your lips if you talk slow," I offer. "And keep your face turned to the light."

She brightens and nods. Thinking for a moment, she pauses again and then begins. "We feel bad that the journey is quiet for you. We can talk but you can't hear us. Is there a better solution?"

Oh. I'm touched. Claire's expression is earnest with her desire to please. Rokan gives my knee a squeeze and I suspect he is glad they're saying something, too. I sign with my hands even as I speak. "I appreciate you asking. I knew it would be quiet. It is okay. Just talk to me now."

Claire beams. "We talked about fruit a lot," she says, laughing. "It has been a long time since we had fruit!"

"Not so long for me," I admit.

"There are not many sweets here," Claire continues. "Have you tried *ra-goo* yet?"

I frown, trying to read her lips. *Ra-goo* doesn't sound familiar to me, unless I'm reading her mouth wrong. Claire glances away, over at Tiffany, who is spelling something out in ASL by the fire. I watch Tiffany's hands as she explains.

*H-R-A-K-U,* she spells.

I shake my head. "I don't know this hraku. What is it?"

Claire grabs my other knee and makes a face of ecstasy, and I laugh at how dramatic she is. "Let me tell you," she begins, and then I'm drawn into the conversation, and things are easy. It's comfortable to sit around the fire, and if I miss some of the conversation, Rokan is right at my side to sign the words and fill in the blanks for me.

It makes me feel included and warm. Happy.

It also makes me realize how absolutely in love I am with my mate. I know that as a deaf person, I should expect to be treated just the same as hearing people. But for Rokan to go out of his way to ensure that I'm included, and the way he watches me so closely so I don't miss a word . . . it makes me feel cozy inside. Like I'm his entire world and he'll burn it all down if I don't get to participate in Claire's telling of a dad joke.

There's nothing sexier than a man who lives for your laughter.

I'm thinking about how sexy Rokan is as we head to bed, yawning. We've signed our good nights to the others and Claire and Ereven have retreated to their bed at the back of the cave. Tiffany and Salukh are in the middle, and we're near the front entrance with Rokan's back closest to the privacy screen and me tucked safely on his other side.

Even though I'm tired from traveling, I'm feeling good. Warm.

Flirty.

Frisky, even.

And Rokan is filling my senses with all kinds of need.

He pulls off his tunic to go to sleep, wearing nothing but his leggings, and I slide in close to him in the furs. I press my mouth and nose to his skin, breathing in his scent. He's so velvety soft to the touch, all that blue skin like suede against mine. I rub my lips against his shoulder, caressing him, and his arm goes around me as he tugs me into the blankets.

Nights without hearing are normally isolated, because I can't see anything in the darkness and the silence added onto it can be overwhelming. But with Rokan's warm body pressed against mine, I don't feel alone. I can press my ear against his chest and feel his heart beat, and the vibrations of his khui pulse through his skin, matching its rhythm with mine.

Even in the darkness, I'm not alone. My other half is with me. He pulls me into his arms, settling in the blankets, and his tail strokes against my leggings. I'm still fully clothed, as I run colder than he does, but I don't mind. I feel good in this moment. I feel sexy despite the fact that I'm covered head to toe in leathers.

And I'm feeling like I want to tease my mate.

I slip a hand over his tail, feeling the new kink in it, where the bone didn't heal quite correctly. He got that in defense of me, and he swears it doesn't hurt, but his tail doesn't look the same. I adore that kink. I adore every bit of him. I trail my fingers up his tail, to the base where it meets his skin just above his buttocks, and he shifts against me in the furs.

A small tap from him would tell me to stop playing, that he's not enjoying himself.

There's no tap, though. He runs his fingers through my hair, and I know he's content to let me touch as I please.

That tells me everything I need to know. With a smile curving my lips, I slide my hand between his thighs, cupping the hard bulge of his cock. He's erect, all right. His khui seems to be vibrating faster at my touch, and Rokan strokes my cheek, then buries his fingers in my hair.

It's silent encouragement of the best kind.

I press a kiss to his chest, burying my face against his warm skin. So warm. Smells so good, like sweat and skin and Rokan, and I love the combination. I kiss down his chest as far as I can go, and when my head can move no lower, I slither my body farther down in the furs, pulling them over my head. Rokan will know what I'm about to do, and when I kiss down his belly, still caressing the bulge of his cock in his leathers, I keep waiting for the tap.

The tap never comes. His fingers tighten in my hair, and then the tip of his tail brushes my arm. It's not a tap, though. It's a caress.

Grinning to myself under the furs, I tug at the laces in the front of his leggings. It only takes loosening a knot or two before I can pull him free, and then his thick, hard erection is pressing into my hand. I rub my cheek against him, enjoying the tactile feeling of the ridges lining his shaft. Still velvety here, I notice.

Velvety and scorching hot and covered in ridges. His scent is stronger here, too. I love it so much.

I kiss the head of him, stroking his length with worshipful fingers. His hand tightens in my hair, his body tensing, but all is good. If he's surprised by my adoration of his cock, he'll tell me so in the morning. For now, I'll be quiet and nibble on him in secret under the furs.

Well, possibly in secret. For all I know, he's making all kinds of noises. The thought excites me, and spurs me on . . . because what if I'm making him bellow and groan so loud it wakes the others? I love the thought of him so into my touch that he loses all control. My Rokan is always so solid, so certain of himself. I like the thought of being the only one that can make him lose himself.

So I kiss the head of his cock again, pressing my lips to the underside. There's a vein there, and I trace it with the tip of my tongue, my hand gripping at the base of his shaft. I lick the flared tip of him again, tasting a hint of salt, and then close my lips over him.

Rokan jerks, his hips flexing, and the hand in my hair tightens and then relaxes. His tail strokes against my arm, and then his hips move again. He's pressing into my mouth, trying to go deeper. I can't stop the moan that rises in my throat, and his hand tightens on my hair again. He thrusts lightly, rubbing against my tongue, and I loosen my jaw, trying to take as much of him into my mouth as I can. I'm thrilled when one ridge pushes past my lips, then another, and another. By the time he's butting the back of my throat with each shuttle of his hips, I realize I still can't take him fully. It doesn't matter, though. I have hands and a tongue, and I can use them both. I cup his sac, stroking him even as I bob my head, working him. I'm lost in the moment, my world reduced down to nothing but Rokan's scent, Rokan's warm skin, and the thick weight of him on my tongue.

When the small warning tap comes, it startles me. The taste of him is flooding my mouth, his movements erratic, and I don't want to stop. I suck him deeper, tightening my grip around his shaft.

A moment later, the hot spurt of him hits the back of my throat. His hips strain against me, his body tense, and more seed floods my mouth. I try to swallow all that I can, but it becomes too much, spilling out of my mouth as he pulls out just before I start to choke. I'm left with a mouthful of salty heat and a smug sense of pride. I swallow, wiping my mouth, and then Rokan's hands are there, brushing my face clean with a bit of leather even as the blankets pull back and cold air hits me like a wall.

I glance up and see the warm glow of Rokan's eyes as they meet mine in the dark, and I'm filled with happiness. Even on a strange, icy world, I feel more "seen" than ever.

# Rokan

I never knew that my Li-lah was such a tease.

Fascinated, I watch as she runs her hand through her mane, combing through the tangles. There's a pleased little smile on her lips as we wait for the morning tea and meal to be doled out around the fire, and whenever I look over at her, she licks her lips, reminding me of last night.

Glorious female. She's perfection, my Li-lah. A teasing, naughty perfection. She surprised me with her hand on my cock last night . . . and then proceeded to take me in her mouth and drive me wild. I had one hand buried in her mane and the other in my mouth, biting down so I did not cry out aloud and wake the entire cave.

I am strangely disappointed we will make it to the fruit cave today. I would love a repeat . . . and then I would love my turn to go down upon her, to tongue her cunt until she writhes underneath me, knowing that the others are close by (and likely doing the same under the privacy of their furs).

But I can just pleasure my mate under the furs *at* the fruit cave. There is no need to be in a hunter cave.

Her hand moves and she has caught me staring at her. *What?* she signs.

*I am just appreciating your beauty.*

She smiles.

I add, *And your mouth.*

Her smile grows even wider and she licks her lips. My cock stirs in my leggings and I press my thighs together. Not now. There is still a long ways to go before we make it to the fruit cave.

The day is a long one. I watch over my mate closely, trying not to get in the way. Today, Claire and Tee-fah-nee walk next to her, practicing their signs, and Li-lah's laughter pierces the air. I want to remain at her side in case she needs me, in case she needs someone to sign for her, but I also do not want to push if I am not wanted. The females are managing fine, sometimes pausing to explain themselves or to allow Li-lah to read lips, which only causes more laughter and jokes to fly.

Salukh shoots me an amused look. "You are worse than the females with their new kits."

Perhaps I am. I rub my chest, where my khui resonates even now. I am attuned to my mate, and of course my focus is on her. "It is still new for me. I am allowed."

"The fascination does not stop," Ereven says from my other side. "You just become better at hiding it."

Well, at least they understand how I feel. I glance over at Li-lah again, my steps slowing. She is moving her smallest finger slowly, trying to show Claire something, and is not paying attention to her steps. I move to her side quickly and steer her back onto the path Salukh is forging for us, so she does not wander into a drift.

Li-lah jumps in surprise at my touch, but her expression changes to pleasure at the sight of me.

*Feet stay in the path,* I sign to her, pointing at the trail Salukh has made. *It is safest.*

*Yes, of course. Sorry.*

"Sorry!" Claire chirps, adding, "We're keeping her distracted."

"It is fine," I say, and sign it as well. "I will watch Li-lah, just as your mates watch you." I smile down at mine, and the knowing feeling moves through me, swift as an arrow. I stare at Li-lah, stunned, as my mind fills with images of her hand on her rounded belly. Of course she will be pregnant. That is the purpose of resonance.

Yet knowing about resonance and *feeling* it are two very different things.

I rub my chest again, wondering if my knowing feeling will tell me more. Is it a boy? A girl? But just as quickly as the image flitted through my mind, it is gone again. I cannot say whether or not it truly was my knowing or if it was just me daydreaming of my mate.

It does not matter. I press a quick kiss to Li-lah's brow since she is watching me closely, and then jog to the back of the group so I can watch the females. As I walk, I rub my chest, where resonance yet sings its feverish song.

I will see if my knowing sends anything else to me.

The heat of the fruit cave is as oppressive as I remember it.

The wall of sultry warmth hits us the moment we enter from outside, and the others in our group make exclamations as they step in. Li-lah walks just ahead of me, with my hand on the small of her back, and when she steps into the cave, she closes her eyes and takes a deep breath, drinking in the warmth.

"It's like a greenhouse," Claire exclaims, peeling off her outer layer of furs as she stares up at the ceiling. "This is incredible."

"I like it," Ereven says, even as he takes his cloak off. "Strange, but enjoyable. Is there a fire in here somewhere?"

"No fire," I tell them. "It is somehow warm on its own."

"You are certain?" Salukh asks, moving instinctively closer to his mate.

"No fire," Li-lah adds, signing the words. "It's electronic. Or a heat vent of some kind."

"Whatever it is, it's awesome," Claire says, and gives an excited thumbs-up to my mate.

I help Li-lah take off layers of furs, folding them and setting them down near the entrance. She piles her mane high atop her head with one hand, fanning her neck. I watch her closely even as the others exclaim over the greenery and disperse into the cave to look at its wonders.

The only wonder I need to see is right in front of me. *Too warm?* I ask Li-lah. *Do you need to go outside?*

She releases her mane, the dark, long strands sliding over her shoulders. *It will be fine. I just need a moment to adjust.*

*Sit and I will braid your mane for you,* I tell her, pointing at the rocky ground.

A smile spreads across her face and my khui sings happily at my mate's pleasure. Li-lah sits at my feet, crossing her legs and facing outward so she can watch the others. I immediately get to work on my task, braiding her mane in a circle around her head so it will not lie against her neck. Claire and her mate are climbing down the vines on one side of the cave, while Tee-fah-nee studies the greenery and how it attaches to the wall of the cave, Salukh hovering at her side.

I loom over my mate, too. It is the nature of the sa-khui male, I think, to obsess over his mate's happiness. I try not to bother Li-lah too much, but I want to ensure that she is not missing conversations, that she feels included. I braid one section and then move into her line of sight, signing that Claire and Ereven are now splashing in the pool at the bottom and I can hear Claire's squeals of delight.

She just grins and rolls her eyes. *They are excited. We should do the same.*

*Let me finish your braid first,* I tell her, and my heart clenches at the thought of her climbing down the vines. I know she is capable, but . . . I hate it. I want to do it for her. Li-lah wants to be treated the same as the others, though. So I bite back my worry and finish her braid, then tap her shoulder.

She gets to her feet, her hand touching her newly braided mane. *Shall we go down to the bottom?*

I nod. *I will go first, so I can catch you if you slip.* I pause, then add, *Do you want to be roped to me just in case?*

Li-lah nods. *Just to be safe.*

My relief is overwhelming.

Once we are tied together, I go down first, our packs on my shoulders, and then Li-lah climbs down after me. I am glad to see she is extremely cautious, taking her time and double-checking each handhold as she moves down. I scarcely breathe until my feet are on the ground, and then Li-lah is there at my side, all smiles.

I lean in and kiss her, just because I am relieved.

*It smells just as good as I remembered,* Li-lah signs to me. Her gaze drifts to Claire and Ereven, who are already eating a piece of fruit, juice dripping down their chins. Ereven holds it so his mate can eat, a grin of joy wreathing his face at Claire's delight. My mate makes a little noise in her throat and then gestures, *I'm hungry, are you?*

*Very. Which fruit is your favorite?* I ask, then reach for the closest one.

*All of them,* she tells me, grinning.

I get one of each kind for my mate, taking bites here and there but making sure Li-lah eats the most. She likes the greenish fruit's flesh as much as last time, but at the reddish one she makes a face, shaking her head and handing it back to me. *Too sour.*

*Is it not ready?*

Li-lah purses her lips, thinking, and then signs, *It's fine. I think I just want raw meat.*

*You want raw meat?* I echo, surprised.

She pauses, and then signs shyly, *I think the baby does.*

My knowing sense flares with confirmation at the same time that joy leaps through me. I did not realize she suspected. *You did not tell me that you knew.*

*Isn't that what resonance does? Get me pregnant?* Li-lah gives me a little smile. *My khui has felt different today. Like something has settled. And I know it's early to be having food cravings, but maybe it's different when the baby is part human and part sa-khui?* She shrugs. *It might also be my imagination, but I like to think it's the baby.*

*I like that idea, too,* I tell her, and move forward to put my hand over her heart. She clasps it and presses the back of my hand to her chest, over her khui, so I can feel the rhythm. She is right, it feels more leisurely, less frantic. Mine is the same. I just didn't realize it until now.

My mate. My beautiful Li-lah.

And my kit.

I kiss her again, overwhelmed with emotion. She smiles up at me, all sweetness, and my heart feels as if it will burst with all the happiness it contains. *I will get you some raw meat,* I sign eagerly. *Wait here.*

*You don't have to go,* she signs back quickly. *I can eat fruit . . . just not the red one.*

She sticks her tongue out and it is the most adorable thing I have ever seen.

# Lila

Several hours later, we're stuffed full of fruit and lying on the warm stones next to the waterfall. Rokan lies next to me on his back, his sticky fingers twined in mine. I've eaten so much fruit that I'm uncomfortable, but my mood is pleasant and languid. It's stuffy and humid in the cave, almost too much so after living in the snows, and there are no signs of the metlak creatures in here.

It's all ours, I guess. There's no sign that anyone else has been here, and some rotted fruit has fallen to the floor, which means no one's coming around very often—if at all. We can do as we please. I'm contemplating dried fruit, maybe some jam, and of course I'll have to bring some back for Maddie. Josie asked for melon, too. That's fine. I figure that by the time we leave here, I'm not going to want any fruit again for a long while.

I turn on my side, watching as Claire holds her nose and jumps into the pool, Ereven's face contorted in a laugh as she splashes him. They're frolicking like a pair of kids, which is cute. Tiffany and Salukh have taken a more measured approach to things. For the last while, Tiffany has crawled everywhere, determined to find out where the light and heat are coming from. Farther down, I can see her pointing out something to Salukh, sketching with her hands the plan for a sled to bring back cuttings of the plants themselves.

Perhaps Rokan and I should be doing something. My gaze settles on my mate. His eyes are closed and his thumb slowly rubs my knuckle, a sign that he's awake and alert.

If I got up, I'm sure he'd help me in whatever my plans were. For now, though, I'm content to lie here and simply think about things.

I feel guilty that Maddie isn't here.

My initial excitement at being apart from my sister and spending time alone with Rokan has modified. I'm not really alone with Rokan. I'm with Rokan and two other couples, so it's not like we're getting a lot of alone time. I guess I hadn't anticipated that when I'd hinted she shouldn't come along. I'd wanted to experience more of being on my own. Of it being just the two of us. But . . . I miss Maddie. Maddie always goes out of her way to ensure that I'm included, even if she makes enemies of everyone else. Maddie would demand Claire and Ereven share their whispered conversations, because I can tell they're whispering even when I can't hear them. It's the look they have on their faces and the way they barely move their lips when they speak. Maddie would demand that no one do anything unless I'm included.

Not that Rokan is doing a bad job of keeping me included. He's been amazing. He's just not . . . aggressive about it like Maddie is. And maybe that's the difference. I've never had to push to remind people to include me. Leaving me out of conversations is not something that people do consciously or out of spite. It's just me reminding them to slow their speech, or that I didn't hear a word . . . or all of them. And while I can do it for a little while, after a time it starts to wear on me. Yesterday I was happy to correct. Today I'm just tired.

I bite back a sigh. It's my own fault. Maddie made it easy and acted as referee. Now I have to do it myself and my desire to please wars with my desire to be included.

Rokan taps his thumb on my hand, pulling my attention to him. *Hungry?* he signs with one hand on his chest. Then it moves to his face. *Sleepy?*

I think for a moment and then pull my hand free from his to do the gesture for *tired/fatigued.* Then I tap my head and continue signing. *Lots in here.*

That gets his attention. He sits up, crossing his legs in front of him and giving me his full regard, and I'm reminded just how easy Rokan makes it for me. I love him so much that I start smiling even before he begins to sign. *What is wrong?*

*We aren't alone,* I sign back to him. *It's tiring to have to pay attention to the others all the time to make sure I don't miss anything.*

*I would not let you be excluded,* he says to me. *I will keep watch and you will be included in all ways. This I promise.*

Here I've been moping that I've lost Maddie and I've neglected to appreciate just how hard Rokan is working to ensure that I'm safe and comfortable. *I know. I just wish we were alone. It feels easy, just the two of us.*

*Do you want to leave? We can go. They know where the cave is now.*

The look in his eyes tells me he would pack up our things and ditch his tribemates in an instant. All I have to do is say the word. Which is sweet, but . . . they're my tribemates, too. If I'm going to be independent, I have to take the good with the bad. I shake my head and sign some more. *It's all right. I think I am just tired. I miss Maddie.*

*I miss my family, but I am also glad they are not here,* Rokan signs. *Because I want to kiss you between your thighs and under the furs.*

My face heats. *With the others around?*

*You were not so concerned last night about them being close.* A sly smile curves his mouth. *But I have a compromise.*

*I'm listening.*

*We will help the others gather some fruit for a little, and then we will take watch tonight at the top of the cave, near the entrance. The others can sleep down here. That way we are alone together, yet we are not abandoning them. Does that please you?*

*It's a perfect solution, I agree. Thank you.*

*I am your mate. There is no need to thank. Your happiness is my happiness.*

He's so sweet. I make the gesture for *I love you* and then get to my feet. *Should we tell the others, then?*

Rokan stands, too. *Are you tired now?*

*I am exhausted,* I confess. It's hard to tell what time it is with the lights constantly on here in the cave, but it feels late. My brain is fried and I want a nap. I don't want to be seen as a party pooper, though, so I add, *But we can hang out if you like.*

Rokan lifts his hands to respond, then glances at something over my shoulder. He gestures that I should turn around.

I do, and there are Claire and her mate, dripping water. Claire has a fur wrapped around her shoulders and she stifles a yawn. "I'm getting tired," she says, making sure to talk slowly so I can read her lips. "What are the plans for sleeping?"

"Rokan and I are going up top," I say, gesturing with my

hands and then indicating with a pointed finger. "We will watch the entrance. You two can sleep down here."

"Perfect," Claire says with a relieved thumbs-up. "I am too tired to climb."

I grin at the exaggerated stagger she makes at the word *climb*, as if just the thought of it is far too much for her. Claire does have a flair for the dramatic.

Tiffany and Salukh come to join us, and when we suggest again that Rokan and I take the top and they can stay here by the pool, she nods. In her hand, she has an open piece of fruit and points at it. "I need everyone to save the seeds. We're going to dry them out and try to grow them back near the cave. We need as many as possible."

"Got it," I say, though secretly I'm a little dismayed. "As many as possible" sounds like we're going to be eating a lot of fruit over the next while. The thought is not nearly as enticing now as it was a few hours ago when we first arrived.

Rokan steps forward into my line of sight and begins to speak aloud, signing with his hands at the same time. "Li-lah is tired," he says, signing my spelled name with speedy ease that makes my stomach flutter with pleasure. "We are going above to sleep and would like privacy."

"Sleep," Claire says, and makes air quotes, chortling. Then she gets confused, her gaze darting to me. "Wait, the sign for 'sleep' . . . " She thinks, flustered, and then pairs her hands by her cheek. "It was a joke, Lila—"

"I caught it," I tell her, my cheeks heated. Maybe we're a little more obvious than I thought, but they're all here with their resonance mates. They know what we do in the furs. It's not as if it's a big secret. Heck, they're probably doing the same thing.

But Claire's panicked signing reminds me that I'm weary, and seeing the others struggle to include me—which they're being very lovely about—feels exhausting after a while. I just want to retreat with my handsome Rokan and snuggle up against him, feeling the beat of his heart against mine. "See you all in the morning." I eye the false lighting, which doesn't seem as if it dims, ever. "Or just . . . later."

When we finally make it back to the top of the strange cave, I'm relieved. It's not that there's anything wrong with the others, but the feeling of having to constantly be alert to catch conversations gets tiring. I know with Rokan he'll always include me, so that "alertness" ebbs and I can relax. It feels as freeing as stripping off a heavy cloak.

For a moment, I miss Maddie again. I'll have to tell my sister how much I love and appreciate her when I get back. Then again, Maddie would be right next to me in this moment, glaring at my mate as he takes off his boots and then unrolls the fur blankets he brought for us.

I watch him, his strong back flexing as he works, and I decide that in this moment, I'm glad Maddie isn't here after all. I can appreciate the view.

When Rokan turns back to me, he catches me staring and a knowing expression curves his mouth. He holds a hand out to me, and I slip my fingers into his.

He kisses my knuckles and then releases my hand. *My beautiful mate,* he signs to me, then takes my hand again. The sign for *mate* is the same one as *wife*, a creation all my own, and it makes my heart flutter to see him gesture it. I step into his arms, sliding my hands over his back. I press my nose to his skin, breathing in his scent, and he strokes my back, holding me close.

I feel safe. Loved. Precious.

Seen.

Valued.

Rokan strokes my cheek with the backs of his fingertips and then taps my shoulder to get my attention. I open my eyes and gaze up at him as he mouths a word I don't quite catch, but the tug of his hand on my tunic tells me plenty.

Nodding, I step back and pull my tunic off as he removes his leggings and tosses them aside, glorious and naked and vibrant in front of me. There's so much gorgeous blue skin laid bare that I want to put my mouth on all of it, and it fills me with emotion. *My beautiful mate,* I sign back to him.

I earn a grin as he approaches, helping me undress. His hands move all over my skin, and he leans in and kisses my bare shoulder. When I'm in nothing but a breastband and the strange, thin leather shorts that pass for panties here, he runs a finger up my spine, tickling me as he kisses across one shoulder and then moves to the other.

Then he pulls away, which surprises me.

*Cold?* he signs. *Hungry?*

I shake my head. *Want you.*

A sly smile curves his lips. *Idea,* he signs quickly, and then gestures that I should get in the furs.

As he turns away, I move toward the bedding he's laid out and pull the last bits of my clothing off. It feels a little strange to be naked inside the big cave, but the silence helps me imagine that we're alone. If Rokan is positive no one is coming up here, I believe him. I lie atop the furs since it feels far too warm and stuffy inside the cave to cover up. If it's warm for me, I can only imagine how hot it feels for Rokan, who strides through the snow in light clothing as if it were as hot as a summer's day on Earth.

And because I'm a self-conscious woman, I try to arrange myself in a sexy pose. I prop up on my elbows, crook one knee, and squeeze my arms tight against my sides to plump my breasts . . . and feel more than a little silly.

The silliness fades when Rokan returns to my side, his eyes bright with appreciation at my posture. That makes it all worth it. In his hands, he has two pieces of fruit, the ones that are reddish and sour and not my favorite. I wrinkle my nose at the sight, a question in my eyes.

*I like this one,* he tells me, setting the fruit down next to the blankets. *It has a strong taste.*

*Yes, but is now the time for a snack?* I want to ask. I thought—I'd interpreted his signals—that we were going to have sex. Maybe that's a newlywed mistake.

He bites into one with his strong teeth and juice spills down his chin. He grins at me, chewing, and then casually reaches over and squeezes the fruit over my breasts.

I gasp as the juice splatters over my skin, as red as blood.

And I gasp again when Rokan leans over and licks a bead of juice off my nipple.

He looks up at me, his eyes heated, and lifts a hand to his chin, signing the word for *delicious*.

My mouth falls open and I watch as he licks one breast clean, while squeezing the fruit over the other. I'm flushed with arousal—especially when he takes his sweet time tonguing my nipple—and watch as he trails a sticky finger down to my navel.

*No lower,* I sign quickly. *Not between the legs.* I can only imagine the infections and I don't want to ruin this sexy moment.

*No lower,* he agrees. *I like your taste there far better than the fruit.*

I blush, and he tosses the wrung-out fruit aside, moving over me to lap at my other breast. My nipple is hard and pointing, and when his tongue teases a circle around it, I'm utterly fascinated.

Rokan lifts his head for a moment and puts a finger to his lips.

Oh. *Was I making noises?*

*You moan,* he signs quickly, and there's a look of pride on his face, as if he likes that very much.

*Sorry.*

He just grins, pressing a finger to my lips in the universal signal for silence, and then goes back to lavishing attention on my breast.

I realize dimly that I'm on my back in the blankets, staring up at the greenery on the ceiling as Rokan's tongue and lips tease my breast. He nips at my nipple with his teeth, just enough to give it an edge but not enough to hurt, and I'm pretty sure I moan aloud again. He gives my shoulder a little tap of warning, and I bury my hands in his hair, arching up against his mouth.

God, his *mouth.* He sucks on my nipple and then circles it with his tongue, and I might spontaneously combust if he keeps that up. He takes my arching as a sign to go lower, and licks his way to my belly button, lapping up the sticky juice as he goes. His tongue dips into my navel, and that feels almost as erotic as his mouth on my clit.

I squirm in his arms, restless as he slowly moves lower, kissing and nibbling his way down my abdomen. My thighs are spread wide in anticipation, and I dig my fingers against his scalp, waiting, waiting . . .

When his mouth clasps over my clit and sucks, the breath explodes from my body.

He gives me another little tap, this time on my hip, but he doesn't lift his mouth. His tongue teases against my clit even as he sucks on it, and I'm absolutely lost. I don't know—and don't care—what sounds I'm making, just that it feels so good to have him touch me like this that all I can think about is the orgasm that's quickly rushing to the surface.

Rokan lifts his mouth just before I come and I know I whine aloud. I grip his arms tightly as he moves over me, his lips covering mine in a quick, heated kiss before he pushes between my thighs. Then he's pumping into me, thrusting with such intensity that I'm breathless. He gazes down at me as he rocks into me, and I'm lost in his eyes. As he fucks me, he lifts one hand and makes the one-handed sign for *I love you*.

I melt. "I love you, too," I whisper. At least, I hope I'm whispering. I'm not sure I care. I wonder if I can dirty-talk him with ASL. He grips my hip, his eyes full of determined lust, and I start signing.

*Big,* I manage. *Big cock*. Then *Hard. Fast*.

The look on his face turns feral. He bares his teeth and hunches over me, pounding harder, and I give up on signing, clinging to him as he drives into me. His punishing rhythm ensures that the orgasm starts building again, until I'm right on the edge.

This time, I come. And I keep on coming as Rokan keeps going. It's incredible, and every time we have sex, it's better. I hold on to him tightly as he races toward his climax, and when he shudders over me, I lock my legs around his hips and grip him in place. He collapses over me and I pant hard, feeling his hot breath stirring my hair as he recovers. His heart is beating fast, and I can feel the rhythm of his khui through his skin. It's agitated right now, but the rhythm still feels different than before, when we were resonating.

I tap on his chest over his heart, and he nods, meeting my eyes.

It's changed. He doesn't have to sign it for me to know. And when he rolls to the side and then touches my belly, I know we're thinking the same thing.

Resonance is fulfilled. We've made a baby.

We knew that, of course. It's just . . . the realization makes me smile. I roll toward my mate so I can watch his face. He smiles at me, a sheen of sweat on his velvety skin, and brushes his fingers over my face.

Our happy ever after is just beginning, I think, and I'm excited to see what the future brings.

# AUTHOR'S NOTE

Hello there! It's 2023 and I'm updating the author's note to reflect the time that's passed. This book was originally written in 2016, and sometimes just realizing that it's been seven years makes me need a moment. Seven years! How!!!

But I love that I'm able to see a fantastic new version of the book. I loved being able to write an extended epilogue for Lila and Rokan. I love how sweet the cover is and that Lila's signing to her mate. The Berkley special editions fill me with wonder every time they come out, and I can't thank the team over at Penguin Random House enough for helping to take my vision to the next level.

But enough about that! Let's talk about the characters.

Writing every book in this series is an adventure for me. I originally ended Josie's book thinking that I'd write one story for the two sisters, entwining their tales and rotating the point of view between sisters and lovers. My readers spoke out—they wanted each sister to have her own book. You guys love your barbarians!

And so I started to pull the story apart to see where I could separate the two. Maybe I could write two short books instead of one long one. However, this story took off on its own! I knew Lila was stolen by Hassen. I knew Rokan would save her. Did I think it would grow to be the longest book in the series? Nope! Did I know that they weren't going to fulfill resonance until the very end? Gosh, no! (Don't kill me—it just worked out that way!)

Did I know that Lila was going to show up in chapter 1, deaf? No! But once I had the idea, it wouldn't let go of me and I had to write it. She's scared of everything—she can't hear. And Maddie's overbearing nature took on its own angle; naturally she's protective of her little sister, given that she's been her champion in the past.

I loved exploring how a deaf/hearing-disabled character would cope with life on a savage planet. While I've always had hearing loss, at around the time of my writing this book it grew so intrusive that I now wear hearing aids. If you have any sort of hearing loss, even minor, you know how isolating it can be to be part of a crowd and not able to participate in the conversation. It's something I've struggled with all my life. I wanted to delve into that, because in a survival situation, everything takes on a new, more profound significance. I also wanted Lila to grow in strength as the story continued. I wanted her to realize how strong she was and how she wasn't a victim, no matter the circumstances. The Lila of the story's start is not the same Lila of the last chapter.

Does her hearing ever come back? From a story perspective, it's entirely possible; if the khui can keep Harlow's brain tumor in check, it could also repair the cilia in Lila's ears that affect the transmission of sound. Of course, this is problematic—"fixing" her hearing assumes that she's flawed. Like Rokan says, she's perfect just as she is.

So will she *ever* get her hearing back? I won't spoil it for you, but she doesn't need it one way or the other. She's strong enough either way, and I hope I've portrayed her as such.

In addition, you'll notice that toward the beginning of the book, there are different spellings of some "common" story words, like *khui*. That's because they're interpreted as Lila would see them when reading lips. I hope it's not too jarring for readers. I spent a lot of time while writing this book with my fingers pressed against my mouth to see how my tongue and lips would move, so I could re-create the experience as faithfully as possible.

As always, thank you, thank you, *thank you* for reading. I really do have the best fans in the universe, and I adore your Facebook messages, your cheery posts, and your enthusiasm. I love writing in this world, and I'm beyond thrilled so many other people love hanging out on the ice planet with me.

<3
RUBY

# THE PEOPLE OF
# *BARBARIAN'S TOUCH*

## The Main Cave

### THE CHIEF AND HIS FAMILY

**VEKTAL** (Vehk-tall)—Chief of the sa-khui tribe. Son of Hektar, the prior chief, who died of khui-sickness. He is a dedicated hunter and leader, and carries a sword and a bola for weapons. He is the one who finds Georgie, and resonance between them is so strong that he resonates prior to her receiving her khui.

**GEORGIE**—Unofficial leader of the human women. Originally from Orlando, Florida, she has long golden-brown curls and a determined attitude.

**TALIE** (Tah-lee)—Their infant daughter.

### FAMILIES

**RAAHOSH** (Rah-hosh)—A quiet but surly hunter. One of his horns is broken off and his face scarred. Older son of Vaashan and Daya (both deceased). Vektal's close friend. Impatient and rash, he steals Liz the moment she receives her khui. They resonate, and he is exiled for stealing her. Brother to Rukh.

LIZ—A loudmouth huntress from Oklahoma who loves Star Wars and giving her opinion. Raahosh kidnaps her the moment she receives her lifesaving khui. She was a champion archer as a teenager. Resonates to Raahosh and voluntarily chooses exile with him.

RAASHEL (Rah-shell)—Their infant daughter.

HARLOW—One of the women kept in the stasis tubes. She has red hair and freckles, and is mechanically minded and excellent at problem-solving. Stolen by Rukh when she resonated to him. Now mother to their child, Rukhar.

RUKH (Rook)—The long-lost son of Vaashan and Daya; brother to Raahosh. His full name is Maarukh. He grew up alone and wild, convinced by his father that the tribe was full of "bad ones," and has been brought back by Harlow.

RUKHAR (Rook-car)—Their infant son.

ARIANA—One of the women kept in the stasis tubes. Hails from New Jersey and was an anthropology student. She tended to cry a lot when first rescued. Has a delicate frame and dark brown hair. Resonates to Zolaya. Still cries a lot.

ZOLAYA (Zoh-lay-uh)—A skilled hunter. Steady and patient, he resonates to Ariana and seems to be the only one not bothered by her weepiness.

ANALAY (Anna-lay)—Their infant son.

**MARLENE** (Mar-lenn)—One of the women kept in the stasis tubes. French speaking. Quiet and confident, and exudes sexuality. Resonates to Zennek.

**ZENNEK** (Zehn-eck)—A quiet and shy hunter. Brother to Pashov, Salukh, and Farli. He is the son of Borran and Kemli. Resonates to Marlene.

**ZALENE** (Zah-lenn)—Their infant daughter.

**NORA**—One of the women kept in the stasis tubes. A nurturing sort who was rather angry she was dumped on an ice planet. Quickly resonates to Dagesh. No longer quite so angry.

**DAGESH** (Dah-zzhesh; the *g* sound is swallowed)—A calm, hard-working, and responsible hunter. Resonates to Nora.

**ANNA & ELSA**—Their infant twins.

**STACY**—One of the women kept in the stasis tubes. She was weepy when she first awakened. Loves to cook and worked in a bakery prior to abduction. Resonates to Pashov and seems quite happy.

**PASHOV** (Pah-showv)—The son of Kemli and Borran; brother to Farli, Salukh, and Zennek. A hunter described as "quiet." Resonates to Stacy.

**PACY**—Their infant son.

**MAYLAK** (May-lack)—One of the few female sa-khui. She is the tribe healer and Vektal's former pleasure mate. She resonated to Kashrem, ending her relationship with Vektal. Sister to Bek.

**KASHREM** (Cash-rehm)—A gentle tribal tanner. Mated to Maylak.

**ESHA** (Esh-uh)—Their young female kit.

**SEVVAH** (Sev-uh)—A tribe elder and one of the few sa-khui females. She is mother to Aehako, Rokan, and Sessah, and acts like a mom to the others in the cave. Her entire family was spared when khui-sickness hit fifteen years ago.

**OSHEN** (Aw-shen)—A tribe elder and Sevvah's mate. Brewer.

**SESSAH** (Ses-uh)—Their youngest child, a juvenile male.

**MEGAN**—Megan was early in a pregnancy when she was captured, but the aliens terminated it. She tends toward a sunny disposition when not abducted by aliens. Resonates to Cashol. Pregnant.

**CASHOL** (Cash-awl)—A distractible and slightly goofy-natured hunter. Cousin to Vektal. Resonates to Megan.

**CLAIRE**—A quiet, slender woman who arrived on the planet with a blonde pixie cut and now has shoulder-length brown hair. She had a failed pleasure-mating with Bek and resonated to Ereven. Her story is told in the novella "Ice Planet Holiday."

**EREVEN** (Air-uh-ven)—A quiet, easygoing hunter who won Claire over with his understanding, protective nature. Resonates to Claire.

**AEHAKO** (Eye-ha-koh)—A laughing, flirty hunter. The son of Sevvah and Oshen; brother to Rokan and young Sessah. He seems to be in a permanent good mood. Close friends with Haeden. Resonates to Kira and was acting leader of the South Cave.

**KIRA**—The first of the human women to be kidnapped, Kira had a large metallic translator attached to her ear by the aliens. She is quiet and serious, with somber eyes. Her translator has been removed, and she gave birth to Kae.

**KAE** (rhymes with "fly")—Their infant daughter.

**KEMLI** (Kemm-lee)—An elder female, mother to Salukh, Pashov, Zennek, and Farli. The tribe's expert on plants.

**BORRAN** (Bore-awn)—Kemli's much younger mate and an elder.

**FARLI** (Far-lee)—A preteen female sa-khui. Her brothers are Salukh, Pashov, and Zennek. New pet parent to the dvisti colt Chompy.

**ASHA** (Ah-shuh)—A mated female sa-khui. She is mated to Hemalo but has not been seen in his furs for some time. Their kit died shortly after birth.

**HEMALO** (Hee-mah-lo)—A tanner and a quiet sort. He is mated (unhappily) to Asha.

**TIFFANY**—A "farm girl" back on Earth, she suffered greatly while waiting for Georgie to return. She has been traumatized by her alien abduction. She is a perfectionist and a hard worker, and the running joke amongst the human women is that Tiffany is great at everything. Resonates to Salukh.

SALUKH (Sah-luke)—The brawny son of Kemli and Borran; brother to Farli, Pashov, and Zennek. Strong and intense. Very patient and helps Tiffany work through her trauma.

JOSIE—One of the original kidnapped women, she broke her leg in the ship crash. Short and adorable, Josie is an excessive talker, a gossip, and a bit of a dreamer. Likes to sing. Family is everything to her, and she wants nothing more than one of her own. Resonates to Haeden.

HAEDEN (Hi-den)—A grim and unsmiling hunter with "dead" eyes, Haeden formerly resonated but his female died of khui-sickness before they could mate. His current khui is a replacement, and he resonates to Josie. He is very private and unthaws only around his new mate.

LILA—A shy, introverted deaf woman kidnapped from Earth with her sister, Maddie. On Earth, Lila had cochlear implants, which were removed by the aliens who took her. She resonates to Rokan after being kidnapped by Hassen.

ROKAN (Row-can)—The son of Sevvah and Oshen; brother to Aehako and young Sessah. A hunter known for his strange predictions that come true all too often. Resonates to Lila.

## THE UNMATED

**BEK** (Behk)—A hunter generally thought of as short-tempered and unpleasant. Brother to Maylak.

**HARREC** (Hair-ek)—A hunter who has no family and finds his place in the tribe by constantly joking and teasing. A bit accident-prone.

**HASSEN** (Hass-en)—A passionate and brave hunter, Hassen is impulsive and tends to act before he thinks. Kidnaps Lila when she first awakens.

**MADDIE**—Lila's older sister. She is tall, full-figured, blonde, and bossy. She is angry at the sa-khui for letting Hassen steal her sister, and feels very out of place in the tribe.

**TAUSHEN** (Tow—rhymes with "cow"—shen)—A teenage hunter, newly into adulthood. Eager to prove himself.

**WARREK** (War-eck)—The son of Elder Eklan. He is a very quiet and mild hunter, with long, sleek black hair. Warrek teaches the young kits how to hunt.

## ELDERS

**ELDER DRAYAN** (Dray-ann)—A smiling elder who uses a cane to help him walk.

**ELDER DRENOL** (Dree-noll)—A grumpy, antisocial elder.

**ELDER EKLAN** (Eck-lann)—A calm, kind elder. Father to Warrek, he also helped raise Harrec.

**ELDER VADREN** (Vaw-dren)—An elder.

**ELDER VAZA** (Vaw-zhuh)—A lonely widower and hunter. He tries to be as helpful as possible. He is very interested in the new females.

## The Dead

**DOMINIQUE**—A redheaded human female. Her mind was broken when she was abused by the aliens on the ship. When she arrived on Not-Hoth, she ran out into the snow and deliberately froze.

**KRISSY**—A human female, dead in the crash.

**PEG**—A human female, dead in the crash.

EXCERPT FROM

# BARBARIAN'S TAMING

AN ICE PLANET BARBARIANS NOVEL

# Maddie

It's weird when you don't fit in.

I thought that once I hit adulthood, I'd be all done with feeling like an outcast. That once I got past those awful high school years when I felt like the round peg in the square hole, it'd all just be a bad memory. That someday I could look back and laugh at how much it bothered me to be the weirdo on the outskirts.

Sitting here in a cave at a party for my sister, surrounded by aliens, I feel like I'm reliving my high school years all over again. It's pretty garbage, I have to admit. I wasn't popular then, being fat and opinionated. These aliens don't care if I'm fat or if I have a big mouth, and yet I'm still on the outskirts.

It's weird.

Someone dances past me, laughing. His tail smacks against my arm and then he spills a bit of his drink on the stone floor in front of me. Lovely. I absently swipe a bit of my tunic on the spilled alcohol because I don't want someone slipping on it in front of me while I sit and hold down a cushion in the corner of the room by myself.

It's not that people are unfriendly. Heck, it's not even that I'd have to sit alone if I didn't want to. It's that I'm really not sure where I stand with any of these people. I stare out at the celebrating tribe, not paying attention to the people who dance past with a skin of sah-sah, or the woman who pulls her top down to breastfeed not one but two blue babies. I ignore the exclamations over the fruit that they've managed to savor all damn night, and I sure as shit ignore when they start singing again.

Everyone's so damn happy. Everyone but me.

Me? I'm struggling.

In the space of the last month or so, my world has been upended. I went to sleep one night and woke up in the arms of blue space aliens on a frozen planet. Apparently I was kidnapped by bad aliens in my sleep. Apparently they took my sister, too. Apparently we were also stuck in sleep pods for over a year and a half and missed out on the bad guys being shot down.

It seems we slept through a lot.

Even if I thought it was all too strange to be believed at first, it didn't take long to realize this shit was legit. There are two suns, two moons, and endless frost and snow. The people here are blue, covered in a downy fuzz, and act like a blizzard is a nice spring rainstorm. Oh, and the parasites. I don't even want to think about the parasites, especially not the one living inside me now, helping me "adapt" to this alien world.

My sister is thriving, though.

It's weird. Lila's always been a shy introvert and even more of an outcast than me. She was born deaf, and though she got cochlear implants at age twelve and no longer needed me to interpret for her when lip-reading was too tricky, I've always felt the need to protect her and care for her. But here? We've been separated and she's been thriving. Lila is usually the lonely, lost one and I'm the bold, outgoing one. I have to be because that's how you Get Shit Done.

Except Lila's doing fine on her own and now I'm just kind of . . . lost. I'm the single human that doesn't have a mate. I don't know the others. They're all pregnant or getting pregnant or juggling babies already and I'm sitting here, twiddling my thumbs with my "vacancy" sign over my vagina.

Not that I want a baby, mind you. Or a mate. But it feels weird to be the only chick who's not hooked up in this place. Even my sister's lovey-dovey with an alien and mated.

She's happy here despite all the snow and ice and man-eating creatures and lack of toilets. She wants to stay (not that we have a choice).

And me?

I'm just kind of here.

Alone.

I rub at the wet spot on the stone floor while one of the humans—Georgie? Megan? I don't know which one—whips out a boob and starts breastfeeding her child mid-conversation with an alien lady. Lila's not attending the party any longer; she ran off to her cave with her alien guy to go make babies with him. Literally. She's literally going to make babies with him. It's something I'm still struggling to wrap my brain around. It seems that if my chest-cootie wakes up and starts purring, it picks a man I should make babies with.

I'm pretty glad mine is deciding to be mute.

Lila's thrilled to be "resonating," though. Of course she is—now she's one of the baby-crazy crowd of human women who've settled in with the aliens. Now she fits in even more, though she wasn't exactly having a tough time with that. She's mated to a popular guy. She showed up with fruit. She's taken to all the daily life tasks like they're a joy for her. Got a fire that you need made? Lila can do it. Skin a kill? Lila's right there. Make dinner? Arrows? Fucking slings or snowshoes or bear traps or whatever else these Grizzly Adams wannabes can come up with? Lila can do it. She can survive just fine because she's been learning how to be like them.

And they love her for it, too. The tribespeople have been learning sign language to speak to Lila and to make her feel welcome. I'm glad they've accepted her so readily, but it also makes me jealous . . . which makes me a terrible sister.

Everyone in the tribe adores her and they can barely tolerate me. I'm like a stinky fart that's lingering in the cave and everyone tries to ignore.

Not that I can blame them for treating me like a turd—I wasn't exactly Miss Pleasant to be around while my sister was gone. I was frantic with worry about her after she was stolen, and when they wouldn't let me go after her? I was kind of not nice about it.

Okay, I was a bit of an ass.

Well, more than just a bit.

But I was worried about seemingly fragile Lila on this hostile, cold planet. So I took it out on everyone else. I might have picked a few fights and dragged my feet, and okay, I threw a few things at people's heads. So what? Anyone else would have done the same if they were in my shoes, uncertain about the fate of their baby sister.

They don't understand what it's like to be so alone, even in a sea of people.

Everyone here's part of a family. There are happy women with babies, and men utterly devoted to their ladies. As I look over, the chief—Vektal—is tossing his baby daughter into the air and giving her exaggerated kisses just to make Talie laugh. And boy, does that baby laugh. It'd be adorable if it didn't make me feel so sour inside. He's got a wife and a baby. All of the humans here have someone.

I have Lila. Like I have in the past, I'm ready to shield her from the world's harms and interpret for her when someone doesn't know sign language.

Except my sister doesn't need me anymore.

Scared, timid little Lila has returned utterly confident in herself and in love with Rokan.

That leaves me . . . well, it leaves me sitting here by myself on a mat, mopping up someone else's spilled drink.

I sigh and stare out at the entrance of the cave, feeling alone and yet trapped at the same time. I don't fit in with these people, but I also don't have the option to find another people. There *are* no other people.

Sometimes I wonder what would happen if I just up and left. Would they hunt me down like they hunted for Lila? Or would they be all "good riddance" and not care because I've been a bitch?

I scowl into the shadows of the cave's entrance. It would be so easy to get up and just walk out while everyone's drunk and partying. But even as I stare, glowing blue eyes blink back at me, and a big, bulky form emerges from the shadows of the cave entrance, spear in one hand, a dead animal in the other. It's a hunter, returning from a late-night jaunt out into the snow.

And not just any hunter.

It's Hassen. The bastard that stole my sister. The one that decided he wanted a mate so much he'd just up and fucking steal her.

Him? He can kiss my fat ass.

Though the look he's giving me right now? That tells me he'd enjoy that far too much. That he'd do more than just kiss it if I bared it for his inspection.

And for some reason, I find myself prickling with arousal at the thought of Hassen folding his big body down to give my plump ass a kiss. Which is all kinds of wrong. He's exiled. He's a dick. He wanted my sister. None of these put him on the "Ice Planet's Most Desirable Bachelors" list.

As I glare at him, his mouth twists into a fang-bearing smile.

I jerk my gaze back around to the fire, scowling. Totally not gonna keep picturing him with his mouth on my ass. Biting one of my rounded cheeks. Dragging his fingers over my body and exploring the fact that I have no tail . . .

I give my cheek a hard slap to bring me back to reality.

Nearby, Farli gives me a startled look. "Are you all right?"

"Just distracted," I tell her. Farli's a good kid, and the closest thing I have to a buddy here, for all that she's, like, fifteen years old. Right now? She's my ride or die, because, well, I don't have anyone else. Even my sister, Lila, is off in a corner somewhere, making out with her new hubby. I can't even be mad about that—she's so happy and she is such a wonderful person that she deserves every bit of joy. I'm thrilled for her.

I'm a little jealous of her radiant happiness, sure, but still thrilled for her.

I'm just a selfish jerk of a sister who doesn't know what to do with herself when she's not needed anymore and suddenly finds herself with no friends. Funny how I always thought I didn't need friends. Funny how being stranded on an ice planet can totally change your perspective on things like that. In a small community like this, not playing by the rules gets you left behind.

Hassen knows all about that.

I peek over my shoulder back at the cave entrance again. Just in case Hassen is still there. But he's not, and I ignore the little stab of disappointment I feel.

The last thing I need is to get involved with the bad boy of the ice planet.

## Hassen

It is a cold night for me.

The laughter coming from within the tribal cave spills out into the snow, and I can smell the burning meat cooking for the humans. Someone is singing, and I hear Warrek banging away at his drum. They are all good sounds, happy sounds. My people are light and carefree and full of joy.

That joy does not extend to me.

I stand alone in the snow on a nearby ridge, a fresh-killed quill-beast in hand. And I am torn, because I do not know if I should ignore the punishment the chief has given me and join the celebration, or if I should turn around and leave.

I am exiled. I am nothing to my people now. I did not think I would care, but . . . I do. Their scorn hurts me.

If I go inside, I will be met with uncomfortable looks, but they will not turn me away. Some will be filled with disgust at how I have behaved. Some will pity me in my punishment, because I risked everything and lost. It would have all been worth it had things turned out differently, but I am empty-handed and alone, and thus a male to be pitied.

I am not one to dwell upon what might have been, but tonight, I wonder. I wonder what it would be like to have the tribe celebrating my resonance. To hold my mate close and bring her to my cave, and together our breasts would sing until our kit was created.

But I am happy for Rokan. He is a good friend and a good hunter. He truly cares for Li-lah, and together they will be very happy.

Li-lah . . . I have mixed feelings about. I am disappointed that she is not my resonance mate and yet I am incredibly relieved as well. I thought upon first seeing her that she was perfect—small, fragile, with dark hair and big eyes. I thought she would be the perfect female for me, and I listened to my heart and not my head, and stole her away. I kept her captive for hands upon hands of days in a hunter cave, and with every day that passed, I became more and more worried.

Li-lah cried. Many, many tears. She huddled in the back of the cave and stared at me, terrified. And me . . . I felt like a monster. I only wished to resonate with her, to cherish her and start a family with her. I want what the others in my tribe have with their human mates. I want to feel the warmth of another body against mine, to have someone to talk to. To see her belly full with my kit. I would never harm Li-lah, yet she flinched away from me every time I spoke to her. And then she would cry again. It soon grew to the point that I was looking for excuses to leave the cave so I did not have to endure her weeping and trembling.

And I was so terrible in Li-lah's eyes that she escaped. Left the safety of the cave and was taken by metlaks. Rokan had been in the area and helped me search for her, and when he returned, resonating to her?

I felt relief.

This cringing, terrified female was not mine. My gladness filled me with even more shame. Should I not be sad that Li-lah is someone else's? Should I not be jealous of Rokan? But . . . I am not. I am glad for him, even as I ache with loneliness. There are not many unmated females in the tribe. If I am to ever have a mate, I will have to wait for one of the other females to grow to adulthood, unless my khui chooses the last human, Mah-dee.

I snort to myself at the thought. Sometimes I wish it had been her I had stolen instead of cowardly Li-lah. Mah-dee does not cringe and weep. She throws things when she is upset, and bellows at all that stand near. She attacked me the last time she saw me. She is fierce.

Now *that* is a female.

I step into the mouth of the cave to deliver the fresh meat to those that sit near the fire. Normally there is a hunter standing on guard at the front of the cave. Tonight it is Bek, his arms crossed and his expression as morose as mine. He is not interested in the celebration, either. Nor is he interested in taking my kill to the others for me. He watches me with disinterest and then gazes back out to the night sky again. I feel a strange sort of kinship with Bek—he knows what it is like to have a human female and lose her. Though I think Bek still has feelings for his; I test mine and still feel nothing but relief that Li-lah belongs to Rokan. My loss is what she represented to me, but I think Bek truly loved his Claire in his way. Claire, however, has resonated to another and even now sits near the fire with her mate, content.

I feel eyes on me and scan the cave.

There, off to one side. It is the human Mah-dee. She is looking in my direction. I catch her gaze and give her a challenging look, daring her to continue staring at me. Does she think her distaste for me will make me scurry away like a diseased metlak?

To my surprise, a strange expression crosses her face and she quickly looks away again.

Curious. Her response reminds me of when Jo-see first resonated to Haeden. She chattered on and on about how much she hated him . . . and yet could not stop watching him when she thought no one paid attention. The hunters noticed, however. It is our job to be observant of our prey, to notice the behavior of others. Jo-see's lips said one thing, but her body language said another.

Could this be the case with Mah-dee? Is she attracted to me?

I feel a surge of pride and run a hand down my chest. My body is a fine one, and I am strong. I am a tireless hunter, and I am sure that if I were given the chance to test my skills, I could be equally tireless in the furs to please my female.

But it does not matter. I can take no mate because I am exiled. I have no cave to call my own. Until the brutal season arrives, my bed is the snow outside, and my task to bring in as much food as possible. Once I have worked hard enough, I will be forgiven for betraying the rules of the tribe.

Until then, I have nothing and no one.

My mood bleak, I toss the kill down in front of Hemalo. "Meat for you and your—" I stop, because Hemalo has broken the bond with his mate. They do not speak, and now he beds with the hunters. It is unthinkable to me—to have a resonance mate and choose to leave her. I do not understand him. "Meat," I say gruffly.

"My thanks," Hemalo replies, ever mild. "Will you join me by the fire for a bit? Rest yourself?"

I hesitate. I would like to join him by the fire. I would like to share a cup of sah-sah and laugh and eat. I would like to sit amongst my tribe and enjoy the evening, even if it is to celebrate the joining of another male to the female I stole. I would like to see if Mah-dee looks my way again.

But Vektal is sitting nearby, his daughter bouncing on his knee as his mate, Shorshie, shares a piece of fruit with other humans. He is watching me.

And his rules must be obeyed if I want to win my place back amongst my people. “I must not.” I touch Hemalo’s shoulder and then head off, back out into the snow and the dark.

Alone.

I have not yet earned the right to return. But I plan to.

# ABOUT THE AUTHOR

**RUBY DIXON** is an author of all things science fiction romance. She is a Sagittarius and a Reylo shipper, and loves farming sims (but not actual housework). She lives in the South with her husband and a couple of goofy cats, and can't think of anything else to put in her biography. Truly, she is boring.


VISIT RUBY DIXON ONLINE

RubyDixon.com

RubyDixonBooks

Author.Ruby.Dixon